Harrison Elkenshaw
323-804-0475

DEER EYES

A Novel

SONIA DAY

Belwood

Library and Archives Canada Cataloguing in Publication

Day, Sonia, author
Deer Eyes: a novel

Issued in print and electronic formats. ISBN 978-0-9936784-0-0 (pbk.)
ISBN 978-0-9936784-1-7 (html)

PS8607.A985D43 2014 C813' 6 C2014-901132-6 C2014-901133-4

Available from Amazon.com as a paperback and an E-book

Editor: Mary-Fran McQuade
Cover design and typesetting: McCorkindale Advertising & Design
Watercolour illustration: Sonia Day
Author photo: Jenny Rhodenizer

Belwood

Belwood Publishing
Box 311
2000 Bloor St. West
Toronto, ON
Canada
M6P 3LC

For information:
www.soniaday.com

For Kathe

Book One

Prologue

It's hard to imagine your parents having sex.

I feel sure I'm fairly typical of my generation when I state that I have never been able to picture mine engaged in the mechanics of lovemaking. Not ever. It didn't enter my consciousness that they "did it," although of course they must have, and on a pretty regular basis. To me, they were just Mom and Dad. Period. They weren't the kind of couple who paraded around the house naked in front of their kids. Neither of them ever left the bathroom door open when they sat on the toilet. They were too private, too reserved. An atmosphere of intimacy wasn't prevalent – or encouraged – when I was growing up. It wasn't until I was in my late teens that I saw my dad's penis. And I confess that the sight kind of shocked me.

It was on one of those steamy nights in July, when the thermometer shot up suddenly and humid air rolled over Fortune Hill like a thick blanket of wet wool, smothering everything in its path. The maple leaves hung limp outside our house. The spruce branches didn't creak. Not a rustle, not a whisper of wind, not a twig cracking anywhere. The air inside my bedroom was as thick as a can of old paint. I couldn't breathe or sleep. So I got up to go to the john. Their bedroom was down the hall and they'd left the door open. They normally never did, but Dad didn't believe in air conditioning, and they couldn't have breathed if it had stayed shut. He and Mom were lying on the top of the bed, without a sheet covering them.

They were asleep, breathing heavily and Mom was turned away from Dad, curled up on her left side, almost falling off the edge of their queen-sized mattress. She was wearing the prissy pink cotton nightgown with bows on the front that I always hated and it had ruchled up, almost to her waist. Her bare, plump buttocks and thighs looked shiny with sweat and very white in the light from the hall. But Dad....

He lay sprawled on his back, buck naked, legs and arms stretched out. He was a burly guy, the kind who fills a room the moment he steps into it, and still very fit at nearly 50, with a broad, hairy chest and muscular thighs and shoulders, because he was always out in the woods, clearing trees and chopping firewood. But what struck me was his penis. It looked so small. Unbelievably small. And shrivelled. Like a balloon after the air's gone out of it. Flopped sideways on his left thigh, enthroned in wiry greyish hair, it made me think of the dead baby bird, poor creature, that I'd discovered lying in a nest that had fallen out of a tree in a thunderstorm that day. I stood there for a few moments, fascinated. Had Dad really once thrust this pathetic-looking object inside my mother, humped up and down and created me? And then Chrissie? It seemed beyond belief – and kind of laughable – at the time.

So when I got the news about what he'd been doing, my mind went blank. Totally blank. I couldn't take it in. I didn't even cry. I remember wandering around stunned for a couple of hours saying no, no, no. This can't be true. Can it? This must have been someone else's Dad, not mine. You're kidding me. That's impossible. My own father? It was too preposterous to contemplate.

I knew, of course, that he and Mom weren't getting along – and that women, all kinds of women, liked him, although I never really thought about that much. Perhaps I was naïve but you don't go there when it's your parents. I was also aware that love between Mom and Dad – if indeed it ever existed, because they'd married far too young, in my opinion – was now as dried up as the lemons she used to leave for months in the fridge. I never saw them kiss. Not once. Never saw them touch or hug, even at times like Christmas or birthdays. And they performed contortions like circus performers to avoid bumping into one another in the kitchen. Even so, I presumed – indeed expected – that they'd just jog along into old age, placid as the dairy cows over at Charlie Cousins' place. Sitting in their armchairs placed side by side in the living room, getting mildly excited on winter evenings about something new on TV or a good book Mom had discovered in the library at Marsh River, as they slid into the difficult years that face all of us when two-thirds of our lives are over and we've begun the slow, inevitable descent to the end.

I was in Africa when Chrissie called me in a state of panic. I'd been there for nearly six months, totally involved in the new school we were building for a village in the Sikasso region of Mali. Our aid project, our modest attempt to make the world a better place, so long in the making, was taking shape at last.

So home seemed distant, detached, a part of my life that I'd put on hold. I hadn't been in touch with anyone in Fortune for months, and I no longer found it important to email my parents or Chrissie, like one of the other aid workers, Rachel Abernethy. She was always Skyping with her family in Wisconsin, annoying everyone in the bunkhouse with her silly chatter. But work absorbed me. I was always so beat at the end of the day, I just wanted to collapse, read a few pages of the books Chrissie sent and pass out. But neither Mom nor Dad bothered to email me either – they never had, even when I was away at university – so I simply took it for granted that everything at home was as it always was, the way kids do.

When Chrissie reached me on my cell phone – I was standing in the schoolyard, the line was crackly, I could hardly hear – I didn't want to believe her. I sank down on the front steps, getting the red African dust all over my shorts and the backs of my calves, shaking my head, trying to convince myself that this was all just some crazy nightmare. Then assured by her that it wasn't, I managed to get a flight to Frankfurt the next day, then another on to Toronto. And there she was waiting for me at the airport, still dazed and uncomprehending, her face ashen. Poor Chrissie.

I didn't cry. Nor did anyone else in the family except Auntie Hanni, who always burst into tears at the slightest thing anyway. The rest of us were all too stunned to get emotional. We didn't even talk much. Perhaps it was that Tanner reserve kicking in. And then it was over, sort of – although, of course, it won't be over for a long while for Tyson. Or Chrissie. She's standing by him, she really loves the guy. I'm not sure I would, after what he did, but then I've never been in love, and I don't want to be. Love does strange things to you. Look at Dad.

But it's all in the past now. Dad's gone. He never let on to anyone what he did at his deer hunting cabin in the woods, and I don't really blame him. If it made him happy, I'm glad. Though I do wonder sometimes… What happened at the end. Was it an accident? Or deliberate?

But I try not to dwell on it. There's no point.

One

Folks in Fortune (population 540) knew it was going to happen. And probably in the fall, before the snow came. After the first mild frost zapped the last of the tomatoes, and scarlet maple leaves started fluttering to the ground like playing cards, was when they could expect it. The arrival of the mystery relative, that is. The one Gow Rivers mentioned in his will. This person would show up and lay claim to Gow's hundred sprawling acres up on Fortune Hill.

Yet some old timers didn't like the idea. Not one bit. A city slicker? Coming from New York? They'd tolerated Gow, but that was different. The prospect of this long-awaited newcomer appearing on the scene filled them with a sense of foreboding.

"You mark my words. We'd all better watch out now," warned Gracie Piloski, after news circulated that the relative had been found at last. "Things are going to change around here. And not for the better."

"You think so?" said Charlie Cousins.

"I know so."

"Perhaps you're right, Gracie," he murmured.

"I know I am," she repeated. "City people always change things, Charlie. They move out to the country and expect us to fit in with them instead of the other way around. Never fails. And this relative of Gow's will set the ball rolling here.

"Just you wait and see."

Gracie made her prediction on a dark, gloppy morning at the beginning of October. An unexpected early snow squall had blown in overnight, throwing a white shroud over the beat-up buildings that constituted the village of Fortune. They squatted at the eastern end of Bounteous Lake, looking ghostly and deserted, like some old abandoned mining town up north. The street by the lake was empty. Not many people had ventured out of doors, the poor visibility made driving dangerous. Yet Charlie, who farmed on Second Line, had climbed into his pickup and headed down to the general store *cum* post office because he'd put off mailing a package of forms to the Farm Credit Program – and if he procrastinated any longer, the bean counters would start pestering him again. Gracie ran the store. He stayed for a coffee, as he often did, and though pretending to agree with the postmistress, inwardly he thought she was being absurd.

Charlie unzipped his grey windbreaker and leaned against the store counter. He was a big bulk of a man with a kindly, florid face. He watched the snow flakes outside the store window form a thick swaying curtain of white, so that the snack bar across the street kept hoving into view, then disappearing again, swallowed up by the dark lake. The place was already boarded up, its red and white sign with the crude illustration of french fries and ice cream cones taken down, because the cottagers and tourists stopped coming to boat and fish after Labour Day. And that wasn't good, in Charlie's view. He thought the mystery relative would be a refreshing new face. Might perk the place up. Inject some new blood and ideas. Tish Boddington thought so too. She'd come home to Fortune – bringing along her son with the weird name, Flavian – and opened a bed and breakfast on the south side of the lake. And she was surviving, but could use more customers. So could Nathan Knockenhammer, respected throughout the county for his skill in renovating neglected old houses. Nathan, known by everyone as Knock, had itched to get his hands on Gow's place for years. "Such a lovely old place," he often wailed, "but it is falling apart."

Yet the amiable farmer wasn't about to make his feelings known that morning. Not to Gracie. He disliked confrontation. In any case, Charlie knew the postmistress to be a sad soul, soured on life after her Polish parents lost their battle to save the family farm – expropriated to make way for a new highway through the province – and then, at only eighteen, dealt another blow when her childhood sweetheart, Bob Lumsden, jilted her for a prettier girl over in Dufferin County. Poor Gracie never recovered. As a consequence, she liked nothing more than making gloom and doom pronouncements about anything that came into her head, whenever she had a captive audience. So Charlie stirred cream and two heaping spoonfuls of sugar into his coffee and waited, snow dripping off his work boots and making a puddle on the red linoleum of her clean store, for her latest diatribe.

It wasn't long in coming.

"Gow's relative will be bad for this place. Bad things are going to happen now. I can feel it in my bones," Gracie declared with relish, taking his package and slapping a label on it.

"You think so?" Charlie said, keeping his expression deliberately blank.

"I know so. I'll have to change. So will you," she shot back. "This person will come in here asking if I stock organic vegetables, free-range eggs and gluten-free this and that. You know, all those trendy things city people insist on eating these days. And I won't have any choice, if I want to stay in business."

Charlie nodded noncommittally.

"And olive oil. Expensive stuff from Italy," she huffed like an old steam engine. "What city folks call extra virgin, whatever that is. Surely a virgin is a virgin, eh Charlie?" She chortled in a coarse way. "Yes sirree. Fancy-schmancy olive oil will certainly be required. As if canola, made from crops grown right here in our beautiful county isn't good enough for them."

"Everyone looks down on canola, not just people from the

city," Charlie murmured. "It's the fault of the marketing guys, Gracie." He sighed. "Canola needs a more glamorous image."

She ignored him and carried on.

"Then there's pumpkin lattes. Mustn't forget their pumpkin lattes. A New Yorker is definitely going to want those."

"Pumpkin what?" Charlie raised his eyebrows, interested now. Five years ago, he'd tried growing pumpkins, then given up after two rained-out Halloweens in a row stuck him with hundreds of the big heavy orange balls he couldn't sell. Even his cattle had turned away, though he'd tried to entice them by mashing the lot to a pulp under the wheels of his tractor.

"Pumpkin lattes. They're the latest thing," said Gracie, scorn in her voice. "You know what lattes are, don't you, Charlie?"

"Yes, I do, Grace," said Charlie. Her authoritarian tone was starting to get under his skin. "But pumpkin? That's a new one on me."

"Well, get with it, you old fogey. You buy some kind of pumpkin powder that you mix in with the hot milk. Weird, eh?" She chortled again. "I saw it last week on TV."

Gracie kept a small TV under the counter permanently tuned to the Food Network. Whenever the store was empty, she watched it with the fascination of a voyeur, and bizarre though this preoccupation was – because she refused to stock anything in her store but standard fare like hot dogs, frozen burgers and chicken pot pies – Gracie had become addicted to watching trends in food.

"Pumpkin lattes are another silly city fad," she pronounced. Then she stopped and put a balled-up fist to her mouth, as if struck by a horrifying revelation.

"Oh my God. You know what Gow's relative coming here is going to mean, Charlie? I'll have to get rid of the old Kona."

Gracie's drip coffee maker was a fixture on the store counter. She kept it on a red and white gingham tablecloth beside the cash desk, meticulously scrubbed the glass container and put the cloth in the washing machine every week. She was very proud of her coffee.

"I do it right," she bragged to any newcomer who dropped by the store. "A fresh pot every half hour. Real spoons to stir in the sugar. No way I'm making you guys use those plastic sticks, like they do at the Kaffee Klatch in Marsh River. Want to try mine?"

"Your coffee is the best," agreed Charlie. And he was being honest now, for Gracie's coffee was indeed good. Always fresh and hot. You could smell it on the street. He took a pleasurable sip. "People in town say it's worth the drive out to the lake just to have a cup."

Gracie beamed – but then her face fell.

"I'll have to replace the Kona with one of those fancy new machines," she said, panic creeping into her voice. "You know. They're all big and shiny, with names like Smashaletti written on the side. They're Eye-talian. Then I'll have to learn how to make espresso and cappucinos and lattes and stuff like that if I want to still have customers...."

"You're being silly, Gracie," interrupted Charlie. "Of course you won't have to change. You know that everyone around here loves your coffee the way it is."

"You do?" She patted her hair, dyed chestnut and permed into tight curls every six months at A Cut Above in Marsh River, then shot him a grateful smile.

"Well, sure. Why do you think I come by and drink so much of it?"

Poor Gracie looked almost coquettish now. Charlie felt a rush of affection for the prickly old postmistress. But it dissipated quickly when she opened her mouth again.

"City people always change everything," she repeated. "And you –"

"Well, Gow sure didn't," he broke in, wanting to stop the flow.

He smiled. "Remember when he showed up in that amazing car? What a day that was."

Gow's car is a red-and-cream Ford Fairlane, a hard top with a retractable roof that folds back like a Venetian blind. And a beauty, in mint condition. The afternoon in the 1970s that he drives it into Fortune, the roof is closed because it's wet and windy. Wads of sodden maple leaves are clinging to the back window. The chassis gleams in the rain. Yet in spite of the inclement weather, people immediately troop out of the Bounteous Bar and Grill – then a popular watering hole on the edge of the lake – to ooh and aah over the car and its polished chrome bumpers. One of the admirers is Charlie. He's back for the weekend from agricultural college in Guelph. Sits having a beer in the bar with his buddy, Shep Tanner, who's also home from flight school in Thunder Bay. They watch as the driver parks in front of the bar and gets out. He's haggard-looking, this newcomer, thin as a beanpole, of indeterminate age, and kind of scruffy, like a hippie. His long hair hasn't seen a comb in weeks. He smiles with the showmanship of a magician as everybody crowds around the Fairlane. Then he goes inside, sits at the bar next to Har Brydges and orders a double scotch.

Lighting one cigarette after another in a feverish way, he tells Har that he's just driven all the way to Fortune from the Big Apple.

"I crossed the border at Buffalo and decided to stop now because I like the sound of Fortune," he croaks through a fog of smoke, with an accent that's hard to pin down. He asks Har how the community got the name.

"Oh it's nothing to do with it being lucky here, my friend. Quite the opposite. It's always been tough in Fortune to make a go of things," says Har sourly, shaking his head. "You can blame Merrie England for that name."

Har explains that villages in this part of Canada, now south-western Ontario, were often named after colonial settlers who were United Empire Loyalists. One, named Rothesley Fortune, originally owned thousands of acres in the area.

"Lord knows what the guy did to deserve it," says Har, with a bitter laugh into his rye as Charlie and Shep sit at the other end of the bar, listening in. "The Brits just swiped a whole lotta land from the Indians back in the 1700s and dispensed it as they pleased. And for sure," he takes a big swallow, "Mr. Rothesley Fucking Fortune had friends in high places."

Gow seems mildly disappointed by this revelation and looks into his glass, rubbing the stubble on his chin. Har says later that he thinks some private matter is troubling the guy, because his eyes water.

But then Gow brightens and says, "Well, to me, Fortune rhymes with opportune. I'll take that to be a good omen. Mind if I stay?"

And Har, who has just got his real estate licence, promptly hauls Gow up to Fortune Hill Road and sells him the old Maxwell homestead, with its hundred acres, on the spot. For the full asking price. Cash, too. Gow shakes his head when asked if he needs financing. Har is thrilled. Everyone in Fortune is agog, particularly the Maxwells. They've been dying to get the uninsulated brick farmhouse, in Laureen Maxwell's family for generations, taken off their hands for over a year. They've built a new, much warmer place with a wrap-around porch next door to Charlie on Second Line, and the land is better for farming over there than around the woods on Fortune Hill.

Then Gow just stays. And stays. He parks the Fairlane at the side of the house. Lets it rust and fall apart until a scrap dealer carts it away. He treats the house the same way – and he allows Laureen's perennial garden, once full of lovely flowers like monkshood and foxgloves, to turn into a tangled mess. He only goes into Marsh River, six miles away, to pick up groceries and booze and visit the library. As the years go by, he stops doing that, too. He calls Gracie instead. Makes do with her scant selection of provisions from the general store. And he gives young Joel Sprauge, who lives up on Sixth Line, a hefty tip for picking up his Johnnie Walker in town and then delivering it in his dad's old pickup.

Gow just sits by his woodstove in winter and swings in a threadbare hammock on the porch of the house in summer, swatting bugs with hunting magazines that Shep, who lives next door, gives him

He's an oddball, all right. Has an aura of something mighty strange about him. Rumours circulate, put about by Gracie. Gow must have run away from something. An unhappy marriage, perhaps. Or a gambling debt he couldn't pay, because he sometimes plays poker with Shep. Or worse, he's a fugitive from justice.

"A lot of American criminals flee up here, you know. I keep seeing them on TV. Perhaps Gow killed somebody," she whispers to regulars like Charlie.

But no one pays much attention. They're all used to Gracie's gloomy pronouncements. They wind up accepting Gow for what he is – a quiet loner who gives them no trouble. People know he's there, part of their little community, but they aren't bothered because they hardly ever see him.

But then he dies. Unexpectedly. Without any warning. Just before Christmas.

"Sure I remember the car," Gracie said, pouring herself a coffee. "Perhaps the relative will arrive in one of those big old American gas guzzlers, too."

"You think so? I doubt it," said Charlie wistfully. "Those days are over, Gracie. Everyone drives little Toyotas and Nissans now."

"Well, let's just hope the guy has plenty of money to spend – and that he doesn't go and die on us like Gow did."

Gracie shuddered, recalling how she sent Joel Sprauge up to Fortune Hill during the worst white-out of the year because Gow hadn't called to order groceries for a couple of weeks and she feared the worst. And Gracie was right for once.

Poor Joel knew something was wrong the moment he pushed open the unlocked front door. The house was like an icebox, the woodstove gone cold. Then he discovered Gow's corpse, slumped on his brown corduroy sofa, clad in blue flannel pajamas. The old man's body had turned the bluish-white of bone china, and mice – perhaps attracted to a half-eaten cheese sandwich lying on the floor – had defecated on his forehead. Joel retched on the spot. Couldn't even face his Mom's turkey dinner the next day. Then when he recovered, he found an empty bottle of whisky and a glass on the floor beside the sofa. Also a pill container with its lid off, the medication all gone, lying in the kitchen sink. It had contained Xanax, an anti-depressant.

This discovery prompted Gracie to assert that Gow had killed himself.

"He must've swallowed the pills and washed them down with the scotch, because he wanted to end it all," she declared. "It's obvious."

But was it? A shadow hung over Gow's death. Now, over two years later, Charlie wondered if the relative could throw light on the matter. He drained his coffee. Said he'd better be off.

But Gracie was reluctant to let him go. She leaned across the counter with a gleeful smile.

"Being as this guy is coming from the city," she said, "you'd better watch your back, Charlie Cousins."

"Excuse me?"

"I said watch your back, Charlie. After he gets here, you're going to start hearing complaints about the smell of cattle manure. And then some meddler from the township office will show up out of the blue to inspect your farm and give you a list of improvements to be made within 30 days, saying that a neighbour – some unspecified neighbour – has complained that you're a health hazard. Not environmentally friendly. Not green enough to operate as a farm anymore."

Gracie paused to catch her breath, pleased by this little speech. She glanced fretfully at the plastic bags of carrots and paper sacks of potatoes piled on a wire rack in the corner of the store.

"City folks sure do love two words. Green. And organic," she declared, frowning. "Guess I'll have to find a supplier of organic vegetables now. Will you grow some organic carrots for me, Charlie?"

Charlie shook his head.

"No way, Gracie."

What with soybeans, corn, winter wheat and 200 head of dairy cattle, the last thing he needed to think about was frigging carrots.

Charlie frowned himself. Gracie had initiated doubts. He wondered for the first time if she might have a point, even though there was no way he wanted to be drawn into a debate. Not now. Not when he needed to get back home and put the blower on the tractor before the snow got heavy. He put his mug back at exactly the designated spot on the gingham cloth (Gracie was touchy about such things), and headed for the door.

But the postmistress had one more shot up her sleeve.

"And something else, Charlie," she called out as he pushed the store door open, letting in a blast of cold, damp air. "You can forget hunting on Gow's land this year."

"Excuse me?" He stopped in his tracks.

"City folks hate hunters. They hate 'em so bad," Gracie said, wagging a finger. "So your days of bagging deer with Shep are over. You realize that, don't you?"

No, Charlie hadn't realized that. Truth be told, he hadn't even thought about it. Outside the store, he brushed the snow off his pickup, digesting this information. He felt perturbed. Gracie had hit a raw nerve.

He wondered if Shep had considered the implications of the mystery relative coming to Fortune – because his property was right next door to Gow's. He'd make a detour on the way home. Go ask him.

Charlie climbed into the cab. Turned the key. Looked up at

the sky. More white stuff lurked up there, waiting to descend. A flock of starlings flew over the lake swooping and diving in unison like a school of fish. Three brilliant yellow leaves, somehow still clinging to a branch of a maple at the lake's edge, provided the only dab of colour in the dreary day. Winter had arrived all right. This weather wasn't going to let up. Then it would freeze tonight. That would mean plenty of business for tow trucks by morning, because not many drivers had bothered to get their snow tires on yet. There'd be vehicles stranded in ditches all over the county. Fall in this neck of the woods was as unpredictable as a buck in the rutting season. You couldn't tell which way it was going to turn next. But people never learned.

As he drove up Fortune Hill, Charlie thought more about Gow's relative.

Who was this person? Would it turn out to be a man or a woman? No one knew. Because what the old guy specified in his will had been tantalizingly incomplete.

He simply said his property must go to someone called A.D. Coulter. That was all. No address, no nothing.

It was a mystery that demanded answers. Perhaps the people of Fortune were finally going to get some.

Two

Where is she? She's late today. Very late. Have I missed her? Eight nineteen... Eight twenty... Eight twenty-one... Eight twenty-two....

At the precise moment that Charlie Cousins was heading up Fortune Hill, a man named Michael Fenster Smith stood peering out of an apartment window on New York City's Upper East Side. He was fifty-six – the same age as Charlie, and even shared a July birthday with him. Yet there the similarities between the two ended. Because Charlie was country. And Michael was as urban as Starbucks.

Tall, thin, self-assured, with an innate sense of being intellectually superior to the world at large, Michael exuded big city sophistication. Yet that morning he was as anxious as a teenage boy going on his first date. Beads of sweat shone on his high, wide, patrician forehead, which he'd scrunched up in a frown while scanning the pedestrians hurrying along the rain-slicked street three floors below him. He kept checking the time on his cell phone. Like a madman he was. *Stab, stab, stab.* All fumbling fingers and thumbs. His heart booming like a cannon in his chest.

Michael couldn't wait for the moment that the girl would come into view on the sidewalk opposite. A stunner of a girl, with fantastic fiery hair, splaying out around her head like a mass of molten gold. He called this girl Sid. His luscious, lovely Sid. His jewel. He had no idea what her real name was. He didn't care. He'd given her that name for a special reason. And he worried now, because it was raining cats and dogs, and she was always so punctual. Always down there on the sidewalk at precisely eight sixteen, striding by his apartment building. She never wore a hat, either, never kept her halo hidden from him, even on wet, windy mornings like this one.

Michael had watched Sid, enthralled, for twenty-three mornings in a row, barring weekends, without ever catching a glimpse of her face – his apartment was too high off the ground for a full frontal view. She could be as ugly as Phyllis Diller under the hair. He didn't care about that, either. Her shining tresses were what he yearned to savour, what transported him to a state of pure, spiritual joy. So he waited every morning at the living room window, watching, hoping, fingers crossed, on tenterhooks for the exquisite thrill of the ten and a half seconds when he could observe her passing on the sidewalk.

But where is Sid this morning? Has she been taken ill? Stayed home because it's so blustery and wet? No, she wouldn't do that. So diligent, so dependable Sid is. Always off to work. Never plays hooky. Her employer is one lucky guy....

Something must have detained her today, he reasoned. The minutes went by. Perhaps she'd taken an alternative route. Michael peered down towards the old J. Braun liquor store on Lexington, the one that always reminded him of an urban scene by Edward Hopper. No sign of her down there. He stabbed his cell phone again. *Eight twenty-nine.* Kept turning his head to the left, then the right, like a spectator at a tennis match. *Eight thirty. Eight thirty-one.* Still no sign. He was getting frantic now. *Dear Lord, please. I love this girl. Find her for me.*

The gusts funneling down 90th Street were getting fierce. The black locust tree outside the window started thrashing about. A woman's scarf snapped up into the air like a sail. Umbrellas turned inside out. An old man's hat blew off and rolled down to Lexington. A youth in tight black jeans and a leather jacket ran after it for him, but the hat got jammed beneath a truck delivering bottled water. The pavement looked slippery, shiny as glass. Had Sid been jostled by somebody? Lost her footing in the morning rush to reach the subway entrance at 86th Street? Yes, that must be it. Right now, his angel was sitting on the curb half a block away, somewhere up near Park Avenue. Screaming with pain from a twisted ankle. Soaked to the skin. Buffeted by the gale force winds. Shivering. What should he do? Go look for her? Call 911?

But whoa, Michael.

A key clicked in the lock at the end of the hall. He froze. Waited for a woman's voice.

And it came, as it always did.

"Hi there. I'm back," the voice said. High, clear, like a flute. And a bit out of breath.

Quickly switching his gaze to the hardwood floor of the apartment, Michael squatted down on his thin haunches, pretending to look for a dropped flash drive under the white IKEA dining table. He felt sheepish now. Caught out. Ridiculous. Ashamed. As if he'd been caught masturbating in public or swiping a package of underpants from the racks in the menswear department at Bloomingdales. He straightened up, shoved the cell phone into his jacket pocket. Sat down at the table and purposefully pushed up the lid of his laptop. Adjusted the glasses on his beaky, Bob Cratchit nose. The glasses had heavy black rims, and he'd bought them hoping to appear hip to his students, yet their only effect was to make him look like a startled, old raccoon, caught in the act of rummaging through a garbage can. Michael stared with deliberation at the screen. He pursed full lips which were turning blubbery and purplish with age. Feigned interest in research he was supposed to be doing about the influence of the German Nazarenes on the

Pre-Raphaelite art movement in England. It was for a lecture he intended to present at Columbia, where he was a professor of art history, yet a blur of Sid's captivating coppery red hair kept blotting everything out. And the Nazarenes, once of interest to him because no other academic had studied them extensively before, had become boring. He wished he could dispatch the Nazarenes to a dark corner of his mind and never have to think about them again.

Michael waited. Held his breath, Listened for what always came next – the fumbling of a fleece jacket being hung up in the hall. Then running shoes being kicked off. And...

But no. Not this morning. Her face, flushed pink from exertion, didn't materialize in the doorway to the living room. He heard the bathroom door open instead. Then, click. Michael counted. One beat. Two beats. Three. The door stayed shut. He exhaled with relief. A deep, audible sound from the back of his throat. Whew. Escaped again. That was close.

Must be more careful. Don't be so obvious, you fool. She mustn't know, mustn't notice. The last thing you need is probing questions about why you keep looking out of the window every morning.

Because Sid, copper-haired Sid, was Michael's guilty secret. His romantic fantasy. His obsession. And he wanted to keep her hidden away in his heart.

Yet, foolish Michael. So naïve, so self-absorbed, so complacent, in spite of his advancing years – or perhaps because of them. Did he really think he could dupe Adie Fenster Smith? After more than three decades of cohabitation, her antennae honed sharp as a hornet's, she recognized only too well what was going on with her husband. Had noticed his eager stance by the window every morning. Noticed the girl, too. And now, in their cramped, windowless bathroom, Adie stripped off her sodden running gear, said "hell's bells" out loud to the mirror over the sink and wanted to slug him

"I hate you, Michael. Why are you doing this to me again?" she said angrily, leaning close to the mirror, her breath steaming up the glass. She hoped he could hear. Knew he couldn't. The living room window was twenty feet away from the bathroom and the walls of their building, constructed in the late 1960s, were solid concrete and surprisingly soundproof.

She rubbed the glass clean with her hand and analysed her wet, shiny face in the ruthless way that every woman past the age of fifty does. Each wrinkle, sag and blemish was duly noted, as anger dissolved into a sense of hopelessness and defeat.

"Face it, kiddo. You are old," she said out loud. "And ugly. And unloved. You're like a roll of brown paper tape, all crumpled up, full of creases, ready to be tossed in the recycling bin – no, make that the garbage bin, because no one is going to find another use for you when you're done with this life."

Counting the deep, vertical lines that were starting to etch themselves, like fine picture wire, around her mouth, Adie wondered if her husband's peculiar penchant was what happened to men – all men – after they hit fifty. Terrified of the inevitable, long, dark tunnel to oblivion that lay ahead of them, they started fantasizing about girls who looked the way their wives looked, back when they were young.

Because she saw the resemblance. Oh yes, it was striking. This girl on the street was exactly as Adie herself once was, years ago. Same height. Same build. Same erect posture. Same habit of swinging her arms confidently when she walked. Same air of happiness with the world around her. Same practical flat-heeled boots. But mostly it was the hair. Girls with flaming mops of flowing carrot-coloured hair had always fascinated Michael. They'd be walking along the street together, en route to a restaurant or a movie, and a freckly girl with a mantle of fiery red would go by, and he'd murmur "Lovely hair" and try not to stare. Then he'd look over at Adie with a sheepish grin, and she'd grin back. And she'd remember when her own hair looked like that. Back when she first met Michael.

London's Tate Gallery in the late 1970s. An unusually warm morning in March, so Adie hasn't worn her duffel coat, although it feels cool, as usual, in the gallery's temperature-controlled halls. She's standing in an old cable-knit sweater and paint-stained brown cords in front of John Everett Millais's oil painting of Ophelia floating downstream to her death, hands poking out of the water – the iconic scene from Hamlet that catapulted the young unknown artist and other members of the Pre-Raphaelite art movement to fame in the late 19th century, and which remains the most popular postcard in the gallery's gift shop.

Adie has a buff-coloured sketchpad balanced on her left arm. She's holding a 4B pencil in her right hand. Chewing her lip, she's trying hard to concentrate on the myriad flowers that Millais painted around Ophelia. Trying, yet not succeeding very well, because of all the other gallery visitors who keep trickling by to inspect his masterpiece. Her intent is to do a detailed sketch of the flowers – the buttercups, daisies, daffodils, fritillaria, violets, meadowsweet, purple loosestrife, cascading, wild white roses and one solitary red poppy – for a class assignment at St. Martin's School of Art, where she's recently enrolled. Yet it's proving difficult, thanks to the rubberneckers. Mostly Americans they are, and such loud-mouths. They keep peering over her shoulder, making idiotic comments. And it doesn't help her concentration when one of them, tall, lanky, in a grubby suede jacket and jeans, comes loping up like a kangaroo, exclaiming:

"Wow, amazing. It's amazing."

"What is?" she says, irritated, refusing to look at him.

"You. Standing there. You're a stunner. You're exactly like Sid."

"What? Sid who?"

"Lizzie Siddal. Her, the girl...." The kangaroo man gestures excitedly

at Millais's painting. "She was his model, you know. She posed for this painting in a bathtub and nearly died of pneumonia because the water went cold. Everyone called her Sid, not Lizzie. And you," he's staring at Adie open-mouthed, "you could be her double."

"Oh, I see." Adie feels nonplussed. Looks up now. Blushes, because he's young and quite good-looking. Returns hastily to her drawing. But he won't stop staring at her in a demented way and now other Americans are stopping and staring too, wondering what the heck is going on.

Adie doesn't understand why he's making such a fuss. But it seems futile to try to continue sketching. So she agrees – reluctantly – to go over to a bench in the middle of the gallery with him. And then it hits her – the firecracker that sometimes explodes when two people look into each other's eyes for the first time. He keeps going on about her hair. Won't stop saying that it's like burnished copper and exactly the same as Sid's. She's embarrassed. Yet she's drawn to his smile, thoughtful yet full of humour, and to his own hair, long and dark brown, curling behind his ears, with a thick lock falling rather rakishly, a la Marlon Brando, over his left eye. And when he smiles, he shows a gap between his two top teeth which gives him a boyish look. She likes that, too. He seems both serious and fun.

"Would you like to go for lunch in the gallery café?" he says, flashing the teeth.

"All right, then," she says, feeling shy.

And over greasy Cornish pasties, which he confesses to hating, "although I've gotten used to them now," he tells her that he's in England taking a master's in fine art at the University of London, and that he intends to write his thesis on the Pre-Raphaelites.

"Everything about their art, its romanticism, purity of detail and heavy use of medieval symbols, like the legend of King Arthur, intrigues me," he explains, his face going serious. "No one has produced art like it. It was unique at the time. It made them famous."

He pauses.

"The artists led fascinating lives too, you know. All kinds of…um…" he looks boyish again now, with a hint of mischief in his brown eyes, "amorous goings-on."

She blushes, because she's heard about those goings-on already, at St. Martin's. Yet she doesn't feel like discussing them with a total stranger. It would be too intimate.

He doesn't pursue the point.

"So what about you?" he asks leaning close. "What's your life plan, if indeed you have one?"

So she tells him, with the hesitancy of a nineteen-year-old who isn't sure yet that she can excel at anything, that she's in her first year at St. Martin's, and that she loves the flowers in the Ophelia painting, because Millais chose them with the story of Hamlet in mind.

"They all have hidden meanings," she says, looking back at the lone poppy, "and the way he incorporated each flower into his composition was very clever, I think. I read that he spent five months working out of doors eleven hours a day, doing the landscape first, before he added Ophelia to the scene. And… it made me decide that I want to become a botanical artist," she says. Then she stops abruptly, expecting this confession to be greeted by a puzzled look. Or worse, a gale of laughter.

But Michael doesn't laugh.

He just nods and says: "That sounds like a fascinating career choice." Then he leans forward, seeming to want to stroke her hair – making her feel awkward again – but he holds himself in check, and finally, after what seems like ages, asks: "So what does a botanical artist do? Enlighten me, please. I've no idea."

So she tells him about her childhood, spent surrounded by plants and flowers because her father was a gardener at Kew, where she was born, but that now she's more interested in how they're portrayed in art – by everyone from George Ehret, a German painter who was around in the 18th century, to Georgia O'Keeffe. And she's in a four-year general art program at St. Martin's and is sharing a flat with three other girls in South Kensington.

"My uncle was an artist," she says. "He didn't paint flowers. He was more of an abstract painter but I guess he influenced me. He brought me up to London when I was eight years old to visit the National Gallery, and I never forgot going there. And now I want to be a painter like him."

Michael nods at the mention of O'Keeffe. Looks thoughtful once more. Says he likes her tulip paintings, then confesses that he's never heard of Ehret, but would like to know more. And he reveals his own ambitions: to go back to the U.S. and teach the history of art in a city like New York.

Then he relates the most famous story about the Pre-Raphaelites.

"Dante Gabriel Rossetti, a friend of Millais's, became obsessed with Lizzie Siddal, particularly her hair." He looks back at the painting as he talks, although most of Ophelia's flowing red locks are invisible under the water. "And they became lovers, which was scandalous back then, but he wouldn't marry her. He finally decided to, but only when she was dying of addiction to laudanum. Then he went mad with grief and guilt after she died, and had her body dug up so he could find a book of love poems that he'd buried in her casket. And get this," Michael pauses for dramatic effect, "the gravediggers discovered that her mane of red hair was still growing."

Adie shivers. "You're kidding," she says, feeling sick and wondering how anyone could become that obsessed by a person's hair.

"Yes, it was described as filling the casket with gold."

Michael laughs now. Then noticing her stricken face, he adds, "Creepy, huh? But don't worry," he says, patting her arm, "it's undoubtedly not true. The Victorians loved melodrama. They were weird. And now," he shoots a glance over to the cafeteria counter, "shall we pay tribute to Signor Rossetti's decadent ways by sharing a slice of the Tate's decadent chocolate gateau?"

She nods happily. "Yes, let's."

What an intense, yet funny, American he is. Such a lot he knows about the Pre-Raphaelites. Adie feels herself falling for him already.

Then the café closes abruptly at three, and a grumpy woman in a blue uniform materializes with a floor mop to kick them out. So they head out, spirits high, down the wide concrete steps of Millbank, to stare at the glistening Thames. Their heads are already bent together like lovers. They're still deep in conversation about art and artists. And they both sense, right there and then, that the first giddy stage of infatuation has gripped them tight – and isn't about to let them go.

It did, of course. And fairly soon. Then a quieter kind of love had come along, nurtured by their mutual passion for art. Conversation between them – often intense and animated, about some piece of art or an artist they'd discovered – didn't flag for years and even induced a sense of smugness about their ability to stay interested in one another. In restaurants, Adie would shoot an amused glance at Michael when she spotted bored older couples, staring blankly across the table at each other's faces, and he would smile knowingly back. They developed an unshakeable sense of belonging, confident that they'd never, in their marriage, run out of things to say.

Yet recently, they had – and the feeling of being joined at the hip for life had been gradually drifting away downstream, to die like poor, demented Ophelia.

Adie now likened life with Michael to the fugitive colours she no longer used in her paintings. Once, they'd been a fixture in her watercolour palette – the gently scented rose madder genuine, derived from the roots of the pink-flowering madder plant that's native to Greece; the gamboge whose main ingredient is the yellow gum of the South Asian tree *Garcinia Hanburyi*; the indigo, sourced at first from a brilliant blue flower of that name, and later from coal tar; and the hue she adored, shocking pink opera, a modern invention but not, alas, light-fast. And how bright, how warm, how passionate such pigments had seemed at the beginning. Yet over the years, that vibrancy fades to nothing, more than a few grey smudges, barely discernable on watercolour paper.

And once fugitive colours disappear, an instructor at St. Martin's had warned her, they're gone forever. You can't bring them back.

You can't bring them back. Adie thought of the instructor's warning again now — and indeed often did when she examined herself in the mirror — because the colour of her hair had gradually faded like the pigments in her early inexpert paintings. It was now a pale orange, with patches of pure white in places. Yet Michael's fascination with vivid red heads of hair hadn't faded. Not at all. If anything, he'd become more fixated with age, living as he did in the idealized, unreal world of the Pre-Raphaelites. He couldn't accept that age changes everything, often in a brutal way. And it no longer seemed like an option to keep turning a blind eye to this strange quirk of his, shrugging if off in the way that a parent glosses over an annoying habit in a witful child, hoping the kid will eventually grow out of it.

Because Michael wasn't going to grow out of it. She realized that now.

So a drastic solution had started to form in her mind.

Three

Fortune Hill Road was slithery with slush. Big wet globs kept splatting on to the windshield. Charlie could barely see more than a few feet in front of him. The sky stayed ominous, roiling with dark clouds. He turned the wipers up high and slowed to a crawl. He was unlikely to collide with anyone or skid into the ditch. The four-wheel drive was on and he'd been dealing with this kind of unexpected change in the weather all his life. Farmers knew the score when it came to Mother Nature. She was a devious dame. She could play tricks when you least expected it.

He relaxed when he turned the pickup into Shep Tanner's long driveway and headed up to the house. He was looking forward to seeing his old buddy. It had been a while.

Shep sat at his kitchen table. The big black hulk of a Dodge pickup materializing through the falling sleet outside the window surprised him. He wasn't expecting anyone, and people usually called before dropping by, because he was often away, flying up north. But as his eyes lit on the familiar shape of Charlie Cousins climbing down from the cab, he put down the gun he was cleaning and felt a rush of pleasure.

He hurried over to the back door and threw it open, shouting, "Yo, Charlie. Good to see ya, man. Come on in."

Shep would never admit to feeling lonely. He wasn't that kind of guy. He didn't have much time for modern girly men, the ones who blubbed on TV talk shows about "issues" and let their emotions hang out like flapping shirttails for all the world to see. Yet he certainly felt disgruntled, out of sorts, eager for the company of another human being, preferably male, that morning.

Charlie filled the bill just fine.

They didn't meet often. Mostly, they hunted together in the fall. Headed out into the woods behind Shep's house, he to a blind high in an old maple, Charlie to another nestled in the crook of a spruce on Gow's land. Yet their encounters always followed a similar pattern. After bagging their limit of deer, after observing the hunter's ritual of frying up the fresh, still-warm heart of a young buck or doe in bacon grease on Shep's woodstove and washing it down with a few beers, they didn't feel the urge to keep on seeing each other regularly. They simply slapped each other's shoulders and said, "See ya around" – which often meant their paths wouldn't cross until the following hunting season. It was the way men liked to do things, Shep told his wife, Mary Ann, when she asked why they didn't see more of Charlie.

"Guys aren't into calling each other to gab and make dates for lunch," he'd grunted. "That's what women do."

Shep lived in a red brick Victorian farmhouse partially hidden in a hundred acres of dense woods on Sideroad 15. It was right around the corner, so to speak, from Gow's identically-sized parcel on Fortune Hill Road – the property that now belonged to the mystery relative. Yet no one would be able to discern where one parcel of land ended and the other began. The whole of Fortune Hill had become thick and shadowy with tightly-packed trees in recent years, because, as family farms in the area died out, the government introduced a reforestation program, paying students to plant tiny cedars, spruce and poplar for minimum wage in the summertime.

And how those trees had grown. They'd developed into dense thickets, difficult to penetrate. Dope growers liked sneaking in there, now. They'd come by at night and surreptitiously cut down a few branches to let sunlight in – but not so many that the RCMP helicopters flying overhead could detect what they were doing – then they'd cram in dozens of marijuana plants, encircling the stalks in narrow-gauge chicken wire to keep four-legged marauders away. There was so much money to be made in cultivating the easy-to-grow illegal weed. It had become Canada's biggest cash crop – although no one in Fortune really talked about it – and motorbike gangs, nasty thugs armed with knives and guns, were busy lining their pockets anywhere they could.

Shep hated the dope growers. He'd never smoked dope. Wasn't even tempted. He'd never been a hippie. Yet he loved the woods with a passion and had lived in them all his life.

Under the thick, dark spruce, cedar and majestic sugar maples was where white-tailed deer roamed freely, making the place a treasure trove for hunters. And what Shep loved as much as his woods was hunting. He kept his freezer stocked year round with game – mostly deer, sometimes wild turkeys, the odd moose. He rarely bought red meat at a supermarket. He went out there – with a gun or crossbow – every day of hunting season, just as his dad, Ottmar, had before him.

"We hunt for food, not fun. We aren't monsters. If we didn't cull a few deer, they'd die of starvation over the winter," he retorted when city folks looked appalled and asked him how he could bear to stalk and kill wild animals.

Nor did the impending arrival of the mystery relative concern him.

"No way," he told Charlie, shaking his head, when Charlie – before he'd even taken his boots off in the mudroom – repeated Gracie Piloski's fears about being banned from hunting on Gow's land. "No way that's going to happen, Charlie. I'll make sure of that."

Shep flashed the smile of a supremely confident man who is used to getting what he wants.

"Wanna stay for a coffee?" he asked.

Charlie hesitated. Gracie's brew, agreeable at the time, was gurgling in his stomach. But he never said no to Shep, because it wasn't worth arguing with him. He always won.

"Just half a cup then," he said, looking at his watch.

"Aw, c'mon Charlie, stay for a while," Shep said. "I'm all alone."

He mimed a fit of weeping, rubbing at his eyes, then laughed. "My sweet Mary Ann has upped and left me, you know."

Charlie smiled uneasily.

The two men went into the kitchen on the north side of the house, facing the woods. Shep's enormous black woodstove, his pride and joy, dominated the room. It was a cast-iron antique embellished with chrome. He'd picked it up from an old Finnish guy at a hunting camp up north, and Shep loved to brag how he got the guy pissed on a bottle of 80 proof rum one bitter night when the coyotes were howling around outside. After the fourth round, the Finn had caved in and agreed to sell the stove for a song, even though he'd loved it like a woman and wept when Shep took it away. But that was the kind of thing Shep did. He was a wheeler-dealer. He searched for the vulnerable side of people to achieve what he wanted. All wit and charm on the surface, yet sly as a fox underneath, people in Fortune said, and well known over the whole of Wellington County for not wanting to pay cash for anything, if he could avoid it. Some locals disliked Shep. But Charlie didn't. They'd been buddies since they were kids – in bad times and good.

The stove made the big old house so warm, Charlie started sweating, beads of perspiration forming on his forehead. But he kept his coat on. He didn't want to stay long. The squall off the lake was a warning. He needed to head back over to Second Line and get his snow blower oiled, then hook it up to the tractor, or there'd be hell to pay from his wife, Nancy, when the first big dump blew in.

Shep lifted the metal coffee pot off the stove and plunked it pointedly down on a trivet on the wooden kitchen table. He got out mugs and spoons and a carton of fresh cream. Pulled a bottle of Baileys Irish Cream from a cabinet by the sink and rummaged around for a new bag of chocolate chip cookies. He was a genial host. He took a cookie out and nibbled on it, because Shep had a very sweet tooth. He was putting on weight. The roll of fat around his middle kept getting larger, spilling over the top of his pants, making him look like his old man did before he died, but he couldn't help himself. And he wasn't going to worry about it. Life was too short. He grinned at Charlie. Plunked himself down on a chair. Stretched out stocky muscular legs clad in dark green overalls under the table, as if the matter of Charlie staying a while was settled. So Charlie reluctantly sat down, too, hot in the bunched-up jacket, but deciding not to take it off, because if he did, he'd be sitting there getting drunk on the sweet, cloying Baileys all day. He accepted a mug, heavily dosed with the liqueur. Said "Mmm. Good," as he always did, though he didn't really like the taste.

The day stayed dark outside. Sleet kept falling. Shep's two shotguns, polished to a shine, gleamed in the light from the woodstove door. Lined up neatly beside them on the big table were a long bore brush like a giant black Q-tip, a bottle of oil, a tube of gun grease and some solvent, Shep was preparing for the deer hunting season. It opened in Wellington County in just over a month, and he fully anticipated that he and Charlie would bag several deer on Gow's land. The old guy had never minded. So why should the new one?

He picked up one of the guns. Stroked the stock, which was made of English walnut. Cradled it with the tenderness of a mother admiring her firstborn.

"A beauty, eh?" he said, handing the gun over to Charlie. "My dad's. An Ackley. It was his favourite. He went all the way to Colorado to meet old man Ackley. I even used to have some of his homemade shells, but they're gone now. And I don't use this gun anymore. I just get it out and polish it now and then."

He sighed.

"Dad was one of the best hunters I know. Did I ever tell you what he said back when I was eight, and I went out with him in the bush for the first time?"

Shep chuckled.

"He said you should cherish a gun the way you cherish a good woman. Give 'em both a lot of loving. Sound advice, eh, Charlie?"

Well, Shep should know, Charlie thought, feeling uneasy again.

So had Mary Ann finally parted ways with Shep? Maybe yes, Charlie surmised. Because it was common knowledge in Fortune – where gossip travelled faster than a pickup with a sixteen-year-old boy at the wheel – that they didn't get along. So with their two girls grown up and gone, Mary Ann had taken a job at the home decorating store in Marsh River's new shopping mall and that had made Shep sore. It wasn't that he objected to women working – on the contrary, relief flooded over him after she got hired, because now he often had the house to himself – but this store was giving her ideas. Expensive, citified ideas. He couldn't see the point of brass table lamps from Thailand, Mexican cushions and all the other pricey paraphernalia Mary Ann kept bringing home in shiny carrier bags. Then, without consulting him, she'd hired a guy to paint the living room walls a colour like baby poop and bought a new black leather sofa. But whatever for? Shep liked his walls plain white. And their comfortable old plaid couch, with the stuffing falling out, had been so relaxing to flop on to when he came in from chopping wood. The rumour at the general store, put about by Gracie, was that they'd had a humdinger of a fight over the leather sofa. Then Mary Ann had moved out. Gone to stay with her sister Hanni in Marsh River.

Yet perhaps that was best for them both, Charlie reflected, sipping his coffee. Shep was hardly ever home anyway. For weeks at a time he went off to work up north. It seemed like an odd way to conduct a marriage. Charlie couldn't imagine being parted from Nancy for that length of time. And whispers had always circulated about what Shep did in those isolated northern communities with names like Attawapiskat and Moosonee, because everyone in Fortune knew something else about Shep: women were attracted to him like bugs to flypaper. They found him irresistible. Charlie often wondered why. His hunting companion was shorter than most men, with a chunky build, a bull neck and an ordinary square face. He certainly didn't fit the "tall, dark and handsome" stereotype.

But Shep was always in control. Perhaps that was his secret, Charlie thought now, appraising his buddy's smiling face as he handed back the Ackley. Women liked men who took charge, who took care of things, who appeared confident in any situation. And that sure fit Shep. The guy was cocky as a rooster. He had powerful eyes, too: a penetrating, pale grey, deep set under his brows and he fixed them on women, staring hard, until they blushed and looked away. Nancy had even fallen for his act after drinking too much homemade elderberry wine at a community barbecue a few years ago. Had said Shep was "sexy" and giggled as they headed home in the pickup, then pushed Charlie away in bed that night. He'd felt hurt. Nancy never did anything like that again, but all the same, Charlie wondered what this guy pouring the coffee had that other men didn't.

"So what's the latest on this relative?" Shep asked, leaning back, tipping his chair on to two legs. He took a gulp of coffee. "Have we found out if it is a guy yet?"

Charlie shook his head.

"Nope. No one knows for sure. Could be a girl or a guy. All we have is the name. It's A.D. Coulter."

"Yeah, I heard that. Well, let's hope we don't get stuck with some cranky old dame. We have enough of them in Fortune already."

The men laughed in unison.

"Yeah, right," said Charlie. "I was down at the store, seeing Gracie this morning. She was in, uh, her usual mood."

Shep shook his head.

"Poor old Gracie. Never got herself laid, that's her problem," he said. "And the relative's coming from New York?"

Charlie nodded.

Shep grimaced. He'd only been to New York once. Back in his twenties. Had hated the place. The crowds, the lack of clean air, the claustrophic skyscrapers. They'd made him feel like an ant that could be crushed underfoot any moment. Now, in middle age, he disliked cities in general. And city people. He always insisted that he had nothing in common with them and only went to a big city to buy something if he couldn't find what he was looking for in Marsh River. It suited him just fine.

"So when's he showing up?"

"Don't know. No one does."

"Well, he better get his ass up here soon, that's all I can say." Shep stared at the wet, white stuff that was starting to accumulate on the window ledge outside. "Sleet in October. It's kinda early, isn't it? Is this an omen or what?"

Shep gave a mock shiver, chuckled and took a big swallow of coffee.

"Mm, we may be in for a bad one this year," Charlie said, glancing at the window himself. "They're predicting more snow than normal."

"Well, could be," Shep snorted. "But those weather guys

always get it wrong. And who's to know?" He fidgeted his feet under the table. "Winter's a crapshoot, Charlie. Always has been, always will be. They can't predict anything beyond a couple of days. Don't know why they get paid so much."

He thought for a moment. "You put the blower on your tractor yet?"

"Nope."

"Me neither."

Reminded of this task, Charlie put his mug down, hoping Shep wouldn't notice that it was still a quarter full. His stomach was sloshing like a drain in a January thaw. He looked at his watch, thinking about Nancy's wrath.

"I was planning to do it today, so I'd better be off or," he chuckled, "my dear wife will have my hide."

He got up from the table.

"Aw, c'mon, Charlie. Pay no attention. Why do we have wives?" Shep grunted. He poured himself another mugful. Held the bottle out again. Bit into another cookie and chewed, dropping crumbs on the table. "There's plenty of time. This sleet today is nothing much. I guarantee it'll melt tomorrow. The real stuff won't come till December."

"You think so?"

"For sure. I'm not even looking at my blower till after hunting's done. It's still in the drive shed."

"Even so, Shep. I gotta get back. Stuff to do."

Charlie stood up, straightened his jacket. Wiping the sweat off his brow, he felt relieved to be going.

"Okay, then," Shep said, getting up himself. He yawned. Stretched muscular, freckly forearms above his head. "Thanks for coming by. I'll call ya in a couple of weeks. I'm going to clean up the cabin."

Charlie headed into the mudroom and started to pull on his boots.

"I want to bag me an eight-point buck this year," Shep called out after him.

"Well, with those deer eyes of yours," Charlie called back, laughing, "you'll probably do it."

"Yeah, hope so. But perhaps you're right," Shep said, frowning. "It'll mean doing some arm twisting with this relative. Because you know what people from the city are like." He sighed. "They ignore the reality of meat, that it means killing animals. They just want to go to the supermarket and buy everything served up to them on a nice little Styrofoam tray. "

"No one understands the life of a farmer, that's for sure," Charlie said, thinking of the feeder calves he was shipping off to the slaughterhouse tomorrow. "But there isn't much we can do about that, is there?"

"Nope. Let's hope it's a good year, then. Seem to be plenty of deer out there. Oh, and I forgot to tell you," Shep paused. "I told young Tyson Sprauge he could join us."

Charlie stopped pulling on his boots.

"You did what?" A stricken look flashed over his face. "Is that a good idea, Shep? Don't you remember that trouble up on Eighth Line last year?" Charlie shook his head. "Tyson kept taking potshots at coyotes from his dad's old pickup and nearly killed a couple of tourists going by on bikes, down to the lake."

"I know, I know, but Tyson's growing up," Shep said smoothly. "Chrissie's influence, I think." He smiled at the mention of his younger daughter. "He's twenty now. They're announcing their engagement soon, you know. She's good for him. He's just landed himself a good job, pouring concrete floors for Bob Marsten. And, you know, he did take the firearms certification course this summer. Finally got his hunting licence. Told me the other day, all puffed up, that the only thing he wants to shoot now is deer."

"Well, let's hope so," Charlie said, frowning, closing the Velcro snap on his boots. "Because we don't want any trouble. Not this year, if that relative of Gow's is going to be around."

"Relax. Charlie. Stop worrying. It'll all be fine. Just fine," Shep said, cutting off the conversation, taking charge the way he always did.

Charlie left. Sleet was still falling. His truck tires dug two dark parallel ruts through the slush as he headed down Shep's long driveway. He was annoyed. He didn't want to go hunting with that hothead Tyson Sprauge. And he disliked having his concerns dismissed by Shep, simply because the boy had got himself hooked up with Shep's younger daughter. Good looking but immature as a young stallion Tyson was, always picking fights with guys in Marsh River bars and threatening to go get his gun to settle things. Charlie sensed danger if Tyson was out in the woods with them. Real danger. And Shep – usually so canny about people – seemed to have a blind spot about the kid.

Shep put his guns away in a cabinet and locked it, then poured another coffee. He polished off the bag of cookies. Threw the empty bag into the woodstove. Tidied up the table. Unlike Charlie, he didn't intend to worry about Tyson. He'd been a hell-raiser himself too, once – and it was just a phase. He and Charlie could smooth the edges off the kid. Show him how to behave responsibly out in the woods.

His thoughts turned to the relative. He had a hunch A.D. Coulter would turn out to be a man. But he hoped not, because Shep preferred handling women. They were more malleable. More inclined to give in, in the face of a disagreement. He knew from experience that he could talk a woman into anything. Persuade her to see a situation exactly his way. Take charge of the conversation. Even get her to open up her legs, so long as he played his cards right.

He laughed softly. Ah yes, he'd shared some sweet times with women. All kinds of women. Up north. Down south. In Marsh

River. That long-ago time in New York. What was her name, Cindy something? And you just had to shave and put on a clean shirt. Tell them they looked beautiful, make them laugh. Women always loved men who did that.

If the mystery relative turned out to be a woman, he'd crack a few jokes. Smile a lot. Make her feel good about herself and her appearance. It always worked.

Four

Another rainy mornng in New York. Adie went on a longer run than usual, not caring if she got soaked. She headed up past the National Design Museum and into Central Park, dancing deftly around the cyclists who habitually ignored stop signs and threatened to mow down every pedestrian who got in their way. She joined the usual throng of runners, all bedraggled because of the rain. In a damp huddle, like a pack of dogs, they climbed the steps at Engineer's Gate, past the gleaming gold bust of John Purroy Michell, a one-time mayor of New York who'd died in the First World War, then the group spread out on the path around the reservoir. The path was soggy underfoot. Shards of rain kept stabbing at her cheeks. It wasn't a pleasant time to be out, but she needed to think – and a long run, all the way around the reservoir, helped her do that. It unscrambled her thoughts. Made her calm. Above all, she wanted to be calm while coming to a decision about Michael.

It was time to act. Being made to feel insecure and unloved was bad enough. But she also worried that her husband might be turning into a real weirdo, a stalker, the kind of man who was watched by the police and wound up being charged with harassment, because this wasn't the first time. Two years ago, he had fallen in love with one of his students at Columbia, after becoming obsessed by her hair. He'd even had the balls to reveal this infatuation to Adie. Chastened and contrite, he'd sat her down one evening, then explained gravely over a bottle of wine that the girl was homely-looking and dumb as a doorknob, but he couldn't help watching her from his faculty office window every day. And though he felt bad about it, he was in love – madly in love – and just couldn't help himself. He'd even trailed her several times across the campus.

Tolerance. Forgiveness. Absolution. Had Michael hoped for such reactions from her, after this confession? Adie presumed so, yet she'd wished that he had kept his mouth shut. For heaven's sake, how self-centred you are, Michael, she'd wanted to blurt out. Why did you reveal this silly little crush to me? Sexual fantasies about people we can't have are part of life, surely. For everyone. Everywhere. They just happen, triggered by hormones or circumstances or whatever. And what's the point of my knowing about yours? I fantasize too, she'd been tempted to say, recalling her erotic longings for a blonde stud half her age, a would-be actor called Sean, who'd lived in their apartment building with his parents. Any time she'd run into Sean in the elevator, she'd picture them ripping each other's clothes off in a frenzy and tangling on the elevator floor. Yet spilling the beans to Michael about this had never occurred to her. It would only have hurt him. And then Sean had landed a gig in a daytime soap and moved out, and the fantasy had died – just as Michael's should have died, without being brought out into the open. His revelations about the red-haired student had been an embarrassment for them both. He'd looked so foolish and abject, pledging to stop, she'd even felt sorry for him. And she resolved never to mention the subject again.

But now here he was, the stupid bastard, behaving like a lovesick puppy over another redhead. And how many others had there been – the ones she simply didn't know about?

Back on 90th Street, wet and chilled, she looked up and saw Michael standing at the window again, watching. He didn't notice Adie. He never did. He always fixed his gaze on the opposite sidewalk. And she was half-hidden anyway by the black locust tree in front of the building. She headed upstairs, the drizzle of resentment escalating into a downpour, and retreated straight into the bathroom, not bothering to call out hi this time. Staring at her reflection once more, she fingered her long, faded strands of hair. Plastered flat by the rain, they looked like rats' tails hung on a line. Then a sobering realization struck her. The person she most resembled nowadays was not Lizzie Siddal but Whistler's Mother. *All you need, kiddo, is the severe black dress. And your hair pulled back into that Victorian white cap with the dangling side bits. The similarity is striking. You have her nose. People will be astonished.*

She laughed. Ha-ha. Pulled a face at the mirror. Yet there was no mirth in her voice. What she ached for at that moment was a Reese's Peanut Butter Cup – or better yet, two or three. Michael indulged in adolescent fantasies about copper-haired girls, but Adie harboured a guilty secret, too. She was addicted to the candy that came in bright yellow-and-orange packages. Those scrumptious little chocolate tarts with fillings of creamy gold. What utter bliss. What heaven. She nibbled on them in private, whenever she felt stressed out. Didn't dare tell Michael, because on his fiftieth birthday, he had looked in the mirror, patted his paunch (which in reality wasn't that big) and announced that he was getting fat. Then came a declaration – voiced as solemnly as his confession about the red-haired girl – that it was time for them both to embrace "healthy eating."

Michael didn't touch anything that contained sugar now.

"I'm throwing out that blue sugar bowl," he'd announced one Saturday morning. "No point in keeping it, is there?"

Adie had been about to disagree – but held her tongue, wanting to avoid an argument – because the bowl was a sentimental reminder of the Scottish Trossach Mountains. They'd gone there on their honeymoon. Michael had wanted to see the spot where Millais painted an iconic portrait of the Victorian art critic John Ruskin, and for years afterwards, every time she looked at the bowl, she'd felt a glow, remembering days of hiking and holding hands in the fine Highland mists, and how they'd stopped one afternoon at a pottery in the village, then gone back to their cold room above a noisy pub to make love for hours. Yet Michael had consigned this memento to the garbage without a thought of what it meant to her.

He'd also started steering clear of carbs – every kind of carb – in the obsessive way he seemed to do everything. And as for sharing a slice of chocolate cake with his wife – another treasured memory of the good old days – that hadn't happened in years. So she'd become secretive, too. She kept the Reese's packages hidden behind a box of oil paints in her studio credenza. Their sinful sweetness was her escape. Her refuge. From him. From the red-haired girls. From every problem in her life.

But no. Not this morning. After the long run in the park, she resisted the urge to wrap her European peasant hips in a towel and go looking for a peanut butter cup. No more seeking consolation of the caloried kind over Michael's fixation. She would take the plunge

She'd do something about the amazing letter that came from Canada about six weeks ago.

Her uncle had, it seemed, left her a house in the country, plus a substantial amount of cash in a bank account. What a total surprise. What a windfall. What an extraordinarily generous gesture on his part. The knowledge had been painful at first. She'd wondered where he'd gone and whether she even wanted to reply to the letter, because it prompted unsettling emotions to flood into her head. Memories of the crime he'd committed. The selfish act that caused so much hurt and anger, affecting so many lives, with no satisfactory answers as to why. Years ago, her only recourse had been to pile the unsettling thoughts into a locked box, then bury the box somewhere deep in her brain and throw away the key. And she had. Her uncle was gone from her consciousness for decades. She forgot him, his whole strange story, the aftermath that affected her own life. And if she went to Canada, she inevitably would have to confront the reality of what he did all over again.

Yet now, spurred by Michael's behaviour, she was feeling braver about dredging up the past. She would go and at least check out her uncle's place in Canada. And perhaps – just perhaps – she might decide to go and live there.

Because the fact was, she could. She had indeed become a botanical artist. The ambition that she'd shyly revealed, all those years ago in the Tate Gallery, had come true. Magazines on both sides of the Atlantic now sought her services. So did book publishers. Her illustrations filled two popular small books – one on orchids, the other on the language of flowers – and reproductions of her intricate, stylized watercolours and acrylics sold in décor stores, all embellished with her married initials, AFS. She painted the monogram in the same flamboyant manner as the Pre-Raphaelite Brotherhood had habitually inscribed the logo PRB on the bottom of their work.

This stroke of marketing genius – Michael's idea, obsessed as he was with the band of Victorian painters – had turned her into a recognizable brand. So much so, where she lived no longer mattered. If she chose to make her home in the backwoods of Canada and work from there, well, why not?

Adie stepped into the shower and turned the dial to hot, fueled by a determination to start over, to build a new life away from the recurring insult of young, red-haired girls. A scalding jet hit her scalp. She flinched as it pricked her breasts and pale, no-longer-taut belly with the force of sharp little pins. The medical mavens insisted that doing this was ruinous for the skin, but so what? Even if she wound up looking like a lizard, nothing could beat the blessed rejuvenation that came from a long, hot shower.

Delighting in the searing heat and steam, she stood under the jet for fifteen minutes. Willed it to wash away the image of Whister's crabby old mother. And it did. When she stepped out, she felt different. Refreshed. Jubilant. As pink, plump and delicious as a plateful of boiled shrimp. Her face was a blur in the steamed-up mirror, but she took a corner of the towel and rubbed it clean. Peered eagerly now, no longer cowed by what she saw. Hmm, not bad. A hint of purplish shadows, yes, but no sagging, no volcanic craters yet, underneath the eyes. Cheekbone structure still noticeable, not buried in fleshy folds. Lines, yes, quite a few lines, but not as many as she'd counted before. All things considered, the happy, positive face of the strong, confident 51-year-old woman she knew she was.

"Here's to Canada. And the life I'm going to have up there." she said, hoisting an imaginary glass of champagne.

"Goodbye, Adie Fenster Smith. Hello again, Anna Dorothee Coulter."

She knelt on the floor. Rummaged in her pants pocket for her cell phone.

It was time to tell Val.

London again. Adie and Val Mendel meet as nineteen-year-olds at St. Martins, shortly before she encounters Michael at the Tate. They bond over a lecherous life-drawing instructor called Dmitri who looks like Rasputin and stinks of garlic. Fed up with his wandering, ink-stained hands during class, they concoct – at Val's instigation – a little wake-up call for him:

You may think you're great
But Dmitri, we have to state
That you'll give us all a big lift
If you start using this gift.

They ink the rhyme on an elegant sheet of paper. Leave it on the instructor's desk one night, folded around a deodorant stick and a

*package of breath mints. But the hint backfires. Dmitri is a melancholy
Russian. He comes to class the next morning. Glances at the note.
Hurls it dramatically into the air. Glares at a gay student called
Martin, whom he suspects – wrongly – of having a crush on him.
Stomps off to the principal's office. Makes a huge fuss. The principal
demands to know who is responsible. Val and Adie snigger behind
their easels but don't own up. Instead, they toast each other that night
with a bottle of Mateus Rosé. And when Dmitri continues to stink like
an alley cat, they switch to other classes and embark on a lifetime of
laughter and friendship together.*

*Their closeness weathers Val's two stormy marriages to lawyers
named Richard – she nicknames them Richard the First and Richard
the Second – as well as Adie's own ups and downs with Michael.
Both know that there is nothing so valuable as a supportive woman
friend, there to weather with you the crises that life flings in your
path. So Val, who follows Adie to New York after marrying Richard
the Second, always listens patiently when Adie bends her ear about
Michael's peculiar peccadilloes.*

Almost always, that is.

"You're really serious about leaving him?" Val said into the phone,
stifling a yawn. It was awfully early in the morning.

"Yes, I am."

Val felt sceptical. She'd heard all this before. Adie was always
saying that she wanted to leave Michael, but then lacked
the courage to actually go.

"But hadn't you better tell him how upset you are about this
new chick, before taking such a drastic step?" Val asked, half-
asleep, glancing bleary-eyed at her bedside clock, wishing she
was still snuggled under her blue duvet.

Plump, curvy, with unlined skin and long black hair that had
kept its curl, Val was a modern anomaly, a woman who felt quite
content with how she looked in middle age. She liked to sleep

late and never exercised. Didn't see the point of it. The only form of physical activity that appealed to her was rough sex with young men, whenever she could find a suitable candidate. Trying to stay slim and youthful by running around reservoirs at the crack of dawn – as her friend habitually did – was, in her view, a cockamamie idea.

"Well, yes, I guess I might let him know I'm upset about the girl, but it's not going to change anything. He's never going to stop," Adie said crossly. "So I've something exciting to tell you. I'm going to check out my uncle's house in Canada. I might even," she paused, uncertain whether or not to give voice to her next statement, "go and live there."

"You're kidding me," Val sat up, wide awake now. "Up there? So fucking cold. You must be nuts. And won't you have to speak French all the time?"

Adie took a breath, perplexed.

"I don't know. Will I?"

"Yeah, think so. Everything's French in Canada. Friend of mine told me who took a trip to Montreal. You go to a museum up there, it's all *parlez francais, s'il vous plait*. No English signs anywhere." She laughed. "But let's talk tomorrow. Come to the opera for free, cherub. Buddy at work – the cute gay guy I have the season tickets with, remember? – he can't make it."

Val had a job in the exhibitions department at the Museum of Modern Art that paid peanuts. But thanks to her divorce settlements from the two Richards, she owned a swanky condo on the West Side near Central Park and bought season tickets to everything.

"I'd love to," Adie said. "What's the opera?"

"Oh, an unusual one," Val chuckled. "About a hunter."

Five

On Marsh River's main drag, Flavian Boddington was thinking about encounters with women. Not of the amorous kind – his preference was for beefy guys with tight abs, like his former lover, a fireman called Jean-Paul – yet at the age of twenty-seven, he had discovered one thing he adored about the female sex.

They bought books – lots of books – while men didn't. At least, that seemed to be the pattern in this small town where he was trying to make a life for himself. Flipping the sign from Closed to Open in the window of Boddington Books, Flavian reflected that at least 80 per cent of his customers were female. Not that he'd be seeing many of those supportive, middle-aged ladies in the store today. The miserable weather would keep them away. They'd be staying indoors, cosy and warm, making soup for their husbands and kids. Or cleaning house. None would venture out to pick up the latest Nora Roberts or Margaret Atwood.

He didn't blame them, either. It was nasty out there, another day of sleet and rain. Flavian lived in an apartment above the store, and he wished he had someone upstairs making a comforting pot of soup for him at that very moment. He watched a car moving cautiously along St. David's with a smartly dressed young couple inside, talking in an animated way to each other, obviously heading off to work. He felt jealous.

And there were only three pedestrians on the sidewalk today – not one of them a potential buyer.

A lumpy girl swaddled in a pink snowsuit was trying to manoeuvre a stroller containing a crying kid up to the intersection with St. Agnes, but its large rubber wheels kept getting stuck in the slush. She said something sharp to the kid, who stopped crying and recoiled under the plastic hood of the stroller, like a tortoise going back into its shell. The girl didn't look like the type who read books. Nor did an older woman with glasses and a purposeful air, heading towards the bank on the corner. Probably a local entrepreneur, he surmised. She had a strong, intelligent face and carried a bulging, black leather briefcase. Once he'd have considered her a possibility, but no, those kinds of women didn't buy books, either. They were too absorbed with proving themselves in the business world and only read summaries of financial and economic news on the Internet.

Then Sam Sorry-for-Himself hove into view. A mournful young guy, overweight and vacant, with a face as pale as a marshmallow, he looked like he suffered from chronic constipation and never even glanced in the window of the bookstore as he trudged by. Sam was on his way to the Kaffee Klatch. Flavian felt jealous of the Kaffee Klatch, too. It was the most popular coffee shop in Marsh River and did a roaring business.

Unlocking the cash register, getting ready for the day, he felt discouraged by everything – the weather, the store, the people he saw outside. Had he been naïve to come here and open a bookstore? His mom, Tish, had encouraged him. She'd come home to Fortune and opened the B & B on the lake, then wanted to have him close by. And after splitting from Jean-Paul, he'd been relieved to get out of Toronto. The memories were painful. But now he missed the buzz of urban life on College Street and the ethnic take-out food. You could always pick up something cool and different to eat in the city for only a few dollars, unlike Marsh River, where the only so-called ethnic restaurant was the Golden Dragon, directly across the street. It served sweet-and-sour everything, smothered in suspicious red sauce. He'd eaten only once in the Golden Dragon and felt guilty about staying away, because the owner, Mr. Lee, was friendly and often waved at him. Yet he suspected Red Dye No. 2 in every dish and worried about getting cancer with every mouthful.

The most disappointing part about Marsh River, though, was the citizenry at large. So welcoming at first, thrilled that he'd taken over the long-defunct hardware store building and restored its antique tin ceiling, they came in regularly for a couple of months. But then his customers had become like Canada geese dispersing over Bounteous Lake. They kept getting wider and wider apart. He wasn't building up the client base he needed to stay alive. Depending upon a handful of bright, middle-aged women who loved reading wasn't going to keep Boddington Books in business.

The bookstore's big oak door, which he'd refinished himself, opened. A lovely young woman hovered in the entrance, indicating that she wasn't sure whether she wanted to enter or not. She had the face of a Madonna, with skin like alabaster. She wore a buttery yellow mohair scarf wrapped around her head that glinted with flakes of sleet. And how encouraging, she seemed to want to buy something.

"May I help you?" he asked. "Please come in."

"Yes, I think I will," she said, whispery and girlish. Now he recognized her. She worked in the hairdresser's further up St. David's.

"I'm getting married soon, and I want to buy a book on how to plan a wedding," she said. She shook the sleet off her head, but kept the scarf in place, gingerly approaching the cash desk.

"Do you like Martha Stewart?" he asked. She looked like the type who might.

"Ooo, yes," she said. "I love Martha. So does my Mom. We've watched her on TV. She has, like, great ideas you can copy about decorating."

Flavian guided the girl over to his non-fiction section, at the back of the store. It was consistently more popular than the novels he placed prominently at the front, and he intended to switch the two sections around soon. Perhaps with more non-fiction titles on display, people walking by the window might be enticed into the store.

The girl bought two books. A big, pricey tome by the decorating diva on the art of floral arrangements, plus another on how to shop for the perfect wedding dress. She also picked up *Wedding Bells* magazine. And to Flavian's delight, she said that she'd be back before Christmas.

"I want some gifts for my sister. She's going off to Africa on an aid project," she said. "And she'll need to take along stuff to read, won't she?"

She smiled, still looking self-conscious, as if she'd come to the wrong place.

"Yes, I would think she won't find much to read over there," Flavian said. "Find out what kind of books she likes, because I can order anything for you. I only need a few days' notice."

"Like, she's serious, you know. Quite different from me. Tells me off for buying *People* magazine at the supermarket."

The girl giggled. Flavian noticed her eyes now. They were heavy-lidded, big and dove grey. Like a Botticelli angel's.

"I can find any kind of book for you." he repeated.

"You can? Awesome."

He examined her Visa card. Christine Tanner. The name rang a bell, though he couldn't recall why. Putting her purchases in a green-and-gold Boddington Books bag, he refrained from saying, "Thank you, Christine," in the pointed way that many store-owners did nowadays. Flavian disliked obsequious salesmanship and resolved that he wasn't going to behave that way himself.

He watched her out of the window as she crossed St. David's and went into A Cut Above, the book bag tucked under her coat to protect it, her yellow scarf the only splash of colour in the grey morning. What a charmer. Even better, a potential buyer of more books. He made himself a coffee. Bustled around the store straightening titles. Flicked at all the shelves with a feather duster, though nothing really needed cleaning.

He felt upbeat now, so he called his mother. He didn't like to bother her when he got down. She worried about him. He told her about Christine Tanner.

"Ah yes, that's Shep Tanner's daughter," Tish Boddington said. "Shep lives up on Fortune Hill. Next to Gow's place."

Flavian remembered now. He and Tish had discussed the whole strange story about Gow and the mystery relative, because years ago, she'd cleaned for the old guy and got to know his neighbour. She'd also told him a secret about something that happened there, insisting that he must never talk about it to a soul.

"Chrissie's a beauty, isn't she?" Tish murmured, wistfully remembering the time when people made such comments about her. "She gets her looks from her mother's side of the family. They're Dutch. But I can't think why she's getting married to that idiot Tyson Sprauge. Sure, he's good-looking, but what a jerk. He'll be nothing but trouble for her."

"Perhaps he's great in the sack, Mom. It's the underlying reason for most relationships, mine included," Flavian said with a cynical chuckle, thinking of Jean-Paul again – and pleased that he could make such a comment to his mother, who hadn't minded when he came out.

Flavian told her about Chrissie promising to come back for gifts for her sister.

"Ah yes, that's Kara Lynn. She's older and quite different from Chrissie. Real smart. At university in Montreal. A bookworm, I should think."

"Perhaps she'll take a whole load of my books with her when she goes off to Africa."

"Yes, perhaps. So cheer up, Flave. Just wait till the beginning of December. Marsh River is big on Christmas. People will flood into the store then. They'll be spending money like crazy, buying lots of gifts."

Tish paused. She swallowed and took a deep breath. Flavian sensed she had something important to tell him. She did.

"Guess what? I have exciting news," she said in a rush. "I got a call from a woman in New York late last night. And I still can't quite believe it, but," she stopped for another breath, "she's Gow's relative. Isn't that amazing? Revealed at last. After all this time. And I'm the first person in Fortune to know."

Tish stopped again. Flavian waited. With his free hand, he straightened some bookmarks in a slot beside the cash desk. He was used to his mother's pauses between announcements.

"She seems to be Gow's niece," she said at length. "And she's coming up here. To stay with *me*," Tish chuckled. "She's made a reservation. For an indefinite period."

"Wow, that's fantastic, Mom. I'm so glad for you."

Customers at his mother's B & B had become as sparse as in the bookstore, with the holiday season on the lake over, and winter on the way.

"Yes, I'm relieved, Flave," said Tish. "But it may be good for you, too, you know. People from New York read. I'll tell her about my son who runs this wonderful store called Boddington Books and how fantastically knowledgeable he is about every subject under the sun and —"

"Okay, okay, Mom," Flavian interrupted. He laughed. "Hold the maternal overdrive."

She laughed, too, pleased that they felt so comfortable with one another.

Flavian looked out at the street again after hanging up. Sunlight was breaking through the lid of sullen clouds that hovered stubbornly over Marsh River. A shaft struck the Golden Dragon's window and bounced back into Flavian's face. He blinked. Then the clouds closed up again, and he noticed Mr. Lee. He was standing in the window opposite, pulling up a blind, waving.

Flavian waved back, feeling the gloom dissipate. Yes, things were going to change once the mystery relative arrived. He could sense it.

Six

BANG! A volley of pistol shots rang out. Six of them, in quick succession, loud enough to burst eardrums. Val almost leapt ten feet in the air. So did Adie. A couple of thousand other people reacted in similar fashion. Then an audible sigh of relief, like a whale expelling air, whooshed around the auditorium at Lincoln Center, and everyone relaxed back into their maroon velvet seats.

Because it was just an act. They weren't being attacked by terrorists or a drug-fueled wacko with a grudge against the rich. The realistic shooting scene was part of the second act of Weber's *Der Freischütz*, a convoluted story about a sharpshooter who makes a deal with the devil. The Met was giving the German romantic opera a rare airing and the setting – a haunted woodland named Wolf's Glen – was suitably scary. So were the shots. Val and Adie sat downstairs, close to the action. When the curtain went up, Val had felt a wave of relief that she could retreat into this high-blown fairy tale about lederhosen-clad huntsmen and simpering maidens in dirndls, because the beginning had cut short Adie's latest recitation of woe about Michael.

Secretly, she was sick of hearing about the guy. The trouble was, Adie never let up once she got started. She would keep going on and on about Michael's obsession with red-haired girls. After they'd met in the lobby at Lincoln Center, she'd bent Val's ear about the latest one for at least twenty minutes, right up until the start bell rang. Then, when the intermission came, she'd launched in again. That was when Val blew her stack.

"Well, for fuck's sake, cherub," she said, her voice rising to a shout, as they stood in the lobby. "WHY DON'T YOU JUST DIVORCE THE FUCKER?"

Other patrons turned around and stared. One over-refreshed man in a rumpled green velvet jacket let out a laugh like a hyena and shouted "Way to go, girl," at Val, flashing the thumbs up sign. A society matron with hair like silvery grey sausages shook her head and slid quietly away, a tuxedo-garbed gent following meekly behind, holding the woman's cashmere coat over his arm.

Chastened, Val slid away, too, to her seat, leaving Adie standing on the red carpet with her mouth open.

When Adie returned to her seat, Val leaned over and whispered, "Sorry." She squeezed her friend's arm, full of remorse, as the curtain went up again. Yet inwardly, she thought she'd done the right thing. Val couldn't fathom why her buddy vacillated, because the two Richards had both cheated on her – the first with a girl at the office, the second with high-class hookers – and she'd divorced them both. Val now preferred the pink silicone dildo she kept in her bedside drawer and casual flings, usually during vacations down south. She never wanted a full-time man again.

"They're all fucking liars, not worth the trouble. And Michael, you have to admit, is a weirdo," she told Adie over a drink in a bar near Lincoln Center after the performance.

Adie blanched at the word "weirdo" and looked offended.

Like many people mired in difficult marriages, she felt free to criticize her spouse's behaviour, yet hated to hear anyone else doing the same.

"But he doesn't have sex with these girls," she protested, springing to Michael's defence. "He's basically a nice guy with whom I have a lot in common. He just fantasizes about their hair. It's harmless, I guess," she sighed. "But I realize now that he's never going to stop and I find it insulting."

"For sure, cherub. Any woman would," Val said, taking a large swig of wine. She drew her head back and laughed. "And c'mon, Adie. Wake up. Whether it's all in his head, or he really is shoving his willy into their ying-yangs, it amounts to the same thing, doesn't it? He's cheating on you. And I wonder why a talented, attractive woman like you goes on putting up with it."

Adie looked peeved. Fiddled with a strand of hair. Stared at her glass and said nothing.

"Stay in New York, but leave Michael, cherub. It's gone on for far too long," Val pleaded. "Don't just run away. That's nuts. You love it here. I'd miss you. And with the money you've inherited from your uncle, plus your share of the condo you bought with Michael, you could buy yourself a really nice place of your own."

"Well, yes, I might do that," Adie said, avoiding Val's gaze. She took a careful sip of wine. "But I *am* going to see what Canada is like. I'm curious about it now. You won't believe this," she turned and smiled, "but I actually called a bed and breakfast last night in this place where my uncle lived – and I'm probably going up there next week."

"You are?' Val was stunned at her friend's decisiveness. It was so out of character.

"Yes. It's time. I heard about the house and money weeks ago. I shouldn't leave it any longer, should I?"

"No. And good for you. I'll be all ears to hear what it's like," Val said, although in reality, Canada didn't interest her in the slightest. What could possibly be of interest in Canada? Up there, that great big country in the frozen north, so far from everything. She never read or heard a thing about Canada or Canadians anywhere – on TV, in newspapers, magazines. It sounded like such a boring place, full of boring people.

To change the subject, she added: "Wasn't that a wonderful opera, cherub? The huntsman who makes a deal with the devil. Such a good story."

"Yes, I wonder why they don't perform it more often."

Leaving the bar, Adie wondered, too, if going to her uncle's house, resurrecting all the flotsam and jetsam of his life, would mean making her own deal with the devil.

But what the hell, she thought. She'd take the risk.

Seven

this

Adie kept her plans under wraps. She always procrastinated when she had a touchy topic to discuss with Michael, because he invariably took offence. The moment she opened her mouth he would interrupt. Tell her she was totally wrong. Childish. That she didn't know what she was talking about. Then he'd stomp out of the apartment and disappear. This lightning reaction of his meant that their marriage had gradually ceased to contain any spark of candour or spontaneity. Adie now knew exactly what set Michael off, what to avoid saying, when it was appropriate to broach a subject and when it was best to keep her lip buttoned, and she carefully rehearsed little speeches over and over again, plotting her strategy like a chess player, alert for exactly the right moment to spill the beans. To behave any other way, to impulsively bring up anything she wanted to discuss, would only make him flee, usually slamming the apartment door behind him.

Yet Tish Boddington, the woman who owned the bed and breakfast, kept creeping into her thoughts. Her place sounded so pleasant on the phone. So did Tish, who had a gentle voice and seemed eager to meet her. She definitely wanted to go and check Fortune out. She just had to wait for the opportune moment to break the news to Michael.

Three days after Adie met Val at the opera, she received an unexpected work assignment. Micheline Fulbrow, editor of a prominent gardening magazine called, sounding – as she always did – as syrupy as a chocolate milkshake.

"*Ca va?* How are you, *cherie?* Long time, no talk," Micheline purred into the phone. "Hate to bother you, but we need an illustration of a turban squash in a hurry." Her tone turned wheedling, as it always did when she wanted something. "It's for a feature on ornamental vegetables, and you're so very good at that, aren't you, *cherie?*"

She paused, hearing no answer. "Are you there?"

Another pause. "*Ca va, cherie?*"

Adie thought for a few moments. She was tired of jumping through hoops for Micheline, tired of her phony solicitousness, tired of her habit of lapsing theatrically into French, when she spoke English perfectly. And why did the silly Parisienne airhead always leave everything to the last minute? With her own future so up in the air, she wasn't in the mood to undertake anything demanding.

"What's the deadline?" she asked sharply.

"Oh, yesterday, of course," Micheline said. She sighed as if the world were ending. "Hate to spring it on you, *ma petite artiste,* but you know how it is in this business. So many pressures, so many…"

"Okay, I'll do it, but it's going to cost you more. A lot more," Adie broke in. "A turban squash isn't the easiest thing to get right, you know."

"Fine. Whatever. Just get it done, *cherie. Tout de suite.* I'll shoot a purchase order over to you by courier today. Bill whatever you like." She sighed again. "And *cherie…*"

"What?"

"Give us something bold and colourful that jumps off the page at you. You know, your usual." Micheline sounded brisk now. She'd reeled her catch in. Time to move on to bigger fish. "By Tuesday. No later. And sorree, *cherie,*" her tone turned breathy, "but I have to run."

Click. Adie looked at her watch. It was just before five. She pictured the fiftyish editor clip-clopping to the washroom in her stilettos. Carefully reapplying her make-up. Adjusting a Hermès silk scarf under her chin to hide the lines. Maybe squirting on some fancy perfume. Then Micheline would be off to a dark, wood-panelled bar where a suave gent in a business suit would have a vodka martini waiting for her in a secluded alcove. Adie knew that Micheline was, like her, unhappy with her husband – it seemed that just about every married woman she knew in New York was – yet unlike Adie, Micheline had no intention of ditching Saul Fulbrow. He was old and fat. He smoked cigars. But he'd made a fortune building shopping malls on Long Island. The couple had a penthouse in New York, a vacation home in the south of France and a Caribbean villa. So his chic French wife, who knew nothing about plants or gardening or editing and had landed the plum job at *Gardens Around the World* simply because of Saul's business contacts, indulged herself in a little *cinq a sept* arrangement now and then. Adie wondered who the lucky guy was this time.

And Micheline's assignment actually delighted her. A turban squash with its extraordinary, bulging topknot and eye-catching stripes of green, scarlet and cream was the kind of thing she loved to paint. She took the subway down to the farmers' market on 14th Street. Found a perfect specimen, with a few inches of stem and a couple of bristly leaves still attached to the top.

"Yeah, that one's a beauty," said the young guy in a Dodgers cap who sold it to her. "I'm kinda sorry to see it go."

On the credenza in her studio, the squash looked perfect. She draped a length of dark green burlap down the wall behind it, then, after fiddling with a spotlight, she felt fired up and ready to go. And work always went better and faster, she knew, when she liked the subject.

She sat down at her art table and completed the preliminary sketches in less than an hour. Next came a black-and-white version with diluted India ink on another sheet of paper. This was important to get the values – the lights and darks – right. She decided she liked the results of that sketch, too. The first gentle washes of diluted aureolin yellow and permanent rose went in next, and tomorrow, she'd get into the stronger hues, the Winsor green and red and Indanthrone blue, which created such lovely darks mixed together on the paper, although you had to use caution. They could so easily turn to mud, if combined in the wrong quantities and worked over too much with a brush. But with luck, she could complete the entire illustration the day after that, she told herself with satisfaction.

Shutting the studio door at nearly six, Adie also realized – with mounting excitement – that this was the kind of assignment she could undertake from anywhere in the world. Micheline liked her work. So did other magazines. She'd still get calls, even if she moved to the North Pole. And with the Internet, it was now a snap to download files anywhere. Adie pictured herself in her uncle's home, which would surely be elegant and turn of the century. She'd install some huge, airy attic studio with exposed beams. It would be three times the size of the cramped cubbyhole she had to work in now, next to the apartment's kitchen. In Canada, she'd have gingerbread trim everywhere and dormer windows looking out on sweeping meadows carpeted in wild daisies. There'd be a backdrop of purple hills. A view to admire every morning, instead of a brick wall only fifteen feet from her face....

Her mind raced, she was so keen to go now.

She resolved to break the news to Michael tonight, over a good meal with a bottle of wine. That would soften him up. Get him to see that this exploratory trip of hers – and then maybe an amicable separation afterwards – was best for both of them. And even if he didn't see things her way, what the heck. She was so sick of the whole situation with the red-haired girls, she'd just go anyway. Adie grabbed her fleece jacket and hurried over to Dean and Deluca's on Park Avenue. She bought, at huge expense, a Styrofoam carton each of marinated poached salmon in dill sauce, braised Chioggia beets, edamame with red pepper, a roasted kale salad, and finally, a tub of fresh cubed Bombay mangoes. It was the kind of low-carb meal Michael loved.

She then detoured to a convenience store on Lexington and picked up three packages of peanut butter cups. These she stuffed into her jacket pocket, telling herself not to touch them. Yet she lasted exactly sixteen minutes. Going past the Church of the Redeemer on the corner of 90th, she almost collided with a little blonde girl in lurid turquoise and pink leggings. The child was in a hurry, weighted down by an enormous backpack, exploding out of a doorway that led into the day school next door to the church. She clutched a pink cell phone in one hand and a Hershey bar in the other. Adie practically drooled, noticing the chocolate. She plunked her shopping bags down on the sidewalk. Leaned against a planter of white begonias and variegated ivy. Rummaged for her peanut butter cups and ripped a package open, breathlessly gobbling both tarts. She watched the kid run to meet her adoring mommy further down 90th, wondering, as the sweet peanut butter hit her tongue, if the kid's mother hated cooking as much as she did. The whole rigmarole of preparing meals – the peeling, the chopping, the dicing, the constant checking of the stove – was anathema to her now. Her interest in cooking had waned, she concluded, when Michael lost interest in what she cooked. She felt glad not to be that adoring mommy, with a demanding kid to feed every day.

Michael seemed surprised by all the food when he got home from Columbia.

"What's this? A celebration?" he said in a jaunty tone, coming into the living room, throwing his tweed jacket with the leather elbows on the sofa.

In the kitchen, Adie pretended not to hear.

He called out that he'd almost finished his research about the Nazarenes. The lecture would be ready to deliver soon. And what a relief to get it over. He sat down on the sofa.

"Mind if I do a bit more work before we eat?" he added, opening up his laptop.

"No, fine. Go ahead. Dinner can wait," replied Adie, surprised, because he usually didn't ask and often dilly-dallied about dinner, so the food spoiled. She wondered what had prompted this uncharacteristic burst of thoughtfulness now.

Michael stared at the laptop screen. He felt guilty about his obsession with Sid and resolved to be more considerate towards Adie, so she wouldn't notice. But then he wished – as he always did – that he had a photo of the girl sitting there, on the screen in front of him. He shot a furtive glance at the kitchen. Adie was bustling around. Putting stuff in the microwave. Taking dishes out of cupboards. Humming an old Simon and Garfunkel tune. Not paying any attention to him. So he was struck by an idea: He'd take a photo of Sid. Stand concealed with his cell phone in a doorway somewhere and wait for her to go by. Do it one morning when Adie went on a longer run than usual, around the reservoir or to visit her friend Val on the West Side. Then he'd download the picture and use it as his screensaver.

Michael knew what he contemplated was dangerous and stupid. Adie might spot the photo when he opened the laptop lid. Might ask who the girl was. Even so, he couldn't wait. The risk inherent in doing such a thing fired his blood and imagination. Made him feel so alive. He was unbelievably excited. He put the laptop aside on the sofa cushions, then got up and crept into the bedroom. Plugging his cell phone into the charger, he resolved that he'd scout out a suitable doorway to stand in tomorrow, and that tonight, over dinner, he would ask Adie about her morning runs, pretending to be interested (though he loathed the whole idea of running), in order to ascertain when she next planned to be out for longer than normal. He hoped it was soon.

Back in the living room, the prospect of being down on the street, close to Sid, filled him with such exhilaration he couldn't face the Nazarenes anymore. He shut the laptop.

"I'm done now," he announced, yawning, making a show of stretching out his kangaroo legs as though he'd been sitting on the sofa working the whole time. "Shall I open a bottle of wine?"

Adie came to the kitchen doorway, smiled and said yes.

"A Cab, then?"

"That would be lovely."

It was a warm smile. The kind of smile he hadn't seen on his wife's face in ages.

Michael smiled back. She could be sweet when she wanted to be. It was nice of her to organize this special dinner.

They could relax together tonight. Then he'd go out and get that photo of Sid. Perhaps even scout out a suitable location tomorrow.

And Adie clearly didn't suspect a thing.

Eight

It was a beautiful evening. The rain had stopped. The sun reappeared. The top floor of the tall apartment building opposite, normally a bland grey, resembled a long, freshly-laundered white sheet strung out on a line, its windows reflecting the pink-tinged sky with the clarity of polished mirrors. Even the locust tree outside the living room window looked clean, green and sparkling again. Adie always loved New York after Mother Nature had given it a good scrub. She wondered how she could bear to leave, and if she really wanted to, because her day in the studio had proven so satisfying.

Yet she felt resolute. Actually saying goodbye to New York... she wasn't yet sure about that, but it was time to take a stand. She folded open the extra leaf of the dining table, right over the spot where Michael stood every day watching for the girl. They could eat dinner next to the window, while she revealed her dissatisfaction with his ongoing obsession – and the decision she'd reached. The view of the tree outside would be calming.

She brought the food in from the kitchen. Michael shot her a wary look. Adie rarely served dinners as elaborate as this – something was up, he knew – but he brushed the thought aside. She sometimes acted in a strange way when preoccupied with a new painting – and he'd seen the half-completed turban squash portrait sitting on her art table when he went down the hall to recharge his cell phone. The painting looked quite promising. Perhaps, he reasoned, she wanted to celebrate her success with it by dining on something more extravagant than usual.

Michael opened the wine. They sat down at opposite ends of the table, oddly formal with each other. She took a sip, said, "Mmm. Good" and smiled at him. But inside she felt so jittery, so anxious to get it over, she launched immediately into what she'd wanted to tell him for so long.

"Michael, we no longer love each other. This is a dead marriage. That's obvious to me. I think it must be to you, too. So it's time we separated," she said, her sentences coming out in flat, staccato bursts, devoid of expression. "I want you to know that I've decided to check out my uncle's house in Canada. And I might go and live there if…"

"You WHAT?" he broke in, flabbergasted.

"I think it's…"

"Have you gone mad?"

Adie expected him to get up immediately and leave the apartment, as he usually did. Somewhat to her surprise, he stayed glued to his chair, his voice shaking with incomprehension. He banged his glass down on the table, splattering wine everywhere, so that it pooled in his plate, like blood leaking from an underdone steak. Michael had never been a good listener to women. At work, whatever the topic, he was always impatient for his female students or faculty colleagues to finish, so he could break in and smother their assessment of a situation with his own vastly superior viewpoint. This time, though, his wife's words so astonished him, he had difficulty getting any words out.

"What's brought this on? You must be… must be, uh…." he spluttered, blinking at her from behind the raccoon specs. "Uh…are you into the change or something?"

Adie barked with laughter and shook her head. "No, Michael, I'm not menopausal. Nor am I mad. And I'm serious."

He turned red in the face now. He blotted at the spilt wine with a paper napkin. Squeezed the sodden paper into a ball.

Hurled the projectile across the room, where it bounced against a framed print of Dante Gabriel Rossetti's most famous portrait, *Beata Beatrix*. He poured more wine into his glass and swigged. The red liquid dribbled out the sides of his mouth and down his chin, on to the white tabletop. He ignored the drips and glared at her.

"You don't have a clue what it's like living in the boonies, do you?" he asked at length, in a dry tone.

"Well no, but...."

"Adie, I do know. And believe me," he sighed, "it ain't pretty."

Adie sighed too. She fidgeted on her white IKEA chair with its striped blue and yellow cushion, knowing she was in for the Let-Me-Tell-You-All-About-My Lousy-Childhood speech, which Michael had trotted out many times during their years together. But she didn't attempt to cut him off. It was pointless. On her husband's taut face, behind the big black specs, she recognized his "lecture look" – the expression he adopted when pontificating on a point to his students. And it was a look that brooked no interruption.

So she fiddled with her own napkin and stared back, sticking her chin out in what she hoped was a defiant pose. Then listened.

Northern New York State, near the border with Canada in 1954. Michael is born there, an only child, in a small town called Ponnetville. A dreary little place, "at the ass end of the Adirondacks" he will later say, with a deprecating laugh, when colleagues at Columbia inquire about his origins. And how he loathes his life. How he aches to leave Ponnetville and move to a big city from the moment he can comprehend where he is.

A prodigious reader, he identifies in his late teens with Baudelaire. He acquires the "horror of home" that afflicted the French writer, a sense of loneliness from early childhood. He feels he is destined to live a solitary existence.

His dad, Herb Smith, doesn't understand. Is not remotely interested in what makes his son prone to black moods. Herb works in insurance. A loud, crowd pleaser of a guy, he also dabbles in local politics, wears flashy ties and drinks to excess. While serving with the Armed Forces in Germany he met Michael's mother, Dagmar Fenster, an aspiring jazz singer, brooding, dark, taller than Herb, with a smoky voice. She entertained the troops in the bar at the forces base and dreamed of making it big in America. Yet her aspirations came to nothing. Michael never learns why she stopped singing after marrying Herb and coming home with him to the backwater of Ponnetville, because fame had obviously been her goal. Indeed, after Michael is born, she insists that he carry both their names "to keep memories of Dagmar Fenster alive." Yet as Michael grows up, he feels mortified by this burdensome name, because it makes him a laughing stock at school. He is the only kid in his class who has two surnames. Everyone – even the teachers – titter when they hear the three words "Michael Fenster Smith" read out loud.

And as memories of her youth shrink, Dagmar's mind shrinks, too. She becomes as suspicious as Herb of anything that could remotely be construed as "artsy". So much so, Michael wonders constantly throughout his childhood how they'd managed to produce a son like him, because his passionate interest in art surfaces early. Had he been adopted? He doesn't think so. He looks like Dagmar, although grows much taller than she is. When his parents imply that there is something strange about him because he doesn't like playing baseball – Herb asks him outright, during one Thanksgiving dinner, if he is "a homo" – it is the last straw. He retorts, "Of course not" and flees to his bedroom feeling wretched. And after that, he becomes obsessed with the desire to leave Ponnetville.

But he can't yet. Michael watches his mother shuffling around in a stained housecoat, her hair in rollers, weeping all over the wiener schnitzel that she beats into submission with a hammer from his dad's toolbox. He witnesses her squabbles with the neighbours when *she gets drunk. He becomes aware that people don't drink openly in small towns because they're scared what the neighbours will think. But he discerns plenty of secret drinkers like his Mom. He hates her. Hates Herb. Hates Ponnetville.*

Even going off to study liberal arts at Syracuse isn't far enough away from his small town. So after getting his bachelor's, he applies to the University of London and flees for England's "green and pleasant land" the moment he gets accepted. He finds part-time jobs, mostly washing dishes in Turkish and Indian restaurants, to fund his studies and shares an apartment in a rough part of Willesden Green with two other grad students. And he never looks back. He never needs to either, because Herb, showing off a brand new Chrysler to Dagmar, collides with a ten-wheeler hauling logs on the Interstate highway near Plattsburgh shortly after Michael arrives in London. They both die in the crash. Their son goes home only one more time — for their funeral at Ponnetville's Catholic church.

Adie hated having to sit still, listening to Michael's sad story once more. The part that always shocked her the most was the loss of his parents. Years ago, after first hearing about their abrupt demise, she had been surprised at his coldness. He expressed no sadness, no regrets, no feelings of remorse, no wish that things could have been different.

He didn't now. He simply compressed his lips into a line after the latest recitation and fixed his gaze on the *Beata Beatrix* print. It was his favourite Pre-Raphaelite painting, because it portrayed Rossetti's recollections of Lizzie Siddal, and her shining red hair, after she died. And what a haunting image. So ethereal, so uplifting. The print came from the Tate Gallery. He'd bought it before they left London, and blown money he could ill afford on an expensive gilt frame at a gallery on Bond Street. Even now, every time he looked at the print, he identified with the romantic Rossetti, revelling in those heavenly tresses that he could no longer caress because his lover had gone. Yet today, the painting unsettled him. The purple mark made on the glass by the wine-soaked napkin was mortifying. He made a mental note to wipe the blemish off immediately after dinner and turned towards the window, to avoid Adie's cold stare. He thought of his own Sid. Ached to see her again. Wished he could be on the street watching her, away from this tiresome discussion with his wife. But he wasn't tempted to look for her down on the sidewalk. He knew better. His jewel only went by in the mornings – a source of puzzlement to him.

Adie let her eyes travel over the back of her husband's large, bony head as he stared out of the window. She took in the thinning salt-and-pepper hair. The coarse grey wisps that sprouted perpendicularly from his temples. The pink, fleshy ears. The ends of the big, black glasses hooked over the folds of those ears. She'd once loved Michael's neck. So long, so graceful, so suitable for the brainy professor he was to become. And what a dashing figure he'd cut back in his University of London days, loping around in a knee-length navy blue wool cape that he threw over his suede jacket whenever the weather got cold, his neck protruding above the collar with the grace of a swan. The cape billowed out in the perpetual winds that blew off the Thames, and he'd seemed to her, back then, like a cross between Rossetti and a youthful Sherlock Holmes. Yet now what she noticed about his neck was a squishy brown mole below his left ear. It looked like a muscat raisin and had a long, grey hair sprouting from its centre like a piece of wire. An urge seized her to lean across the table and tweak the hair, just to annoy him. It was a symbol of how unattractive he had become. How pompous. How prematurely old. How exactly like the caricature of the stuffy academic that ordinary people made fun of. She pondered the nature of physical attraction – and why, over the years, this man whose body she'd once lusted after with a passion that was sometimes overwhelming had become so utterly repulsive to her. They hadn't made love for years. She felt no desire to. Nor fortunately, did he.

Michael turned back to face her with an edgy smile.

"Listen, Adie," he urged, leaning towards her, over the table top, his lips stained with the red wine. "I can understand that you want to go and see your uncle's place. But you won't want to live there. I know you won't. Because it'll be like Ponnetville. No culture. No life beyond sports and small town gossip. And pickup trucks everywhere, going too fast, driven by uneducated, boorish people like my Dad.

"Oh, and don't forget the broken-down farms, and ugly mobile homes, surrounded by stacks of firewood. It's not pretty and pastoral, the way you think it is. City people always make that mistake," he laughed mirthlessly and poured himself more wine. "And the locals, well, they're very suspicious of outsiders. They won't like you on principle."

"Why?"

"Because you're from the city."

"So?"

"Country people are inherently conservative. They don't like our liberal values. They feel inferior and defensive – and they resent the power that cities have."

"Perhaps it's because we act in a superior way towards them. We imply that we're better than they are."

"Well, yes, I guess we do, when you put it that way. City agendas do tend to dominate rural ones."

"Because we're in the majority. It's not really fair, is it? Huge cities like New York and Chicago dominating government policies."

"No, but it's just how it is. It's not going to change, either. City people and country people inhabit two different worlds."

Michael shook his head.

"And look, here we are, sitting and enjoying this very pleasant Cab from California that cost us — what? ten bucks a bottle." He held up his glass up to the light, swirling the ruby liquid around. "And we have a huge selection of wines like this in a liquor store that isn't even a block from where we live. But just try," another mirthless laugh, "finding anything like that up there."

"I don't care," Adie shot back. She looked down at her glass but felt no urge to pick it up. "I can live without wine."

"Oh, sure, you think that now," he said contemptuously. "But you'll soon miss it – and the ease of getting it, too. Because it's all jug wine and lurid coolers made from sugary pink and green stuff in country towns. And don't forget," he chuckled at the memory, "the guys with beer bellies swaying up to the liquor store counter in the strip mall, saying 'gimme three cases of Bud, man.'"

He shook his head. "Believe me, Adie, I know."

Michael changed tack now. He stuck his fork into the food. Seemed anxious to strike a conciliatory tone.

"Mmm, this is delicious," he said, lifting a morsel to his lips. "From Gristedes?"

"No, Dean and Deluca," Adie snapped. "I'm tired of Gristedes. Their stuff all tastes the same and I didn't want to cook."

"Fine with me," he countered smoothly. "Whatever's easiest for you. Thanks for picking it up."

They resumed poking at their plates in silence.

"And that reminds me of something else," Michael said, after chewing a mouthful. "It's the same with the food in places like Ponnetville. I mean, we're kind of fussy about what we eat now, right?"

"You sure are."

"Okay so I am. I admit it. But we both prefer organic, right?"

Adie nodded. Thought guiltily of the two packages of peanut

butter cups, probably turning into a squishy mess in her jacket pocket.

"You won't find take-out stuff like this," Michael motioned at his plate, "in the country."

He forked a leaf of arugula into his mouth. Chewed it slowly and contemplatively, like a cow masticating cud.

"You'd better get used to hot dogs and burgers up there, Adie," he said. "Even my mom got fed up with the selection of stuff in Ponnetville supermarket. That's why she took to making her own wiener schnitzel. And in the fall, well," he snorted, "get ready for *them*."

He stopped and shot her a look of triumph, as if he'd just administered the coup de grace in a Presidential debate.

"So, who?" Adie said, turning away uninterested, looking out at the locust tree.

"The hunters, my love. The yahoos riding around in those pickup trucks, banging away at everything they see, hauling the deer carcasses along on their truck hoods, blood dripping everywhere."

Michael shuddered visibly. He picked up the wine bottle. Held it out, eyebrows raised.

"More?"

Adie shook her head and put her hand over her glass. She didn't want to help him finish the bottle. Drinking more than a couple of glasses of wine made her giggly. Inclined to blurt out silly, facetious things. That would only bring on another lecture.

Michael filled his own glass and sipped, staring up at the sunlit apartment building opposite.

"What's prompted this crazy idea to go and live in Canada, anyway?" he said at length, turning away from the window, as if it had only just struck him to ask. "I thought we both loved New York. I mean, look at what we have here, so close to this apartment. There's Central Park. You'd miss running.

Country people don't run, you know." He shook his head again. "And there's the Met, the Guggenheim, so many restaurants to choose from. And look how you regularly go down to Lincoln Center to the opera with Val. You went just last week, didn't you? You won't be able to do that out in the boonies."

He stopped and stared at her, baffled.

"I thought you'd decided to sell your uncle's place anyway," he added in a flat tone. "Wasn't that the plan?"

"Well, yes, but…"

Adie suddenly found herself unable to say a word. She'd intended to tackle Michael once more about his peculiar obsession, but now couldn't summon the energy. It didn't seem worth bringing up, because it was such old news. Stale. Tired. Redundant. Not worth the pain of resurrection. And she'd learned one thing: People don't change. If someone indulges in a habit that makes you wary at the outset, be prepared for a repeat performance during the years ahead, because it is bound to occur. Michael's obsessive interest in her own hair had vaguely disturbed her the day they met, but she'd dismissed the doubts. Foolishly, she now thought. She pictured his latest, the one he'd be watching for at the window tomorrow morning. And the one before her, the student whose name she'd forgotten now. And the faceless others, the unknown intrusions into their life together, those copper-tressed goddesses who'd kept fuelling his unfathomable yearnings for something he couldn't have – and didn't really want, anyway. She recalled Val's outburst at Lincoln Center. Agreed with Val, now.

Drastic though it was, she'd just go, without a discussion or a fight. Far better to just remove herself from the constant compromises and seething silences. She only wanted it to be over.

She put down her fork. Took a deep breath. Announced with a vehemence that mildly surprised her: "I hear you Michael.

You're probably right. You usually are, about everything, aren't you?"

She smiled.

"But so what? I don't care. I'm going to Canada, whether you like it or not. I'm keen to see what it's like up there. And you…" She felt as serene and calm as the oyster pink sky floating over the apartment building across the street.

"…you can go fuck yourself."

Nine

Right from those first mornings before dawn when he'd crouched, frightened as a field mouse, in the snowy, dark woods with his dad, Shep Tanner had learned two important lessons. They were that – to a hunter – sight and sound matter. In equal proportions.

"To be successful, you must develop what I call 'deer eyes,'" Poppa Tanner had counselled, raising an index finger like a stern schoolteacher at his young son. "Now watch, Shep, watch what I'm doing now…."

And Shep had stood rapt while his dad scanned the woods around them with his sharp, dark eyes, not moving his head an inch, yet going over and over the same area several times, silently taking every detail in.

"Keep your eyes focused every second you're out in the woods. Watch for any hint of movement, however small," he'd stressed.

And then Poppa Tanner had grinned, mussed Shep's hair and said that sound was important, too. Very, very important. A hunter had to train his ears to perform at the same high standard as his eyes, because it was imperative to stay alert for the slightest possible sound in the woods.

"Any noise – even something you can barely hear, that lasts for less than a half a second – can be crucial," he'd said.

A twig snapping. A startled bird taking flight. A loud snort from somewhere close by. The crack, sharp as a rifle shot, of heavy hooves breaking through a patch of ice down by the stream. Or, in milder weather, a clumsy splish-splashing, like a kid in a bath, followed by the soft thud-thudding of a heavy four-legged animal moving away through wads of fall leaves. These all signalled that a deer was close by. So he'd better sit tight. Not move a muscle. Play a waiting game.

Shep adopted similar tactics anticipating the arrival of the mystery relative. He watched. He listened, as often as he could. After Charlie's visit, he kept both those faculties razor-sharp, poised to pick up any indication this much-ballyhooed individual had shown up next door. Though Shep couldn't see Gow's house from his – they were too far apart, the woods too thick – he could still sometimes discern the shape of a car proceeding up Gow's driveway behind the trunks of spruce. And he invariably heard the faint drone of any vehicle.

Two mornings later, it happened. Outside the mudroom, stacking cut lengths of a big dead elm that had crashed down in the woods – and that he intended to barter for an almost-new chainsaw that Cliff Sprauge up on Sixth Line was selling – he stopped. Because yes, he heard it – the distinct sound of an engine being revved, then shut off.

The day was warm and hazy, tiny yellow flies buzzing in circles, making the most of any patch of late fall sunlight that managed to penetrate the spruce. His prediction to Charlie had proved correct. The sleet did melt overnight. Fall was back in all its glory, thumbing a defiant nose at winter. Brilliant reds and golds lit up the sugar maples around the house. The air was heavy with the smell of the earth: rotting leaves, overripe fruit falling from abandoned apple trees and a flower he didn't know the name of, which turned the ditches and open areas along Fortune Hill Road into a haze of purple at this time of year.

When Shep recognized the sound of a car pulling in next door, then two doors being slammed, he felt absurdly excited and hurried along the trail to Gow's house. There was a path through the woods that he'd slashed years before, so he could get over and check on the old man – he'd been fond of Gow

– without having his eye poked out by overhanging branches.

He saw two men, slightly built, wearing identical dark suits. They looked sinister, like undertakers. Carried slim black briefcases. Stood ramrod straight outside the old house. The shorter of the two was rapping a pasty knuckle on the peeling blue paint of the front door, while his rail-thin companion clutched a Bible close to his chest, as if wanting to demonstrate his devoutness to the occupant of the house the moment the door opened.

He realized, with a sinking heart, what they were: Jehovah's Witnesses.

"Hey, you guys," Shep called out. He disliked the way these proselytizers roamed around the countryside in pairs, pestering people. He felt reluctant to approach them. Decided to stay on the edge of the woods.

"Forget it. The old guy died," he said. "And do me a favour, will you? Don't come round to my place next. God and I don't get along."

The men turned and stared, poker-faced, as pale and silent as ghosts. They slid noiselessly back to the car, their black shoes not making a sound on the gravel. The car left.

Shep trudged home, deflated and disappointed.

Then it happened again. Twice. A vehicle that sounded like a tank chugged in. Shep rushed along the trail. Outside Gow's house, he encountered a mud-splattered UPS van, the engine still running, the muffler shot, by the sound of it. At the wheel sat a bad-tempered young guy in cargo pants, pushing buttons on an electronic device.

"I'm trying to deliver a package to someone called Cliff Sprauge on Sixth Line," he said. "And I'm lost. Goddamn GPS doesn't work."

Shep provided directions. Said "Good luck, buddy," and slapped the side of the van. The kid looked blankly at him.

Muttered, "Sure," then hurtled off without so much as a thank-you. The van sent great glops of mud flying into the air as it headed down Gow's driveway. One landed on Shep's jacket. He shrugged. Brushed the mud off. Went home. Made himself a big pot of coffee. Got the Baileys out again and tore open a new package of chocolate chip cookies.

After that, a couple of hippies showed up one weekend. They came in a rusty white minivan. A bumper sticker in the back window said, Save the Whales. He found them at the rear of the house, standing on tiptoe in the long grass, peering in the bathroom window, the only one on the ground floor that wasn't obscured by plywood or curtains.

"Can I help you?" he asked, thinking that one of this pair had to be the mystery relative.

"Oh, hello, is this place for sale?" the guy asked. He had long, tarry black hair and a spotty complexion. He spoke in the drawly, disconnected way of a dope smoker. Shep disliked him on sight.

"Yes, we were wondering if it was abandoned," the girl chimed in. She was younger. Had perky eyes like black buttons. Wore tight blue jeans and a pale blue hoody.

"It's neither," he snapped, thinking the guy didn't deserve such a sharp-looking chick. He turned and retreated through the woods again.

Shep waited for the sound of more cars stopping. Didn't hear any. He dropped by the general store in Fortune to ask Gracie if she'd heard anything.

"Nope, not a dickey bird," said Gracie.

"Shit," said Shep.

Hunting season was due to start in four days. He thought about calling Tish Boddington, because she'd known Gow. Or the lawyer guy in Marsh River where he'd made his will. What was his name, Wickenheiser? Shep badly wanted to meet the mystery relative before hunting started, just to make sure it was okay for him, Charlie and Tyson to be out there. Then he decided, what the heck. Gow's next of kin wasn't going to show. He'd just carry on the way he always had.

He got his shotgun ready. Took his green-and-brown camouflage gear out of the closet. Brushed it off. Tried everything on. The tunic top felt uncomfortably tight across his middle, but at least he could still do the buckles up. He hadn't gotten as fat as he thought, barbecuing all those deer burgers, eating too many potato chips, shoving down Mary Ann's awful zucchini bread when the girls came home for family get-togethers over the summer. He lined up his ammo on the kitchen table.

Then just after six one morning while he was buttering toast, he heard a shot. Followed by another. And after that, a whole barrage of shots. *Pop. Pop. Pop.* They came from Gow's side of the woods, out back, not far away. Shep felt alarmed. The sun wasn't even up yet. Who could be out there so early? He shoved his feet into the felt slippers he kept by the woodstove and raced for the mudroom door.

Then, on second thought, he went back. For his shotgun

Outside the mudroom, Shep stopped, debating whether to get his ATV out of the drive shed. Decided, no, there wasn't time. He had to investigate – and fast. He hurtled along the trail in his flannel pajamas, peering ahead of him through the spruce, gun at the ready, searching for the person who'd fired the shots. He saw a flash of something red behind some tree trunks. And yes, there near Gow's house, he discerned a tall man with broad shoulders, dressed in a black jacket and a scarlet baseball cap. He had his back to Shep. Was holding a rifle in the air, the barrel of the gun pointed straight upwards into the thick evergreens.

What the...? This couldn't be Gow's relative, could it? Shep wanted to call out and challenge the stranger, but hesitated. He knew enough about guns and trigger-happy jerks to be wary. The stupid fucker clearly was a novice and potentially dangerous, waving a loaded gun around like that. If the guy heard a noise unexpectedly he might turn around and fire in Shep's direction.

The stranger inclined his head slightly, intent on looking up into the tree, still pointing the gun skywards. A wave of shock went through Shep. He recognized that profile. It was Tyson Sprauge.

"Tyson!" he roared. "Tyson! Jesus Christ, man, what the fuck are you doing out here with that loaded gun?"

Tyson turned to face Shep. He dropped the gun to his side and clicked on the safety catch. Hung the barrel over the crook of his arm. Ambled closer, the insolent self-assurance of the young evident in his gait and in the smile spreading over his handsome, twenty-year-old face.

"Oh hi, Shep," he said casually. "Take it easy, old buddy. I was, like, just trying my new rifle out. Decided to come up here this morning and knock off a few rats in fur coats. I need some practice before hunting season starts. Got two so far. See?" He pointed downwards with the gun and grinned. "Like, I don't want you and Charlie showing me up, do I?"

He kept on grinning. Shep didn't grin back.

"I parked my van over there, in front of the house. Just walked in, around the back. Like, it's okay, isn't it?" Tyson spoke quickly, nervousness creeping into his voice. "Chrissie told me that no one's living there. The place is empty. So I thought it would be all right." He paused. "It is, isn't it?"

"No, you fucking asshole," Shep shot back. "It is definitely not all right. You're trespassing. What you're doing is illegal. If the person who owns this land shows up and discovers you fooling around with that gun, shooting at squirrels, you could ruin everything for us. Do you want to get us banned from hunting here?"

Shep was tempted to grab the kid by the shoulders and

shake some sense into him. He restrained himself. Turned away instead to simmer down and catch his breath. Bloodied bits of a grey squirrel, its head blown off, lay on the spruce needles a few feet away. Spotting the squirrel, he swung around angrily and faced Tyson again.

"Put that gun away at once, or I'm going to take it away from you. Forever," he ordered. "And get rid of that fucking squirrel. And Tyson…"

The kid looked scared now.

"…get out of my sight. Right now. This instant. Now. I don't want to see your stupid face around here… "

Shep wasn't sure what he wanted to say next. He backed towards the trail. The felt slippers made a squelching sound. His feet and pajama bottoms were soaked with dew.

"Okay, Shep, I'll go. Like, I'm sorry, man. But can I still come out with you guys?" Tyson was pleading now, whiny as a five-year-old whose privileges had been taken away. "Can I still go hunting with you and Charlie? Please?"

Shep didn't answer. He recalled what Charlie had said. Wanted to kick himself for being so soft. Wondered whether Tyson should be allowed to get away with this or not. Concluded that he wasn't going to decide now. He heard the van start and leave, but didn't look back. He felt weary. Back in the kitchen, he kicked off the sodden felt slippers and undid the string on the pajamas, letting them drop to the floor in a heap. His bare butt felt cold in the morning air. He wished he hadn't allowed the stove to go out yesterday, but the weather had turned so warm, and he hadn't envisaged getting soaked in heavy dew like this. Stiff, cold and angry, mostly with himself, he stepped out of the pajamas and sank down on a chair at the kitchen table. The toast was cold, the butter on top dried to a thin, yellowish sheen. He threw it out, then discovered too late that it was his last slice.

Cursing, he found a new bag of chocolate chip cookies and gobbled half a dozen, one after the other, very fast, still fuming about Tyson.

Jesus Christ, what an idiot. And this was his future son-in-law. It didn't bode well. He'd better call Chrissie.

Time to give her a reality check about the love of her life.

Ten

Quinacridone Gold. Quinacridone Burnt Orange. Winsor Yellow, Red, Blue and Green. Indanthrone Blue. Alizarin. Hooker's Green, the hue that always made people chuckle

Adie was in her studio before seven. She pulled out tubes of her favourite watercolours – the regulars, the transparent pigments which made her botanical paintings so luminous and instantly recognizable. Outside the apartment, it promised to be a glorious fall day in New York. Sipping her tea, she'd watched fingers of sunlight creep across the top of the building opposite and felt tempted to go out for a run. But, no. Not today. She had to knuckle down. Glue her bum to the stool in the studio and complete the assignment for Micheline. She couldn't waste even half an hour.

She squeezed small amounts of each colour into the compartments of her white John Pike palette. Placed the palette on the credenza beside her wooden art table. Took out a fat sable brush next and shook a few drops of water into each compartment. It would take about twenty minutes for the pigments to juice up and soften to the texture that made them luscious and luminous when they dried on paper.

While waiting, she went over to her laptop, which sat on a small desk in a corner of the studio. Above it was a banner emblazoned with the words: "As the sun colours flowers, so does art colour life." An eccentric British baronet called John Lubbock was responsible for the quote. She'd found it in an art book while at St. Martin's and made the banner herself. The paper was a bit dog-eared now, but Lubbock's sentiments always inspired her to get going in the morning. Today, however, she felt more excited Googling flights to Toronto. Tish Boddington had told her to fly there, then rent a car. She found a flight from Newark, leaving at 8 a.m. tomorrow, and, to her surprise, it took only an hour and a half to reach its destination. This refuge of her uncle's clearly wasn't as far from New York as she'd imagined. She booked the flight and a car. Entering the numbers of her credit card and printing out her boarding pass, she realized with a thrill that she was definitely committed to going now. So no dilly-dallying with Micheline's assignment. She couldn't break off halfway through and finish the portrait of the turban squash the next day. She wouldn't – yikes – be here.

Yet the pressure felt good. Fuelled with purpose, she had a goal to work for. And her composition was sound, she knew, the preliminary pale washes laid down already. The rest, the crucial part, would proceed like clockwork. It always did, whenever she worked out what she wanted to do in advance. The drawback to botanical painting in watercolour was that you had to think ahead, you couldn't get sloppy, because laying in the pigments required knowledge of how they would work together on paper. Yet she'd become a pro. A recognized expert in the technical aspects of manipulating colours so that they didn't turn to mud. She hardly even needed to look at her "model" now – the squash with its brilliant orange, cream and dark green stripes, sitting on the credenza. Everything was ready inside her head. All she had to do was let the creative energy flow out.

Then, mission accomplished, she could get the hell out of New York.

And there would be no interruptions, no meals to prepare today. She could just paint, paint, paint, because last night, Michael had risen from the dining table, pink in the face with rage after she swore at him. Then he'd grabbed his jacket and briefcase and stormed out. And he didn't come back. At 6 a.m., she got up and checked the sofa cushions to determine if he'd slept there, even though she knew he'd done no such thing. She concluded that he'd taken the subway out to Brooklyn to stay with Dan Wagstaff, a faculty friend, with whom they'd spent Christmas a few times. Dan had a bubbly blonde wife called Jolanta, who shared Michael's German background and often felt isolated in New York. She also loved cooking and didn't mind unexpected visitors. Michael had retreated there before, following some marital spat. If Dan and Jolanta had taken pity on him now, she felt relieved, yet she wasn't about to call their house to find out. She didn't care where Michael was. Or what he was doing.

Next, she emailed Micheline.

"M: Got the purchase order. Completing turban squash today. Finished work coming tomorrow as agreed. I'll courier it over, as I'm going away. Not sure when I'll be back. A bientot. AFS"

Finally there was Val.

But, whoops, Val hated emails. She never sent them to Adie or anyone else, although she did own a computer. Val used the phone instead. If friends were worth having, she insisted, then people should make the effort to call and have a proper conversation, not hide behind emails and text messages. And thick-or-thin friends like Val were as rare as gold dust.

Yet the hour was so early. Val always slept late. And it was imperative to stay focused, to not speak to a soul. She resolved to call Val later.

The pigments in her palette looked juiced up now. She filled a large yoghurt container with water from the bathroom tap. Next, out came her hairdryer, the indispensable tool of every watercolour painter because each layer of pigment must be absolutely dry before going back in with another layer.

She sat down on her stool. Squinted critically at yesterday's black-and-white value sketch, then at the big sheet of water-colour paper, stapled to a drawing board. She worked out where the curves of the squash would flow into one another and where she'd lose an edge or two, so the transitions appeared soft, making the big spherical shape meld into the green burlap backdrop. It had taken her years to learn the art of "losing the edges," so that objects in a painting didn't look as if they were pasted on the paper. But now she had it down pat. Finally, she decided on the intensity she'd aim for with the crucial darks.

Satisfied, she picked up a brush and took a deep breath. She felt unaccountably nervous. With this plant portrait, there could be no second or third attempt.

She simply had to get it right the first time.

The day dissolved. Night started to close in. Adie's stomach rumbled like a subway car going over Brooklyn Bridge. Yet even the thought of a peanut butter cup didn't make her budge. She got up from her stool only once – to pee.

Her back ached. Her right hand felt stiff, fingers tingling with fatigue. She flexed them to get the circulation going and looked at the studio clock. It was just before seven. She'd been at it for nearly twelve hours. In the kitchen, she tossed a teabag into a mug and brought the tea back to the studio, feeling like she'd just run in a marathon. Her hand wobbled as she put the mug down. Scalding tea spilled into the palette. *Bugger, bugger, bugger.* She mopped the pigments clean with a rag, so hungry now, she almost shoved the rag in her mouth and chewed on it. Instead, she rummaged in the credenza for peanut butter cups but found only one package left. Ripping the paper off, she nibbled absently, without savouring the cups' golden centres this time, because analysing the completed painting in front of her was the only thing on her mind.

Yes or no? Would Micheline like it? Determining whether a

painting made the grade or not was always the worst aspect of an artist's life. It required guts. And ruthless self assessment Too many amateurs kidded themselves that their work passed muster, when they knew all along that it didn't. They just couldn't face the task of starting over. Yet Adie had never fallen into that trap. It was why she'd risen to the top of her field. If necessary, she'd done paintings over and over again. They had to satisfy her, before the client even saw them.

She held her breath, chewing her lip.

And relief. Huge, heart-rending relief. Yes, it was okay. Not brilliant, but okay. The orange stripes on the squash shone. The darks had wound up luminous and lush, not muddy. Micheline would be satisfied, if not ecstatic. She picked up a brush with a fine point to sign the corner of the painting with her monogram, AFS. Then she stopped in mid-air. Hold on a minute. She wasn't going to be Adie Fenster Smith anymore, was she? With the decision solidifying in her head to part ways with Michael, she'd better start using her maiden name.

She put ADC – for Anna Dorothee Coulter – on the bottom of the painting instead, even though it felt odd. She'd been AFS for so many years. Yet, as she carefully inscribed the three new letters, elongating the D as she'd done with the F in her previous incarnation, a great weight started falling from her shoulders. She was reinventing herself. Embarking upon a new image and a brand new life. This changed monogram merely signalled the beginning.

She called a courier. Dispatched the package to Micheline. Pulled on shoes and went downstairs, glad of the walk over to Modell's, the sporting goods store on Third Avenue where she'd bought her running gear. She knew they stayed open till nine. The cavernous store, bright with fluorescent lights, hurt her eyes after the controlled spot lighting in her studio. Racks of dazzling shocking pink and orange sweatshirts and multicoloured sports bras confronted her. Yet the place was empty of customers. She wandered around, dying to get the shopping over and done with. She'd never liked shopping for clothes. At one end of the store, she finally tracked down a fat black youth in a lurid lime green T-shirt. He was playing with a cell phone, had three rings in his right ear and a sizeable belly on him. He looked all wrong in this emporium dedicated to the art of staying fit. But he had a cheerful grin when she approached and shoved the phone in his pocket, clearly pleased to have a customer.

"I'm taking a trip – possibly a long one – to Canada," she told him.

"Hoo, man, it'll be cold up there. Lots of snow," he said, leading her over to a display of boots. He picked up one and held it out. The boot was made of undyed sheepskin and had a thick, fleecy lining. She noticed the "Made in Australia" label and realized it would cost a fortune. But, Yes, fine, she said, after trying the lone boot on. There was no time to debate the respective merits and prices of boots. Next, she slipped on a bright red jacket, heavily padded, which gave her the proportions of the Michelin man. The young guy stifled a grin when she stood in front of a mirror, wailing that she looked fat in the jacket. But it went into her shopping cart, too, along with some thick men's wool socks and sheepskin mitts.

It was nearly ten when she got back to the apartment. She called Val and told her about the purchases.

"Well, good luck, cherub," Val said. "If it all works out, I'll get myself some swanky boots like yours and a big fur coat. Then I'll fly up to the frozen north to visit you."

"Yes, but I'm coming back soon," Adie protested. What Val said sounded so scary, so final. Was she really going to leave New York? She reiterated where she would be staying.

"The lawyer who handled the will recommended this bed and breakfast nearby. And the woman, Tish, who runs it sounds very helpful. She knows my uncle's house. Says I can't live there yet. It needs work. But in any case, even if I do decide to take that step," she looked around the little studio she loved, faltering at the prospect of packing up her paints and leaving it permanently, "I'll have to come back and settle things with Michael, won't I?"

"Yes, and be warned. It'll be messy," Val said, remembering the two Richards. "But if it's what you want, then go for it, cherub. I'm not going to try and dissuade you anymore. And before you leave, you just gotta hear this," she rustled some pages, chuckling. "I found this old book in a thrift shop on Second Avenue. It's called *Strange Superstitions*. And there's some amazing stuff in it about red hair."

Val cleared her throat.

"Seems that Michael isn't alone with this fixation. People have been been hung up on redheads for centuries. It was considered unlucky by the early Christians, because Judas was thought to have hair that colour. Witches, too. People even killed red squirrels in England once, because they were thought to be in league with the devil. Can you believe that?"

Val chuckled again and continued.

"Egyptians burned red-haired women alive in an attempt to wipe them out, and sailors refused to go on voyages with redheads. Then Queen Elizabeth the First finally made red hair okay in England, and people became fascinated by it. The writer Jonathan Swift thought redheads were more libidinous and mischievous than other people."

Adie yawned.

"Hey, Adie, are you listening, cherub? Are you libidinous and mischievous?" Val laughed. "And as for Michael's Lizzie Siddal," she paused, "well, she got teased about her red hair as a child, but then all those Pre-Raphaelite guys went gaga over it. Almost all their paintings were of girls with red hair."

"Yes, I know," Adie murmured.

She wanted to hang up and collapse into bed. She didn't have the heart to tell Val that she'd read the book herself. Years ago. And that none of it mattered anymore.

She was beginning her new life tomorrow.

Eleven

November 6. Two days before the start of hunting season in Wellington County. Weather still unseasonably warm and sunny, according to the forecast. Shep took his ATV out of the drive shed in the late afternoon. Piled logs and kindling into a plywood box he'd built behind the bench seat. Headed into the woods, happy to be alone, the problem of what to do about Tyson Sprauge temporarily shelved. The cabin that his dad had built down near the stream was his destination. He and Charlie retreated there to warm up any time they got chilled to the bone, waiting for the deer to show, because the biggest drawback to hunting was that it involved spending hours sitting still as a dead man. And in November, when snow carpeted the woods in white, or a heavy frost descended, your feet soon turned into blocks of ice, even in top-of-the-line insulated boots. So the cabin, equipped with a small woodstove, was a lifesaver. Shep recalled how once, sitting motionless in a tree blind for hours, his hands had become so numb, he couldn't even pull the trigger when a big buck wandered by below him. So now he made a point of stocking the cabin with dry firewood before hunting season got underway.

The trail veered close to the edge of Gow's land, where the vegetation was dense with dogwoods and weedy willows. A large fallen poplar blocked his path. He swore. Poplars were useless trees, no good for firewood, always crashing to the ground whenever the wind blew hard. He cut the ATV's engine. Cleared the tree away with an axe he carried on his belt. Climbed aboard again. Leaned forward to turn the key.

Then he heard it. A voice. Definitely a voice. Unmistakeably human. Quite high-pitched. And female, by the sound of it. It was a surprise, hearing that voice out here in the woods. It occurred to him that there might be two people standing somewhere behind the dogwoods in front of him. And they were arguing, it seemed, because he thought he picked up the words "…get it RIGHT, will you?"

Twice.

Was Joe Perri, over on Second Line, out back of his barn, having a difference of opinion with the woman who milked his cattle? No, Joe's barn was a long way off, on the other side of Fortune Hill. Voices, even when raised in anger, wouldn't travel that far. Besides, Joe's woman had a voice like carrots being grated, whenever he'd run into her at Gracie's. This person wasn't like that. Her voice was clear as a bell.

Had some tourists found a way in off the road, perhaps? Ridden their bikes up from the lake and taken it into their heads to go hiking, even though No Trespassing signs were posted all along Fourth Line? No, they wouldn't come this late in the year.

It was odd in the silence of the woods, hearing that voice. Bothersome. No one ever came out here but him and Charlie. He'd only once met a stranger, a would-be dope grower, a fat guy with a woolly beard, and he'd sent him packing. Shep wondered if he could have imagined the sound, because it stopped now. Was it simply the shriek of a blue jay?

He got off the ATV. Walked closer. His sharply-tuned ears detected stamping in long grass, as if a deer were turning round and round, making a place to bed down for the night. The noise came from behind a dense tangle of brambles, over where Gow's property ended and bordered his. The grass there was long and overgrown in fall, and whoever was doing the stamping sounded frustrated, trying to flatten it, but not succeeding very well.

Because then he heard the word, "Bugger."

Then again, "Bugger. Oh, bugger."

It hit him then. Who it must be.

"Oh. Hello," she said. And after a pause, "You scared me."

"Sorry about that," he said with a grin, "but you scared *me*."

"I did?"

She didn't apologize. Just looked him up and down, her eyes alight with speculation and curiosity.

Then, after a couple of seconds, grinning herself, she said, "Scared one another, did we? Well, I guess that makes us even then, doesn't it?"

Her voice was crisp, eyebrows raised in a cheeky way.

And his interest was immediately aroused, because spirited women always appealed to Shep. She had a pretty face too, framed by lots of pale hair, and shrewd eyes. He noticed how she let them rove over the whole length of his body, taking everything in.

She looked to be about his age, or a bit younger, and was short, clad in an unzipped red padded jacket and swanky hiking boots. Both items of clothing appeared brand-new, not a mark on them. Her hair shone, whitish-orange, with streaks of gold, in the evening sun and was piled up on top of her head. Wayward tendrils had escaped and were flopping about her face as she fiddled with an old aluminum lawn chair. Shep noticed her close-fitting jeans as she bent over the chair.

"Nice ass," he thought.

The chair was from Gow's woods. It had once sat on a wooden platform high in a spruce tree – one of Shep's favourite places to wait for deer – but had fallen to the ground years ago and stayed there, its green webbing torn, half-hidden in spruce needles.

"You shouldn't appear so suddenly, coming up behind me like that," she said now in an accusing tone, turning to face him

Then she sloughed the jacket off in an irritable way and flung it on the ground.

"Boy, that jacket is hot," she said. "Stupid salesman in New York. Didn't know what he was talking about. Said it would be freezing in Canada. But it isn't, is it? The weather's glorious here." She took a deep breath and exhaled, staring in a satisfied way around her.

"But you," her gaze was steady, "you nearly gave me a heart attack. You are...?"

"Shep Tanner." He stepped forward, uncertain whether to put out his hand. "I'm your neighbour. I live in a house over there," he gestured through the trees. "And you must be," he spelled out the initials in a deliberate way, "A.D.... Coulter."

She seemed somewhat surprised at this enunciation of her name. As they shook hands, she said: "Well, yes. I guess I am, now. How did you know?"

"This is a small place, ma–" He was about to say ma'am, but checked himself in time. She didn't look like the type of woman who'd like being called ma'am. "News travels fast around here."

"Obviously, yes."

"We wondered when you were going to show up."

"Oh, so I'm a big object of curiosity, am I?"

"You could say that." He hesitated. "A lot of people thought you were going to be a man."

"Well, sorry to disappoint you."

"I'm not disappointed."

"You aren't?"

"No." He switched on his best smile, the one he assumed whenever he met attractive women for the first time. It always made them melt like lard over a camp fire.

But she appeared not to notice. She turned away again. Looked down at the chair.

"Well, er, Shep," she said, the hair flopping in her face. "Perhaps you could help me with this bloody chair."

"What do you want to do with it?" he asked, stepping closer. "The frame's bent. The seat's gone. It's broken."

"It is? Oh, I had a mind to squat myself down here on it for an hour or so. I wanted to do a quick sketch of the Michaelmas daisies before the light went."

"The what?"

"These," she gestured at a cloud of purplish-blue stretching all along the edge of Joe Perri's field. "You call them New England asters over here. Don't they look glorious?"

Shep shrugged. "They're just purple flowers. They come up here every September."

"Well, you're lucky. They're dying out where I come from, in England. Farmers get rid of them. They think they're a nuisance, getting in the way of their crops."

She shook her head and sighed. "Yet they're so beautiful, I want to paint them."

He'd been puzzled by her accent, her precise way of talking. It clicked now.

"You're British," he said. "And you're an artist?"

"Yes, on both counts, but I've lived in New York for years. I guess you knew that too?"

She regarded him with amusement.

"New York, yes," he said, feeling uncomfortable. "I did hear about that part."

"Oh, boy," she said. "What a gossipy place this is. I'm going to have to watch what I say and do around here, aren't I?"

"I guess you are. Yes."

"Well, then, I'll remember. Better not get myself into trouble. Better not..." she smiled in a mischievous way and stopped. Seemed to be sizing him up again. He wondered if she found him attractive. Suspected that she did, because she went kind of pink in the face. Then she looked away at once at the flowers, as if annoyed with herself.

"I tried just standing here for a while, holding my sketch pad in my hand. But I'm not very good at doing that. Never have been," she said with a wry laugh, as if remembering something pleasant that had happened a long while ago. She kicked at the aluminum chair. "I got quite flustered. Thought it might be easier if I sat down to draw, so I've been trying to flatten the grass out. And to fold out this stupid chair. But I can't see the flowers properly when I sit down low, so it was a daft idea anyway." She paused and looked around her. "It's very overgrown here, isn't it?"

"Yes. And that chair is broken," Shep repeated. "You should find another one. I can help you, if you like."

He gestured into Gow's woods behind her. "There's lots of old chairs lying around in there. I collect them."

"You do? Why?" Without waiting for him to answer, she glanced at her watch and said, "Well, that would be great some other time, thank you." She squinted at the sun, which was starting to dip down behind Joe's cornfield. "But I guess I'd better give up now, hadn't I? It's getting late."

She picked up her red jacket and put it on.

"Yes. It'll be cold once the sun goes down. When did you arrive?"

"Oh, about two. I was surprised to discover that Marsh River is only a couple of hours from the airport. But then I got hopelessly lost, trying to find this place," she added with a chuckle. "I finally went back to that store down by the lake and asked directions from a nice woman at the counter."

Nice? Gracie must have been on her best behaviour for a change, Shep thought. He realized why he hadn't heard the woman's car. He'd gone into Marsh River at about 1:30 to get a jerry can of gas for the ATV.

"You're not staying in Gow's house, are you?"

"Heavens, no." She rolled her eyes. "The house is a mess, but do you think it has potential? I confess that I don't know much about these things."

"Well," said Shep. "It's certainly solidly built, like my place. But it does need some work. Gow neglected it. You got big bucks to spend?"

"A reasonable amount," she said, laughing again.

There was a small sketchpad on the ground near her feet. She squatted and put it away in a green nylon backpack and appeared ready to depart. He suddenly didn't want that to happen. He was eager to know more about this strange woman, who'd shown up only a few hours ago and had immediately wanted to sit down in a field and paint flowers.

"You're not going back to New York right away, are you?" he asked.

"Oh no. I'm staying with someone called Tish Boddington, at the other end of the lake. I'm not sure for how long. I want to see what it'll cost me to fix the house up – and if it's even possible."

"Yes, I know Tish," said Shep, pleased. So she was going to be around for a while. He wondered if she'd travelled up here alone – and if there was a husband hanging around somewhere, perhaps looking over Gow's house at that very moment. He hoped not. She was interesting. Unusual. Obviously adventurous. He liked that in a woman. She didn't look like the type who got in a lather about brass table lamps from Thailand. And something told him that she was alone.

"Yes, Tish is a sweetheart," she said. "She's cooking me a meal tonight. And...."

Her face lit up.

"...I've discovered that she knew my uncle. I'm so glad to hear that. I'd love to know more about him."

"I knew him, too. Gow was your uncle?"

"Yes, but he disappeared when I was a kid. I haven't seen

him for years and years. It's a long story…" she stopped, clearly reluctant to go any further.

Her face clouded over. Her expression became tense. Shep wondered what she was reluctant to tell him about Gow. Was Gracie right after all? Had his long-time neighbour committed some awful crime?

Perhaps if he got to know this woman better, he'd find out.

There was an awkward pause. Usually not at a loss for words when women were around – his charm invariably won them over – Shep felt uncharacteristically hesitant faced by this one. She had a sharp, dry manner of speaking that unnerved him. Yet he decided to take the plunge.

"Would you, er…." He wasn't sure what to call her. Opted not to call her anything at all. "Would you like to come over to my place for a coffee before you go back to Tish's? We could ride over there on my ATV."

She looked puzzled.

"What's an ATV?"

"An all-terrain vehicle. You've never heard of them?"

Shep raised his eyebrows. Wondered if she was kidding. Glanced at his own ATV.

"No, sorry, I'm a city girl. Or at least, I have been for a long time. You don't see things like that in New York City," she said, with a chuckle. "But I've seen them in movies. I do know what they are."

He waved a hand in the direction of the machine.

"Won't take long. It's not far," he said, hoping he didn't sound too pushy.

She glanced at her watch again. Looked hard at him. Seemed to be of two minds, sizing him up once more.

"Nice of you to ask," she smiled. "But I don't really drink coffee at this time of day. And I'd best get back to Tish's."

"Tea, then?" He didn't want to let this woman go. "I have Earl Grey."

She wrinkled her nose. "This is going to sound rude, Shep, but I hate Earl Grey tea. People always think we Brits like it, but I prefer plain old black tea."

Shep liked her even more. He hated that Earl Grey stuff himself. The perfumey smell permeated everything else in the kitchen cupboard. It was only there because Mary Ann and the girls liked it.

"What about a drink then?" he said, turning on his best smile again. "I'm sure you like wine. Come on. Just one glass?"

He stared back at her.

She blushed then. Definitely blushed. Yes! He felt exultant. But then she looked away again, pushing her hair out of her face. The escaped tendrils were clearly annoying her. He wondered if he was annoying her, too.

She glanced doubtfully over at the ATV.

"I've never been on one of those things, you know. It's like some big, black-and-red insect. Um... I don't know..." she said, hovering and pushing at her hair.

"It's quite comfortable. You'll like it," he interjected.

"All right, then, thank you. I'll come for just one glass."

His heart did a little skip.

"Great," he said quickly, before she could change her mind. "Let's go. Hop on. It's going to be dark soon."

"Hang on a minute."

She went over to the ditch, clambering down into it. Picked a stalk of the purple flowers.

"I'll bring this with me. Perhaps I can paint it at Tish's. Did you know, Shep..."

She pulled gently at one of the layered petals.

"...that North American Indians used to burn these asters before they went out hunting? They did it to attract deer. The animals were drawn to the smell."

"Wow, that's a new one on me," he said, raising his eyebrows. "I'll have to bear that in mind."

"I'd love to see a wild deer," she said scanning the woods around her. "I never have. Are there any deer here?"

He smiled.

"For sure. This place is crawling with them. They come for the corn."

He gestured at Joe Perri's field. In the waning sunlight, the dried corn stalks resembled rods of gold, adorned with ribbons that rustled and crackled in the breeze.

"I want to take some pictures of deer," she said. "I've brought my camera in my backpack."

She straightened the backpack and hoisted it on to her shoulders. Then she stopped halfway towards the ATV.

"You're not a hunter are you?" she said, with a horrified look. "Because I hate the idea of anyone hunting deer here, on this land, *my* land," she added.

Shep didn't answer. He kept going ahead of her towards the ATV, his mind racing. With hunting season about to start, what should he do? Be honest? Stay silent? He opted to play a waiting game. For now, anyway. Because she was bound to come round. Women always did. They were all alike, especially after you plied them with a drink or two. He'd get a good bottle of wine out. One that women seemed to go for. A white. A Sav something. Mary Ann's favourite. He had several bottles down in the cellar.

He swung his chunky legs on to the ATV and motioned for her to get on behind him.

"Hang on to me," he commanded, "or you might fall off the back."

Obeying, Adie clasped each side of Shep's thick waist. She liked feeling his flesh through the coarse fabric of his jacket. Sensed that she'd been stupid to ask him about hunting. Because of course he was a hunter. You just had to look at him — and this machine, and this place he lived in, and the authoritative way he talked about deer — to know.

She remembered what Michael had told her about the men in New York State. How they were all ignorant yahoos, drunk half the time, hauling around deer carcasses on the hoods of their trucks, blood dripping all over the place.

So should she be going off to drink wine with this man? This hunter? Who seemed intent on flirting with her? His woods looked hostile now. Full of shadows. Dangerous. And where was his supposed house? She could discern no evidence of such a place in the dark woods ahead of them.

What if Michael was right?

Yet she had a hunch there was no reason to worry. Some dirty, wild-eyed hermit he wasn't. She doubted if he intended to cart her off to his lair in the woods to commit unspeakable deeds, although he certainly did seem a tad arrogant and pushy. But, at the same time, he looked clean and respectable. She liked his open, friendly face, pink from the sun, and the very ordinariness of his looks — the short, sandy hair going grey at the temples, the freshly shaved chin, which had a dimple, and the stocky, chubby body, which gave him the demeanour of a cuddly teddy bear. He projected an air of being so different from Michael, who'd become all bones and sharp, unfriendly angles, thanks to his stringent low-carb regime. But what struck her the most were the guy's eyes. Not particularly big, they were a pale blue-grey, deeply set under his brows, and he kept fixing them on her in a compelling way.

A little thrill ran through her body — the kind of thrill she hadn't felt in a long time — as he turned the ignition key.

He yelled, "Ready, girl?" over the sound of the engine.

She felt glad she'd said yes.

Twelve

The sky was a black velvet curtain. Adie saw not one star. No lights of houses, either – just the occasional oncoming vehicle, its headlights so glaring, they forced her to look away. The Canadian countryside seemed devoid of people at night. Incredibly dark, too. It felt strange – even eerie – after the bright lights and constant hum of humanity in New York City.

This road around Bounteous Lake – the same one she'd followed a few hours earlier, after visiting the lawyer's office, then checking in at Tish's bed and breakfast – turned into a taunting, twisting demon in the dark. It went this way, then that, then back again. It seemed to go on forever.

All around her were woods. Frightening shapes, crowding in on the road. Rarely, she caught a glimpse of something inky black and flat between the trees, which she took to be the lake. But mostly, she just saw trees. And more trees. They made her feel very small.

She also felt immense relief not to be driving. Shep sat at the wheel. He'd offered to take her back to Tish's place, and she'd said yes. So they'd gone outside to his big, dark green four-by-four with the huge, shiny mag wheels and splatters of mud on the chassis and fenders, and climbed in, even though, as she slid her backside over a jumble of papers, tools, discarded Styrofoam cups and cookie crumbs, she told herself *Kiddo, watch it, this isn't the smartest of ideas.*

A little bell kept ringing in Adie's head, counselling caution about this man with the smiling friendly face who kept pouring wine – a good Sauvignon Blanc, she'd swallowed two glasses quite quickly – and fixing his eyes on her in a pointed way.

"You need a driver. I'm not going to let you go off by yourself," he'd declared, swigging his own wine in big gulps.

"Oh, I'll be fine," she'd replied. "Please don't worry. I'm a careful driver."

"I'm serious, girl. You aren't going," he'd said, leaning forward and putting a hand on her knee. "Deer wander out into the road here. They get stunned by the headlights. People smash into them and break their own necks. Do you want to wind up a quadriplegic?"

He'd added, in an irritated way, "Even if you don't get injured, that car of yours could be a write-off. And then you'd get into all kinds of hassles with the rental people at the airport. Buddy of mine lost a brand new truck hitting a deer. He's still waiting for the money to buy a new pickup."

His eyes had met hers again. Then he'd said softly, leaning closer:

"And we wouldn't want that to happen, would we? Just as we're getting to know each other."

Adie had felt her cheeks going hot. She hoped it was due to the wine.

What happened to the poor deer his buddy ran into? She'd wanted to quiz him about that. Visions of a mangled animal with broken legs, dying in agony on the shoulder of the road came to mind – but concerns about wildlife casualties on country roads dissolved with that look of his. Was he hitting on her? Yes, he was. But why? Women of fifty-one didn't get treated as objects of lust. It just never happened. Did it? If a man took a shine to you, it was because you had money. Or he thought you might take care of him in his old age. Or he loved your pot roast.

The nurse or purse factor. Val Mendel always brought it up,

with a cynical chuckle, when people asked her why she never intended to marry again.

"Older men are invariably looking for either of those things – or both," she declared. "And I've no intention of giving them what they want."

Yet nurse or purse or not, Adie found herself wanting to respond to Shep's overtures. He had an animal magnetism about him, even though the vibes he gave off were confusing. They made her wonder what his intent was. As she sat in an old armchair opposite him, enjoying the warmth of his woodstove, sharing the wine, their eyes glued to each other, she sensed right away in the suggestiveness, the innuendo and the unspoken things they left dangling in the air, the potential for something that both excited and scared her.

Shep mentioned his wife in a cursory way, as if he wanted to get it over. Said her name was Mary Ann and that she was currently staying at her sister's. Then he took a framed photograph off the top of a cupboard near the woodstove and held it out.

"These are my girls," he said with pride, handing Adie the frame. "It was taken a few years ago."

Two smiling teenagers, both wearing shorts and halter tops stood on a beach holding paddles. A green fibreglass canoe was pulled up on the sand beside them. What looked like Bounteous Lake shimmered in the background.

"Kara, with the dark hair, she's the brainy one," he said, standing close to Adie as she examined the photo. "Well, we christened her Kara Lynn, but she doesn't like that much, so she's plain Kara now. She's finishing a master's in international development in Montreal and going to Africa after Christmas on an aid project. Very clever and serious, she is. Wants to save the world." He shrugged. "And the one in blue," he beamed, "well, that's my Chrissie. My little princess. Goodwill Ambassador at the Marsh River Fall Fair last year, you know."

"Yes, she's very pretty," said Adie, examining the photo. The daughter called Chrissie was clearly Shep's favourite. She felt a twinge of sympathy for the other one.

He took the frame back from her. Gripped it in both hands. Stared silently for a few moments.

"Chrissie's a hairdresser. Lives with her boyfriend, Tyson, in Marsh River now. He's a handful, always getting into scrapes." Shep thought of the squirrel incident a few days before. "But she'll straighten him out. They're announcing their engagement soon."

He turned to her. "You got kids?"

"No."

It was always difficult when people asked. She dreaded what came next. Often it was a hostile accusation. "Oh, so are you one of those DINKS who hates kids?"

Yet Adie didn't hate children. There was a much deeper reason why she'd never become pregnant, but she wasn't about to tell Shep.

Fortunately, he showed no interest in pursuing the matter. His daughters restored to their place of honour on the cupboard, he focused his attention on her again.

"I suppose I should ask you," he said slowly, lips curling into a sly smile, "if you have a husband?"

"Yes, I do."

Adie inwardly winced and provided the barest of details about Michael. She didn't want to talk about him. And once again, Shep nodded and seemed satisfied by what she said. They resumed their armchairs by the woodstove.

Both of Shep's daughters were pretty girls, she thought, picking up her wine glass again. Pretty and intelligent-looking. She felt irked by the way he had defined them. It sounded so paternalistic and old-fashioned.

"Beauty and brains aren't mutually exclusive, are they?" she asked at length, sharpness in her voice. "Surely it's possible for your daughters to have both?"

"Yes, of course it is, girl," he said, after a pause for more wine and another long gaze. "Well, look at you."

That was a bit over the top. She blushed anyway. To cover her feelings, she said, even more sharply, "Well, thanks for the compliment, Shep, but what's with this calling me 'girl' all the time? I'm not sure I like that. I'm hardly a girl anymore, you know."

He grinned and looked surprised.

"No, I guess not. But it's just a thing country people say. If it offends you, I'll try to remember to stop. I'm sorry." He thought for a moment. "Perhaps you'd prefer it if I called you 'woman' instead?"

He held out the bottle, his grin even more flirtatious.

"May I pour you some more wine, woman?"

"No, no," she said, laughing. "That sounds even worse. How about I call you 'boy' whenever you call me 'girl?'"

"Deal."

"All right, *boy*. You can refill my glass now, please."

"Sure, *girl*. Your wish is my command."

They chuckled and drained their glasses.

Now, leaning back in his pickup, woozy from too much wine, blasts of hot air hitting her cheeks from the heater vents, she watched Shep's square, workmanlike hands on the wheel and decided to enjoy the attention that he was lavishing on her. What the hell. This was fun. Being chauffeured around the countryside by a macho guy who owned an ATV, who called her "girl" and displayed a sense of humour about her objection to the word, was a surprise. A whole new experience for Adie. It made her feel young again. Attractive. Free. Even desirable. In a matter of hours, she'd sloughed off her mature, citified skin and become a carefree country babe, out for a wild night ride with an admirer who apparently had the hots for her.

"Some music, *girl*?" Shep said, putting a CD into the dash. She nodded and giggled.

"Why not, *boy*?"

The boom-chick-boom-chick freight train sound of Johnny Cash flooded the cab. Michael had always loathed what he called "the whiny warbling of white trash." He pressed the off button or changed the channel the moment any country singer came on the radio or TV. His vehemence had made Adie think for years that she loathed country music too. But cruising along a rural road in the darkness, the rhythm and sentiments seemed so fitting. Shep tapped his foot on the floor of the pickup. She joined in. They kept looking over and grinning at each other. Then they started belting out the Cash hits, yelling "…because you're mine, I walk the line" at the tops of their voices.

Neither of them could hold a tune. Yet how exhilarating it was, her thigh brushing against his thick muscular one whenever the pickup went around a bend. Another thrill shot through her. It fluttered around in the pit of her stomach as they drove along the lake road.

Tish Boddington's grey clapboard house stood close to Bounteous Lake Road, a mile outside Marsh River, where the town's new subdivisions abruptly dissolved into a patchwork of fields backed by dense woods like the ones on Fortune Hill. Her home – a farmhouse in another life – now stood only a couple of hundred yards from a busy bridge that trucks rumbled over, day and night, en route to Northern Ontario. Yet the owner of Bounteous Bed and Breakfast had tried hard to lessen the impact of the traffic. Tish's eye-catching sign, painted in curly blue italic letters on white, bordered by delphininium flowers, hung in the narrow front garden, impossible to miss, and made her little establishment look inviting. Shep stopped the pickup in front of the sign. He leaned over towards Adie and patted her arm, apparently about to kiss her. But then he glanced at the farmhouse and clearly thought better of it. He pressed a button to release the passenger door, saying with a grin that he'd be back in the morning.

"Nine o'clock, okay?" he said. "You can show me what you'd like to do with your uncle's house."

She nodded. Clutching the wilted stalk of Michaelmas daisies, she stood in the empty road, pondering, as the red rear lights of Shep's pickup disappeared around a bend.

What did this guy want?

Adie rummaged for her key, but before she had a chance to insert it in the lock, the blue door of Bounteous Bed and Breakfast swung open. Tish Boddington filled the doorway, pink, perspiring, plump as a puffed-up pigeon. Wrapped around her ample middle was a white chef's apron with the words "Meet Me In Marsh River" superimposed in big blue letters over a picture of an old mill. A black-and-white cat hovered in the hall behind her.

"Come on in, lass." she said, wiping floury hands on a red-and-white tea towel. "Supper's almost on the table. And I hope you don't mind Sammy coming to greet you, as well. He always does it to my guests."

"Not at all," Adie said. "I love cats." She remembered the cats of her childhood, and wished she still had one. But Michael wasn't fond of any kind of pet, and in any case, whenever he was around a cat, his eyes watered and he started to sneeze.

Tish sounded warm and welcoming, yet her tense expression betrayed something else. The speed with which she'd opened the front door indicated that she must have been watching out of the window.

"Sorry, Tish," said Adie, looking at her watch, realizing that people in the country ate far earlier than in the city. It wasn't even six-thirty. "Sorry I'm late. I got detained."

"So I see," said Tish, amused now. "Was that Shep Tanner's truck I saw driving off?"

"Yes, he invited me over to his house for a drink."

Tish opened her eyes wide.

"Oh my, so he's sweet-talking you already, is he? Well, trust Shep." She laughed and threw the tea towel over her shoulder. "You better watch him, you know. He always gets what he wants."

He always gets what he wants. Adie felt stupid and wished she'd stuck to her plan to drive over to Tish's in her own rental car.

"He's being very… er… helpful," she said hastily. "It will be useful to have him as a neighbour if I decide to move up here."

"Yes, but he's away a lot, you know," Tish said with a smirk. "Up north. Did he tell you he's a pilot? He works on contract for the government up in Moosonee. It's all Cree Indians up there and not accessible by road, so he flies them to hospitals by helicopter when they get sick or injured or something. And when there's huge bush fires, he goes up in water bombers and flies right over the fire to put it out."

"Yes, he told me about it," Adie said. "It sounds very exciting."

Tish snorted.

"Dangerous, more like," she said. "But that's Shep. He likes adventure. Always wants to walk on the wild side."

He likes adventure. Was that what she was – simply a new adventure for Shep?

"He crashed once," Tish went on. "It was in the Caribbean. He was working for some shady operation down there – I think they were probably smuggling drugs – and his plane ran out of fuel. He had to land in a swamp. Hit a tree and broke his leg and some ribs. Came home all beat up. Hobbled around on crutches for a while, but just laughed it off." Tish shook her head in amazement. "Then after a couple of months, he went back because, he said, the money was good."

Laughed it off. Would he laugh her off too? Adie was glad when Tish changed the subject to Shep's wife.

"Mary Ann's a sweet woman," she said. "Works at the decorating store in our new mall. She helped me choose colours and furnishings for this place. She's real talented at that. You'll have to go meet her."

"Mm-hm" said Adie, not wanting to hear what a paragon of virtue Shep's wife was. "I'll go wash my hands for supper, shall I?"

"Good idea. It'll be ready in a minute."

Tish served hearty country fare: braised pork with carrots, mashed turnips and potatoes, followed by her own blueberry pie. Adie was surprised how much she ate. The repast was a pleasant change from skimpy containers of take-out – mostly salads, endless salads – the kind of meals she and Michael existed on now. Tish explained that the meat came from her cousin's farm on Eighth Line. Adie resolved that she'd do more of her own cooking and seek out local ingredients if she moved to Fortune.

As they ate, they talked about Gow.

"Tell me what you know about him," said Adie. "I'm all ears. I know very little, except that he was my mother's half-brother."

"He was? Well," Tish said, "I don't know much, either. Probably no more than you. He was a funny guy, eh? I don't think anyone here ever got that close to him."

Adie swallowed. Put down her fork. Sat back to listen.

Tish repeated what everyone already knew in Fortune, that Gow showed up one day in a big American car. That he met Har Brydges in a bar and bought the Maxwell property on the spot. And that he said he'd lived in New York for a while.

"We heard that he was a famous artist there. Was that true?" she asked.

Adie looked doubtful.

"Well, he certainly became an artist. When I was small, I remember him working on a big abstract painting and spilling a whole can of red paint on the wooden floor of his flat in London. It made a terrible mess. And he certainly loved cars. He had a sports car, a pale blue Austin Healey Sprite, that he took me for a ride in once. We went to an art gallery."

She paused, smiled at the memory and dabbed her lips with a napkin.

"But I don't think he made a lot of money in the art world. His father was very wealthy, you see, and always supported him financially and…"

She stopped again, suddenly nervous about going further.

"Did he tell you he was French?"

"You're kidding. I sometimes thought he had a funny way of pronouncing words."

"Yes, his real name was Guillaume and his father – my grandfather – was an aristocrat called Didier Cresson de Rivery, who owned vineyards in Bordeaux. He and his wife had Gow – er, Gully to me, I always called him that – but the marriage wasn't happy, and she ran off with one of her husband's clients, a wine importer in London. Gully would have been about ten years old, then, I think."

Adie paused, mentally counting off the sequence of events.

"And he stayed in Bordeaux. Then my grandmother had a daughter by the wine importer – my mother, Sophie. But Didier refused to give her a divorce so she was never able to remarry or see Gully for years, because of bitterness about the break-up. His papa wouldn't let him come to England.

"And then," she took a breath, "when he was about twenty, I guess he rebelled, because he did come on a visit. My mother would have been about fourteen then. And, well," she paused, "something happened."

"What?"

Adie stopped, wondering whether to continue. She decided that she didn't know Tish well enough.

"There was some, um, trouble in the family. It seems Gully refused to fit in. My English grandfather didn't like him. The French and English never really get on do they? Even here in Canada, I hear."

She smiled.

Tish nodded and said: "Yes, I confess I never learned to speak French properly at school."

"You didn't? Before I flew up here, a friend in New York told me that everyone in Canada speaks French."

"Oh, that's just in Quebec, eh? They're like a different country. A different world. I've never even been there. Most of Canada is English..." She trailed off. "But carry on with your story."

"Right. So Gully moved out, got himself an apartment and hung around for a while. I have a picture of him at my mum's wedding to my dad when she was only sixteen. Imagine that. So young. But then I came along soon afterwards, and after that my brother, Philip. And when I was about eight, there was some huge family row. I don't know the details. After that, Gully just disappeared. I never saw him again."

"Sad."

"Yes."

"And he went to New York?"

Adie shrugged.

"I presume so. I didn't know it at the time."

"Why did he come up to Canada?"

"No idea. But listen," Adie said hurriedly, "I want to hear your half of this story. How did you get to know him?"

Tish explained that she'd cleaned house for Gow.

"He put an ad up for a cleaning lady at Fortune general store," she said. "And I answered it. I was having problems with my husband, Donny, eh? He's a bully. He's a telephone lineman. I still see him sometimes up in the buckets, installing the lines around here. Well, we got married when I was only nineteen, and then he started beating me up." She shrugged. "That's men for you. You tell 'em you love 'em and they treat you bad, eh? So I left him only a year later. Just walked out. Didn't take a thing with me. And Gow helped me get through it."

She smiled and seemed near to tears.

"He paid me well. Gave me books to read. History books. And he encouraged me, taught me things, the way no one else ever has. I never finished high school, you know, Adie, I have no education..."

She faltered.

"...and then I started seeing this other guy, another good-looking bastard. But that wasn't going well, either – I've always had awful taste in men – and Gow told me I should get away. And I..."

Again, she hesitated.

"... I took his advice, even though I was scared to death of going to a big city. You live in a small town all your life, you don't think you're capable of handling anything else. And of course I was still just a kid." Tish cleared her throat. "But I went to Toronto, like he suggested, and then only a few weeks later, found I was pregnant. I wanted to have an abortion, but I didn't know where to go, and then the baby was born, and I decided to keep him. I found work flipping burgers, waitressing, clerical stuff in a data processing centre, things like that, so I could raise him. And I gave him the name Flavian because the name means 'golden,' and he had hair that colour when he was born. Gow was reading a book about the Flavian Empire in Rome at that time and I just liked the name, I guess. It's too bad..."

She sighed

"...that ignorant people here make fun of it."

She paused.

Adie smiled. "It's... a distinctive name," she said, thinking she'd never saddle a child with a name like Flavian. "And I'd like to meet your son."

"You will. He runs the bookstore in Fortune. But you know what happened after that?" Tish's soulful brown eyes opened wide and her voice shook. "It was awesome. Such a total surprise. I lived in Toronto for years. Didn't come home much. Only saw Gow a few times, because I didn't have a car, eh? I couldn't get up here to Fortune. And then I hear from my aunt that he's died. She saw an obituary in the local paper. And after that, this letter comes out of the blue, saying he'd left me money in his will. I couldn't believe it. Did you know?"

"No. But I only found out myself a few weeks ago about the house. They couldn't find me, because I changed my name after I got married."

"Well, I decided to keep quiet about the money he left me. People are such gossips around here. That Gracie Piloski at the general store," Tish pulled a face, "she's the worst. And I came home because the money was enough to put a down payment on this place. I could start my own bed and breakfast, something I've always wanted to do. There was even a bit left over so I could help Flavian get his bookshop started. Amazing, eh? He was a lovely man, your uncle. Sad, though. Always something sad about him."

"Yes. It was..." Adie stopped. Her mouth puckered. Her face darkened. She looked down. Picked up her fork again and stirred her food in an agitated way.

"Do you think, um, he killed himself?" asked Tish, fingering the tablecloth with her hand, wondering whether to ask. "It's what Gracie down at the general store says."

Adie thought for a moment and looked up.

"I suspect that it was just a mistake, mixing booze with pills. But who knows for sure?"

"It might just have been that he was ready to go."

"Right."

They both sat back.

"You've eaten enough?" asked Tish, dabbing her lips with a napkin.

"Mmm, thank you. That was wonderful. You're a great cook."

Adie brushed her teeth in the bathroom next to the kitchen, then dragged herself up the narrow, steep stairs. Tiredness was invading her body like an illness. Tish had two attic bedrooms with sharply sloping ceilings tucked under the eaves. She'd given Adie the smaller, pink-themed room at the back, which was a relief. The traffic on the highway was barely audible there. The room looked out on a long, narrow garden. At the end there was a fast-moving river, rippling like crackly foil in the light from the kitchen. She resolved to take a look at the river tomorrow.

She dropped the shrivelled Michaelmas daisy stalk on the bedside table. The leaves were limp now. The bluish-violet petals had almost all fallen off. Staining flecks of yellow pollen had somehow found their way on to her white sweatshirt. What had possessed her to pick it? The appearance of a new flower in your life is an omen, her Scottish horticulturist dad had told her once, only half joking, and she believed him. Adie also knew that the Chippewas used the flowers as a love charm. So subconsciously, was she doing the same? Trying to work some magic on this man called Shep? She couldn't stop thinking about him. She laughed and told herself to stop being absurd. She was simply overtired. She curled up naked beneath the salmon-pink duvet and sought sleep.

Yet it wouldn't come. Conflicting emotions, unanswered questions, they kept going round and round in her head like a hamster trapped on a wheel. Love was so strange, so unpredictable, so impossible to figure out. It defied analysis, because people seemed to fall in love for the oddest reasons, and the objects of their affection were often so wrong for them. Why was Tish drawn to men who treated her badly? What had impelled Michael to become obsessed by girls with red hair?

There was also Gully.

Adie had never told anyone but Michael what Gully did. Yet the woman with the rather sad face who was washing dishes in the kitchen below her deserved to know. She'd been one of Gully's few friends.

Perhaps one day she'd pluck up the courage to tell her.

And Shep? Whatever was brewing between her and him, she felt powerless to stop it happening. Her heart jumped every time she thought about the guy.

Sammy pushed open the bedroom door. He bellowed – commandingly, in the sergeant-major manner of all cats – demanding to be stroked. Then he hurled himself up on to the bed with a thump and flopped down beside her. His warm, plump body felt comforting after the turbulence and hectic happenings of the day. So she allowed the cat to settle in, snuggled into the curve of her hip, his purr like a motorboat.

They both slept well.

Thirteen

An alien atmosphere takes over a house when it is empty. And the longer it stays uninhabited, the creepier it gets. Shep realized that as he stepped into the living room at Gow's. When the old man was alive, he'd enjoyed dropping by. The place was a break from Mary Ann's decorator cushions, which always bugged him, getting in the way when he wanted to lie down on the sofa and watch TV. But here he could keep his boots on. Sprawl about, his muddy feet propped up on a milk crate. Not worry about beer cans left lying around. Because Gow, a lifelong bachelor, didn't give a hoot about housekeeping after Tish stopped coming by with her dustpan and brush to clean for him. His house was a perpetual mess. Piles of his sloughed-off clothes – even, on occasion, soiled underwear – lay all over his own sofa. Yet Shep didn't give a hoot about the disorder, either, because he could relax in this house, something he could never do at home.

There was no relaxing now, though. The empty house on Fourth Line seemed as dead as its former owner. Sealed off from the world, like a coffin. Sinister, even. When Adie turned the key in the lock and pushed open the front door, the smell hit them both – of damp, decay and something more rank, like death. Shep recognized that smell at once. Dead mice. Or squirrels. Or rats. Probably all three. With Gow gone, they'd multiplied, legions of them, leaving their urine and droppings everywhere. Then the critters had died and turned into dessicated bits of fur and bone in the walls, under the floorboards and up in the attic. An empty country house that was overrun with rodents always had that foul smell of decomposition.

It was dark inside. Only a smidgen of sunshine, like a small spotlight, illuminated the sleeve of Shep's blue denim jacket. It came from the front window, which someone had covered in black plastic. The plastic had rotted, and a tiny slit, sharp as a knife blade, had appeared.

"Phew. Let's get some light in here, shall we?" Shep said. He went quickly across the room and yanked at the dark shroud. The plastic shredded in his hand, like a Kleenex that's been thrown into the washing machine by mistake. Fine black powdery dust flew into the air.

Adie coughed and put an arm over her mouth. She looked about her, blinking. Hazy sunlight flooded in now, through the dust, but she almost wished Shep had left the plastic where it was. How old, tired and decrepit her uncle's house looked, so different from yesterday, when she'd only peered briefly in the front door, then headed off on a trail through the woods, watercolours in her backpack. After living for years in the cramped confines of the Upper East Side, it seemed so amazing that all this land was hers. All one hundred acres of it. The reality had been hard to take in. The house and its interior had seemed secondary. Driving over with Shep this morning she'd also been bursting with excitement, humming along to Willie Nelson this time, on the edge of the seat in his pickup. But now her heart sank.

The enormity of what needed to be done made her want to flee back to Tish's cosy little farmhouse, with its frilly pink curtains, pink duvet and pink stuffed animals sitting on the chest of drawers. Back where she could just crawl into bed with fat old Sammy and nibble on a peanut butter cup. She wanted to retreat to a place where she could feel warm and unworried about anything, and forget the whole absurd idea of fixing up this house.

"Cheer up, girl," Shep said. He put an arm over her shoulder. Look on the good side. At least you're starting from scratch. There's nothing in here that you have to get rid of."

It was true. The large living room was surprisingly empty. No furniture, no old picture frames on the walls, no nothing. The wooden floors even looked fairly clean, with just a layer of dust, and the cast iron woodstove, its door left open, had been emptied of ash. The clean-up happened the first summer after Gow died, because the house kept being vandalized. Word soon got around Marsh River whenever there was an empty house to party in, and local teenagers had headed up Fortune Hill like lemmings every weekend to get drunk, smoke dope, have sex and just hang out. They broke in through windows on the ground floor. Slashed open the old brown corduroy sofa where Gow had died. Left the sofa's foam stuffing to spew everywhere and become nesting places for mice. Scribbled obscenities on the walls. Peed in corners, making smelly, sticky stains on the baseboards. But the worst part was what they left behind – liquor and wine bottles, crushed pop and beer cans, Styrofoam containers from McDonalds, broken electronic equipment, used condoms and small plastic bags that had the skunky smell of marijuana. The kids had also brought along boom boxes and made such a racket into the small hours, Shep finally bugged the township to clean the place up and make it impossible for anyone to get in. Somewhat to his surprise, they did. A carpenter came to nail plywood over the windows on the ground floor. A cleaning company emptied the house, top to bottom, hauling over twenty bags of trash away, along with Gow's old furniture. No Trespassing signs were posted.

Not that these efforts had much impact on the kids. What had really stopped them coming was Shep himself. Every time they'd careened crazily up Gow's driveway in cars and trucks borrowed from their parents, he'd gone over on his ATV and threatened to call the cops if they didn't leave. And once, on a Saturday night, he'd followed through on his threat because the kids laughed at him and called him a stupid old fucker. Then one of them had backed up and tried to run him over. So at two in the morning, a black-and-white cruiser had materialized, lights blinking through the trees, whoo-whoo siren waking up everyone on Fortune Hill Road. Five boys, all under seventeen, got busted for possession of marijuana, and Shep agreed to go to youth court in Guelph and testify against them, a move that didn't make him popular with the kids' parents. But he wouldn't back down. He endured the whole rigmarole, feeling vindicated when the kids got slapped with probation, community service and fines. He told Gracie, dropping by the general store afterwards, that too many people made excuses for teenagers nowadays, that they got what they deserved. And Gracie agreed. After that, the parties did stop. Gow's shuttered house retreated into silence, just another abandoned farmhouse on a quiet dirt road in the country.

"Who paid to clean up the mess?" Adie asked, after hearing this story.

"You did, girl," said Shep with a cynical chuckle. "You probably didn't notice, but when you received your final reckoning from the lawyers, there'd have been a bill for cleaning this place up tacked on somewhere, probably with the outstanding taxes. But if I had my way," he swung an imaginary stick, "I'd have hauled those spoilt brats up here. Given 'em buckets and scrubbing brushes and said: 'You did it, you filthy little pigs. Now you get down on your knees and clean it up.'"

He laughed.

"But I guess that makes me a rural redneck right?" he said, his look accusing. "That's what you city liberals would call me."

Adie wasn't sure what an appropriate response was to this tough-talking guy, this law-and-order advocate who was undoubtedly politically conservative and carried a gun, just as

Michael had predicted. But he'd saved Gow's house and she felt grateful. She smiled at him.

"Thank you for protecting my uncle's house," she said.

"You're welcome," he said in a sharp tone, uncomfortable now about his outburst. He grabbed her hand and headed towards the hall. "Come on. Let's go take a look around, shall we?"

She liked having his big, rough hand in hers. It had been years since Michael held her hand. She liked the kitchen too, because it reminded her of Shep's place, a hundred yards away through the trees. A sheet of plywood had been nailed over most of the kitchen window, so it wasn't possible to see much. But the space seemed big and roomy and undoubtedly had the same pleasant view of the woods from above the sink as he did. She pictured herself sitting in this kitchen, at a pine table she'd polished with lemon oil, sharing a glass of wine with Shep, laughing, telling him about a flower painting she was working on. The prospect made her feel fluttery inside. Yet those warning bells kept going off, sounding awfully loud in her ears, as they had yesterday. *What are you getting into, Adie? This guy is married. So are you. Aren't you asking for trouble, wishing, hoping for something that isn't yours to have? And isn't this all a bit sudden?*

The kitchen cupboards were old, with cream paint and round chrome handles from the fifties. A couple of the doors hung crookedly, hinges falling off. Adie resolved to give the kitchen a complete facelift and replace all the cupboards. The same went for the worn Formica countertops, marked with the stains and knife cuts of decades of chopped and spilled meals. Little black clumps of mouse droppings speckled them now. Spotting the deep white enamel sink, she gulped and backed away. At the bottom was a shrivelled pile of corpses.

Shep squeezed her hand.

"Just mice, Adie," he said, gently. "You'd better get used to seeing them, girl, if you're going to live in the country."

"I know," she said. "But I just pictured the poor things struggling to get out of the sink and…."

She let her words trail off, conscious that she must sound so naïve and citified to a guy like Shep. But he just smiled.

The bathroom stank. A quick glance in through the doorway revealed a cracked, pale-green fifties toilet minus a seat. The toilet bowl, empty of water, was stained a dubious dark brown, from what she wasn't sure. The sink and bathtub didn't look much better.

Shep let go of her hand and went ahead of her up to the second floor. She watched his legs. Like most men over fifty, he didn't have much of a backside. It just kind of melted away under the edge of his jacket, but she sure liked the look of those legs. Muscular, hard, capable, the kind of legs she saw on construction workers in New York. A sudden urge seized her to unzip his dark green work pants and peel them down to his ankles, nice and slowly, taking her time, so she could run her hands up and down his bare thighs. She wondered what kind of underwear she'd find underneath the pants. Hoped he didn't go in for baggy boxer shorts like Michael.

Then she blushed and told herself not to be stupid, relieved that he couldn't see her face. The faded wallpaper that lined the staircase had a bilious design of cabbage roses in pale pinks and greens, and she tried hard to concentrate on that, but someone had peed against the wall and the stain made her gag.

The upstairs layout was much like Tish's house, only twice the size, with four bedrooms, two each at the front and back. All of them had faded wallpaper, identical sash windows and sloping ceilings. The floors were bare. But in the biggest bedroom, some furniture had been left behind. There was a huge iron bedstead – obviously where Gow had slept, although his mattress had gone, making Adie mentally thank the cleaning company. People were always dumping old mattresses on side streets in Manhattan, and she'd developed a phobia about walking by them, their pale, puddly stains displaying evidence of sexual activity, leaky bladders and other human intimacies she didn't care to know about. Whatever private acts her uncle had performed, lying alone up here on a mattress for years, she felt relieved not to have to speculate about those either.

Next to the bed was a tall old dresser of dark wood, with four drawers and a badly cracked mirror. It looked Victorian to Adie. She stroked the wood, beaming at Shep.

"Wow. This is beautiful, Shep. Solid walnut, I think," she marvelled. "Just try finding something like this in New York. It would cost a fortune. Amazing that it's been left here. I wonder," she tried to pull open the top drawer, but it was stuck, "why nobody stole it."

Shep shrugged. City people always went wild over furniture like this, yet he couldn't understand the fascination. He loved his antique woodstove, but that was different. A woodstove was practical. It kept his house warm. Saved him money. All these heavy old relics from bygone days did was break your back when you tried to lift them. They took up too much space and their drawers always seemed to stick when you needed to grab a pair of clean socks in a hurry.

All the same, he liked the way Adie stood with her back to him, bent over the dresser's bottom drawer, because her posture made him fantasize again about her ass. She had the kind of ass he liked. Round and shapely, buttocks curvy like peaches, the crack obvious in those stretchy jeans. She wasn't slim-hipped and boyish, like the skinny chicks he saw nowadays on TV. He wished the bedstead still had a mattress because he wanted to put his hands on her hips, push her on to the bed, pull the jeans down and fuck her. Hard. He wondered if she wore a thong. Hoped she didn't go in for big white cotton granny pants like Mary Ann.

It wasn't a ridiculous notion, either, he told himself. She wouldn't say no. Wouldn't push him off in horror. He could always tell. There was an eagerness in her eyes now, lighting up her whole face. It was a familiar look, the one he saw on many women when they were around him.

But not yet, he told himself. Bide your time, buddy. Handle the whole thing the way you hunt for deer. Slowly, with methodical steps. And of course, there is that little matter of access to her land that has to be settled first.

"Well, what do you think?" Shep said, when they were back sharing coffee and cookies in his kitchen. "Do you want to take the plunge and renovate? Because if you do," he sloshed Baileys into her mug, "I know the perfect guy."

"Good. Who?"

"His name's Knock. Well, it's Nathan Knockenhammer, but everyone calls him Knock. He loves renovating old houses and does a real nice job. He doesn't cut corners." He paused to help himself to the Baileys. "He's a Mennonite."

Adie looked puzzled.

"You mean he belongs to that sect who wear black trousers and suspenders and go around in horse-drawn buggies?"

Shep laughed. Tasted his coffee. Added more Baileys. Bit into a cookie.

"No, no, nothing like that," he said, chewing and swallowing. "Those are old-order Mennonites. Knock's not one of those. He doesn't look any different from you and me. He drives a truck like mine. There's many different factions of Mennonites around here. My wi–" He was about to tell Adie that Mary Ann was a Mennonite, but thought better of it. He swallowed. "Uh, we have a lot of Mennonites in this part of Canada. And they're very good at construction."

"Sounds great," Adie said. "How do I get hold of him?"

"Do you have a cell phone?."

She shook her head.

"Not with me."

Her cell phone was in her studio. Deliberately left behind, because she'd wanted to dodge any messages that Michael might leave.

Shep pulled out his own cell and called. He left a message for the Mennonite builder to call Adie at Tish's place, or to call him.

"I tell you what," he said, restoring the cell phone to his back pocket and draining his coffee. "Knock's difficult to get hold of. You could wait for him to call back for weeks. But he's usually on site, at one of the houses he's renovating. And I think I know where we can find him. So if you like," Shep glanced at a clock on the wall of the kitchen, "we could go out and look."

"Oh yes, let's," Adie said, clapping her hands together. "That would be great."

"Shall I bring along the cookies?" he said, grabbing the bag of chocolate chips and grinning at her. "I have to confess that I can't survive for long without something sweet to nibble on."

"You can't?" The revelation astonished her. "Wow. I'm the same."

As Shep headed to the mudroom door, clutching the cookie bag, she wanted to run up behind him and throw her arms around his neck. Because how refreshing. How candid. How unaffected this country boy was. No one she knew in New York would ever admit to having a sweet tooth. Revealing that you snacked on empty calories, that you loved candy or any kind of junk food, was an admission of failure. It instantly branded you as low class, trashy, one of the tiresome slobs who didn't know or care about what they ate and who were destined to become obese and unhealthy and a burden on the taxpayers. A waterfall of relief flooded over Adie, hearing Shep's confession. She rummaged in her jacket for a peanut butter cup to offer him, wanting to unload to a sympathetic soul about her own secret craving.

Yet she found no Reese's packages. She'd pigged down her last one yesterday. On the drive up to Fortune.

It was six miles into the centre of Marsh River. They sang along to Shep's country music CDs, swigging cans of Coke and nibbling more cookies as if they didn't have a care in the world. Leaning back on the seat of the pickup, Adie relaxed at last. Shep followed the twisting route around the lake once more. Yet in daylight, the scenery on either side – so threatening last night – showed itself to be merely a thin strip of woods backed up by expansive fields where a crop grew that she didn't recognize. The crop's colour captivated her. It looked like the Quinacridone Gold she incorporated into almost all her paintings. Depending upon the light, QG, as she called it, could be a golden brown. Or a rich, dense butterscotch. Or a luminous gold. Or a streaky blend of all three. And if heavily diluted with water, it had the clear, punchy yellow of a daffodil. Now, a great rainbow of those hues undulated all the way to the horizon on either side of the road. She asked Shep what the crop was.

"Soybeans," he said. "Why?"

"They're such a lovely colour."

"They are?" Shep laughed. "They're just soybeans to me. They look like this before they're harvested."

"But they're like a painting," she protested. "You have no appreciation of the finer things in life, boy."

"Yes I do, girl. Look who's sitting in the truck beside me."

"Oh, stop it."

They were joshing and laughing like lovers now. Yet Adie no longer worried about the consequences. He obviously liked her. She liked him. So why not enjoy the experience for what it was? Reaching the town centre, she sat up straight on the seat, pleasantly surprised. How pretty, how charming, Marsh River was. Driving in yesterday morning, she hadn't appreciated its virtues, because Bill Wickenheiser's law office was in an ugly shopping mall in the suburbs. Yet the downtown reminded her of Vermont. When Val was with Richard the Second, they'd often rented a car at weekends so Val could go antiquing. She collected old duck decoys back then, and they'd explored a lot of New England together. Now Adie detected distinct similarities to Vermont in this part of southern Canada. Century-old, three-storey buildings, built of grey stone, lined the wide main street. In front of the stores, the falling leaves of towering old sugar maples carpeted the sidewalks in scarlet and gold. Slowing the pickup, Shep pointed out the Kaffee Klatch, where three laughing middle-aged women sat on stools in the front window, heads bent, sharing a joke about something. Then he slowed still more, going past a brightly lit hairdressing salon.

"That's where Chrissie works," he said, pride in his voice. "She'll be there now, probably giving some old lady a perm."

He halted outside a store further down the street. The façade was smartly done up in new magenta and deep green glossy paint. A man in his twenties wearing jeans and a checkered flannel shirt stood outside, polishing the big plate glass window.

"Yo, Flavian," Shep called out through the driver's window. "Come over and meet Adie. She's staying at your mom's. She's Gow's relative, you know."

So this was Tish's son, Adie thought approvingly, opening the pickup door and getting out to shake Flavian's hand. He had close-cropped brown hair and a round, likeable face. She saw a slight resemblance to Tish in the big, brown eyes. His store sign, Boddington Books, hand-carved in wood, the letters picked out in gold leaf, looked as tasteful as any she'd seen in Vermont.

They exchanged pleasantries. She told Flavian that she'd drop by and look for something to read during her stay.

"I'll look forward to that, Adie," he said. "It's a pleasure to meet you," and got back to his squeegee mop.

The other end of Marsh River was more crowded – and an eyesore. In common with the outskirts of any city or small town across North America, it revealed itself to be a mish-mash of parking lots, aluminum-clad buildings without a shred of charm and tacky signs, blaring deals on everything from plumbing supplies to pet food. At the end of this visual chaos stood Marsh River Mall, where Adie now realized she'd headed to take possession of her uncle's house. The long, rambling row of boxy buildings had a supermarket at one end and a lumber yard at the other. In between the two, there were smaller establishments. She spotted Wickenheiser and Ecclestone's offices, while next door was Three Brydges Real Estate and beyond that, a home furnishings store called Home and Heart, with lamps and multicoloured cushions displayed in its window.

Shep shot a furtive look at Home and Heart, then drove on, out to the country again. The roads became straight once more, lined with trees and more fields of soybeans and corn, backed by woodland. Here and there were red brick farmhouses rather like hers, but she saw none of the tacky mobile homes that Michael had talked about. This was obviously a more affluent area than Ponnetville. Most of the farmhouses looked like pieces on a Monopoly board, squatting at the end of remarkably long driveways that stretched like white ribbons between the fields. Shep slowed in a hamlet where the road ran, zigzag fashion, along the banks of a river and pulled up beside an old stone property in the centre of the village. An enormous yellow dumpster filled the front yard. Two men in hardhats and work boots were trekking in and out of the house, throwing its ripped-out innards high into the air and over the sides of the metal bin, where they kept landing with a crash.

Shep leaned out of his window and called one of the men over.

"Knock around? I've a lovely lady sitting here in my truck who'd like," he grinned at Adie, "to make the acquaintance of Marsh River's renovation king."

The man laughed and shook his head. Said Knock was probably over at a house on the other side of Marsh River. In a village called Southwood. So they drove back again through the town, along more straight country roads and wound up beside another gutted house.

Yet Knock wasn't there, either.

This happened once more, east of the town.

"This Knock sure is a popular guy," said Adie, her good humour flagging. She felt tired now and thought longingly of Tish's place – and perhaps a mug of tea.

"Yes, he must be getting a lot of business. I'm glad for the guy. He's been through some rough times when he had no work at all. Want to give up now?" Shep asked.

She nodded.

"I'm not used to racing around all these roads. It's exhausting," she said.

Shep looked mildly surprised, as though this was the kind of thing he did every day.

"You get used to driving when you live in the country," he said. "But you don't really need to chase after Knock. He'll certainly call you when he has the time."

On the way back, taking a different route, Shep drove beneath a flock of big black circling birds that resembled eagles. The birds were high in the air, above a flock of grazing sheep. Their dark shadows fell over the truck as Shep proceeded at a fast clip below them.

"Shades of Alfred Hitchcock," Adie said with a shiver, looking up at the sky.

"Turkey vultures," Shep said. "A sheep in that field probably got killed by a coyote. We have a lot of coyotes around here.

I shoot them sometimes and the farmers are grateful because they're a real nuisance." He peered out of the driver's window into the ditch alongside the road. "But it could be that a deer got hit by a car as it crossed the road. Just remember, Adie," he added, turnng towards her with a strange smile, "whenever you see those birds up in the sky, it's a sign of something dead close by."

She felt relieved when they left the circling birds behind.

As Shep turned back on to Bounteous Lake Road, she expected – indeed hoped – that he'd drop her at Tish's. The sun was now a ball of fire behind the black spruce trees and sinking lower. She worried about the lateness of the day.

Yet he didn't stop. He put his foot down hard on the gas, and drove straight past the B & B's blue-and-white sign.

"But I'm tired, Shep. I'd like to –" she protested.

"There's something I want to show you, girl," he broke in, sounding mysterious. "It's out in my woods." Noting the apprehension on her face, he leaned over, grabbed her hand and said: "There's no need to be scared. You aren't scared of me, are you?"

He grinned.

She shook her head. Yet as he pulled into his driveway, a little coil of fear unravelled inside her.

It was getting dark. What was his plan now?

Fourteen

Mist thickened the air. Long white skeins of wool threaded themselves around the pickup as Shep parked. Sliding off the seat, Adie shivered. A clammy feeling enveloped her. She wanted to hurry away along the trail, over to her uncle's place. It was time to take a breather. To think things over. To escape in her rental car, back to the comfort of Tish's warm little house. Shep's overpowering presence, coupled with his apparent eagerness to help her, was tying her stomach in knots. She realized that she also missed running. After two days of sitting in a plane, vehicle or on the ATV, she was like a cut tulip deprived of water. Withered. Droopy. Unsure if she could summon the energy to hoist herself upright again.

Adie had taken up running because of a remark from Michael. One afternoon, while they were dressing in their bedroom for a faculty dinner, he'd looked her up and down and said that she was putting on weight. And that he was surprised "because we always eat such healthy food." They were well into his low-carb regime by then, existing mostly on take-out salads and grilled chicken, with, at Michael's insistence, every smidgen of the skin removed. Frightened that he would discover her guilty secret – or worse, make her see a doctor – she'd gone out and bought running gear the next day. And though her new running routine didn't make her drop any pounds – she nibbled on too many peanut butter cups for that to happen – she stopped gaining them too. Then Michael, to her relief, seemed to forget the matter.

But now, feeling flabby and out of shape, deprived of her

morning ritual in Central Park, Adie realized that she'd have to stop running if she came to live in Fortune. What Michael had declared so vehemently – that country people and city people inhabited two different worlds – was true. Rural roads were devoid of pedestrians. The locals didn't run. Nor did they ride a bike or walk to a store. Those were things city people did. Here, you drove everywhere, even if sitting in a car made you fat – and in Marsh River, many people did indeed look monstrously fat, poured into their minivans, all double chins and dimples and big round protruding bellies, as they waited, engines running, in drive-thru line-ups at two coffee and doughnut franchises Shep drove by in the pickup. These overweight country folk made her think of paintings by Fernando Botero, the Colombian artist who loved painting obese people. And part of Adie loved them too, because, unlike city people, they seemed so cheerfully unbothered by their excess poundage. They accepted imperfection. Had no interest in conforming to some unattainable body image. Ate what – and when – they pleased. And judging by the smiles on their faces, they seemed to enjoy food far more than their urban counterparts. Adie resolved to be more like them, to stop worrying all the time that she was overweight, something she always did at home in New York.

Shep had descended from the pickup and was waiting impatiently by the ATV.

"C'mon, Adie," he cajoled, as she vacillated between leaving and staying. "It's not far. I want to show you something back in the bush."

He hurried over to his drive shed, a modern boxy building with orange siding, and came back carrying a yellow jerry can. He siphoned some gas from the can into the ATV's tank and continued beaming in a hopeful way at her.

"I think you'll like what I'm taking you to see," he said.

"And it won't take long, I promise."

He held out his hand. "Won't you come? Please? It'll be fun."

He was persuasive, all right. Not the kind of guy you argued with. And the prospect of putting her arms around Shep's chunky middle once more did somewhat revive Adie's spirits. She climbed on. Yet as the engine roared into life, sending out a spume of blue smoke that made her cough, that annoying little bell went off in her head again. *He's hauling you out into the woods now, Adie. And it will be very dark out there. Doesn't that strike you as mighty strange? What is this guy after? Why did you agree?*

"You're not going to tell me what this something is?" she asked in his ear in a teasing way, to hide her nervousness.

"Nope," he said firmly, looking straight ahead. "It's a secret, girl. You'll have to wait."

With Adie hanging on to his waist, Shep steered the ATV towards a trail behind his house. It was through denser woods than the one he'd followed yesterday on the edge of Joe Perri's field. As the machine's fat black rubber wheels bounced over the bumpy terrain, long overhanging branches of prickly spruce reared up in Adie's face. Very little light penetrated here. She shivered again Pushing away the sharp, stinging evergreen needles, she sensed a presence of something. Malevolent or friendly? She wasn't sure. It hung around them like a fog, enveloping everything with probing fingers and was more evident in some places than others. But then the trail broke into dappled sunlight, and the feeling evaporated. Shep steered the machine along the banks of a stream, where water trickled over fallen tree trunks covered in such thick coats of moss, they looked like slumbering animals. Bright green, rounded leaves that might be wild North American ginger appeared. Then a scarlet cardinal flower, standing ramrod straight like a soldier, on the edge of the stream. Tall Joe Pye weed, topped with fluffy, light-as-a-feather seed heads, she spotted next. And at the base of a pine tree, a cluster of brilliant red. The berries of Jack-in-the-Pulpit perhaps? Or wild ginseng? The amazing variety – like nothing she'd ever seen, living in New York – banished her tiredness. For her botanical illustrations, she was often restricted to working from photographs. She itched to bring her sketchpad and watercolours out here again, to capture these real live plants on paper.

"The stream is the dividing line between our properties," Shep yelled over the roar of the engine. She had to lean against his cheek to hear. As her bare skin touched his, her heart danced like a butterfly. "There's never been a proper survey done, but my land is on this side of the stream while yours is over there."

Over there. Adie peered into the woods. The marvel of the place – or simply fatigue, or the roar of the ATV – induced a kind of trance. She was sitting on the bank of the stream, a long, Victorian skirt of grey silk spread about her, while a side-burned John Millais, garbed in a frock coat and cravat, peered over her shoulder frowning. He seemed to be criticizing her efforts to paint some heavily-scented white flowers bordering the stream, but she couldn't hear what he was saying. Then behind them Lizzie Siddal reared up, demonic, terrifying, flapping her arms and shouting gibberish as ten-foot-high flames shot skywards from her uncombed tangle of copper-coloured hair.

The image dissolved. She came back to earth as Shep braked the ATV and cut the engine. The machine stopped sharply, making her almost fall over backwards. He leaped off, did a mock bow like a coachman from another era, and helped her dismount.

"At your service, your ladyship," he said, tipping an imaginary hat.

"Thank you, kind sir," she said, and performed a mock curtsey in her jeans.

They both laughed.

They were in a small clearing. With the engine noise stopped, she felt unnerved by the utter silence of the place. They had clearly travelled a long way off the road because she could hear nothing except the gentle trickling of the stream.

He gestured and there it was. The secret that he'd wanted her to see. A beautiful old log cabin. A Hansel and Gretel dwelling in the dark forest, with a front door painted red, four tiny windows set deeply into the logs and matching red shutters. The shutters made her think of the Alps and of a skiing holiday she'd taken with Michael, back in the years when they still liked each other. He'd schussed confidently down the slopes, having learned the technique in the Adirondacks. All she managed to do was crash into a barn and bang up her knee, provoking laughter from their toothless old ski instructor, who'd smelled of gin. Michael found her inept performance funny, too. Back at their little hotel with red shutters, he'd bathed her knee tenderly. Then they'd made love all afternoon under an enormous feather-filled duvet that made him sneeze.

Click. She switched off the memory.

"Oh wow, it's lovely, Shep," she marvelled, staring open-mouthed at the cabin.

"It was built by my dad," he said. "Let's take a look, shall we?"

The path was covered in a thick layer of spruce needles that felt like a soft wool carpet underfoot. At the entrance, Adie stopped, surprised. Painted above the door, in neat red Gothic lettering, almost obscured by the overhanging roof, were two words: Wolf's Glen.

"Hey, that's a coincidence," she said, turning to Shep excitedly. "I've just seen an op –"

"You got it, girl," Shep interrupted, laughing. "The German opera Der Freischütz. I had a hunch you'd know. You're the first person I've ever brought out to this cabin who's known the significance of the name Wolf's Glen."

"Well, a few weeks ago, I wouldn't have known either," she admitted. "But I've just seen that opera in New York. It was fascinating. Have you…"

He shook his head.

"I've never been to a live opera. There's not much opportunity for that kind of thing out here, although I do know the story of *Der Freischütz*. And anyways," he shrugged, "I'm a country boy, you know. I don't do city stuff."

"Why?"

"Cities are so crowded, so suffocating. All those people crammed together in a small place. They scare me."

"You don't look like the kind of guy who'd be scared of anything," she teased.

"Ah, you'd be surprised, girl," he said. "People aren't always what they seem, are they?"

They went inside. The cabin was low, with only one room. Shep wasn't tall so he didn't have to duck, but even so, his short hair almost grazed the ceiling. The interior smelled of smoke and mould. There were two bunk beds constructed from the same rough-hewn logs as the cabin. A rolled-up sleeping bag lay on the top bunk. On the bottom was a neat pile of folded grey blankets. She loved the woodstove: small, pot-bellied, its fat black chimney rising into the apex of the roof. Smooth deer hides the colour of butterscotch hung on the walls, along with some faded photographs. A triangular wooden cupboard with a small rack of deer antlers on top was squeezed into a corner. The cabin had only one chair. It was roughly made of pine, with a patchwork cushion, clumsily sewn. The cushion had been squashed flat by years of use.

Shep motioned for Adie to take the chair.

"My dad was German. He made that chair. Even sewed the cushion himself," he explained, squatting beside her, next to the stove. He picked up a small metal shovel and opened the stove door, then started scraping powdery white ash out of the firebox into a container on the floor.

"He was a cultured man, you know. Not like me," he said with a chuckle. His expression turned serious. "He came to Canada in the 1950s with dreams of becoming a concert pianist. But he wound up working in a tannery in Acton – it's a town near here – because he didn't have the right connections, and jobs were hard to get. He even changed our family name from Tantzel to Tanner, because there was a lot of prejudice against Germans in Canada after the Second World War and he wanted to fit in.

"But as often happens in life," he went on, continuing to scrape out the firebox, "he wound up staying at the tannery. He never played a piano again. He hated the work and his one consolation was this land and the house I live in now. He saved and saved to buy the place because he'd loved the German forests, and land here was pretty cheap back then, so he eventually could afford it. And then..."

He put the shovel down and glanced around the cabin, as if searching for memories within the walls.

"...he built this little place. As a hunting cabin. He'd gone hunting when he was young in the Black Forest, see, so he took it up again here. Lots of people hunt, you know. Your royal family does. We aren't all a bunch of yahoos," he shot Adie a challenging look. "And after he was done, Dad would come here by himself and play his German music – Beethoven, Wagner and that opera by Weber, *Der Freischütz*, things like that – on an old record player. He'd brought the LPs over with him from Germany. I still have some of them, back at the house."

He paused.

"And he decided to call the cabin Wolf's Glen. Because of the opera, you know? He loved the instrumental music in it."

Adie nodded in recognition.

"He worried about the place being haunted by ghosts, as it was in *Der Freischütz*. But in the end he decided he didn't care."

"And is it haunted, do you think?" Adie asked, looking around the small room.

"Oh yeah, I think so. But in a good way, because sometimes...."

He stared out of the cabin door, where night was closing in. "Sometimes I do feel a presence around the cabin and this part of the woods, and I wonder if it's perhaps my dad. It's hard to explain, but I sense him or something else hanging around, particularly when it's getting dark."

"Yes, I felt it too, coming along the trail just now."

"You did?"

Shep looked pleased.

"This is a magical part of the woods," he said. "Maybe the spirit of my dad has stayed around and is protecting us. Or do you think," his nostalgia gave way to a cheeky grin, "that there's a devil out here, getting up to naughty tricks?"

Nervous again, Adie looked out of the cabin door herself. The sun had slipped away. Only a glimmer remained, lighting up the western horizon behind the spruce like a slash of pink, transparent watercolour. The woods were taking on an entirely different dimension now. They seemed larger, darker, full of menacing shadows. Was the Black Huntsman about to materialize out of the gloom, as Samiel did in *Der Freischütz*? Had Shep planned some crazy stunt like that, to scare her? The feeling of being overwhelmed by so many trees that she'd experienced last night, when they travelled back to Tish's along Bounteous Lake Road, returned. She looked at her watch. Said they should be getting back. But Shep, lost in thought, staring at the cabin wall, was in no mood to hurry.

"My dad loved these woods," he went on, "even though my

mother hated them. She never came out here. She thought the cabin was too dark and German. She still does. She's from around here, see. Lives in an old folks' home in Marsh River now. Sits there all day watching Lawrence Welk reruns," he chuckled and shook his head. "So Dad would come and play his music in the cabin, out of her way, because they weren't happy together. And he'd think about the *Der Freischütz* story, about the sharpshooter who had to make difficult choices, and the struggle between dreams and reality. He related to that. This place became Dad's retreat from everything in his own life that disappointed him. And then, he taught me how to hunt when I was eight years old and I shot my first buck...."

Shep paused, put the shovel down, and nodded towards the cupboard.

"That's the buck's antlers, on top there. Real proud of myself I was. We hunted a lot together, and after we'd been out, he'd bring me back to the cabin and tell me the story of *Der Freischütz*. And he'd play his classical music, too, even though it drove me nuts."

He shook his head and laughed.

"Poor Dad. I've always been a Johnny Cash kind of guy, myself. I take after my Mom. But I've learned to like some of that serious stuff since he died. You like Beethoven?"

She nodded.

"Very much."

"Thought you would. Dad used to play the Eroica symphony after we went out hunting. That one I do like."

He hummed a few bars of the third movement, then stopped and looked expectantly at her.

"I love the Eroica too," Adie said smiling, "but sorry, Shep, I'm tone deaf. I haven't a clue how to hum it."

"No?" he looked mildly disappointed and got up. Over at the triangular cupboard, he pulled out a liquor bottle.

"It's rum," he explained, brushing dust off the bottle neck. "Dad used to keep schnapps out here, but I prefer rum."

He looked hard at her.

"Want some?"

"Um, don't you think we should be getting back?" Adie said, examining her watch again. She longed for a cup of tea at Tish's. Her throat felt parched in the claustrophobic cabin. She didn't want to linger in the dark, drinking liquor in this apparently haunted place.

Shep held out the bottle at her.

"Aw c'mon," he said, shifting on his feet, with a persuasive, almost petulant, look. "Let's have a drink to celebrate our being here together." He switched on the disturbing gaze that was becoming familiar. "We're discovering that we have a lot in common aren't we, girl?"

"I guess we are, boy," she said, picking up the cue again with reluctance.

"Yes, and I want to listen to the Eroica and some of the music from *Der Freischütz* with you. Out here in the cabin. Just you and me."

His eyes bored into her now. They were an odd grey, not really infused with blue, she noticed for the first time. And they had flecks of amber. Average-sized eyes, but quite mesmerizing. The intensity she saw in them both repelled and excited her. A little coil of fear started unravelling again and she looked away, uncertain what to say.

"So let's drink to that, shall we?" he insisted.

"All right."

He took two small glasses out of the cupboard, poured liberal measures of dark brown liquid into both and handed a glass to her.

"*Prost* as they say in Germany," he said. "Here's to us."

"Yes, *Prost*."

The dark rum tasted like maple syrup that had been boiled too long, then stored for years in a jar. It was strong and thick. She felt a buzz almost in seconds and wondered for the hundredth time what she was getting into. She debated telling Shep about Michael, that his mother was from Hamburg and his middle name was Fenster, which meant window in German. It seemed appropriate, given the revelation about Shep's Teutonic origins. Yet Michael was so radically different from Shep, and the last thing she wanted, sitting there in the cabin, was to bring up the subject of her marriage. Or his, for that matter.

He stood up, drawn to a faded colour photograph hanging askew on the wall.

"Here. Come take a look at this," he said.

"Isn't he handsome?" His grin turned roguish. The photo showed a child in a navy blue snowsuit standing outside the cabin, dwarfed by a big brown-and-grey dog sitting at his side.

"You mean the dog or the boy?" Adie teased.

"Ah, that's for you to decide, girl. Personally, though, I'd opt for the boy." He slid an arm over her shoulder. "Because it's me when I was four. And the dog was a German Shepherd. So I called him Shep. I loved that dog, and we were inseparable. He went everywhere with me and people started calling us the two Sheps. The name somehow stuck, even after he got killed by a truck."

"So that's how you got your name."

"Yes, I've been Shep ever since."

"What's your real name?"

"Believe it or not," he looked embarrassed, "it's Max."

"Like in *Der Freischütz*?"

"You got it, girl. The sharpshooter."

"And do you always hit your target, Shep?"

"Well now, that depends," he paused, looking hard into her eyes, "on what the target is, doesn't it?"

Adie went crimson, floundering for words.

"And what's *YOUR* real name?" he said, still staring.

"Anna. Well, Anna Dorothee really."

Shep took a sip from his glass.

"Hmm. Anna Dorothee. Sounds like some prim English lady," he said, his eyes not moving from hers.

"Yes. I mean, No. I… I was named after my two grandmothers. One was Scottish. The other was… um… French," she said, hesitating and feeling stupid. "But I've never liked either name so I just shortened it to Adie and –"

"And you've never been prim I guess. You don't strike me as prim." He raised his eyebrows in a questioning way.

"No, I guess not." she said, not moving her own eyes now.

"Well, good. No point in a woman being prim." His voice was soft as velvet.

One of his brawny arms still hung over her shoulder. Their faces were close. Adie felt as shy as a young girl. Was that genuine longing she saw in his eyes? Or was she wishing and hoping for something that wasn't there? The rum was making her head spin. She couldn't think straight. The cabin walls started going round and round. She thought she detected something calculating in the way he stared, a deviousness, as if he'd figured out the role he was going to play with her in advance and was now methodically putting it into action. And, uncertain of her ground, she was terrified of looking foolish. Though she wasn't sure why, she wanted to touch this man's skin, to feel his fingers roving over her body and his mouth hard against her own – but did he want that too?

Apparently not. The intimacy of the moment seemed to embarrass him, for he removed his arm from her shoulder and went deliberately back over to the stove, carrying his glass. He squatted. Started fiddling with the shovel in the firebox again, looking down, so she returned wordlessly to the chair and sipped the rum. They went silent now, as he continued emptying the stove, the shovel sounding loud and harsh in the small cabin. Then, he took a deep breath and turned back to her, his voice sounding different, as if he'd been building up to tell her something.

"Now listen, Adie," he said, his tone becoming as oily and unctuous as the real estate salesman who'd once hauled her and Michael all over Manhattan, trying to sell them a condo. "I know you told me you didn't want anyone hunting deer on your land. And I respect that. But now that you've heard the story about my dad, won't you change your mind? I've hunted here for years and it never bothered your uncle. There are so many deer in these woods. They'd die of starvation if we didn't cull a few. And of course," he leaned close to the chair again, "I'd give you some of the of the best cuts of meat in return for permission to hunt. What do you say?"

He put up the palm of his hand and switched on a silly grin.

"Deal, girl?" he said.

She ignored the cue this time.

"Do we have a deal, girl, or don't we?" he repeated.

Adie felt perplexed. Railroaded. Indignant. Taken for a fool. Anger and bewilderment rose in her throat. She kept her right hand gripping the wooden arm of the chair. An urge seized her to leap up and run away – away from the horror and humiliation of realizing that this man didn't want *her*. He'd pretended to find her attractive. Flattered her. Tried shamelessly to win her confidence. And it was simply because of his desire to have free access to her land.

Hell's bells, the idiot even wanted to seal the agreement with the repugnant macho gesture of slapping hands together.

You sneaky bastard. You con artist. You deceiver. You scumbag. You fuck....

Adie opened her mouth to voice every insult she could think

of, but she didn't get the opportunity.

Because at that moment, his expression changed once more. She detected longing – genuine longing – now in his eyes. He leaned forward, put his arms around her neck and kissed her roughly on the mouth.

The glass fell out of her hand, on to the floor. It rolled away splattering the syrupy rum on to the side of the woodstove.

He ignored the glass. So did she.

"You're beautiful, you know," he said softly. "I…"

He clamped his mouth on hers.

She wanted to push him away.

But didn't.

Fifteen

"..and then in 1809, six students at the Vienna Academy formed an artistic cooperative initially known as the Brotherhood of St. Luke, or Lukasbund, and in 1810, four of them, Johann Friedrich Overbeck, Franz Pforr, Ludwig Vogel and Johann Konrad Hottinger began living in the abandoned monastery of San Isidoro in Italy and…"

A youth with stringy blonde hair yawned. Another doodled on a pad. A third had his laptop open and was smirking at something on the screen. Probably a pornographic video, Michael thought with disgust. Two girls in the front row, who usually brought notebooks and scribbled furiously with ballpoint pens, were staring at the ceiling, fidgeting in their seats. Several others hunched over cell phones, texting. Then a cell phone went off. *Da-dee-da-dd-dd.* Someone answered it, even though it was forbidden in class. Another cell phone played a tune. And another. The little plastic devices stayed pasted to ears, their owners chatting in hushed tones.

Boring, boring… Michael knew he was turning off his students, droning away in a monotone, padding this lecture with laundry lists of names and dates. In all his years of teaching, he'd never presented such a dull dissertation on a subject that he'd once found fascinating. Yet now he just wanted to be done with the Nazarenes. Forever. Who gave a rat's ass about an obscure German art movement that might have influenced the Pre-Raphaelite Brotherhood in England? No one sitting in front of him, that was for sure – and now he didn't, either. He checked the clock on the wall at the back of the lecture hall. A quarter to three. Only fifteen minutes to go. Then he could escape. Go home. Focus on what mattered more to him at that moment than anything else in the world.

Getting that picture of Sid. With Adie gone – she'd vanished three days ago without even leaving a note – he'd run through a gamut of emotions. Shock first. Then fury. Then relief. Because he'd spent a couple of nights with Dan and Jolanta Wagstaff and that had been a refreshing change. Dan was a Dickens scholar. While Jolanta cooked beef stroganoff, they'd engaged in a lively discussion about the British author's prurient interest in the prostitutes who modelled for the Pre-Raphaelites. And now – well, he could bask in the simple pleasure of being alone, something that rarely happened in their rather cramped apartment. Even better, Adie's absence meant he could stand at the window every morning and watch Sid go by with no qualms about being caught in the act. And tomorrow…. Yes, tomorrow…. He'd be able go downstairs and get that photo.

"Er, sir…" A woman's voice broke in.

"What?" He looked up from his notes, irritated.

"Would you say that the Nazarenes' art movement was a reaction against Neoclassicism?"

"What? Oh, yes. Yes, of course, it was…." Michael ran a hand through his sparse hair, flustered. He always reacted that way whenever anyone caught him off guard. The question came from a scholarly young woman with thick-rimmed black glasses like his own. She wore a purple hijab. He blinked in surprise because she appeared genuinely eager to hear what he had to say.

"Yes, yes, it was unquestionably a reaction," he reiterated, smiling in a vague way at her, fiddling with the cap of his pen.

He looked down again, shuffling his notes. He straightened his own specs once more. Tried to appear as if he was reorganizing his thoughts. Then he cleared his throat and resumed:

"The Nazarenes rebelled against the stultifying art embodied by the academy system of teaching. They hoped to return to art that had spiritual values and sought inspiration in artists of the late Middle Ages and early Renaissance, rejecting..."

The blonde boy in the front row yawned again. He opened his mouth so wide, Michael could see his ruddy pink tonsils. The little creep. Just hang on, he told himself. Only a few more minutes. Then you can get rid of them.

At four-thirty, Michael returned to the apartment. He felt drained by the lecture. He boiled a kettle of water. Poured some in a teapot, then tipped the water out before spooning two teaspoons of loose tea into the bottom of the pot and adding more bubbling water. Then he left the brew to steep for precisely six minutes while he changed into jeans and a sweater. Michael considered himself a connoisseur of tea. He'd acquired the habit while living in London and now religiously prepared it the way the British did, usually twice a day. He never used teabags. Every month he made a special trip down to Zabars on Broadway and bought their loose tea – expensive blends like Irish Breakfast, smoky Russian Caravan and even smokier Lapsang Souchong. It came in shiny silver and orange tins and over thirty of those tins now stood in a row on top of the kitchen cabinets. The look of them sitting there pleased him. He also kept another supply – and a Brown Betty teapot – in his office at Columbia. He liked the ritual of making the tea as much as the drink itself. And he got irked whenever Adie made him settle for a teabag tossed into a mug.

"Teabags are made with sweepings from the factory floor," he'd reminded her reproachfully more than once, "and they taste like it. You're a Brit, Adie. You should know better."

"Yes, but you've come home so late today, Michael. There just isn't time to make a pot of brewed tea," she'd say with a sigh. "Dinner will spoil."

How great it was that she'd gone away. For how long he had no idea, but she was bound to be back. She loved New York, even if she didn't love him anymore. Whatever happened to her up there in the wilds of Canada, her interest in the place wouldn't last. That was a given, because life had become so comfortable for them both in New York. Couples became tied to one another through habit, circumstances, sheer inertia and – most important – financial considerations, Michael often thought. When you reached middle age, love didn't play much of a role anymore. What had far more significance were the little routines and rituals the two people in question established over the years – and, of course, where they lived. He and Adie had bought this apartment together – chipping in an equal amount of money for the deposit – and they both loved it, especially the location, close to everything they enjoyed on the Upper East Side. He felt confident that she'd never give that life up for a radically different one out in the boonies – even though the inheritance from that dubious uncle of hers was undoubtedly putting such ideas into her head.

Lifting the teapot lid to check if the brew was dark enough, Michael concluded that all couples needed to take a break from one another and that he intended to make the most of this one. It would be like a vacation. He didn't miss Adie in the least. Yet he would be pleased to see her when she came back.

Putting half an inch of milk in the bottom of his mug, he poured the tea. In the living room, he settled down on the sofa and sipped slowly, savouring the exquisite flavour, debating whether to put on Shostakovich's Second Symphony or not. Adie hated modern composers, and he could never listen to any of them when she was around. He opted for silence.

It was far more agreeable to just sit, without any distractions, daydreaming about Sid. His harmless little fantasy. His escape from a world that he had accepted long ago and had no desire to change.

It got dark. Michael jerked awake, realizing that he'd dozed off. He switched on a lamp next to the sofa. Checked the time on his cell phone. Dammit. Nearly seven – and this was the evening he'd intended to scout out a concealed doorway on the street below, where he could wait to take that photo of Sid walking by. Should he postpone the search now? Find an ideal spot in daylight tomorrow?

No. He'd been excited about this for too long already. He slipped on loafers and hurried downstairs.

East 90th between Park and Lexington was all residential. Medium-sized apartment buildings like the one he and Adie occupied stood on both sides of the street. Hawk-eyed doormen hovered behind all their plate glass doors, so there was no point in seeking a suitable spot there. And simply standing on the street in full view of everyone, waiting with his cell phone, was risky. New Yorkers never paid attention to people who did such things – they were too busy with their own lives to worry what others did with theirs – but what if Sid, his angel Sid, noticed him pointing the cell phone at her? She might wonder if he was a pervert. Shout at him. Call him a voyeur. Try to summon a cop on her own cell. He couldn't lay himself open for that. How absolutely mortifying to have her – the girl he adored – discover his secret.

He turned down Lexington. Walked slowly up and down between 90th and 87th, checking both sides. There were virtually no recessed doorways where a person could hide. He stopped by a mobile phone store near 89th. A possibility? Its entrance was set back a couple of feet from the sidewalk and looked ideal. But, no. Dangerous idea. A belligerent-looking young guy with a shaved head ran the store, and he always came to work early. He'd certainly create a fuss if he encountered Michael standing there, hovering in front of the plate glass door. He'd want to know why.

And then he found it by accident. The perfect spot. Outside Lucinda Nails and Spa, near 88th. The entrance was up three steep steps, and the tired-looking Filipino women who sat behind the big plate glass window all day, painting green and purple on the extended fingers and toes of bored New York women, didn't start work till ten. Besides, if they arrived earlier than usual and discovered him standing in their deeply recessed entrance, they'd be unlikely to mind. Yes, Lucinda's. He could wait there quietly for Sid, and no one would notice. Then when he spotted her coming by, en route to the subway, he'd hold up his cell phone and go click. Just like the paparazzi did with celebrities. It would be so simple. Only take a couple of seconds. And what a perfect position, standing at the top of those steps, pointing the cell phone downwards. He'd get a great shot of her hair from there.

Michael picked up a carton of angel hair pasta in tomato and caper sauce from Gristedes on the way back to the apartment. He ate standing at the kitchen sink, too excited to sit down. The scarlet sauce dripped on to his brown sweater. He left it there. He made a pot of Lapsang Souchong, then went to bed early. It was crucial not to oversleep.

Overnight, rain returned to Manhattan. Not the downpour of a few days ago, but drizzle – dreary British drizzle. The stuff that turns skies grey as battleships, penetrates coat collars and makes every item of clothing, as well as limbs and torsos, feel perpetually clammy. One of the few things Michael had disliked about life in London was the rain. He watched it with dismay, while sipping his Irish Breakfast in the living room. He dreaded going downstairs. Damp weather seeped into his bones. It gave him arthritis. Made him feel like an old man. Should he postpone his little photographic expedition to another day? No, he was too keyed up. Too eager. He'd waited long enough.

He got dressed. Pulled a raincoat out of the hall cupboard, stashing his cell phone in one of the coat's baggy side pockets. He headed downstairs at precisely eight-oh-five and joined the throng of pedestrians hurrying along Lexington in the rain.

At the corner of 89th, he ran into a bottleneck. People coming down that street were blending into the crowd on Lex. It was always like this in the rush hour. Everyone in a hurry. No one caring about anyone else. The pavement dipped sharply at the intersection, because of a drain situated in the northwest corner. As he neared the drain, some jerk jostled him from behind. Michael slipped. He toppled forward in a heap. Heard a strange popping noise in his right foot. Then pain, incredible pain, shot all the way up to his knee. He cried out and grabbed at the foot, massaging it like a madman through his sock, half lying, half kneeling on the drain, getting soaked to the skin. He couldn't seem to get up.

A young dark-skinned man in an Aquascutum raincoat, carrying a briefcase, stopped. He crouched down. So close, Michael could smell his fruity deodorant. Rain dripped from the lapels of the coat into Michael's face as he tried to help. When getting up proved too agonizing, the man asked what he could do.

Michael gulped. He felt stupid crouching there, rubbing his foot. "Do you have a cell phone?"

He couldn't reach his own cell. It was at the bottom of the raincoat's deep pocket, bunched up beneath him.

"Sure," the man said.

"Well, could you call my wife? Ask her to come down here

right away. We live just a couple of minutes away, up there." He gestured with his free hand in the direction of 90th Street.

"Sir, are you sure you don't want me to call an ambulance?" The man looked at Michael's foot with a doubtful expression.

"No, no," Michael smiled weakly. "My wife will know what to do. I'll just wait here till she comes, then we'll decide."

"Sure, if that's what you want."

The man held the phone to his ear, putting his free hand over his other ear to blot out the noise of the traffic. After what seemed like an eternity, he raised his eyebrows and pulled a face at Michael.

"Sorry, sir. There's no one there. Just a message," he said.

Michael remembered then.

Adie had gone. He missed her now.

And at that moment, the red-haired girl walked right past him. Her brown leather boots almost brushed his back.

Crumpled over the drain, he didn't notice.

Sixteen

Aaark. Aaark. Aaark. A shrieking bird woke Adie. Buried beneath a puffy duvet patterned in ten shades of pink, she immediately thought of Shep and felt hot all over. She wriggled her toes. Ran her hands up and down her body. Let them linger on her nipples, her stomach and between her legs, recalling the previous evening. Oh, how delicious. How wonderful. How unexpected. How utterly amazing. Last night, an attractive guy had actually told her twice that she was beautiful and then made it obvious that he desired her. She couldn't quite believe it.

But yes, it had happened. He didn't seem to be stringing her along, either. Adie sat upright and watched the bird's brilliant blue feathers flashing through the tree branches outside the window. She croaked, "Aaark. Aaark. Aaaark," out loud, back at the noisy bird, feeling so happy, recalling their adventure in the cabin. They'd necked for a long time like teenagers. Awkwardly, sitting side by side on the bottom bunk. Smooching, Sucking. Nibbling. Groping each other through their clothes. Then, disaster. He'd made a move to push her backwards on to the mattress and pull down her jeans. but she'd hit her head on a wooden post supporting the top bunk. *Crack.* Ouch. She'd almost blacked out. The cabin interior went round and round. She'd sat up, dazed, clutching her temples. Took a few minutes to recover. And that had sort of spoiled the moment, because her head hurt like hell for ages, so neither of them had wanted to resume. He fussed over her, worried. Then they'd laughed about it and left the cabin.

But who cared that they'd failed to complete the experience? Adie reflected, propped up against a pillow, that being close to a warm, lusty man who found her desirable, who had a sense of humour and who didn't take himself too seriously, meant more to her than the actual act of sex. She'd forgotten over the years how that kind of intimacy could make her feel.

At his house, they'd shared some snacks and a modest amount of red wine. Then he'd driven her in his pickup back to her little red rental car.

"I guess it's okay now if I go out to hunt on your land tomorrow? Hunting season opens then. You won't mind?" he said, kissing her forehead gently through the driver's window.

"Of course not," she said. At that moment, she'd have cheerfully agreed to strip and run naked along the main drag in Marsh River if Shep had asked her to.

"You'll be all right, driving back to Tish's by yourself in the dark?" he said, anxiously. "I would offer to take you but…"

"I'll be fine," she broke in. "I'm used to the road now. And I'll drive slowly, don't worry. I'll watch out for deer."

"Okay, I'll call you tomorrow."

She had indeed been fine. Had felt like a local, tackling the twists and turns back to the B & B. Now she sprang out of bed, her heart as light as a feather. She practically skipped down the steep stairs into Tish's kitchen.

"Oh my, but aren't we the happy one this morning," Tish said, with a hint of sarcasm. She was at the sink, chopping vegetables on the draining board and listening to the radio. "I heard you come in quite late. I presume you were out with our Mr. Tanner again?"

Adie blushed.

"Yes. We had a lovely evening, thank you," she said, annoyed by the question. What business was it of Tish's who she spent time with?

"I saw this beautiful blue-and-grey bird outside the window this morning," she added, to change the subject. "What kind of bird is it?"

"Oh, it's probably just a blue jay," Tish said, in a dismissive tone. "I don't like them much. No one does. They're quarrelsome birds. But just wait till you spot a pileated woodpecker. They're big, black and white with a red ruff on top, and they look awesome. They're becoming rare now. But I've seen them up at your place, because there's lots of woods up there," she shot a sly smile in Adie's direction, "and of course, they're in your friend Shep's woods, too."

Your friend Shep. Adie blushed again. Would the woman never let up? She took a shower and dressed, then carried her toast and coffee outside to avoid any more needling from Tish. The air felt chilly, but she went down to the river bank where there was a concrete patio with a white plastic table and chairs. The chairs were wet with dew. She dried one off with a corner of her sweatshirt and sat down. Brownish-green water was gushing down towards the bridge outside Marsh River where the trucks roared along. But if you shut your ears and ignored the traffic noise, it was a lovely country scene. Like something Constable might have painted in another era, with that old graceful stone bridge. Open fields spread out along the opposite bank. Further upstream, she saw a fisherman in olive-green hip waders, casting out a long line over and over again. Fly fishing. Michael had always been so contemptuous about fishermen. Careless and unthinking yahoos, he'd insisted. They caused nothing but trouble, their fish hooks constantly getting caught in birds' beaks. Yet this old guy looked harmless enough, and the way he stood there, knee-deep in water, casting and concentrating, struck her as relaxing. She would ask Shep to teach her how to fly fish.

She went back to the house to wait for his call.

The phone didn't ring. Back in her bedroom. she straightened the duvet and tidied up her clothes, then got her sketch pad out. There was a clump of Michaelmas daisies growing at the end of Tish's garden. She sat in the garden with her pencils, but couldn't seem to settle down to draw. And she knew why. She was starting to get edgy, waiting for the sound of the phone, back at the house.

At noon, she got up from the chair, uneasy now. Where was Shep? Hadn't he said he'd call in the morning? She decided to drive into Marsh River and have a look around to stave off the doubts that were starting to grip her heart. No way was she going to pick up the phone and call him herself. Chasing a man like Shep was not a good idea.

"I think I'll go and check out Flavian's store. I met him outside yesterday, and I need a book to read," she called out.

Tish was upstairs, putting sheets on a bed in the room opposite Adie. A new guest was scheduled to arrive that night.

"Great idea," she called back. "He has all kinds of books. And drop by the Kaffee Klatch afterwards. They make pretty good sandwiches."

Adie drove into Marsh River. She parked on the main street, right outside Boddington Books, beneath a towering maple tree. Flavian was delighted to see her. His store was empty. He stood organizing a display of non-fiction books in the front window.

"Here, take a look," he said, holding up a hardcover with a photograph of an old house on the front. "It just came in and you may like it. It's a funny story called *Middle-Aged Spread*. Written by a woman who buys an old house in the country like yours, then goes through hell fixing the place up."

"I'll probably be able to relate to that," Adie said wryly, realizing that Knock hadn't called her, either.

She crossed the street and sat on a stool in the window of the Kaffee Klatch after buying the book and nibbled half-heartedly on a chopped egg sandwich. Her spirits sank even lower as she drove back to Tish's.

Had Shep made a fool of her?

"No, no calls," said Tish, with an I-told-you-so kind of smile, in the early afternoon on her return to the B & B. Adie went upstairs and lay on the bed. Felt comforted by Sammy, who pushed open the door, motorboat purr going at full throttle. She tried to read the book she'd bought from Flavian but couldn't get interested in it. The cat kept butting the book out of her hand. She fell asleep after a couple of pages.

It was getting dark when the phone finally did ring. Adie leaped off the bed, pushing Sammy away. The book thudded on to the floor. She almost tripped over the cat in her mad rush to make it down the steep stairs. She could hear Tish talking on the phone, giving directions to someone called Mr. Brainerd. He was apparently on his way to the B & B but couldn't find the place. He must be the new guest.

She retreated back up the stairs. Collapsed onto the bed again. The man arrived about half an hour later. She heard him come up the stairs, banging a bag against the wall, then he went down again. Tish called out to her.

"Supper's on the table, lass."

Adie went to her door and opened it a crack.

"I don't think I'll come down, if you don't mind," she called back. "I have an awful stomach ache. I think the eggs in that sandwich at the Kaffee Klatch must have been off."

Under the duvet, Sammy snuggled in her arms, Adie allowed herself to shed a few tears. Quietly. She felt so stupid. She didn't want Tish to hear. She ached for a peanut butter cup to nibble on.

Next morning, still no call from Shep. Adie sat at the table in Tish's dining room with Gerry Brainerd, a rather pompous, middle-aged man who worked for a bank and travelled around the province, conducting inspections of branch procedures.

"I'm delighted to have discovered Tish's little place," he said in a plummy tone. "I travel a lot in this area and there aren't any decent motels. And her eggs and bacon look like the best. Almost as good as my wife's." He beamed at Adie and dipped his toast into runny egg, practically drooling on the plate. "But you aren't having any, Mrs. ..."

"Coulter," Adie said, picking at her own toast, not bothering to explain that she was a Ms. not Mrs. This kind of guy wouldn't understand the difference anyway. "No, I'm not that hungry."

"Well, you're missing a treat, let me tell you. And what brings you to these parts, Mrs. Coulter?"

"Oh, family business." She spoke vaguely, not wanting to get into a discussion about the reason why she'd come to Fortune, because she was starting to wish she hadn't.

He nodded, satisfied, and mopped the toast around his plate.

Adie excused herself and went back to her room. She heard Mr. Brainerd go out. Then Tish departed, too – calling up the stairs that she was off to the supermarket. So she seized the moment and hurtled down the stairs. She picked up the receiver in the hall. Heart pounding, she called Shep's cell phone.

It clicked straightaway to his message pickup. She tried again an hour later. The same thing happened. At noon – having dithered away two hours, sitting in the garden, trying and failing to do a decent sketch of the Michaelmas daisies – she called once more. There was still no response. She decided not to leave a message.

Feeling annoyed now, she got into her car and drove out to Fortune Hill. En route, she heard a volley of shots – *pop, pop, pop* – in the woods at the side of the road. Then she remembered: hunting season started today. So did that mean Shep was out in her woods at that moment with his buddies, trying to bag a deer? Was that the reason why he hadn't called her? He'd been too busy getting ready to hunt?

It seemed not. Her woods — and his — appeared silent and deserted when she parked outside her uncle's house. She decided not to go inside — it was impossible, anyway, unless she pried open a window, because she'd left the key at Tish's — but she did pluck up the courage to walk along the trail over to Shep's house. An old white minivan, with rust around the doors, stood in the driveway. His green pickup wasn't there. But a light shone in the mudroom, so she knocked on the door.

After a minute or two, a girl — a startlingly beautiful girl — wearing a pink terry bathrobe, with a white towel wrapped around her head like a turban, opened the door.

"Oh, hello," she said. "Have you come with the flowers?"

Flowers? What flowers?

"No...um... I own the house next door and I was wondering if Shep was home and..." Adie stumbled over the words, realizing that the girl must be one of his daughters. Probably Chrissie.

"No, my dad isn't here."

"Well, do you know where he is?" Adie said.

The girl giggled.

"No idea," she said. "I never know where my dad is or what he's doing. He just, like, goes off."

She adjusted the towel around her head.

"But shall I give him a message when I do see him?" The girl sounded more friendly now. "I can, if you want."

"No. I don't think so. Thank you."

Adie turned to go, but a tall youth materialized in the mudroom at that moment, directly behind the girl. He was about twenty, as handsome as the girl was beautiful, with film star features and thick, dark, wavy hair. He peered over the girl's shoulder at her.

"Oh, hello. Who are you?" he said.

"Shh, Tyson, it's our new neighbour," the girl said, giggling again. "Don't be rude."

"Well, invite the lady in then, Chrissie," he said expansively, pulling the door open wide. "You're being the rude one, babes. You gotta be nice to your neighbours. You never know when they can be useful to you. Right, Mrs... er?"

He beamed at Adie and winked.

"Oh, please call me Adie," she said, feeling out of place, conscious she was interrupting something. Smells of marijuana and chicken take-out wafted from the room. Rock music was blaring.

She turned to leave again, but Tyson grabbed her arm and propelled her into the kitchen.

"Don't go yet, ma'am," he said in an exuberant tone. "Have some coffee with us. Or do you want something stronger? We have the hard stuff, beer, everything you can think of," he laughed, "because we're getting ready for our Stag and Doe tonight."

He blew a kiss at Chrissie and added, "Aren't we, babes? And it's going to be awesome."

Chrissie's eyes lit up.

"Yeah, totally awesome," she said, giggling again, and blew a kiss back.

"It was going to be at the Legion in Marsh River, but now that her old man isn't around," Tyson told Adie, grinning gleefully as he went over to a black cabinet to turn the music down, "we're saving ourselves a whole lotta dough and having the bash here."

Adie wondered where Shep was – and what he thought about this turn of events.

Tyson filled a kettle at the sink, plugged it in and kept insisting that she stay.

"You're really welcome ma'am. Our buddies aren't coming for a while," he said.

The way he spoke made her feel very old.

Stag and Doe? This must be some rural rite of passage. She pictured a scene out of *Midsummer Night's Dream*: a rowdy, drunken crowd of youths, their identity hidden by papier maché stags' heads, cavorting in Shep's woods like Bottom and the Rude Mechanicals, making crude rutting movements at young girls like Chrissie, who lay languidly on logs arranged in the shadows.

And even if that wasn't the case, a rowdy all-nighter was clearly in the offing. Big trays of cocktail sandwiches, plus bowls of dips encircled by raw vegetables, were arrayed on every table top and even the black leather sofa. Two stacks of beer cases, three feet high, stood piled in a corner, along with more boxes containing hard liquor, pop cans, paper napkins and plastic glasses. Paper streamers in yellow and red had been draped over the light fixtures. Clothes – obviously Tyson's and Chrissie's – covered the old armchairs by the stove where she'd sat with Shep. A very short white dress lay spread out on an ironing board, waiting to be pressed. Presumably, some flowers to pretty up the festivities had also been ordered.

"Thanks for the invitation, but I'd better not stay," she said, as Tyson extricated a coffee mug from a heap of dirty dishes in the sink. "You two clearly have a lot to do."

"It's no problem, ma'am," he said.

"Even so, I'd better go," she insisted.

"Okay, then," Tyson said, winking at her again and kissing her cheek. "Till next time."

"Sure," she said, thinking what a nice young guy Chrissie's fiancé was.

Before Adie could say goodbye, a dark-haired girl in jeans appeared, moving noiselessly down the staircase that lead to the bedrooms. She was frowning, her body language taut, as if she'd been hiding upstairs, reluctant to get involved in the preparations for the party.

"Wait a minute, ma'am. Come and meet my older sister, Kara," Chrissie said to Adie, with a nervous smile. "I insisted that she take the train from Montreal for our party, but she doesn't really like parties, do you, Kara?"

Kara hovered beside the woodstove, rubbing her hands up and down her arms as if she felt cold.

"No, not particularly," she said.

"Oh, lighten up, Kara," Tyson called out in an exasperated tone from the sink, where he stood with his back to the girls, washing dishes. "Why can't you have some fun for a change? It ain't good to be a saint all the time, ya know. Some of my buddies would love to get to know ya."

He chortled in a lascivious way but there was no response from Kara. The three women continued to stand awkwardly by the woodstove, looking at each other.

"He's right, you know," Chrissie said at length, in a pleading tone, smiling at her sister. "Don't spoil our party, Kara. It's just for a few hours, and we'd like to enjoy ourselves, even if you hate every minute of it."

"I shouldn't have come," Kara said softly, looking away, out of the window. "It was a bad idea. I had to break off from studying for an exam, you know."

"Well, sorry about that, but I didn't know," Chrissie retorted. She flounced over to Tyson's side seeking moral support. "Sorry I persuaded you."

"Yeah, sure was a dumb idea," Tyson said, craning his head sideways from the sink to smack a noisy kiss on her hair.

Kara retreated upstairs. Adie was struck by how different the two girls were. This older sister looked intelligent and interesting, and quite attractive, too, but she was as tense as a kite string in the wind and didn't have an engaging personality like Chrissie.

She recalled how Shep seemed to prefer his younger daughter and sympathized with him now.

"Thanks, but I really must go," she told Tyson.

He escorted her to the mudroom door with soapy fingers and gave her a hug.

"Well, it was a pleasure to meet you, ma'am," he said. "We'll see you some other time, won't we?"

"Sure."

Adie headed back along the trail, picturing the lovey-dovey young couple getting ready for their engagement party in Shep's cosy kitchen. She felt lonely and desolate, wondering again where he was, puzzled and hurt by his silence. It was a relief to reach her own property. Some monkshood was in full, glorious bloom at the side of the old house, and its elegant spires of purplish-blue were cheering. Beautiful flowers always had that instant effect on her. All tangled up with the monkshood, she noticed, to her delight, some stalks of a tall wild herb with tiny white flowers. It was wild catnip. She remembered picking it in her dad's garden at Kew the last time she'd owned a cat. Her mother had made a sedative tea with the leaves. She stuffed some stalks into her pocket to take back for Sammy.

Back in her car, she drove on to Fortune Hill Road. That's when she noticed the turkey vultures. They seemed to be hovering right above where Shep's cabin was located. Menacing, big and very black against the sky, there were three of them. They looked alarming. Had there been some kind of hunting accident out in the woods? Was that why he hadn't called? After all, he had told her only yesterday that the birds were a sign of a death close by. She headed into Fortune in a tizzy, wondering if she should tell someone, and pulled up outside the village store to ponder the situation. But no. It was probably just her imagination running wild. She wouldn't say a thing to anyone because there was probably some simple explanation for the birds. And for Shep's silence. She didn't want to look stupid in front of country folk who were probably used to these occurrences. And his daughter would surely know if something had happened to him.

She went into the store, aching for the consolation of a peanut butter cup melting on her tongue.

The same woman with the old-fashioned perm whom she'd met when she arrived in Fortune was there again, slumped on a stool, watching a television behind the counter. As Adie walked in, she clicked the TV off and waved in the direction of a coffee maker.

"Freshly made less than half an hour ago. And very good," she said, her tone aggressive. "Want some?"

"Sorry. Not right now," Adie said. "What I'm looking for is Reese's Peanut Butter Cups."

"You are? Well, now that surprises me," the woman said, her expression changing. She sat up straight, seemingly delighted. "I expected that you'd come in bugging me about organic vegetables. But I have plenty of candies, my dear. I stock all kinds. Right here. Help yourself."

She pointed at the packages on a shelf in front of the cash register.

Adie bought all six Reese's Peanut Butter Cups.

"You're Gow's relative, aren't you?" the woman said, all smiles now, leaning forward on the counter, eager to talk.

"Yes, that's right, I am. But sorry, I have to run."

She didn't feel like talking to anyone.

Stuffing two peanut butter cups into her mouth at once, chewing quickly and swallowing in great gulps, she drove on to Tish's. Putting her key in the lock of the B & B, suppressing a burp, she heard the phone ring. Her heart started beating fast. Shep at last? Tish came out of the kitchen to take the call, wiping her hands on a tea towel, and listened to what seemed like a rambling message. Her face fell.

She held out the phone to Adie.

"Oh dear, it's for you, lass," she said. "A friend of yours called Val, in New York. It seems your husband has had an accident."

Adie's face fell too. She took the phone.

"Adie, cherub," said Val in a gentle tone. "Sorry to have to spoil your fun up there in the frozen north, but I think you'd better come home. Michael's holed up in the apartment. He's broken two bones in his foot. Can't put any weight on it for at least a month. He's so pathetic and helpless. He called me to ask if I knew how to track you down. I got this number from information."

She paused. "He needs you right now, cherub. Truly he does."

That night, winter arrived in Fortune with a whomp. Adie went to bed early. Unable to sleep much, she pushed back the duvet and padded over to the window when dawn started to creep in. She peered out, down the garden, towards the river, shocked. A great sweeping mantle of white confronted her. It covered everything. The patio chairs and table. Tish's flowers. The lawn. She searched for the Michaelmas daisies she'd tried to hard to sketch. They were gone, too, under the thick snow. Flattened. Obliterated. Buried.

Like her dreams.

Biting back tears, she threw her clothes into her carry-on bag.

As more snow fell, she drove to Toronto airport and fled back to New York.

Book Two

I wish I hadn't met her. When you can connect a real person to a bad situation, it becomes harder to forget what happened. For a long while afterwards, I kept seeing her face in front of me – although truthfully, the image was hazy and probably not a true representation of how she looked, because we encountered one another for only a couple of minutes in the kitchen before Chrissie's Stag and Doe.

What I do remember is that she wasn't young. In fact, she seemed quite old to me – probably over fifty – and she had long, messy hair that was once red but had faded to a sort of whitish-orange. She'd have looked younger and more attractive with short hair. And she was a surprise because Dad always gravitated towards pretty young women at parties. He couldn't be bothered with the older ones. He made rather cruel jokes about them, behind their backs. So I wondered, when the truth came out, what he had seen in her.

Chrissie said that she'd seemed very anxious about Dad, that it was obviously on the tip of her tongue to ask where he was. Yet she didn't. She held back. Something was probably going on between them even then, Chrissie concluded afterwards. She just didn't realize it at the time. Nor did Tyson, who tends to pick up on things like that, between men and women. He was very nice to her, Chrissie said, and asked her in for a coffee. But she wouldn't stay and when she left, he felt sorry for her because she looked so sad and lonely.

Chrissie keeps talking about closure now. But what exactly does that mean? Closure is such an overworked word. There can never be closure for me, probably because I'm not religious in the way Chrissie is. I never liked going to church, although I do feel deeply spiritual when I'm in Africa. I stare up at those vast, open skies, and it's like God is reaching out to touch me. I want to grab his hand and fly up to join him. I can't wait to go back there. I'm hoping to hear soon about a new project in Senegal.

But in the meantime, forgiveness as the Christians preach? Well, no. I know it offends Chrissie, but I'm of the opinion that the concept of forgiveness is overrated. I think it's best to just move your mind into a radically different place when something like this has turned your life upside down.

Because some memories don't fade with age. They get sharper. They cut into you like a knife.

Seventeen

Michael sat in a chair next to the apartment window. Hunched over, stony-faced, unshaven, staring into space, he had all the melancholy of an Edward Hopper painting. He wore his grey bathrobe. His right leg, thin and papery white, the calf stippled with long black hairs, was bent at the knee under the chair. The other leg he'd hoisted on to the stool from Adie's studio, and his broken ankle, encased in a long white cast, dangled off the chair's edge. The room was gloomy, in virtual darkness, apart from a street lamp outside. He didn't have his glasses on.

Arriving at the apartment just before midnight, Adie felt a surge of guilt, because he barely acknowledged her presence. He just glanced over, mumbled, "Oh, hi. It's you," then stared into space again. She switched on a light and dropped her luggage on the floor. Debated telling him about her awful flight, how the aircraft had circled for more than an hour and a half over Newark, unable to land because there was some unspecified problem – she suspected with the landing gear – and that she thought they were going to crash. But, no, not a good idea, she decided, looking at his wan face. *Better concentrate on him. Better be nice, even though you don't particularly want to be.* She went over to the chair. Hugged his thin shoulders. Kissed the top of his thinning hair.

"You poor thing, Michael," she said. "Val got hold of me. I came straightaway when I heard."

"You did? Well, I'm glad you're back," he said, looking up at her. Purple hollows hung under his eyes. He clearly hadn't eaten or slept much since she left. "I'm sorry about this, Adie." He nodded at his foot. "Sorry you had to interrupt your trip."

Sorry? Michael rarely said he was sorry. In all their years together, he'd apologized only a couple of times. She was invariably the one who ate humble pie following an argument. This new-found penitence was alarming. It prompted an unfamiliar flush of maternal solicitousness. She grabbed a cushion from the sofa and pushed it gently under his raised leg. Turned on more lights. Squeezed another cushion behind his back.

"How did it happen?" she asked gently, sitting down beside him.

"Oh, I was stupid." he said. "So utterly stupid. I... er... slipped at the lights on Lex. It was raining and I... er...." He heaved a huge sigh that made his whole body shake. "So stupid. I'm such a fool. I'll tell you about it sometime," he looked up at her anxiously, "but not right now, if you don't mind."

"Sure, whenever you're ready. Do you want some tea?"

"I'd like nothing more than that."

"Does your ankle hurt?"

"No, not really. Not anymore. But it does if I try to walk on it."

"What damage did you do?"

"I twisted my foot somehow, stepping from the road on to the sidewalk. It was raining and slippery, I guess. Two bones in my ankle snapped. I even heard them break. It was weird. And one splintered, so they had to put two screws in."

"Sounds nasty. You'd better stay off the foot. Shall I help you move over to the sofa?"

"No, I'm more comfortable sitting upright in this chair. But thank you, Adie. Thank you for coming back."

In the kitchen, putting a teabag in a cup, Adie thought how pathetic Michael looked. How sad. How old. Something must have happened to plunge him into this strange mood of despair and hopelessness. It couldn't simply be his broken ankle, could it? He was in no apparent physical pain now. Whatever, he did seem moderately glad to see her – and she felt glad that she'd come home.

Over the next few weeks, as she nursed Michael back to health – sometimes with a willingness that surprised her – Adie realized that relinquishing a long, shared life with another person is a hard thing to do. You can't just swat those years away, as if they're some annoying bug that has landed on your arm. The bug gets under your skin. It burrows deep. Settles in. Makes itself comfortable. And sometimes, the sheer constancy of that bug can be as comforting as a pair of old slippers.

Michael needed her – and she liked knowing that he did. Plumping up pillows. Bringing him his laptop or a bowl of soup on a tray for lunch. Escorting him to the Mount Sinai outpatient clinic. It felt reassuring. Sometimes there was resentment at being forced into this role of nurse, but it also struck her that togetherness, even with all its flaws, was preferable to the frightening prospect of being alone in middle age. Panic and despair had gripped her that last morning in Fortune, after Shep hadn't called. She'd felt so alone, so lost. And a new Michael did appear to be emerging as his ankle started to heal. He became warmer, less critical, and almost pathetically appreciative of everything she did for him. Had he put the red-haired girl out of his mind? It seemed so. Adie was cynical enough to wonder if that was for practical reasons. The plate glass windows of their apartment only went down to waist level and observing the pavement below required a person to be standing up. Yet Michael couldn't stay on his feet for more than a couple of minutes at a time. So had he, frustrated, simply given up his peculiar fixation? Perhaps. He stayed upright in the straight-backed chair from morning till night, the injured foot propped up, reading or surfing the Web. Columbia had granted him a leave of absence. The possibility that he might resume watching the girl once the broken bones had healed did cross her mind, but for now there was peace between them, and that felt good.

Christmas neared. They'd always drawn close at Christmas, for the simple reason that they both hated it. They felt shut out, perpetual outsiders – or worse, hangers-on – at the time of year when it seemed that the entire world worshipped at the hallowed altar of "the family." Neither of them had any family. Adie's dad had been felled by a heart attack in his greenhouse in his early sixties. Her distant, depressed mother, with whom she'd never really gotten along, had died just before Gully. That left Adie's brother, Philip, but he'd gone off the rails following a bitter divorce and moved to an island in the Outer Hebrides. Like her, Philip had no children, and he never wrote. She hadn't heard from him for years. Didn't even have an address for him anymore. And Michael had never bothered to keep in touch with an aunt and uncle in Ponnetville, either. Although they were his only living relatives, he confessed that he couldn't stand them.

"We were born to be together," he had once laughed, "because we both want nothing to do with Christmas."

This year felt no different. Adie shut her ears to Jingle Bells, to Bing Crosby warbling "Chestnuts Roasting On An Open Fire," and to the parum-pum-pum of the insufferable little kid with the drum. She ignored the throngs of shoppers staggering around with bags stuffed full of gifts. She didn't tune into the Christmas specials on TV where celebrities grinned like morons beside fake evergreen trees, gushing about their supportive moms and dads. And when she picked up food at Gristedes, she listened politely as Jose, the man behind the deli counter, told her how he and his wife couldn't wait to have all six kids and fourteen grandkids together at their home in the Bronx on

Christmas Day. Then she went home, grateful to have Michael, because if she were on her own in the apartment at this time of year, she'd probably have jumped under a subway car.

They regretfully declined an invitation to join Dan and Jolanta Wagstaff's waifs' and strays' dinner on Christmas Day (the couple had no children either), because of Michael's broken ankle. He couldn't walk far. Adie planned a modest meal of roast chicken that she'd cook herself and invited Val to join them. But Val always flew the coop at this time of year. She disliked the family-centred hoopla as much as they did. It didn't matter whether the occasion was Thanksgiving, Chanukah or Christmas, she maintained.

"It's a rough time for people like us, cherub, so I'm taking myself off to a resort in the Virgin Islands. Going to find me a pretty young waiter to lie with under the stars," she said, chuckling. "Haven't tasted that kind of honey for a long time."

When Christmas morning dawned, cold and bright, Adie went out for her usual run. Back at the apartment, she rubbed the chicken with salt to make the skin crisp, prepared mashed potatoes and green beans, and on impulse cut the turban squash that still sat on her studio credenza into quarters and put that in the oven, too. By mid-afternoon, everything was ready. She lit a solitary red candle for the dining table. They'd agreed that they wouldn't exchange gifts, because Michael couldn't get out to buy anything for her. When she brought the squash out of the oven, dripping with butter and sprinkled with brown sugar, he launched into a moan about the "overload of carbs," and she suppressed an urge to kick his injured foot under the table. Yet his delight and gratefulness at dessert – a brimming bowl of sliced Bombay mangoes decorated with dried unsweetened cranberries in honour of the season – mollified her. They sipped a pot of Lapsang Souchong, because Michael couldn't drink wine while on medication, and Adie had no desire to imbibe alcohol anyway. After dinner, they watched a DVD – a British movie about a spy – instead of sitting through *It's a Wonderful Life*, which always held sway on every TV channel on Christmas Day, and which neither of them could stomach anymore. By ten, they were in bed. They shared a chaste goodnight kiss. Felt calm, at peace, and reasonably content with the world and each other. But also – though they didn't express it – overwhelming relief that Christmas was over for another year.

Michael went to sleep at once. Adie lay awake. Right after coming back to New York, she'd tossed and turned for a few nights thinking about Shep. Then she'd told herself sternly to stop. It was nothing but a funny little fling, kind of like Val's. An ego-booster, but no more than that. *So end it, kiddo. Grow up. Act your age. All the scumbag had wanted anyway was access to your land.* The self-administered pep talk worked. She forgot Shep and resolved to sell the property in the New Year once Michael was better. The keys were with Tish. It wouldn't be difficult. Bill Wickenheiser could handle the deal for her. She never wanted to go near Fortune again. The house on the hill seemed unrealistic now, a place of soured dreams and infinite loneliness – for her, for Gully. Nothing good could come of allowing it back into her life again.

As Michael gently snored beside her, Adie glanced at the illuminated digital clock on the bedside table. After midnight. She cursed under her breath. Rolled on her stomach. Punched the pillow. Rolled back again. The elusive mistress of sleep was playing tricks on her. With a sinking heart, she knew why.

Shep. Cunning, stealthy, like a panther stalking prey. He crept back into her head and made himself at home. He wouldn't go. She envisaged a family dinner on Fortune Hill, a big, joy-filled affair, similar to the one Jose and his wife had planned with their offspring. Shep's daughters were present. Probably his wife, too. Plus various other relatives. And the merrymaking was still going on, at that moment, while she lay sober as a judge in bed. Everyone was sitting around the big kitchen table, animated, laughing, swapping jokes, their faces lit up in the flickering orange light from the wood stove's glass door. On the table she saw empty bottles of wine and Baileys Irish Cream, plus the remains of a huge, calorie-laden feast. There were the picked-clean bones of a wild turkey and a rack of deer, both shot by Shep on her uncle's land. Plates smeared with traces of sweet potatoes, dressing and thick gravy. A stack of smaller, sticky plates with little forks piled on the top plate, indicating that the guests had also tucked into desserts. Delicious, sweet desserts. Cakes and pies. His chocolate chip cookies, of course. Probably a box or two of chocolates. But she saw no remains of Bombay mangoes. A country boy certainly wouldn't include those in his Christmas dinner. Shep had probably never eaten mangoes. And the only cranberries consumed on Fortune Hill tonight had doubtless been in a sauce served with the turkey.

Adie longed for him then – the rural redneck who had a sweet tooth like her, who loved both Johnny Cash and Beethoven, who made her laugh and who hated city life. Her mouth filled with saliva, thinking of his lips on hers. *Stupid, stupid, kiddo.* But she couldn't help it. She saw his compelling eyes, their strange shade of grey, his penetrating smile. She felt his rough hand in hers as together they climbed on to the ATV. She heard the engine roar as they sped off to the cabin, deep in the woods, leaving the stresses of the world behind.

She punched the pillow again, unable to stand his presence any longer. Then, a few minutes later, she folded herself quietly out of bed, taking care not to disturb Michael. She pattered along to her studio and pulled a packet of peanut butter cups out of the credenza. Tearing the packet open, she gobbled both the candies like a starving child.

And she wept.

Eighteen

In the New Year, snow fell on Manhattan. Not the smothering blanket of white that had filled Adie with wonder and a sense of despair on her last morning in Fortune, but a sprinkling, more like sugar spilled from a bag. It clung to the trees and benches in Central Park and along Park Avenue, creating a surreal winter wonderland that triggered impulsive behaviour for a few brief hours. Kids threw snowballs. Total strangers smiled at each other, commenting on the beauty of it all. Then the temperature plummeted. Things turned nasty. Wind whisked all the whiteness off the trees and whooped along the hard, bare concrete pavement in great gusts, making noses red, rattling windows and turning New Yorkers back inside themselves again. Adie ignored the chill and continued running every morning. She swathed herself in thick, black leggings, plus two layers of fleece and a snug wool hat that covered her ears. Though she sometimes hesitated to venture out, she steeled herself to go, because the exercise kept her sane and banished memories of the person she was determined not to think about. And Michael resumed teaching part-time at Columbia, hobbling there on crutches via a taxi to start with, but after the cast was taken off, graduating to a cane and the hazards of the crosstown bus at 86th Street.

His mental state improved too. The frightening deadness in his eyes disappeared. Yet the biggest change, Adie noticed with relief, was that he no longer stood by the window in the morning, watching for the red-haired girl. His disposition seemed to change as a result. He was calmer, less inclined to be moody and preoccupied and didn't pick on her about trivial things. He obviously wasn't adrift in his private world anymore. Then one evening, when they were sharing supper, not saying much, in a quiet old-married-couple kind of way, he put down his knife and fork and shot her an odd look across the table.

He cleared his throat nervously.

"You knew about her, didn't you?" he asked.

She waited for a moment. Put down her fork.

"Yes, I did, Michael," she replied. "I'm afraid it was obvious."

"Well, I'm... er... sorry," he stammered. "So sorry that I've hurt you again. I'm an idiot. I don't know why I keep doing it...." He flexed his hands in a helpless way, then closed them into fists on the tabletop. His eyes wandered around the room. "I just couldn't stop myself, Adie. I hope you'll forgive me. Perhaps I need to see a shrink or something?"

She nodded. "You do seem to have... um... a problem."

"Yes. I can't explain it." He glanced at the *Beata Beatrix* print, then looked quickly away. "I... er...."

Michael did not come clean with the full story. He still felt mortified and foolish about going out to get a photo of Sid and injuring himself in the process. He resolved never to reveal that part of his fantasy to his wife.

"I promise you," he reached for Adie's hand across the table and gripped it, "it's over now, for sure. I won't ever do it again."

"Right then," she said squeezing back. "We'll forget about it. But make an appointment to talk to somebody, won't you? Because I think you need help."

Michael promised that yes, he would see a shrink. He would call their doctor the next day for a referral. He would, he would. But then he let the matter slide, as he often did with things they'd agreed upon. Adie decided not to press the issue. They settled back into the comfort of the familiar: him at Columbia most of the day, her in the studio, followed by quiet evenings together in the apartment. Sometimes a sense of disquiet gripped her, a feeling that something remained bubbling beneath the surface of their lives which wasn't quite right, but after he'd pledged so sincerely to take action himself, she was loathe to allude to his "problem" again.

She met Val for lunch. Heard about her trip to the Virgin Islands.

"Found myself a real cutie. Worked in the pool bar. Had great buns. But otherwise, the place was a total drag. Full of fussing parents with bratty kids who kept whining that their cell phones didn't work," she said. "It's good to be back in New York."

How invigorated and alive Val looked, after some sun and her casual roll in the hay, Adie thought. She wished she could treat sexual encounters in the same light-hearted manner. Memories of the strange little episode with Shep still stung, so she sought refuge in work. She bought an expensive potted amaryllis from Windsor Florist on Lexington. It had a bevy of beautiful buds and an appealing name: Rosalie. She positioned the plant on the studio credenza with a backdrop of creamy silk, then as the huge trumpet-shaped blooms started to unfurl, revealing themselves to be salmon-pink shot through with scarlet, she began a big acrylic, strictly to please herself, because a break from the pressure of watercolour commissions would recoup her enthusiasm for making art. If it turned out well, she'd order another limited edition print. A new one would delight the décor stores that sold her work.

At the end of January, a manila envelope plopped through the Fenster Smith brass mail slot down in the lobby. Adie retrieved it breathlessly, after her morning run. The envelope carried Canadian stamps. It had been addressed by hand. Inside was a note from Tish on perfumed, pale blue notepaper bordered with delphinium flowers, plus a long white envelope.

"A hasty note. This was dropped off for you yesterday. I thought you'd like to have it. Let me know what your plans for the house are. I enjoyed having you here. We're getting lots of snow this winter. Flavian sends regards. Sammy loved the catnip. Yours, Tish."

Adie realized, feeling guilty, that she hadn't been in touch with the owner of Bounteous Bed and Breakfast since coming back to New York. She'd wanted to forget Fortune. Her insides wobbled as she turned the other envelope over. Could this be some note, some kind of explanation from Shep? No. It was addressed to Mrs. Adrian Coulter in neat handwriting and in the top left hand corner, in small italic type, she saw a logo with the words: "Knock Has The Knack."

So. The Mennonite with the funny name. After all this time. She'd almost forgotten him. Knock wrote that he had "taken the liberty" of getting the keys to her house from Tish, and after a thorough inspection, had determined that the place was structurally sound, but required a daunting list of improvements. Adie ran a finger quickly down the list: new furnace, new windows, new roof, new electrics and plumbing, various updates to the kitchen and bathroom, new wood trim on the front porch. Phew. Although Knock attached a price list and concluded his letter, "I am not busy in the winter and could give you a discount if we start the project soon," she felt glad she wasn't going to renovate Gully's house, after all.

That evening, she'd send emails to Tish and Knock, saying she was going to sell the place. And then perhaps she and Michael could take a trip to London, back to their old haunts.

In her studio, the phone rang just as she about to start work on the amaryllis painting. She picked it up reluctantly.

"Ah, bonjour, ma cherie. Ca va?"

It was Micheline Fulbrow.

"*Et Bonne Nouvelle Annee,*" Micheline trilled. "You are so clever, *ma petite artiste.* We loved your turban squash. It is beyootiful. It will appear in our spring edition."

"Oh, I'm glad you liked it," said Adie, putting a tube of paint down and mentally kicking herself for not billing *Gardens Around The World* fifty per cent more. Then she remembered why. The illustration wasn't, in her estimation, one of her best.

"But *ecoute, ma cherie*, what's with the new signature?" Micheline sounded injured. "Why did you write ADC, not AFS on the bottom? Are you changing your name? People know you as AFS. And *cherie*," she gushed, "we prefer that people can recognize your wonderful work."

"Ah, sorry, Micheline," said Adie. Her idea to start a new life seemed absurd now. "It was an error, a passing fancy. I'll come in and change it back, if you like. ADC stands for my maiden name of Anna Dorothee Coulter. But don't worry, I'll put AFS on anything I do for you in future."

"Well, that is good to hear. But *ecoute cherie*, it is not the reason for my call. I have exciting news," Micheline burbled. "Our book publishing arm, Sumac Books, is planning to produce a beautiful new book. And," she paused for dramatic effect, "they would like you, *ma petite artiste*, to illustrate the book for them."

"Oh," said Adie. A book project. A huge amount of work. Probably for low pay. She wasn't enthusiastic. "What kind of book?"

"On native North American plants and flowers. They are becoming very, very fashionable, as I'm sure you know, and we at Sumac aim to capture the high end of the market with a wonderful coffee table book. We want illustrations that are *absolumment merveilleux*, so they will take your breath away."

She paused. "And you, *ma cherie*, are the one who can do this for us. I would like you to come into the office today and discuss it with our publisher. *D'accord?*"

Adie thought for a moment. She disliked Micheline's Parisienne arrogance and her presumption that she had nothing else to do. The acrylic of the amaryllis was progressing. Breaking off for even a single day would destroy her focus. Yet paying work wasn't to be sniffed at. And it was never a good idea to get on the wrong side of valuable clients.

She sighed. Said, "*D'accord* Micheline. All right, I'll come in this afternoon."

She glanced at the amaryllis. Whispered, "Sorry, my ravishing Rosalie. Gotta abandon you for a while," because Adie often became attached to the plants she painted and conducted conversations with them while she worked.

"But I'll be back, don't worry." She blew a kiss at the plant and shut the studio door.

In the bedroom, she rummaged in her closet for something decent to wear. Settled on a black pantsuit. Black always made her look and feel old, she thought, looking in the mirror. Shades of Whistler's Mother again. But at least the outfit was clean and not too tight. An orange, pink and green scarf brightened it up.

The headquarters of Sumac Publishing occupied two floors of a glass-and-steel edifice on 59th Street. Micheline and her minions at *Gardens Around The World* had half of one floor; their sister magazine devoted to upscale country homes, the other half. The book publishing arm took up the entire upper floor. Although Adie had produced a number of illustrations for the gardening magazine, she rarely went to Micheline's office in person – and had never visited the books section. So she was curious to see inside.

Micheline escorted her upstairs, clip-clopping like a little show pony in her crocodile-skin high heels. She wore a chic, black-and-white check suit with a white silk scarf at the neck and reeked of an expensive perfume. Feeling dowdy, Adie wondered which swanky fashion designer was responsible for the suit, what the shoes cost and if Micheline was indulging in a *cinq a sept* this evening. The editor made introductions. Then, to Adie's relief, she trotted away.

The publishing boss, Blair Rountree, occupied a large corner suite and sat behind a big, messy, old-fashioned wooden desk covered in papers. Adie was surprised to discover that she liked him at once. He was a New Englander, tall and preppy, with laughing blue eyes, untidy blonde hair and a flamboyant purple and green tartan bow tie. He welcomed her warmly and said he loved her work, but unlike Micheline, wasn't gushy or irritating. The editor's habit of throwing French words into her conversations, even though she had lived in New York for years, got on her nerves.

Blair escorted Adie into Sumac's boardroom overlooking the Hudson River and served mint tea in bone china cups. He showed her eight pages of roughs of the proposed book, each of which had a dummy illustration, then explained that the tentative title was *Beautiful Natives*.

"What we have in mind is an elegant collection of about 35 watercolour portraits of native North American plants and flowers in the manner of George Ehret or Alexander Marshall," he said. "I'm sure you know them both?"

Adie nodded, impressed on two counts. It was always a good sign when clients commissioning a project knew exactly what they wanted, because so many didn't. Yet equally encouraging, this guy with the colourful tie seemed to be familiar with the icons of botanical art. The paintings and sketches of plants by George Dionysius Ehret, who lived in Heidelberg, Germany, in the 18th century, were still acknowledged to be among the best in the world. Adie loved their precision and meticulous attention to detail. But in her own work, she strove to emulate the bolder, more colourful style of the British painter Alexander

Marshall, who was around even earlier than Ehret, and who had included his pet greyhound in a magnificent portrayal of a sunflower – a plant that was then new to Britain, imported from North America, and causing a stir.

"Is this something you think you want to tackle, Adie?" Blair continued." "We're looking for high class work which I know you're capable of." The merry eyes surveyed her with a respectful smile. "And, as you can see, the illustrations are going to be the most prominent part of the book. The text will be secondary and quite short, at the bottom of each two-page spread. And we expect the book to sell well. You'd be working with a garden writer named Maggie McCorkindale. Know her?"

"Vaguely," said Adie. She recalled a hearty woman with a braying laugh and a big backside, who'd drunk a lot of wine and tripped over a potted poinsettia during a *Gardens Around The World* party one Christmas.

"Maggie's a fun gal and a real good writer. She lives in Vermont, and you probably won't even have to meet. She rarely comes to New York. She can simply email you the text. What do you think?"

"The project does look interesting, Blair," Adie hesitated. "But, yikes! Thirty-five large, detailed illustrations. That's an enormous amount of work, you know."

"Yes, we realize that. So we're allowing two years for the art, although of course we'd like to get it earlier than that."

"I see. And if you don't mind my asking, what are you paying?"

Blair took a fastidious sip of tea and returned the cup to its gold-rimmed Royal Doulton saucer. He made a steeple with his long elegant fingers on the boardroom table and observed her over it.

"Of course, yes, I was just getting to that," he said. "We normally pay a flat fee, but because we want you, we're willing to offer a generous cash advance and royalties of fifteen per cent on all sales."

Oh my. An advance. And fifteen per cent. Her interest escalated like a rocket going to the moon. This was a switch from the take-it-or-leave-it terms that publishers usually offered to artists. She recalled her painstaking work on the language of flowers book. It still rankled that a famous publishing house had sold more than two million copies around the world, yet she'd received only a paltry fee for her efforts.

"All right, I do like the sound of it. I'll take it on," she said, "so long as I can have two years if I need them."

"Absolutely, Adie," said Blair. "I'll have a contract stating those terms drawn up. But there is," he paused, wrinkling his broad forehead in a frown, "just one obstacle that we foresee."

"Oh, what?"

"Well, take a look at the list of plants we want to feature." He pushed two typewritten sheets of paper across the table. "I understand that you like working from live models?"

"Yes, of course. It's always easier to capture the vitality of the plant when it's a real, live specimen, sitting in front of you."

"But the problem will be getting hold of those live specimens. It's going to be difficult, I think. They are unlikely to be available at florists or garden centres in New York. And we want very precise botanical illustrations. Can you work from photographs?"

Adie frowned now.

"Sometimes I can, Blair," she said, scanning the list. "But it depends on the plant – and how tricky its structure is. For an unusual plant that's not been painted before in watercolour, I'm probably going to need the real thing as a model."

She scanned the plant names. Several jumped out at once: Jack-in-the-Pulpit. North American wild ginger. Cardinal flower. Joe Pye weed. New England asters. Well, how amazing. And how exciting. These were all plants she'd seen growing wild on her land, when she took that jaunt on the ATV with Shep.

A plan formed quickly in her mind. Perhaps the idea to renovate Uncle Gully's house wasn't such a crazy one after all. If the place was made liveable, she could maintain a second studio there. Spend months at a time up in Canada. Find all the plants she needed for this new book in her own woods and the countryside around Fortune.

The more she thought about it, the more enthusiastic she became. She tucked the list into her shoulder bag and smiled confidently at Blair as he escorted her to the elevator. They shook hands. He promised to get the contract to her in a week or two and returned to his office. Practically shaking with excitement, she headed down to street level.

Bouncing along to the subway at the corner of Lex and 59th, humming Beethoven's *Ode to Joy* to herself, she felt hardly able to believe her luck. Yes, yes, YES! It would be wonderful to have that house of her uncle's now. She forgot the sense of desperation that had gripped her on her last morning in Fortune. Pushing the doubts aside, she realized that she'd missed the wild beauty of Canada since coming back. All those amazing woods that belonged to her, the burnt sienna of the soybean fields, the endless vistas undulating towards the horizon. New York's skyscrapers seemed so claustrophobic, so clingy now. And so dark. You hardly ever saw the sun on 90th Street. Yet up there… how different it was. So tonight, she'd email Knock. Call Tish, too. Go ahead with her original plan. Because the fact was, she did have sufficient money to fix the place up. Dear Uncle Gully had been rich. The vineyards in Bordeaux he inherited from his father must have brought him a tidy pile, yet obviously he spent very little money on himself after he disappeared from London. And apart from his bequest to Tish, she'd received the lot.

This new assignment seemed like a stroke of fate now, pointing her in an altogether different direction from what she'd envisaged on her fiftieth birthday a year ago.

She gave Michael the news the moment he came home. He put his cane down and sat on the sofa, stretching out his leg with the injured ankle and propping it up carefully on a chair. Then he listened without interrupting for a change, but with a grave expression.

"Well, if you really want to do this, Adie. And it seems that you do," he said, "I'm not going to stand in your way."

"You won't?" She went over to the sofa and hugged him. "That's fantastic. And it'll be your place too, you know. You can come up in the summertime, when you've finished the teaching year. Escape the heat in New York. It's not that far away. And I promise you that the place isn't ugly. It's rural for sure, but I'll bet it's not at all like Ponnetville. The countryside is so beautiful and there's a town called Marsh River nearby that reminds me of Vermont, where I met a young guy who has a bookstore you would like and…."

As Adie burbled on, Michael reflected that he still hated everything about the country. His repugnance was ingrained, like the grass stains that always wound up on his pants when Adie insisted on hauling him off to outdoor concerts in Central Park. He was a city person. Period. He couldn't fathom why people blathered on about the joys of woods and fields and wild open spaces, when life was so much more vibrant, stimulating and comfortable in the city. Yet he didn't interrupt. He smiled and nodded. He let his wife carry on, because, after the humiliating episode with his ankle, he knew he'd be lost without her.

So Adie set her plan in motion. She contacted Knock and arranged to fly to Toronto. They agreed to meet in Fortune in a few days. Then she called Tish and told her about the book.

"It's very cold here right now, you know," Tish said, sounding dubious. "And the roads will be bad. I'm thrilled, of course, that you're coming back – Flavian will be, too – and the book sounds so exciting. Perhaps he can sell it in his shop. But are you sure you don't want to wait until April or May?"

"Nope," said Adie firmly. "I can't wait that long. I need to start painting in spring, and Knock says he can get started on the house now."

She pictured three native North American wild plants — Jack-in-the-Pulpit, wild ginger and trout lilies — that were on the list Blair Rountree had given her. They all apparently came up in early spring. She couldn't wait to discover if they were growing on her land.

And if Shep Tanner were around, so what? She'd simply stay on her side of the woods and ignore the bastard.

Nineteen

Shep climbed into his pickup and turned the key. Fortunately, it started. After an absence up north of over a month, in some of the worst weather of the year, he'd expected the battery to be dead as a doornail. But no, he didn't need a boost. Good old Ford. It sure beat Charlie's temperamental Dodge every time. As he manipulated the vehicle around the crowded parking lot at Toronto airport and reached the exit, he felt glad – as he always did – to be hitting the highway for Fortune.

It was still snowing. It had been a trying winter so far. Way too much white stuff, and on the first day of hunting season in Wellington County, he'd been called away to Moosonee to fill in. The chief pilot at the air ambulance station had taken sick and needed to come down south for tests. Then the guy hadn't returned. So he'd been stuck up there, in the dumpy little northern outpost on the edge of James Bay for nearly two weeks, airlifting people back and forth to the hospital in Moose Factory by chopper, because you couldn't get there by road. Once he'd enjoyed flying in the Arctic and the wild, free atmosphere of the north. The crummy bars with loud music. The dark-eyed, plump Cree girls, with their long, glossy black hair and big soft breasts, giggling, always giggling, but willing to be talked into having a good time by a white guy with a pocketful of cash. Yet the place had lost its allure. Cree men didn't like their women hanging around with anyone from the south now. As far back as he could remember, there'd been drunken brawls in the bars over the women, but now it felt different. More tense. Less friendly. The locals tended to pick on the whites for the sheer fun of it. Just last week, some young smart ass from Winnipeg had got himself beaten to a pulp for hitting on a pretty young Cree waitress at the Muddy Creek Bar. He no longer felt welcome there himself, although he'd been a regular for years.

Not that home had been a heck of a lot of fun lately, either. He'd upset Chrissie and Tyson, missing their Stag and Doe because he had to go up north. Missed hunting too, apart from the last day, which turned out to be a waste of time. He'd sat in a blind for hours near the cabin. Froze his balls off. Didn't see one frigging deer. Tyson and Charlie had been luckier, earlier in the week. Tyson had bagged himself a six-point buck. The kid had turned into a crack shot. And Charlie had brought down two does, whose meat would be very tender. Then Christmas had come and Mary Ann had refused to come home. Insisted she was staying on at Hanni's. So he'd gone over there with the girls, and the whole thing had been a pain. Everyone sitting around the table in the fancy-schmancy house with the chandeliers in Marsh River, eating over-cooked slices of a Butterball turkey from the supermarket and making polite chit-chat about nothing much. Hanni was boring and her old man, Walter, was brain dead. So was their good-for-nothing wimp of a son, Caleb. They'd all gone off to the Mennonite church before dinner, taking Mary Ann and Chrissie along with them. And neither Hanni nor Walter drank and they got pious and preachy with anyone who did, so he'd had to settle for sickly apple cider with the turkey. Once he got home, he'd poured himself a double rum and swallowed it down in a couple of seconds, standing by the woodstove.

About the only thing he'd enjoyed about Christmas was seeing Kara, back from university. What a smart, bright kid she was turning out to be. She was far too serious and needed to loosen up sometimes, but her optimism about changing the world made him feel old. He'd been more interested in having fun at her age.

He'd also shared a few beers and laughs with Charlie and talked about turkey hunting in the spring. But then he'd had to fly back to Moosonee in early January – poor Bob Wilkie, the absent pilot, had received a diagnosis of advanced prostate cancer – and so he'd missed saying goodbye to Kara when she left for Africa.

Then there was her, of course. Adie. His new neighbour. He'd sure liked her. She'd seemed to like him too. Something had sparked between them in the cabin that night. He hadn't felt that drawn to a woman in a long time. It was a surprise to hear that she'd gone back to New York. When he'd called Tish's place from Moosonee to explain the reason for his sudden departure, Tish said Adie was out. And then when he'd called back a day later, she'd left. For good, Tish thought, but she wasn't sure.

Of course she had a husband back in New York. She'd told him so, the day they met. And she was of two minds about fixing up her uncle's house. So it was probably best to forget the whole thing. It wasn't a good idea to hope for anything to develop there.

Still, too bad. She'd seemed kind of special. And what was she going to do with the property?

Shep wondered, driving home to Fortune, if he could buy Adie's house and hundred acres himself.

It was early afternoon. Snow suddenly swirled around the pickup. Thick, heaving clouds of white blotted out everything: fields, farms, woods, the road, the sky, even the telephone poles. It always happened at exactly this spot, Shep thought, as he took the turn-off from the highway and headed towards Marsh River. It was as if someone drew a magic line between the snow belt that started here and the warmer weather that drifted up from Lake Ontario down below it. Once you crossed that line, you could go from sleet or freezing rain to blinding snow in a flash. It was happening now. A classic white-out. He could hardly see a thing in front of him. He slowed down. Crawled along for a few miles, running into no other vehicles, not even a snow plow. The drifts were piling up, whipped into peaks by the wind. He put a Hank Snow CD in his player but turned it off after a couple of minutes. The guy was putting him to sleep with his whiny laments about love gone wrong. He ached to get home and put his feet up.

Ahead of him he saw the blurry shape of a car tipped sideways into the ditch, its nose deep in a snowdrift. All-season radials aren't good enough here, you jerk, he wanted to tell the driver. You need snow tires. Coming closer, he realized that the car was a red compact, exactly like the ones he saw all the time parked outside the Red Auto Rentals franchise in Toronto airport. A squat figure stood beside the car in a red jacket. A woman. She was flapping her arms above her head. Wore no hat. And her long hair flew wildly around her face in the wind. She was trying to flag him down. It couldn't be.... could it?

It could.

"My God, I don't believe it. It's YOU," she said, her face almost blue with cold.

"I don't believe it either," he said.

"Where the hell did you go?"

"No, where the hell did you go?"

"I waited for you to call me at Tish's."

"I did call."

"You didn't."

"I did."

"I don't believe you, you liar. Tish said there were no calls. So I went back to New York."

"Perhaps Tish didn't want to tell you I called. Perhaps she doesn't like me."

"Perhaps I don't like you either...."

"Okay, so you don't like me. Fine. I'll accept that. But Jesus Christ, girl, why are you standing at the side of the road in weather like this?"

"I should think that's obvious, *boy*. You moron. I slid into the ditch. I didn't realize there'd be so much snow. I'm not used to… to driving in this kind of…." Her nose and cheeks were going cherry-red with rage now. Snow flakes glistened on her lashes and her upper lip. She seemed about to cry. "I was hoping someone would stop and help me."

"Have you called a tow truck?"

"No, I didn't know how to. And I couldn't get my cell phone to work."

"Well, then, unless you want to freeze to death, I'm going to have to be your helper. Come here, you silly…."

He strode forward and put his arms around her. She felt as cold and stiff as a popsicle on a stick. She was shivering. She leaned against his chest. Let him pull her close. Yet at the same time he sensed her reluctance, as if what she really wanted to do was pound the shit out of him.

"Look, Adie," he said, holding her back for a moment so he could look into her face. "Don't be mad, please. Let's get into my truck so you can warm up, at least. Then I'll explain everything."

"Okay," she whimpered in a little girl voice he hadn't heard before. The tension in her body loosened. "But what shall I do about the car?"

"I'll handle it. I'll call the car rental place on my cell phone and get them to send a truck. Where were you heading?"

"To Tish's."

"Why did you come back now? Seems kinda crazy to me. This is Canada, girl. It's February. You aren't in Florida."

Flakes whirled wildly around her, settling on her coat sleeves and hair. She looked quite pretty now, he thought. Like an angry snow maiden.

"Yes, I know, but I heard from Knock," she said. "And he said he'd give me a good deal on fixing up the house if he started in the winter. So I decided to fly back and see him."

Her teeth chattered as he led her over to the pickup.

" I'm sup-p-posed to meet hi-hi-him at the house to-tomorrow morn—"

"Well, you better not think about doing any such thing, girl, till you've warmed up," he said, opening the passenger door. "You could have the beginnings of hypothermia. Get in."

She obeyed. He'd left the engine running. He got in the other side. Turned the heater up full blast. Called for the tow truck. Then he found a squished chocolate bar in the dash and insisted that she eat it. The cab windows steamed up with their breath as he talked. She listened, teeth still chattering, not saying a word.

He told her about the emergency in Moosonee and the sick pilot, his awful Christmas at his sister-in-law's, that he'd missed practically the entire hunting season. Then he said that he'd missed her.

When he stopped, she said, "Oh."

Just that: Oh.

And after a long pause: "I thought you might be dead."

"Dead?"

"Yes, I saw some of those big black birds circling over your cabin. I wondered if there'd been a hunting accident or something."

He laughed.

"No one was hunting out there that day, girl. You have a colourful imagination. It was probably just a dead rabbit they were after."

"Oh."

She looked sheepish now. Said that it felt so good to be thawing out. Unzipping her red jacket, she exhaled a deep breath, her eyes properly on his for the first time.

"I'm sorry," she said in a small voice, smiling feebly. Then she flicked her tongue along her bottom lip. Very slowly. And something about the way she did it made him interpret it as an invitation.

So he moved nearer to her on the bench seat, sliding his bum over a claw hammer and an empty cookie bag. He put his arm along the back of the bench and pulled her to him. Their mouths met. And it was a long kiss, hard and sustained, tongues exploring, arms and hands finding their way around each other's necks in their eagerness to reconnect. It was sweet, too. So sweet. He tasted the chocolate bar she'd eaten. Felt his body grow hot, oppressed by his thick parka. With his mouth still glued to hers, he slid his hand under her jacket and encountered what felt like a wool sweater. He pushed it up. Fumbled for the top of her pants. Thrust his hand in, down between her legs, feeling warmth and wetness down there. He pulled the hand out again and leaned back, his eyes not moving from hers. He smelled the ends of his fingers. Licked them. Pushed two of them into her mouth. She closed her lips around the fingers, sucking slowly, deliberately, flicking their length gently with her tongue as she moved her mouth up and down, up and down. When she stopped, he pushed his face under her messy hair and nibbled her neck, her nose, one of her ears. The ear felt very cold, oddly like a cube of refrigerated cheese he'd eaten on the flight back to Toronto from Moosonee. Yet how aroused he felt with his lips on that ear, filled with longing, wanting to have the rest of her, yet at the same time not wanting to, because this teenage petting at the side of a snowy road in the middle of nowhere excited him in the way it had at the cabin. It was like nothing he'd experienced in years. Her smell on his fingers. The smooching. The sucking, The squirming on the seat of his pickup as their bodies sought each other.

Then, whoops. There was a noise. *Thud, thud.* Someone was rapping with a mitten on the driver's window.

He pulled back and rubbed the window clean with the hand that he'd pushed into her pants. A pale young face was peering in, encircled in the fake fur of a parka hood.

Shep opened the window.

"Well, hello folks," the guy said, smirking. "Sorry that I seem to be interrupting something, but I've come about the stalled car. I presume you want me to tow it out of the drift. But hey… would ya like me to wait till you've finished?"

He leaned in through the window, grinning broadly now, enjoying his little joke.

Adie cringed and shrank into the seat of the pickup. She straightened her jacket and pants. Kept her eyes downcast, refusing to look up at the young guy.

But Shep just grinned back. He felt wicked. Young. And on top of he world.

Twenty

The snow wouldn't let up. Shep stood, a stocky figure in a mud-coloured army surplus parka, smack in the middle of the road, playing traffic cop, ready to put his hand up at any oncoming vehicles that might careen into view while the tow truck – blurry and barely visible – inched Adie's car out of the ditch. Yet the operation took only minutes, and no other drivers materialized. The road stayed deserted, ghostly, obscured in its wedding veil of white as the afternoon light descended into dusk. Watching out of the windshield of Shep's pickup, Adie once more marvelled at the emptiness of Canada. Then at the competent way he handled everything. She felt so happy, so safe, sitting inside his warm, cosy cab. Having to cope with a nightmare like this on her own would have turned her into a gibbering wreck. He was right. She'd probably have frozen to death, waiting for help that never came.

Shep got into the rental car when it was hoisted back on the road. A cloud of exhaust smoke spewed out of the rear and she relaxed. Good. Sliding into the ditch hadn't done something diabolical to the engine. Shep reappeared and left the car running, then shook hands with the tow truck driver. They laughed together about something. She hoped the joke wasn't about her. He rummaged in his parka pocket, gave the guy a tip, and the tow truck rumbled away, lights on the top of its cab flashing in circling patterns of red and white that mesmerized her in the receding light.

Back in the cab, he asked for Adie's cell phone next. Punched in some numbers. Said, "See, it's working now. So call Tish."

"Yes, I'd better tell her I'm arriving later than I thought today."

"Oh no, girl," he shook his head. "You aren't going to Tish's. You better make up some story that you've decided to stay in a hotel at the airport tonight because of the snow and that you'll see her tomorrow. Because you," he grabbed her still cold hand and kissed it, "are coming to my place tonight."

"I am?" Adie blushed.

"Yes." He grinned. "You want to, don't you? I want you to come." He leaned over and kissed her cheek. "You need someone to look after you, girl. You know nothing about winter in this part of the world. You should be wearing a hat to keep the warmth in, for a start." He stroked her hair gently with his hand, pushing a loose strand out of her eyes. "And I'll bet the rest of your body still feels like a block of ice under those clothes.

"But don't worry," he added, tweaking playfully at her red jacket. "I promise you that I can warm it up very nicely."

Yikes. She blushed again. The kissing and groping had aroused passions in her that she hadn't experienced for a long time. Her stomach still felt trembly at the closeness of his chunky body on the bench seat. Yet the prospect of sharing a bed with Shep... how nerve wracking. Michael had been her only lover. They'd stopped having sex so long ago. Would she know what to do after all this time? Would she disappoint Shep? Would it *hurt*?

And what would he think of her flabby stomach and thighs?

She missed Val now. Wished her New York buddy were around to consult, because Val was so worldly, so up-to-date, so matter-of-fact about the whole wretched business of sex. Val knew everything there was to know about different kinds of dildos and condoms, lubricants and massage oils, S & M equipment, any kinky stuff you could name. She made it her business to find out at a store called "Naughty Little Me" down near Times Square. Adie always felt as innocent as a nun when Val related details of her casual flings, like the one at Christmas. After dark, the young pool bar guy had led Val over to the trunk of a coconut palm on the beach. He'd tied her securely to the trunk with some sashes from the terry cotton bathrobes that were kept by the pool for guests. Then he'd fucked her from behind. And Val had liked it. Said it gave her an incredible high having his willy (she always called it that) thrust inside her while she was spreadeagled, unable to move, against the palm's trunk. The story, told in whispered giggles over lunch, had made Adie wince. Even so, she'd listened, fascinated.

And now it seemed that she was about to engage in a fling, too. The thought made her almost shake, and not from the cold. Would Shep want to tie her to the handlebars of his ATV? Or do something equally weird?

She wanted to say no. But a part of her – a sneaky, annoying part that wouldn't go away – wanted to say yes. He insisted again that she call Tish. So she did. She told her that she'd decided to spend the night at a hotel in Toronto, that she'd arrive tomorrow, instead. And Tish swallowed the lie, agreeing that yes, it was wise to stay put when the weather was as bad as this, and that was fine with her.

Adie felt panicky again. Shep noticed. He seemed to think she was having a fit of nerves at the prospect of driving on the slippery road.

"Don't worry. You'll be fine, girl. Just follow me," he said putting a protective arm around her shoulder. "The road is icy as hell, but I'll drive very, very slowly. You do the same. I'll watch out of my rear view mirror. If you feel yourself skidding, don't put your foot on the brake. You might go into the ditch again. Just steer the car straight, right through the skid. Keep going, but take your foot off the accelerator and change down. Remember, steer through the skid."

"Okay," she said, taking a deep breath

It was a relief to have to concentrate on driving. She could shut out her fears about what else she might have to do in the night ahead.

They reached Fortune Hill in only half an hour, just before it got dark. Shep crawled along at a snail's pace, as promised. Following him in the rental car, Adie realized that she hadn't been far from her uncle's house when she slid into the ditch. But everything looked so different in this weather. Ghostly, remote, the thick, white snow transforming the countryside into a sort of dream world she'd only seen in movies. In Fortune village, she saw just one light. It gleamed in the window of the general store, making the falling flakes outside glint like pearls on a necklace. No cars were parked in front. The woman who ran the place sat at the counter. She always seemed to be there, a sad, solitary figure, like someone painted by Andrew Wyeth. Adie felt a twinge of sympathy driving by.

Climbing Fortune Hill, the car slid sideways, out of control. Heart in her mouth, she almost put her foot on the brake. But then she remembered. *Don't brake. Steer through the skid. Steer through the skid.* It worked. She felt quite proud of herself. She was learning a new skill: driving in snow. Yet how comforting the presence of Shep's big, green pickup truck was, out there ahead of her. She shivered with delight, not cold.

Their mini-convoy moved slowly by her property, and her mouth dropped open. A mountain of snow was plugging the driveway. So how was Knock supposed to get up to the house tomorrow and meet her? Just looking at the size of the drift made every bone in her body ache. She decided to worry about it in the morning.

Shep's house was an ice box. He explained that he'd left his oil furnace on low while he was away. Adie started shivering again and kept her jacket on, stuffing her hands into her pockets.

"I'll make you a hot rum toddy in a minute," he said. "Just let me get the stove going first."

Down on his knees in front of the big black stove's glass door, he opened the damper, placed some newspaper and twigs inside the fire box and struck a match. As the fire flared up, he added two split logs of maple. Adie warmed her hands over the top of the stove, admiring the skilful, efficient way he worked. She recalled a trip she and Michael had taken once to a cabin belonging to some friends of Dan and Jolanta Wagstaff in the White Mountains of New Hampshire. What a fiasco. Neither of them could figure out how to keep a fire going in the cabin's small woodstove, and there was no other heating. The temperature dipped so low during the night, their breath came out in clouds the next morning. They hardly slept because mice kept running over the comforter they pulled up to their chins to stay warm. Then some hunters materialized in the woods at dawn and started going *bang, bang, bang,* at the back of the cabin. So they'd packed up and driven right back to New York. Adie had never again toyed with the idea of going to see the maple leaves change colour in New England.

How different it was, being around a guy who was country born and bred. Who made his home here. Who had the skills to cope with this kind of life. Shep was an expert at mundane matters like getting a woodstove to work. It warmed her chilled body, hands and feet in minutes, so she took her jacket off and relaxed into one of his old armchairs by the woodstove, feeling glad she came.

Then the apprehension returned. She saw a photograph on a dresser that she hadn't noticed before. Of Shep with his arm around an attractive woman about her age. Obviously his wife. Other photos – lots of them – of their two daughters stood on the dresser, too, at various stages in their development. They were a nice-looking family. She tried to ignore the photos as he made them both hot toddies with liberal shots of rum, big spoonfuls of honey and a pinch of cinnamon.

When he brought the mugs over and sat down in the other armchair, she said, "Thanks, Shep. This is wonderful. Just what the doctor ordered."

"Yes it'll warm you up," he said.

"Um…" she said after a couple of sips. "Shep, I'm terribly tired and wrung out by what happened with the car. Where am I supposed to… um… sleep tonight?"

He regarded her calmly and smiled.

"Well, I thought with me. But if you don't want to," his expression was mischievous, "that's fine. I understand. I won't hold it against you."

"It isn't that I don't want to. It's just that, well, I don't think it's a very good idea." She took another awkward sip. "Is it? I mean, my sleeping with you here, in your home, surrounded by all these pictures of your family."

She gestured at the dresser.

"If you don't mind my asking," she went on, "what is the situation with your wife?"

His face became a mask.

"Wish I knew," he said tersely. "She's still at her sister's. We are kind of separated, I guess."

"I see."

He turned edgy now. Put his mug down and stared at her.

"Well, since you've brought the subject up, what's the situation with you, girl? Seems kinda strange to me that you're up here without your husband all the time. Does he mind that?" He regarded her coldly now. "I have a right to know, too, you know."

She averted her gaze, feeling sheepish.

"Truthfully, I don't know either, Shep. I'm sorry," she said.

"Well then," he said, pushing back from the table, irritated, "perhaps you'd better sleep in one of my daughters' rooms tonight."

"Fine," she said.

He gave her Chrissie's bedroom. The décor was pink again, suffocatingly pink, as was her room at Tish's. They hardly spoke as he brought out clean sheets and made up the bed. She wished that she hadn't lied to Tish. She wished that she'd headed straight to Bounteous Bed and Breakfast after he'd helped get her car going. But most of all, she kicked herself for bringing up the awkward topic of his wife, because it had destroyed the growing rapport between them.

Stupid, kiddo. Stupid, stupid.

She declined anything to eat. Went upstairs to the bedroom, wrung out with fatigue and depressed. She fell asleep quickly, still in her underwear. During the night something woke her. She sat up with a start but could hear nothing except the woodstove going *plick-plick* downstairs in the kitchen and Shep's heavy breathing down the hall, in his bedroom. Everything was pitch black. She couldn't discern even a smidgen of any light anywhere. It felt lonely under the Hudson's Bay blanket. She half hoped he'd creep into her room and snuggle up under the covers with her.

He didn't. He slept like a baby.

Twenty-one

Adie woke to a white world. Everything outside the window was blanketed in snow. The morning sun, blindingly bright, thrust itself into the room where she lay, softening the lurid effect of the pink. Every wall glowed, like a watery wash of permanent rose dropped on to watercolour paper, making her surroundings seem not quite so alien as last night, when she'd crawled unhappily into bed.

Feeling more at ease now, she snuggled under the covers and looked around her, taking in where Shep's younger daughter had grown up. Everything about the room was ultra-feminine. Although Chrissie now lived with her boyfriend in Marsh River, she'd left behind plenty of evidence of her ascent to adulthood. Stuffed animals sat on a chest of drawers and a child's wooden chair. Posters of hockey players and male movie celebrities, their mouths full of capped teeth, were duct-taped to the walls. On top of a dressing table lay some hairbrushes, plus a small bottle with the desiccated remains of electric-blue nail polish inside. On the bedside table she saw a framed photograph of Chrissie's future intended, who'd invited her in for coffee when she came to the house looking for Shep in the fall. Tyson had been effusive in his welcome back then, she remembered. Yet now, picking the frame up and peering at the glass, which was covered in sticky finger marks, it struck her that that perhaps Tish was right. Tyson had a handsome face, certainly, yet in the photo he was scowling and gave the impression of wanting to reach out and punch the person who had the audacity to wield the camera. Adie wondered if Shep liked the idea of his treasured daughter marrying a guy with such an aggressive temperament.

She felt hungry. Two packages of peanut butter cups, some pretzels on the plane and Shep's stale chocolate bar were all she'd eaten yesterday. She presumed he was still in bed and that she'd have to wait a while for breakfast. In the meantime, everything remained so still and quiet in his house. Then she heard something outside. She threw back the covers. Winced as her bare feet hit the cold floor. Padded over to the window. Down at the end of the driveway, what a surprise. Shep sat on top of a yellow-and-green tractor, clearing snow. A device on the front of the machine was cutting a swath through the high drifts, like a knife going through some massive angel food cake, and a great fountain of white was leaping up in the air in front of him. Yesterday evening they'd had to leave her car and his truck at the end of the driveway, next to Fourth Line, and stumble up to the house through the drifts. But now most of the snow had disappeared. So he must have been up very early.

She pulled on clothes that felt icy cold on her skin and shivered, hurrying downstairs to the warmth of the woodstove. A note was propped up against a salt shaker on the kitchen table.

"Help yourself."

Sliced bread in a plastic bag. Some butter. A half-full pot of strawberry jam. A box of Earl Grey tea bags. She winced at the Earl Grey, then reproached herself, because Shep had saved her life, hadn't he? By amazing coincidence, he'd gone by in his truck. If that hadn't happened, she'd be dead by now. Frozen solid, her hair standing on end, eyes glazed over, like the dead Arctic explorers she'd seen in a movie once.

"So don't fuss," she said out loud, "because he doesn't have black tea."

She boiled water and put a hated Earl Grey bag in a mug,

It didn't taste too bad. She was very thirsty. She made some toast, then started fretting again about meeting Knock. He'd suggested in an email that they get together at her house at ten a.m. It was only eight-thirty, but how was she supposed to get over to her house, with the snow thigh-deep in the driveway? She spotted two old wooden snowshoes hanging on the wall of the mudroom. Could she strap those on and walk over there instead? Perhaps. But she'd have to ask Shep.

The tractor chugged up the driveway twenty minutes later. Shep pushed open the mudroom door, his cheeks pink, the short brown hair crisped into mini-icicles by the cold.

He beamed.

"So you're up. Have a good sleep?" he asked, pulling off his boots. He came over to kiss her forehead as if they'd been married for years.

"Yes, thank you," she said, relief flooding through her. "I feel great."

"Well, good," he said. "You needed to sleep. There's a time and a place for everything, isn't there?" He smiled in a flirty way. "And it sure is a beautiful morning. What time do you have to meet Knock?"

Feeling reassured, she told him.

"So, plenty of time," he said. "I've cleaned the driveway to your house as well as mine, so neither of you will have any problems driving in."

"You have? Already? How long have you been up?"

"Oh, since before six. I'm a country boy, you know." He grinned. "We get up early."

He headed over to the fridge.

"And now I'm starving. Shall I make us a big pot of coffee and a mess of bacon and eggs?"

He was a surprisingly good cook. As they ate, Adie kept looking at the snowshoes on the wall. She wanted to try them on.

Heading on foot over to her own house, using the snowshoes, seemed like more fun – and vastly easier – than driving to meet Knock. She was a bit scared of driving after her slide into the ditch. Yet Shep had probably laboured for over an hour cleaning out her driveway. Would she offend him by not taking the car?

She broached the subject of snowshoes as he poured her a second cup of coffee.

"Shep, I'd love to try those," she said, gesturing at the wall.

"What, the snowshoes? Yes, of course you can. They belong to my daughter Kara. I'm too lazy to use them myself. The snowmobile's easier." He laughed and wiped coffee off his lips with the back of his hand. "But Kara loves snowshoeing. She was here at Christmas. Very briefly, though. I didn't get to see her long." He frowned. "Hers will probably fit you. You can take the trail to your uncle's – I mean your house."

"That would be great."

"You don't want to take your car?" he asked. "The driveway's real clean now."

"No, thanks. It looks like perfect weather for a walk."

"Well, okay." He looked doubtfully at her, "But you'll have to bundle up. Wait a minute."

He disappeared and a few minutes later returned clutching a thick Arran wool sweater and some pale blue underwear lined with fleece.

"Long johns," he said, grinning and holding the underwear out. "Standard wardrobe for Canadians at this time of year. They'll fit you, I think. And you'll need them out there today."

She laughed. "I've seen those in sporting goods stores, but never worn any."

"I guess you don't need to, living in New York."

"No, it sure is a different life."

She changed in the bathroom, wondering if the underwear belonged to his wife. The thick, honeycomb cotton felt awkward bunched up in her crotch, underneath her jeans. Yet it would undoubtedly be warm. At the mudroom door he helped her strap on the snowshoes and kissed the top of her head. Then he patted her behind and said, "There. You're a real country girl now. Off you go."

She ventured out. The big wooden frames felt strange and clumsy on her feet. Yet they sank only a few inches into the deep drifts before holding firm. It was like walking on pillows. Great big, feathery pillows. And such a breeze, quite unlike her disastrous attempts to downhill ski in the Alps with Michael. Holding her knees apart, as Shep had instructed her – so the wooden edges of the snowshoes wouldn't collide – she strode confidently along the trail. *Clump, clump, clump.* She breathed in deeply, feeling satisfied by the dish-shaped areas she kept flattening in the snow. Yet it was cold out. Amazingly cold. The icy air hit her lungs with the thrust of a knife. Her chest hurt. The insides of her nostrils prickled. Even so, she liked the way the Arctic chill sharpened her senses. She felt ultra-alert now, all the little anxieties clogging her mind vanishing with every step.

She followed animal tracks through the snow. Stopping to examine some, she wished she knew what kind of animals made the tracks. She felt so ignorant about the natural world, but she could learn lots from Shep. A cardinal flashed through the spruce trees, its brilliant red feathers matching the colour of her jacket. She spotted a blue jay, the bird Tish didn't like. An enormous, long-legged grey rabbit, larger than a small dog, bounded across her path, then disappeared beneath a mound of white. She thought of Michael, at home in Manhattan. Felt sad that he despised the country – and country people – because she was coming to the conclusion that she loved them both.

Knock showed up promptly at ten, in an old beige pickup, its muffler rumbling like thunder on the quiet hill. The renovation whiz was about the same age as Shep. Stocky, too. Quiet-spoken.

She decided that the name Knock didn't really suit him, because his face was cherubic – unlined, cheeks pink from the cold, lips pursed into a sort of rosebud. Adie thought of frescos around altars in Italy. He carried a clipboard under his arm.

"How do you do, Mrs. Coulter," he said, in a precise way, with a hint of a German accent, as he held out a gloved hand. "I've heard a lot about you from Tish Boddington."

"Oh, please call me Adie," she said, wondering what Tish had told him.

"I hear you're an artist," he said. "I'd like to see your work sometime. We need more people like you in Fortune. You are very welcome in our community."

He gave an old-fashioned bow, as if he were addressing the lady of the manor.

"Well, thank you," she said. "It's a pleasure to come here and to meet you."

"The pleasure is all mine, Mrs., er, Adie," he said, lifting up the clipboard in front of his chest and taking a pen out of his pocket. "I am delighted that you've taken it upon yourself to rescue this lovely old Victorian house from ruin."

"Yes, but I wonder if it's such a good idea," she said, with a rueful laugh. "It does seem like such a huge task."

"It will take time, of course. These renovations always do. I estimate four to six months for the project, maybe even longer." Knock spoke crisply now, his manner formal and businesslike, as he examined his notes on the clipboard. "But right now, I would like to go around the house with you, so you can tell me where you'd like to begin."

"Let's go upstairs, then," she said, "because what I want more than anything else is a studio where I can work."

She told him about the native plants book. How she needed to start working on the illustrations the moment the spring came.

He nodded and looked thoughtful.

"And do you require a lot of space for this studio?" he asked, when they stood in the small room containing the iron bedstead and chest of drawers.

"Yes, preferably. The bigger, the better. I like to work at a big art table."

"Then I suggest that we get rid of the wall between this room and the next," he said. "Removing it will open the space up for you and make the room brighter. You will have two windows for your studio instead of one. We can install a support beam if necessary."

He walked over to the wall, rapped it with a knuckle and seemed satisfied by the sound.

"I have done this in many old Victorian houses that have small bedrooms," he added.

"Fine, I love the idea of changing the layout of the room."

And for more reasons than one, she thought. Seeing the chest of drawers and iron bedstead once more prompted a flood of memories about her uncle. She didn't want to be reminded of his lonely, unfulfilled life every time she sat down to paint.

Knock cast an appraising eye over the chest of drawers. "That's a very fine piece of Victoriana you have there."

"Yes, isn't it?" she said. "I'm definitely keeping that. Not sure about the bedstead. Just put them both in another bedroom while you're working in here."

"I will do that, Mrs., er, Adie."

They toured the rest of the house. Knock made suggestions everywhere. Adie agreed to all of them. Finally, they stood in the kitchen, saying goodbye, and Knock explained that he'd like her to visit several stores in Marsh River and in a nearby town before she returned to New York.

"Please go and pick out the styles and colours of tiles and plumbing fixtures and so on that you prefer. You should do it now, rather than later, so I can order them," he said, handing her a list. "And you may like to drop by and see this gentleman."

He held out the business card of someone called Mervyn Baumann.

"Mervyn is a master carpenter. A Mennonite like me. And a cousin," Knock said, pride showing in his voice. "He's a meticulous craftsman. He has a workshop near here, and he can recreate wooden cupboards and doors for you so that they look exactly like they were in Victorian times. That is, of course," his face took on an inquiring look, "if you want that style for your house."

"I think that would be perfect. I'll certainly go see him," she said, charmed by the courteous renovator. "And Knock, do you want me to give you some money up front?"

"Oh no, that's all right. Not right now. I trust you," he said, shaking his head. "I'll tell you when I need a cheque."

She couldn't imagine anything like this happening with a renovator in New York.

Standing at the front door, ready to leave, he shook her hand and said shyly:

"I am looking forward to seeing your beautiful new book, Mrs., er, Adie. I will buy a copy for sure. My wife and I are big gardeners. We are very fond of native plants. We have many in our garden."

"Oh, so do you have one called Jack-in-the-Pulpit?" she asked.

"Ah yes," he said. "The Arisaema. Such a strange-looking plant with that striped hood. We do indeed grow Mister Jack. It is one of the first plants to come up in our garden in spring."

Wow. Great. This was amazing. She already had her first model for the book.

Twenty-two

A black-and-silver machine sparkled in the winter sunlight outside Shep's drive shed. Adie spotted its gleaming hulk through the spruce trees as she returned on the snowshoes from her meeting with Knock. The machine seemed – as the ATV had, the day she met Shep – like some huge insect hovering there in his cleared driveway, waiting to pounce on her and crush her to a pulp. Shep stood to one side, pouring gas into the tank from his yellow jerry can, beaming like a seven-year-old.

"My new boy toy," he called out, slapping the side. "A beauty, eh? Picked it up last fall. Bartered five bush cords of firewood for it. I had to twist the guy's arm because he wanted six cords. But I wouldn't budge, and he let me have it in the end."

He grinned. "I guess you've never been for a ride on one of these things?"

"No, never," said Adie, recalling Michael's distaste for snowmobiles. He threw a fit every time an ad for one came on TV, ranting that they were smelly, noisy and polluting – and that they should be banned, because the people who rode around on snowmobiles were drunken yahoos.

She'd always agreed. Yet now an entirely different emotion took over as she watched this chunky, cheerful man showing off his so-called boy toy. She wanted to climb on board with him and go for a ride. Because, why the heck not? It looked like fun.

"Let's take a ride out to the cabin," Shep said. "You'll love it going through the woods. I've already been out this morning, while you were with Knock. I lit a fire, so the place will be warmed up by now. And since you're discovering that you love snowshoeing, you could take a little hike down to the stream while I make lunch."

"Mmm. Sounds perfect," she said. "But you do know I'm supposed to be going to Tish's?"

"Oh, it's early, girl," Shep waved her objection away. "Not even noon. You didn't give her a specific time, did you?"

She shook her head.

"Well, then, if you get to her place by late this afternoon that should be fine."

His smile turned flirtatious now. The compelling message in his gaze made her heart do a little dance.

A wave of self-consciousness followed, because as she bent over to unfasten the snowshoes, her bum stuck up in the air, and she realized that he was staring at it. But he averted his gaze quickly and threw the snowshoes into a box on the back of the snowmobile. They climbed on. Adie clutched him, thinking how shocked Michael would be if he could see her now, going off on a machine like this, with some hick in the boonies. Yet she didn't give a damn what he thought anymore. She leaned close to Shep. Even plucked up the courage to kiss the back of his thick neck. He responded by reaching behind him and squeezing her arm. She chuckled. The thought of what was going to happen once they got to the cabin made her shudder.

But the shudder was of excitement, not fear.

Wolf's Glen looked like a ski chalet in an ad for winter holidays in the Alps, its Gothic lettering and door stark-red against the snow. The heat was indeed high inside. Behind the woodstove's glass door, an inferno of fiery red and orange glowed, as it did in the pizza oven at her favourite New York restaurant, San Matteo's on Second Avenue. Shep had pushed the beat-up old chair into a corner. A thick, creamy white polar bear pelt took up most of the floor. Some kind of meat stew, with the scent of rosemary, bubbled in a big, black pot on top of the stove, while on a low folding table close by, was a cast iron frying pan, two tumblers, an opened bottle of rum and a stack of plates, soup bowls, knives and forks. She noticed a pile of split logs stashed in one corner. He had certainly been busy.

The smell of the stew made her hungry, and her heart did a little skip again, because she'd read somewhere that if a man wanted to cook for you, it meant he was smitten.

"You like?" he said, spreading his hands out, wanting her to be pleased.

"Oh yes, it's lovely, Shep," she said. "Thank you for doing this."

He beamed, feeling happy too, because Mary Ann had never liked coming here. Finally, he'd met a woman who did. He bent over and took off his boots. Hung his parka on a nail on the log wall.

"But you haven't noticed the best part," he said, pointing to the triangular cupboard where the deer antlers had been displayed.

In their place was an old phonograph player, its lid pushed up, with an LP on the turntable, ready to play.

"It's battery-operated. My dad built it himself. He was clever with things like that. And the LP is of the Eroica, conducted by Karajan with the Berlin Philharmonic. Dad always said that version was the best. But of course, he was German, so he was biased." He laughed. "The record is a bit scratchy now, but I thought we could listen while we eat."

"Oh yes. Fantastic," Adie said. She made a move forward to kiss him, but he held held his hands in front of his face and backed away.

"Later, girl," he said with a chuckle. "No offence, but be careful of my polar bear pelt with those boots of yours. It's my most treasured possession. I did a barter for the skin with a Cree hunter up north. Took him some plaid shirts and a parka from down south in exchange. Now I can't bear for anyone to walk on the pelt unless they've taken their shoes off. So why don't you go out on the snowshoes now, while you still have your boots and jacket on? Then we can lounge around on the rug and have something to eat."

He waved a spatula at the frying pan.

"But don't be long. I want to make you some bannock. It's a hunter's staple. Tastes great, dipped into deer stew."

Adie pushed at the cabin door. It blew wide open, creaking like a farm gate in the wind. An icy blast filled the room. She shivered and hastily pulled the door shut again. Did she really want to go out after all? It felt so cosy with Shep in the cabin.

"Whew, it's cold out there," she said.

"Yep, the coldest day of the winter so far," he said. "So be careful down by the stream, won't you? The water doesn't completely freeze underneath the snow, and you can't see where the bank begins and ends."

"If you fall in," he added, "it can be hard to get out."

Shep threw more logs into the firebox and started preparing the meal. He hummed, enjoying the rhythms of cooking. Pottering here alone, without any women around, felt good, because Mary Ann and her sister always complained that he made a mess if he tried to cook anything at home.

He took a plastic Baggie containing a mixture of flour, lard, salt and baking powder out of the cooler he'd brought along. Added a few drops from his water bottle. Kneaded the dough into balls and put them aside. Dropped a piece of lard into the frying pan. Slid the pan on to the stove so the lard could melt. Then he poured himself a stiff shot of rum and set the table with the plates, bowls, knives and forks.

Everything was ready for her now.

He checked his watch. Adie had been gone about half

an hour. She was obviously having a good time on the snowshoes. A new experience for a city girl like her, of course, and it would be beautiful down by the stream on a cold day such as this, the black water sparkling like diamonds against the stark white, untouched snow. She might spot a few birds. She seemed to love birds and all kinds congregated in the spruce branches each side of the stream, wanting to be protected from the elements, yet close to a water source. She may even run into a wild turkey. He chuckled, thinking that she'd love that.

The lard melted. He took the fry pan off the stove and set it aside on a trivet. He gently lifted up the turntable arm on the old phonograph and placed the needle on the LP. As the scratchy strains of the Eroica filled the cabin, Shep sat down in his dad's chair and leaned back, sipping the rum and remembering the days and nights they'd spent together here. The first movement of Beethoven's intended tribute to Napoleon always transported him back to his childhood. Back to the happy time when he'd shot his first deer. He loved the majestic German music. He'd heard it so many times. So he knew the first movement lasted precisely fourteen minutes and three seconds. Then the tempo changed to the slow, dramatic funeral march. As the transition took place, he looked at his watch again. Adie had been gone over an hour now.

Over an hour. He thought about that again and a terrifying realization hit him. Where the hell was she? She should be back by this time, shouldn't she? She can't have….

He grabbed his parka off the wall. Shoved his feet into his boots without bothering to do them up. Rushed outside, stumbling along. He took great breaths of the icy air, gasping like a wounded deer and followed the indentations her snowshoes had made in the drifts. But the boots kept sinking in. He needed snowshoes too, yet had none. The snow filled his boots, making his feet go instantly numb. He fell over. Got up. Fell over again. Every second seemed like an hour. Pains shot through his feet. His progress was slow. So frighteningly slow.

"Jesus Christ, no," he screamed out loud. "No, no, NO!"

His voice echoed around the silent, empty woods.

"Adie! Adie! Where are you, girl? Tell me where you are."

He heard nothing. Not even the shriek of a jay.

"Adie! Adie!"

Panic consumed him now. He couldn't scream. He could hardly breathe.

You fucking asshole. You fucking, fucking asshole. Why did you let her go out? Why, on a day like this, when you can freeze your face in seconds? Were you crazy? Living in la-la land? Because she's a city girl, asshole. She isn't used to being in the woods in the winter, you fucking jerk. You should have known that. You, you....

Then he practically vomited, because what he spotted ahead confirmed his suspicions. Her red jacket. Some strands of her long hair draped over a deep drift. Her head lying sideways at an awkward angle. Her whole body bent out of shape and leaning, too, as if she'd been struggling to pull herself out of the snow, but had given up.

She had fallen into the stream.

Twenty-three

The onset of hypothermia is insidious. Sometimes it goes undetected and kills in a matter of hours. Other times, victims last longer but still succumb. Shep knew from all the time he'd spent working in the Arctic that there are three distinct stages to dying from exposure to intense cold. Years ago, he'd witnessed a drunken Cree breathe his last after being tossed out of a bar in Moosonee into a snow bank. The guy reached stage three quickly, because his blood was saturated with alcohol. He'd gone to meet his maker by the time the bar closed in the early hours. And Shep had fallen into an icy creek himself once while hunting moose up north and experienced mild – or stage one – hypothermia. A buddy saved his life by ripping off his frozen clothes and getting into a sleeping bag with him.

Now, as he pulled Adie out of the stream and extricated her feet from the snowshoes, he realized, with mounting fear, that she had reached stage two. She wasn't shivering anymore – a stage one symptom – but was drowsy and had a bluish-white face, her breathing coming in short, shallow bursts. She opened her eyes but appeared not to recognize him. She mumbled something and shut them again. Though he slapped her cheeks, her eyes stayed shut.

He scooped her stiff, cold body up into his arms. She felt incredibly heavy, her feet like blocks of ice, as he staggered back along the trail. He prayed for the first time in his life. He practically wept.

"Please God, don't let her die. Please, please, God...."

Then he felt like a hypocrite, because Shep had never believed in God, and in spite of everything, he still didn't. This had happened simply because he was stupid. So fucking stupid.

His progress was easier going back. He'd stamped down a lot of the snow following her to the stream. But it was still agonizing. It seemed like hours before he kicked open the cabin door. Warm air hit him. He felt glad that he'd piled so many logs into the woodstove. It was as hot as hell in the cabin now and intense, steady heat, as hot as he could make it, was what he needed if he was going to save her life.

The last strains of Eroica faded away as he put her down on the polar bear pelt. Roughly, in a hurry, because there wasn't a second to lose, he ripped off everything she was wearing – the muddy, icy boots, the red quilted jacket, her wool hat, scarf, two sweaters, mitts, socks, jeans, Chrissie's long johns, the panties underneath, her bra. Every item of clothing was stiff as a board, like washing hung on the line in winter. She didn't protest. She barely opened her eyes and felt limp in his arms, her flesh cold and clammy. She looked at him once, but seemed disoriented. A bad sign. He wondered how long she had been there, half immersed in the stream, probably screaming for help but he couldn't hear her because the cabin door was shut tight, and he'd been playing the Eroica so damn loud. Her naked body looked so white, so pathetic, so vulnerable, so utterly lifeless, stretched out on the floor in front of him. A terrifying fear clutched his heart. Was she going to die right there? He grabbed the sleeping bag from the top bunk and the three wool blankets from the bottom one and piled them all on top of her, bunching them around her head so that only her face showed. Then he ripped off his own clothes, keeping only his underpants on, and got under the heap himself. He moved his body right on top of hers, willing it to warm her. She mumbled something again. Opened her eyes. Stared blankly at him. Then she drifted off again.

A wild impulse struck him. He crawled out from under the blankets, over to the table and dipped his hands in the half inch or so of melted lard that lay in the frying pan. The warm fat might help. He pulled the blankets over the top of them again and knelt above her. Rubbed the lard into her chest and stomach, but not into her hands and feet, because he knew that it was important to warm the body core first, not the extremities, otherwise she might go into shock. She opened her eyes again, so he felt encouraged. He rubbed some more. But she didn't respond the second time. Her breathing was still shallow.

He got up again. Made her sit up. Tried to spoon some of the warm gravy from the deer stew into her mouth. But she was so limp and lifeless. Then she drifted off again, seeming unable – or unwilling – to swallow. The liquid dribbled out of the sides of her mouth, down her neck and chest. So he threw more logs into the stove, relieved that he'd piled enough in a corner of the cabin to keep the stove going all afternoon and night.

He should get her to a hospital, so they could put her on intravenous fluids. But no, how could he? Her slumping body would have to be strapped to the snowmobile. She wouldn't be able to cling on to him, not in her condition. She'd fall off the back. And in any case, she'd get chilled to the bone again, if he carried her outside. She might die right there and then, in the snow.

No, they had to stay here. In the cabin. Together like this. Alone, out in the woods. It was all up to him. If she wasn't alive by morning, it would be his fault.

He got under the blankets again and pulled her towards him.

"Live, Adie. Live. Please, please live," he whispered in her ear. "Don't leave me, girl."

Twenty-four

Shep lay holding Adie all afternoon. He watched out of the small cabin window as the sunlight faded away through the trees. He didn't dare move. He crawled out from under the blankets only to throw more logs in the firebox. He peed once, fast, through the half-open cabin door. Her breathing became more steady after dark. Her body felt slightly warmer. So he slid his own body out, tucked the blankets securely around her and lit a portable kerosene lamp. Then he scooped some stew into a bowl and ate hungrily himself, standing by the stove, not letting his gaze move from her face for a moment.

He'd almost finished eating when she opened her eyes. She let them rove around the cabin, the way a deer takes stock of its surroundings. He thought what lovely eyes she had. Big and blue green, like precious stones shining in the light from the lamp. Then she glanced up at him with a puzzled expression.

"Oh. Shep. Hello. Where am I?" she said. Hearing her voice made him want to jump for joy. She was coming back to life. She was going to make it.

A pan of water bubbled on the stove. He'd kept it going all afternoon, waiting for this moment. He mixed some of the water with a couple of spoonfuls of the deer gravy into a mug.

She seemed surprised by his unclothed body as he came over with the mug. He knelt down and helped her sit up.

"What's going on? Why are you undressed?" she said, looking confused. "I feel awfully stiff."

"Here, drink this," he said.

"What is it?" she said, staring suspiciously into the mug, then up into his face. "It smells funny. And I smell funny too." She bent her head over and sniffed at her chest. "I smell like pastry."

"Just drink. Don't argue, girl," he said. "You need to get some hot liquid inside you," he said.

She sipped, wrinkling her nose.

She looked at him again, bewildered, her eyes searching his. So he squatted down on the rug and explained about finding her down by the stream. And of trying to warm her by taking off his own clothes and rubbing her body with the melted lard.

She remembered then and recounted, in a shaky voice, the sequence of events before he came to her rescue.

"I stepped into a pile of deep snow, and whoosh, I sank right down into the water. Up past my knees. It was so sudden. And, God, that water was freezing. It took my breath away," she said. "Then I found I couldn't pull myself out. I was stuck in the mud. And there was nothing to get a grip on. The trees were too far away from the edge of the stream. And…." Her voice trailed off. "I was stupid, wasn't I? You did warn me."

"No, I'm the stupid one," he said, leaning forward and kissing her forehead. "I blame myself. I should never have let you go out. And now I think you should get into that bunk," he motioned at the lower one, "and have a proper sleep. You need warmth and rest after something like this."

She didn't argue. Even in the yellow light of the kerosene lamp, she still looked pale. He noticed how wobbly she was on her feet when he helped her to stand up. He smoothed out the zipped-open orange sleeping bag on the bunk mattress. She lay down on it without saying a word. He piled the blankets on top of her, tucking them in.

Then he got dressed, threw more logs in the stove and bent over her.

"Listen, Adie," he whispered in her ear. "You probably need

to go to a hospital, but for now just lie here and sleep. It's the best thing. I'm going back to the house to get some more water and food and dry clothes for you. But I won't be long, I promise. We're going to spend the night here."

He placed his lips on her forehead again. But she didn't respond. She was already asleep.

Shep raced through the woods on the snowmobile, his breath before him in billowing clouds of white. Back at the house, in Chrissie's room, he yanked opened the carry-on bag Adie had brought with her from New York. Found spare pants, a sweater and a long-sleeved T-shirt, plus some thick wool hiking socks and underwear. Then he rummaged in a drawer in Kara's room for her old long johns. He grabbed a parka and a wool hat belonging to Chrissie in the mudroom and some sheepskin boots that Kara rarely wore anymore. They looked to be about the right size. He was careful not to select any of Mary Ann's clothing. He knew Adie would be reluctant to put anything on that belonged to his wife. He piled the clothes into the big travelling bag he took along when he was flying for the air ambulance station in Moosonee. Then in the kitchen, he filled the cooler with more water, Earl Grey tea bags, a tin of baked beans, sliced bread, cheese, eggs, sausages and chocolate chip cookies. But no coffee. He'd learned while working up north that people recovering from hypothermia shouldn't drink any alcohol or stimulants until all the warning signs had dissipated.

Anxious about her now, left alone in the cabin, he climbed back on the snowmobile, the clothes and provisions stashed in the box behind him. He gassed the engine, going as fast as he dared along the trail. The headlights were bright, lighting up the woods, and he felt glad because he rarely went out snowmobiling on a moonless night. The organized nature of clubs devoted to the sport had never appealed to him, and there were too many hidden dangers – rocks and gullies, fallen tree trunks, barbed wire fences that could rip a man's head clean off – to ride around alone after dark. Thank God he'd swapped the firewood for this quality, dependable machine. His old machine was much slower and often broke down. But there was no likelihood of that happening tonight.

Adie was awake when he got back. Pleased to see him, she still looked dazed, her speech slurred, which made him anxious again. She lay half asleep, half watching, as he heated the deer stew and fried the bannock balls, pressing them into the hot lard with a spatula. She ate reluctantly. Then he prepared a mug of Earl Grey tea with boiling water from the stove.

She pulled a face.

"I hate Earl Grey," she said.

"I know, girl, but it's all I have. Just drink it. You need warm liquids and protein in your body right now, and you can't have coffee or rum. In the morning, I'm going to cook you a big breakfast of eggs, sausages and baked beans."

She smiled at that. He ate himself. Sipped a big shot of rum and heaved himself on to the top bunk. It was stifling up close to the cabin ceiling, and he lay in his underwear sweating, still worrying about her, listening for her steady breathing. Assured that it sounded normal, he sank into a slumber himself.

Twenty-five

Adie survived. The next morning, she ate and drank with obvious pleasure. Her speech came back. So Shep helped her put on dry clothes and wrapped her in blankets like a mummy, and they headed back to the house on the snowmobile.

She shook her head back and forth when he kept asking how she was, repeating that she was fine. Just fine, thank you.

"But I still think you need to get checked out at the hospital," he insisted, putting his hand on her forehead. It felt cool. "You could be dehydrated, or something. We can go to the emergency clinic."

"All right, but let me take a shower first," she said, chuckling for the first time since she fell into the stream. "I must stink, from all that lard."

Shep's heart leapt, hearing that chuckle. She was going to be all right.

"And I need to call Tish. I feel terrible about not showing up yesterday. But I'm not sure what to tell her. It's probably best that she doesn't know I'm with you." She regarded him in inquiring way. "She doesn't seem to like you, does she?"

"Adie, there's something you should know about Tish," he said warily. "We were an item once. It was many years ago. But I wasn't as interested as she was. Tish is," he sighed, "I don't know what the word is... needy? And, well, she never got over it."

"Were you married at the time?"

"Yes, kind of." He turned defensive, his tone curt. "But things weren't going well with my wife and so ..."

"I know. It happens," Adie said, mentally absolving him, thinking guiltily of Michael. She wondered how his ankle was and realized that she had hardly thought about him since leaving New York. She sighed. "It would be good if Tish could meet some nice considerate man to settle down with, wouldn't it? But she seems to have a knack for picking the wrong one."

"Gow was keen on her, you know."

"He was? She never told me that."

"Yes, he was lonely here and she was the only woman he saw regularly, when she came to clean for him. I wondered at the time if anything went on between them. But I think she thought he was too old for her – he was almost twice her age – and she went off to Toronto."

"Yes, and then she discovered she was pregnant by some guy who..."

"Listen," Shep interrupted, looking at his watch, "we should go. There's always long line-ups at emergency, and if we don't leave soon, we'll probably have to wait the whole goddamn day."

She made a quick apologetic call to Tish. Told a half-truth. That she'd had an accident while driving up from Toronto yesterday. That Shep had happened to drive by and rescue her, but it was so late in the evening, she didn't want to show up at Bounteous B & B and disturb Tish. So she'd stayed the night at his house and was now going with him to the hospital to get checked out.

"But I'll be happy to pay you for last night," she added.

"Well, yes, that is normally required when you have made a booking," said Tish stiffly, privately thinking that Adie's story sounded like a load of horse feathers. "Will you be coming here after going to the hospital?"

"Not sure, Tish. They might want to keep me in for observation."

Another lie. Adie knew that no doctor was likely to want to

hospitalize her, because she felt fine. Yet she didn't want to go to Tish's. All she cared about was being with Shep now.

Marsh River hospital was a long, low, red brick building on the outskirts of town. Great mounds of dirty grey snow stood at each end of its big parking lot. Atop a bulldozer, a middle-aged man in a navy blue snowsuit was pushing the snow that had fallen yesterday into another pile. His face was white as the snow, every drop of blood drained out of it in the cold. Shep squeezed his pickup into one of the few parking spaces available and ordered Adie to do up her jacket, pull her hat over her ears, then wrap her scarf over her mouth and nose. She obeyed. It was bitter out, the icy tarmac in the parking lot gleaming like a sheet of tin foil, a wind blowing. He took her arm as they headed gingerly to the packed emergency department. He didn't want her to slip and break a bone. She still seemed so fragile.

The place smelled of sweat and antiseptic. The injured, sick and their relatives sat hunched over in chairs, fiddling with cell phones, or stood propped against the walls, staring ahead, lost in private pain. Several people were coughing, trying to be unobtrusive, putting hands over mouths. A couple of kids screamed around the rows of chairs, bored with waiting. Occasionally, someone glanced over at the reception desk, then up at the clock on the wall and let out a deep sigh.

Adie found the only free chair. She sank into it beside an obese woman, her bleeding forefinger wrapped in a tea towel. The knife had slipped, the woman said, while she was peeling carrots to make a carrot cake for her son's birthday.

"Guess he ain't going to get no cake now," she said with a cackle that made everyone in the room look up. "What're youse in here for then?"

Adie explained.

"Hypothermia, eh?" the woman grunted. "I had a brother-in-law who died of that. Drove his snowmobile across a lake up north during a January thaw. Fell in. He always was a useless piece of crap."

Adie suppressed a giggle and tried to look sympathetic. Then she watched, fascinated, as the circle of blood on the woman's tea towel kept expanding. Bright red splots were starting to drip through the fabric, on to the grey tiled floor.

The woman yelled loudly in the direction of the reception desk, "Fuck, Maria, this hurts, eh? How much longer, for chrissakes? Am I gonna bleed to death sittin' here?"

She cradled the injured right hand in her left one and rocked her massive body too and fro.

"Shall I try to get her to come over and see you?" Adie asked.

"Nah. Think I'll go raise some hell myself. I know that nurse. And I'm fuckin' sick of this."

Breathing heavily through her mouth, the woman waddled over to reception, her massive thighs rubbing together with a zizzing sound. She thrust the hand with the soaked tea towel in the nurse's face and swore at her. The nurse, poker-faced, backed away and said, "Now, now, Mrs. MacFarlane, there's no need for that." Then she produced a wad of cotton, telling the woman to press it down hard on the cut. The woman came back to her seat, rolling her eyes at Adie.

"Sure sucks, waitin' like this, don't it?" she said, plunking herself down. The chair squeaked in protest. "I've bin here nearly three hours."

At that moment, two youths exited through the double doors leading to the examination room. A nurse beckoned the woman over. She waddled like a performing seal, shouting, "Yay! Yay! Yay," her injured finger and the one next to it raised in the air in a Churchillian victory salute.

Shep took her vacated chair. The youths went by en route to the exit. The taller one was limping, his arm in a sling. His face resembled a boxer's after a lost bout. He had a black eye and a plaster stuck across his nose. A massive bruise, quickly going purple and yellow, was spreading all down one cheek. His top lip was badly swollen.

"Jeezus… It's Tyson," Shep said, leaping up. "What happened to you, buddy? You get beat up or something?"

"Oh hi, Shep," Tyson said wearily, lifting an ice bag to his eye. "Yeah, like I was at a party last night, see, with Chrissie. And this older guy from Guelph, he starts hitting on her, and he doesn't stop, eh? So I punched him real good. But then the fucker gets me pinned against the wall and, like he starts punching me back…." His voice faded, as if he couldn't summon the energy to say another word.

"Let's go, Tyson," said his companion, pushing him gently from behind. "Sorry, Shep," he smiled and shot a curious glance at Adie, "but he needs to get home. He's doped up."

Shep walked with them to the exit. Then he returned and settled down with Adie again.

"Wow. That was Tyson?" she said. "He looks terrible. I wouldn't have recognized him, although I've only met him once. What happened?"

Shep told her, grimacing.

"Who was the other guy?"

"His brother, Joel. He used to deliver groceries to your uncle. Joel was the one who found him dead on the sofa."

"Joel seems like a nice kid, coming with his brother to the hospital like that."

"And Tyson is a good kid, too, underneath it all. He's just immature."

"Yes, he was very nice to me when I came over to the house looking for you."

"Oh sure, he's like that. Gets on well with people of all ages. But he's impulsive and he doesn't think things through." Shep recalled the time he found Tyson shooting at squirrels. "But he's young. I guess he'll settle down one day."

Shep sighed and mopped his brow with his sleeve. He was sweating. He sloughed off his parka and pushed it over the back of the chair.

"How do you feel about Chrissie marrying him?" Adie asked.

"I'm not sure anymore. He's nuts about her and she really loves him. They've been sweethearts since Grade 11. Never been anyone else for either of them. And I want to see her happy with somebody, because my wife and I…," he hesitated. "Well, let's just say it hasn't been great. You know what I mean?"

"Yes, I do. Exactly."

He reached out and squeezed her hand.

Twenty-six

Another hour of waiting. Adie finally made it into the examination room and encountered an alarmingly young doctor. A Dennis the Menace lookalike, he had reddish hair, freckles, a white lab coat three sizes too big for him and a mischievous air. He also seemed quite unruffled by the rigours of coping with a nonstop stream of sick people every day, because he grinned broadly, and he shook her hand. He told her to remove "everything on top," and her shoes and socks. A middle-aged nurse materialized at his side to check her temperature and blood pressure. Then the doctor probed in her mouth with a tongue depressor, examined the ends of her fingers, pulled at every one of her toes with his own none-too-warm hands and felt the sides of her neck. Finally he listened to her back with a stethoscope and made some notes on a clipboard.

"You're fine," he said, grinning again. "No real harm done, but your blood pressure is fairly low. So keep warm. Drink lots of warm liquids. And get some exercise, although don't be in situations where you'll be exposed to the cold. I know that's easier said than done at this time of year." He glanced out of the window, where the sky was turning the greenish-black of a frozen pond. "But I don't recommend that you take part in any outdoor sports for a couple of weeks."

"Right," said Adie, remembering the stream. The last thing she wanted to do was go snowshoeing or even take a walk. But where was she supposed to exercise? At some fitness club, no doubt, yet she hated them. So full of germs. Always packed with competitive people, showing off, the sour smell of their sweat pervading everything. Her horror of fitness clubs was the reason she'd taken up running. And what she ached for more than anything at that moment was not exercise, but tea. Black and hot, with milk, the stronger the better.

She rejoined Shep in the crowded waiting room. Saw the woman with the cut finger heave her ham-slab thighs towards the double entrance doors. She was waving at Adie and holding up two fingers – one now ornamented by a big white bandage – in a V-for-victory symbol once more. Adie waved back and gave her the thumbs up sign.

"You're okay, then?" said Shep, getting up.

She nodded.

"Thought so. Good. Let's go home."

Home? It sounded funny, his saying that, because it wasn't really her home. The statement had a cosy, domesticated ring that made her uneasy. Yet she couldn't wait to return to the intimacy of his quiet house in the woods, away from all the sick and injured souls waiting at the hospital.

"Bundle up," he ordered, as they went outside. "It's cold out there."

He wasn't kidding. The sun, dipping low, was now no more than a thin slice of orange, barely visible behind some trees. The buildings in Marsh River's downtown had become black silhouettes against the receding light. Stark spumes of smoke, very white and straight, shot up from their rooftops. The man on the bulldozer had gone. Long, purple shadows of trees each side of the parking lot made wiggly patterns like snakes over the heaps of white snow he'd pushed into big piles. As they went outside, Adie took a deep breath, glad to be out of the stifling emergency department, then she wished she hadn't, because the air was embedded with icicles now. They stabbed at her chest and made her gasp. She peeled her sheepskin mitt back from her wrist to check the time and was shocked by the shortness of the day. Only just after three p.m., yet already getting dark. So this was what people meant by the frozen north. Biting cold enveloping you the moment the sun went, then a quick descent into night. Hurrying over to Shep's pickup, she hoped he'd invite her to stay. The prospect of having to gather up her belongings in his house, climb into her own freezing car, then drive herself all the way around the lake to the B & B wasn't a pleasant one. But how would she explain her second consecutive absence to Tish?

Shep took a detour to Marsh River Mall on the way back, but he didn't follow the road that went past the home decorating store where his wife worked. He entered the parking lot at the other end of the mall, then pulled up in front of the supermarket.

"Wait in the truck, girl," he said. "I thought I'd go get you some tea. Real tea, the kind you like." He leaned over and kissed her cheek. "And I'll make it for you."

She forgot all about calling Tish.

They sat in the old armchairs by the woodstove. Sipping the scalding tea, she watched him make a rum-and-coke with lots of ice. Just looking at the ice made her shudder, although it was comfortably warm in the house. She admired his competence once again, this time with omelettes. The way he cracked the eggs on the side of a bowl with one hand, without getting any bits of eggshell in the mixture, as she always did. Then he poured the bowl's slippery contents into the omelette pan at exactly the right moment, when the butter was hot, but not about to burn. He took two trays and plates out of a cupboard and buttered slices of bread. Then he slid the omelettes on to the plates.

He suggested that they go over to the sofa. They sat side by side, watching TV, eating in silence. A silly sitcom was on. Neither of them had any interest in watching it, yet they did.

He got up the moment the show ended and returned their trays to the kitchen counter. Then he excused himself and went into another room, saying he needed to check his email. Returning with a frown, he shot her a sideways glance. Sat down again, felt jittery. So did she. Because all the time, an unanswered question was hanging in the air between them, like a suspended balloon, with neither of them knowing quite how to reach up for the string of the balloon to bring it down to earth. Were they finally going to make love? Or weren't they? After her refusal to join him in his bed, Shep was surprisingly unsure of himself. Not many women had turned him down. And now, for the first time in his life, he felt at a loss about what to do next. Though they'd been virtually naked together in the cabin, he'd not been aroused then. The only thing on his mind had been keeping her alive. But now he wanted her, ached to feel the closeness of a woman he genuinely liked. And she wanted him, he could tell. Yet she kept looking at a clock on the dresser, as if wondering if she was supposed to she get up and climb the stairs to Chrissie's room. Or pack up and depart in her car for Tish's place.

Ah, the awkwardness of new love in middle age. After what seemed like hours, he slid his arm along the back of the sofa and leaned close, planting a clumsy kiss on her cheek. Shyness consumed him. He felt like a teenager wondering if he should put his hand up the prom queen's skirt. He was half-drunk too, because he'd downed three double rums trying to summon the courage to approach her.

Be direct, he told himself. Don't turn her off with silly compliments. This kind of woman won't go for that.

"Will you make love with me tonight?" he said at length, reaching for her hand.

She turned and looked at him. He wasn't sure what to read in her expression.

"After all," he added in a nervous rush, with what he hoped

was a cheeky smile, "we've already been naked together, haven't we? Well, practically naked. Out there, in the cabin."

"Yes," she said and seemed embarrassed. "I know. Amazing what you did. Thank you." She shook her head then added with a chuckle. "Too bad I don't remember much about it."

She fixed her eyes on his now.

"And I want to, Shep. Really I do. But not in your bed. Not where you sleep with your wife."

"I understand," he said

He kissed her head and relaxed. He got up, clicked the TV off and went out into the mudroom, returning with the rolled-up polar bear pelt. He'd stashed it there after returning from the cabin. He shook out the pelt by the woodstove and held out his hand.

She took it. They lay down. He undressed her slowly, kissing everywhere on her body for a long time. Her long hair got in his face and tickled his nose. He smelled Chrissie's shampoo as he pushed it out of the way and caressed her neck. He hastily pulled off his own pants, kicking off his socks at the same time, because he'd read somewhere that women hated men to make love to them with their socks on. She helped him yank his shirt over his head. He placed his lips on hers. Their tongues tangled together, flicking, probing, sucking. Then he had another attack of nerves.

"I'm not sure I'm going to be good for anything," he mumbled into her ear. "But I just wanted to hold you."

She surprised him then with her directness. She spread her legs and drew his head down.

"Do this then," she said, gently. "It's been so long."

So he buried his nose in her. Relished the fragrance that came from the depths of her, as he tasted, kissed, swallowed. For a few minutes, he forgot about everything, submerged in the moment, absorbed by the sensation, wanting so badly to give her pleasure. Then as he felt her climax, he lifted himself up and penetrated her gently, with great care, controlling himself, not moving his eyes from hers, watching her face for signals that she wanted him to go further.

She flinched.

"Ouch," she whispered. "It's been a while since I did this. I think I'm kind of fragile down there. Go easy, won't you?"

Yet she didn't really want him to go easy. And she wasn't fragile. As he pressed in further, carefully, slowly, she found it easier. She wrapped her legs around his and made a strangled sort of moan. She urged him on, saying, "Oh, yes, that's good now, Shep. Fine now. Oh, yes, please. Fuck me, fuck me."

So he gripped her tightly to him, caressing her, biting at her neck, feeling her arch her back and join his rhythm. Then he came with a shudder, and they both collapsed, panting, on the polar bear pelt.

Twenty-seven

Adie woke in Chrissie's pink bedroom feeling sore between her legs. Then she remembered and didn't mind. The soreness would subside. But memories of the previous night wouldn't. She'd forgotten how wonderful, how utterly exhilarating it was to have sex with someone you loved. And how the physical act relieved stress like nothing else. Afterwards, they'd lain on the rug beside the woodstove for a long time, stroking each other, not saying much. Then they'd retrieved their discarded clothes, gone upstairs, kissed gently on the landing and retreated chastely into their separate bedrooms. She'd fallen asleep at once, in her boudoir of pink. Drifting off, she realized that she no longer had a craving for peanut butter cups. Being with Shep had cured her of that.

It was another frigid morning, yet the sun shone as brightly as yesterday. There was a blue jay in the spruce branches outside the window picking at the cones, just like at Tish's. Getting out of bed, she almost squawked again like a demented idiot at the bird. She felt so full of life, so energized, so deliriously happy, so in love with the whole world. She wanted to grab the bird and waltz around the room with it. Yet the smell of coffee lured her downstairs. As she went down, she heard Shep roving around the living room, talking in an agitated way to someone on the phone.

He put the phone back in the cradle when she came through the door.

"Sleep well?" he said, smiling.

"Oh yes, like a top," she said.

"Me too." He came over and kissed her on the mouth.

"Mmm," he said. "Now do you want tea or coffee, girl?"

"Oh, coffee's fine, boy."

He made toast. They sat down at the table.

Then he said, "I have bad news, Adie. Well, it's not bad, I guess. Just annoying. I got an email last night. I have to go back up north today."

"You do?" Adie said. "Why?"

He sighed, putting his coffee mug down on the table.

"Oh, it's the air ambulance service I work for. They're totally screwed up. There's normally two pilots based in Moosonee, but one of them is on sick leave, getting treated for cancer. And now the second one has called in sick, too, and I have to go up there right away and fill in for him. And, you know," he sighed again, "I don't think the guy *is* sick. I think he's on the verge of quitting, because the whole operation is so badly run. But I can't. I'm still on contract. And...." he took a swig of coffee, "..the money's good. I make enough in sixty days of work up there to keep me here all year. So I put up with their crap."

He laughed.

"Is this house costly to run?" she asked.

"No. I don't spend much. I heat with wood and, as you may have heard, I'm the biggest cheapskate in the world," he chuckled, "because I barter a lot."

She thought of the polar bear pelt and the snowmobile.

"It makes sense," he went on. "The less the damn government knows about your business, the less they come poking around, wanting to grab your money. When you barter, you don't leave a paper trail."

He laughed again. Then his expression turned anxious. Draining his coffee, he glanced up at the clock on the wall and pushed back from the table.

"I'd better go," he said.

"You're leaving already?" she asked, surprised, leaning back on her own chair, still sipping her coffee.

"Yep. Right now," he said, getting up. "Have to. There's only one flight to Moosonee from Toronto today, so I better go throw some things in a bag."

He headed for the stairs. As he went around the table, he impulsively grabbed her hand and kissed it.

"Sorry, girl. I hate to leave you like this. I wanted to come along with you today and give you the benefit my rural redneck opinion," he chuckled again, "on the fittings you should choose for your house."

"Yes, I was looking forward to that," she said, putting her coffee mug down. "I haven't the faintest idea about that stuff."

"Well, ask Knock. He knows everything there is to know about fixing up old houses."

Shep disappeared upstairs. Adie cleared the coffee mugs away and washed them. A cardinal came to the kitchen window ledge, its vermilion feathers brilliant against the greenish-brown spruce needles. The woods here were so full of birds, all kinds of birds. Soon she'd have a view like this from her own kitchen window. She couldn't wait.

He returned in only five minutes carrying the bag he'd brought back from the cabin. He was wearing a pilot's uniform. The authoritative air of uniforms did give men sex appeal, she thought, wishing for a wild moment that she could rip off the uniform and make love with him again, right there on the kitchen floor. Yet he was clearly in too much of a hurry to entertain such a notion. He'd changed and packed with remarkable speed. He was obviously used to going off like this regularly.

"Now where are my damn keys?" he said, pausing for a moment, shuffling his hands in an exasperated way through a pile of papers at one end of the table. He located the keys under the blue wool hat he'd given Adie to wear, tossed the hat at her and headed for the mudroom door.

"When are you coming back?" she called out.

"No idea. I never know," he said over his shoulder. "You're welcome to stay on. Just shut the door when you leave. I never lock it. And I've left the furnace on low."

"But Shep," she said, bewildered. "I have to go back to New York in a couple of days. When will I see you again?"

"I don't know, girl," he said. "Email me. I'll email you. And after last night, I'll think of you every time I see a polar bear."

He laughed again. Then he seemed to have second thoughts, because he turned back to her and said, "Come over here, girl."

She did. He hugged her fiercely to him, kissing the top of her head and mussing her hair. Ordered her not to go near any frozen streams. Said he was sorry again. Then he was out of the mudroom door, the carry-on bag slung over his shoulder. She watched from the window as he climbed into his pickup. There was a puff of exhaust smoke. Then he was gone.

Adie took a few minutes to gather herself together. This was so abrupt, so offhand, as if she were simply a visiting relative or friend, nothing more. She reassured herself that his work must be to blame. He had a plane to catch. And after that he had to go fly a helicopter himself, taking sick people to hospital. So there must be a lot on his mind. Well, fine. She'd go to stay with Tish now, because lingering alone in his house would feel strange. It was awkward enough being there when he was around. What if his wife – or Chrissie and Tyson – suddenly showed up?

She called Tish. Lied again.

"Is it okay if I come to your place today?" she asked. "The hospital did keep me in last night, but now I'm fine. And I plan to stay a couple more days, then head back to New York."

"Of course you can come, lass," Tish said warmly. "I'm just sorry it wasn't earlier. But how great that you're feeling better, and it will be lovely to see you. Mr. Brainerd's here again, and he has the back room. But the front room is free."

The noisy room, Adie thought to herself, but then felt ungrateful. At least Tish had somewhere for her to stay. She showered and dressed, then gathered up her things, thinking of Shep's edict to wrap her scarf around her mouth and recalling the exquisite pleasure of last night. A mixture of emotions swirled in her head – contentment, longing for him again, but also self-pity. She was going to miss him. Yet she told herself not to brood. That was what silly lovesick teenagers did. Theirs was an affair between adults. And she had to leave for New York herself soon, anyway. They would meet up again in the spring.

Anxiety gripped her, walking down the long icy driveway with her bag to the rental car. Ice glistened on the hood. Would it start? The temperature was still awfully low. She recalled that Shep's truck was equipped with what he called a "block heater." She'd never heard of such a thing, yet he plugged it in every night when the weather was as cold as this and told her everyone did. So what about her car? Since she'd arrived, it had stayed parked at the bottom of his driveway, untouched by either of them. And it had no such heater.

She got into the car and turned the key, heart in her mouth. The engine choked like an old man with a bad cough, but then came alive. "Thank you, thank you," she said out loud, her breath steaming up the windshield. No wonder the Red Car Rental place at the airport used these dependable little vehicles. She revved the engine. Scraped the ice off all the windows with a plastic tool she found in the dash and turned the heater up full blast. Driving cautiously away, feeling both pleasure and relief as she watched Shep's house recede into the snow-covered woods, she wondered if she'd hear from him once she was back in New York. A little voice told her that she'd have to make the first move.

Going past the driveway to her own house, she saw, parked outside the front door, a big white van with the words "Knock Has The Knack" painted in green letters on one side. Wow. Astonishing. So the Mennonite renovator had already started work on the interior. He sure didn't drag his feet. This wasn't like New York, where you could wait for weeks for even a telephone repairman to show up. Curious, she almost turned into the driveway, drawn by the faint sound – or so she thought – of someone hammering inside the house. But then she remembered the flood in the apartment above her and Michael years ago. Great chunks of their ceiling had fallen down, and a couple of guys did eventually show up to make repairs, but they arrived with a ghetto blaster, turned it on to maximum volume and quickly made it obvious that her presence wasn't welcome. She'd had to retreat to Val's to work for a couple of weeks, her paints spread out with difficulty on a big oak dining table. So today, she wouldn't get in the way of Knock's construction crew. It must be freezing inside the house, anyway.

She drove down the hill, into Fortune, but felt no urge now to stop in at the general store for peanut butter cups. She wondered vaguely if the lonely old woman was in there, sitting at the counter, and if she should be kind and buy something, but drove on by. The lake road was shiny with ice, yet the twists and turns were becoming familiar now. They gave her no cause for alarm.

Bounteous Bed and Breakfast looked like a Currier and Ives picture postcard, ensconced prettily in the snow. Though it was February, a Christmas wreath with blue, shiny baubles and a matching satin bow still hung from the front knocker. More baubles and bows embellished a spruce tree near the front entrance. Tish threw open the door and welcomed her with a hug, as if she were a long lost friend, and her effusiveness made Adie feel guilty again for lying about Shep. Sammy appeared in the hall behind her, ecstatic. The big black-and-white cat rolled on the rug and rubbed around her legs, purring. Then he followed her up to the front bedroom, sniffing at her bag, looking for more catnip. She lay on the bed petting him, listening for the roar of trucks heading along the Marsh River bypass. But to her relief, she could barely hear any. The heavy drifts that lined Bounteous Lake Road in winter helped to muffle the sound.

Tish asked if she'd like supper tonight. Adie said yes, please.

"Mr. Brainerd will be joining us," Tish said.

Hmm. A dull evening making small talk with the boring bank inspector. Yet Adie realized Mr. Brainerd would be useful. His presence at the dining table, pompously pronouncing on anything and everything, might deter Tish from asking probing questions about the one thing she didn't want to discuss.

Her relationship with Shep.

Twenty-eight

Rubbed bronze or French country? Pull-out touchless or articulating deck mount? Grip-tight seat or dual-flush apron front? Adjustable kinetic full-spray or Italian circular?

Ordering faucets, sinks, toilets and showerheads was complicated – far more complicated than she'd ever imagined. Adie smiled awkwardly at the eager young man standing beside her in an orange shirt. She hoped she didn't appear too old and foggy-brained. That she wasn't annoying the hell out of him. He wore a plastic name tag that said Doug: Here To Help. And she needed help from Doug for sure, but she felt paralyzed. Unable to make a decision. Thoroughly stupid, too. After living in the same unrenovated apartment in Manhattan for over two decades, her world revolving around botanical art, she'd become immune to fashion trends in virtually everything. They simply didn't interest her. And now she was being asked – of all things – to decide on the respective design features of plumbing fixtures. She stood in the cavernous home renovation warehouse, its myriad offerings piled up to the ceiling in big cardboard boxes, and felt overwhelmed, wishing Shep was with her. He was so practical. He'd know what to choose. She didn't have a clue. And Michael would have been even worse than her. He lived in the 19th century with the Pre-Raphaelites. He couldn't even screw in a light bulb.

The store was in a big town half an hour's drive from Marsh River. She'd enjoyed the journey. The car was warm and easy to handle. She no longer felt cowed about venturing out on the road in winter. The expansive fields that had contained the golden soybeans in the fall were now quilted in enormous white comforters that sparkled like diamonds in the winter sunlight. So much pure, clean snow. She'd never seen snow like it. It always looked grubby and grey in Manhattan. She wanted to drive around aimlessly and savour the beauty of the day. Take time to explore the countryside, now that she'd recovered. She dreaded having to go through the rigmarole of making decisions about fixtures for her house. Yet Knock was a gem. He would undoubtedly do a fantastic job with the renovation – and in speedy fashion, too, because he'd already started. So she had to grit her teeth and go shopping for the long list of items that he gave her.

"Um, what do you recommend?" she asked hopefully. The sales clerk, all smiles, was brandishing an antique-looking faucet in one hand and an ultra-modern gizmo, consisting of a polished chrome block with a long spout, in the other.

"What kind of house is it?" he asked.

"Oh, Victorian," she said. "Over a hundred years old."

"Then definitely go for the rubbed bronze," he said in an authoritative tone. "That's going to fit in. Although," he paused, "people sure like modern bathrooms nowadays, with up-to-date appliances. So if you want to sell the place, ma'am, this design from Italy," he held out the strange shiny contraption, "is going to suit your purposes better."

Sell the place? Was the guy nuts? She hadn't even started to live there herself yet. She settled for the rubbed bronze.

Mervyn Baumann's workshop was a long, white building with a green roof on the main street of Fletton, a hamlet outside Marsh River. Adie dimly remembered driving by it before. She'd gone through Fletton with Shep in the fall, trying to find Knock.

The building looked immaculate, as all Mennonite properties

did, with window frames and double doors painted in the same green as the roof. Despite the chill out of doors, the interior was toasty, thanks to a massive, black cast iron woodstove, even bigger than Shep's. It was positioned in the centre of the building and had a shiny steel chimney soaring through the roof. She was starting to understand why people heated with wood in the country. The warmth penetrated right into a person's bones in the way gas or oil heat never could. She resolved to keep the old woodstove in her house, whether Knock installed a new oil furnace or not.

Mervyn Baumann sat hunched over a steel work bench. He was sanding the spokes of a buggy wheel with gnarled, wrinkly hands. Behind him, two old buggies, the kind drawn by one horse, reared up. They were black, oblong boxes on wheels and looked faintly sinister, with little peepholes for the person holding the reins. Mervyn had taken the wheels off one. Seeing the buggies here, stored in the high-ceilinged building, made her think of props backstage at the Met. She and Val had taken a tour once, before a production of *Der Rosenkavalier*, and seen a similar buggy waiting in the wings. Then they'd been delighted when it was wheeled out, creaking and wobbling, during the performance.

The Mennonite carpenter stood up and shook her hand. He was somewhat like his cousin. Same chunky build. Same round, cherubic face. Same thick lips. Yet he looked much older, with clipped grey hair and fingers swollen with arthritis.

"Please sit," he said in a soft voice that sounded faintly German or Dutch. "Nathan told me that you'd be dropping by. Tell me what I can do for you, Mrs. Coulter."

She explained about inheriting the house, that it was over a century old. He nodded and went over to a metal filing cabinet. Out came some ancient file folders with torn edges. They were full of drawings of antique wood cupboards, mouldings and doors, every one meticulously executed in pencil. He'd obviously done them himself.

"Please take a look through these," he said. "There may be something in there that suits you. And take your time, Mrs. Coulter. There's no rush. I'm going over to feed the chickens."

He pulled on a black overcoat and shuffled outside. Adie relaxed, thinking how agreeable this was, picking out cupboards, doors and mouldings for her house in an unhurried way, ensconced in the old man's warm and tidy workshop while he tended to his livestock. It sure beat the high octane atmosphere of the brightly lit home renovation store. Though the young guy in the orange shirt had been pleasant, she'd felt pressured. The whole experience was an ordeal. And now she had doubts about the rubbed bronze faucets. Would they look okay in the bathroom? She hoped so. There was no way she intended to trek back to the store to change her order.

All afternoon, Adie visited other stores that sold tiles, flooring and kitchen appliances, steeling herself to make selections in every one. She wished once more that Shep was there with her. Daydreamed about his arrival in the place with the strange name Moononee wondering how cold it was up there, so far north.

Dusk was falling by the time she headed back to Tish's. As the blue delphinium sign came into view around a bend on Bounteous Lake Road, she warmed to the sight of the cosy little farmhouse, where there would be someone to welcome her. Returning to Shep's empty cold home up on Fortune Hill, then sleeping in Chrissie's bedroom alone, would have made her feel wretched.

She took a cup of tea upstairs and lay on the bed, stroking Sammy. Trying to stop thinking about Shep, she resented the way he kept intruding into her thoughts. He just wouldn't go. She heard Mr. Brainerd come in and climb the stairs to his room.

She wondered if he ever cheated on his wife when he was away from home doing his bank inspections and suspected that he didn't. He didn't look like the type and he was very unattractive, anyway. The only extra-marital activities available to him would be of the paying kind. Restlessly, she wondered once more what Shep was doing, and if he missed her. When Tish called up the stairs that supper was ready, she felt glad to kick him out of her head for a while.

"It's salmon, but just the farmed kind," Tish said, as she brought supper to the dining table. "I know how you city folk insist on eating only wild salmon, but I'm sorry, I can't get that here."

"It looks perfectly delicious to me, Mrs. Boddington," said Mr. Brainerd pompously.

Adie agreed and praised the dish extravagantly. She said that it made her mouth water and concluded that Shep was right about Tish. The plump woman with the soulful eyes, nervously doling out portions of farmed salmon, was needy – and needy people tended to exude an aura that repelled others. She wondered how long Tish was involved with Shep, if she fell in love with him and how badly he had hurt her.

"Flavian is looking forward to seeing you, Adie," Tish said, as the three of them ate, mostly in silence.

"Yes, I'll drop by and see him tomorrow," Adie said.

At least Tish had her son. That must be a comfort to her.

Twenty-nine

Flavian was feeling more upbeat about his move to Marsh River. Business had improved at Boddington Books. Although he hadn't met anyone to replace Jean-Paul, he no longer missed his lover or their city life. He was building a new one in this small town. As he unlocked the oak front door of the store, he waved at Mr. Lee opposite – his custom every morning now, after coming downstairs from his apartment – and reflected that book sales in the past couple of months had been far stronger than he anticipated. First, there was Christmas. His Mom's prediction about the holiday had been correct. The people of Marsh River did indeed go in for big family celebrations, and they bought lots of gifts. They'd started coming into the store in late November – so many, he'd been forced to hire a teenager from the local high school for a couple of weeks over Christmas to help out, re-stocking shelves and gift-wrapping purchases. She was a sweet kid. They'd enjoyed working together.

He was also developing more regular customers. The hairdresser from A Cut Above, Chrissie Tanner, returned to buy an entire carton of mostly non-fiction biographies and adventure titles for her sister to take to Africa. Then she'd dropped in again to pick up a slim volume called *The Secret Life of Deer* for her dad as a Christmas present, plus Martha Stewart's holiday special edition for her mom.

Things were slower now, but he'd expected that. January and the first part of February were always the slackest times of the year for booksellers. Yet Valentine's Day was ahead: he had high hopes for a cute new gift book on chocolate and love. Chrissie Tanner had already bought a copy and said she was going to read it out loud to her boyfriend, Tyson. Flavian had met the guy once outside the store – he sure was a piece of straight bait – but it seemed, alas, that Tyson was only interested in girls. And today, Marlene Knockenhammer, president of Marsh River horticultural society, was going to drop by and pick up the twenty copies of *Perennials For Picky Climates* that she'd ordered as prizes for a gardening event planned by the club in March at the community centre. A roster of speakers was coming from out of town. Flavian had been gratified to discover many enthusiastic gardeners in Marsh River. Mostly middle-aged women, they were big buyers of gardening books.

Yet his first customer of the day was unexpected: Adie, the artist from New York, currently staying at his Mom's.

"Well hi," he said as she pushed open the door. "This is a welcome surprise. But I did hear you were back. You're brave, aren't you, coming up here in February?"

"Yes, either brave or totally mad," she said, pulling a blue wool hat off and tossing her head, so that a cascade of long hair tumbled out. "It's been quite eventful to say the least. I, er...." She laughed uncertainly and seemed about to reveal something to him, then clearly thought better of it because she continued in a breezy tone, "It's good to be back here and to see you and your mom again. How are things going with the shop?"

"Oh, better than I expected. I'm happy," he said. "And I hear that you're fixing up your uncle's house after all and may be spending a lot of time here with us."

"Yes, I hope the place will be in liveable condition by the spring. I've hired Nathan Knockenhammer, the guy everyone calls Knock," she laughed again, "and he's already started work."

"Mmm, he's a good guy, I hear. When I can afford it, I'm going to buy a fixer-upper myself and call him too. But I think that's going to be a while yet."

He looked around the store with satisfaction, reflecting that Boddington Books was certainly going to make it through the first year, but it would be a couple more before he turned a profit.

Flavian told Adie about Knock's wife. He said the members of her gardening club would probably be interested in her new book on native plants and added that a woman called Dorothy Sprange, who lived on the other side of Fortune Hill, had just formed a book club which she might like to join.

"Yes, I'm sure I'm going to find plenty to keep me busy when I come back here in the spring," she said.

In more ways than one, she thought, Shep on her mind again – and almost blushed.

In the back of the long store, she browsed through Flavian's display of recently published novels. She wanted to buy a couple for the journey back to New York. She liked reading on planes and while sitting around waiting in airports. It was easy to concentrate then, because there was nothing else to do.

To her mortification, Shep's daughter suddenly pushed open the door of the bookshop and walked in. Adie turned crimson, thinking of the lusty sex she'd enjoyed with the girl's father the previous evening. Did it show in her face? Could people tell? She hoped Flavian would keep Chrissie busy down at the other end of the store and quickly grabbed a novel about vampires off the rack. She bent her head over, so tendrils of hair obscured her face, pretending to be captivated by the book, although the subject didn't interest her in the slightest. She wondered if Chrissie was like other girls her age, turned on by the concept of blood-sucking Romeos biting their necks at night. She tried to hover unnoticed.

No such luck.

"Oh, hi," Chrissie called out, chirpy as a sparrow, heading up the aisle to the novels section. "You're, like, the lady with the house next door to my Dad aren't you? You came by one morning when Tyson and I were getting ready for our engagement party."

"Yes, that's right," Adie said, hoping she didn't look as embarrassed as she felt. She was struck by the girl's beautiful mop of hair. It had been hidden under a towel when they'd met briefly at Shep's mudroom door.

"Tyson said he saw you at the hospital yesterday with Dad."

"That's right. He, er, helped me with my car," she said. "I got a mild case of hypothermia after going into the ditch when I was driving up here."

If the girl suspected anything, she didn't show it.

"That's easy to do at this time of year," she said with a laugh. "I'm always going in the ditch myself. Tyson gets mad at me. Says women don't know how to drive in winter. So does Dad."

"How is Tyson?" Adie said, anxious to get off the topic of Shep.

"Oh, silly boy," Chrissie giggled. "He gets all jealous if I talk to other guys at parties. And that's all I was doing, just talking. And now he's all beat up from trying to defend my honour." She sighed. "He's doing okay, I guess. But he won't be pouring any concrete floors for a while. His boss has given him a couple of weeks off."

"I see," Adie said. Then for lack of anything better to say, she added, "Tell him I hope he'll be better soon."

"Thanks. He's hanging around in our apartment now, bored out of his skull. Expects me go home and, like, make him lunch because we live five minutes away." She giggled again. "Men, eh? I told him, You get your own lunch, boy. I'm busy working."

She picked up a book and glanced idly through it. "How long are you staying, er...?"

"Adie. Just till tomorrow. Then I'm flying back to New York."

"Yes, Dad's gone away, too. Up north. He called Mom yesterday. She might be going over to live in the house while he's away."

Adie's stomach lurched. She remembered now. How Shep

had replaced the phone in the cradle the moment she came into the living room. How he'd conveniently avoided saying anything to her about the call. So devious. So crafty. He hadn't wanted her to know that he was talking to his wife.

Chrissie wandered back to the cash desk to chat with Flavian. She told him that she needed more books to send to Kara.

"She's already read all the books I gave her at Christmas. They don't seem to have a thing to read in this place she's in. Africa, eh?" She shook her head in amazement. "What a place. Wouldn't suit me. No TV, no nothing, but Kara's loving it."

"What about this new biography about a British woman explorer who went up the Nile in Victorian times?" Fabian said, holding up a thick tome with a black and white photo on the cover. It showed a woman in a pith helmet and long, voluminous dress, sitting in a dugout canoe. "She apparently had all kinds of exciting adventures."

"Cool," Chrissie said. "Kara will think that's awesome."

Chrissie ambled around the store, picking more books out. Adie watched her from behind the vampire book. How beautiful Chrissie was. So dainty in her movements. So like a china doll. Such a delicate nose. With a stab of jealousy, she thought of Shep's wife. She must be beautiful too, to have produced a daughter like that. She put the vampire book back on the shelf and hastily grabbed two other paperback novels, barely glancing at their titles. She headed to the cash desk, telling Flavian she'd better go.

"So soon? You aren't going to stick around and meet Knock's wife?" he said. He glanced at his watch. "She's due here any minute. And I know she'd love to meet you."

"Um, no, sorry. Next time, perhaps," Adie said in a rush. "I have to go do some more shopping."

She fled the store, still fretting about her red cheeks. Had Chrissie noticed? Did she suspect something?

Mr. Brainerd wasn't around when she returned to the bed and breakfast. Tish said he was working late at a bank branch in another town and probably wouldn't be back in time for supper. Too bad, Adie thought. The bank inspector seemed to have only two topics of conversation – how his bank could stay competitive in a global economy and his suburban lawn – yet even they were preferable to being alone with Tish, because of the inevitable question. The one so obviously hovering on her hostess's lips. So evident in her taunting little smile. The one she clearly was dying to ask.

At seven, Tish summoned her downstairs, saying that they wouldn't wait for Mr. Brainerd any longer. They sat down at the table.

Adie wondered how long it would take.

She got her answer in precisely sixteen seconds.

Tish passed her a plate with a helping of steak and kidney pie on it and said, "And how is our friend Mr. Tanner these days?"

"Shep? Oh, he seems to be fine," Adie replied, prepared for this, keeping her voice nonchalant, determined not to go red in the face. "He was a big help when I wound up in the ditch. I don't know what I'd have done if he hadn't come by. And he's gone away up north now."

"Oh has he?" Tish smirked, proffering mashed potatoes and carrots. "And did he take you out to the cabin before he left?"

Oh God. She couldn't help it. She felt her face redden.

A strained silence filled the dining room. She stared at the mashed potatoes. Tried to concentrate on the patterned dish. Thrust a spoon in, but had no urge to scoop out any of the contents and eat. Ditto for the slice of pie. A lump of crumbling kidney, immersed in thick, brown gravy, was oozing out from under the pie's pastry covering, bringing back memories of her mother's cooking, of the urine stink of kidneys that filled the kitchen of their bungalow at Kew – and of being ordered to eat this same pie when she was ten, even though she'd detested the smell. Now, captive at Tish's table, it was like returning to childhood, with Tish playing disapproving Mummy, interrogating her about "unsuitable" friends and making her eat food she didn't like. She wanted – as she had years ago – to leap up from the table, then run upstairs to her bedroom.

But she stayed put.

"Listen, lass," said Tish harshly, leaning forward on the table, willing Adie to look up and hear her. "Let me tell you something about Shep. He's an attractive man, and there have been plenty before you. I know. I was one."

She paused to let that sink in. Stuck her fork into her mashed potatoes. Her gaze held what seemed like pity now.

"And he does the same thing to all of us, you know. Don't think you're any different. You go out to that cabin with him, he gets what he wants, then he drops you. Just like that."

She threw her head back. Her laugh had a bitter edge to it.

"There are rumours that he has women up north, too. Young aboriginal women, in that town he goes to. And you want to know something else?"

Adie ached to say, "No thanks. I don't care. Please shut up and leave me alone." She stared dumbly at her plate.

"He'll never leave his wife. Not for you, not for anyone. He can't stand her, but the only thing he really loves in this world is that place he inherited from his dad up on Fortune Hill. And he knows that if his wife goes, the property goes too. He'll have to sell it and give her half the money. And believe me, our boy Shep hates spending money on anything." She laughed again, without mirth, as if recalling an unpleasant example of his frugal habits. "He's well known throughout the county for being real cheap."

Tish thrust a forkful of potato in her mouth.

"If you're smart, you'll forget about him," she said, chewing with her mouth open. "I did."

She swallowed.

"Now, eat up, lass, won't you? Your supper's getting cold."

Adie's gravy was starting to congeal. A fatty sheen had appeared on top of the kidney. She felt ill, sticking her fork in.

But she ate.

Thirty

Every moment of that evening was hell. Yet back in New York, Adie did heed Tish's warning. She forgot about Shep. The country boy who'd cracked open a crevice in her heart was pushed down a deep hole and ordered not to come out. She willed herself to stop thinking about him. There wasn't any point. She felt confused about him anyway. It wasn't as if she'd wanted to make a life with the guy. There was just this strong sexual pull that had overwhelmed her. Now she returned to Michael, grateful to see him again. And he welcomed her with a hug, obviously pleased at her return. He was in good humour now, his ankle almost back to normal, and he was back full-time at Columbia. The night after she flew home, they went out to dinner at San Matteo's to celebrate his recovery and ate a swanky pizza with an expensive bottle of Barolo. They found plenty of things to talk about for a change. Life was full.

The contract arrived from Sumac Books. Blair Rountree had indeed fulfilled every promise he'd made to her over mint tea in his boardroom. She went through every clause carefully: the cash advance, the royalties, two whole years, if necessary, to complete the illustrations. It was all there. Everything looked fine. She signed, content, and sent the contract back, dying for spring to come, so she could head up to Fortune, track down her first flower model and start work.

She emailed Maggie McCorkindale and suggested doing a portrait of Jack-in-the-Pulpit to initiate the project. Maggie emailed back: "Good idea. I'll get to work on the copy for that.

But look out for trout lilies on your land. They come up real early in spring here in Vermont. Blair would like us to feature those as well, if you can find any."

Trout lilies? She consulted her native plants encyclopedia, *Botanica North America*. And yes, there they were: trout lilies, *Erythonium americanum*.

"Pretty, nodding yellow flowers with spotted leaves. They bloom very early in spring, under deciduous trees like maples. Then the flowers vanish the moment the trees leaf out," the encyclopedia said.

Aha, she remembered some maples on the edge of her land, near where the Michaelmas daisies grew. If she got back to Fortune early enough in the year, she would go looking for trout lilies.

A couple of days later, more good news came via an email from Knock. Things were progressing fast with the house. Her studio was finished, and his crew had started on the bathroom and kitchen. The kitchen cabinets and doors that his cousin Mervyn was making were coming along fine, too. And, hallelujah, Knock approved of the rubbed bronze faucets. They will suit the style of the house, he wrote. She smiled with relief, remembering the Mennonite, his courtesy, his trusting nature, his desire to get the job done. She pictured the big white "Knock Has The Knack" van parked outside the house in the snow, and a crew in navy blue overalls busy inside, ripping down faded fifties wallpaper, heaving the stained brown toilet into a big yellow dumpster like the one she'd seen driving around with... the person she no longer allowed herself to think about. She wished she could be in Fortune to see the transformation taking place.

On the bottom of Knock's email, there was a note from his wife: "Sorry to miss meeting you at the bookstore. Nathan tells me you're interested in the Arisaema. I'll be happy to show them to you when you come back. They usually bloom in early May. –Marlene."

May! It seemed so far away. She was impatient to be off. Yet in the meantime, there was plenty to keep her busy. She resumed running every morning. A British botanical magazine commissioned a watercolour portrait of a twig of sugar maple in winter, and wanted a scarlet leaf to be dangling from the twig. She hunted around and found a perfect specimen in the grounds of the National Design Center. The job was done in a couple of days. Then she returned to the big acrylic of the amaryllis. Ravishing Rosalie's salmon-pink petals had long gone, yet she found a similar plant in full, lusty bloom at the upscale florist's and worked like a maniac for a week, trying to capture the glorious trumpet-shaped blooms before they shrivelled into nothingness. The results weren't bad, she thought, standing back from the huge canvas and surveying it with half-shut eyes – her habit after finishing every large piece. Yet none of her paintings ever completely satisfied her. She remembered her equivocation about the turban squash, yet Micheline had loved it. She invited Michael into the studio to get his opinion.

"Oh, it's perfect, Adie," he said immediately, standing back to admire it. "One of your best. Don't do a thing more. It's fantastic."

"You mean that?"

"Of course I do. You're so talented. Congratulations."

He hugged her.

This was a surprise. Michael wasn't given to superlatives or demonstrative gestures. His devastating criticism of her paintings had often been hurtful in the past. But he had changed now that he no longer watched out the window for the red-haired girl. He was more upbeat. More positive about everything, not just what she did. They were back in sync. Settled, living in harmony once more, the way couples were supposed to be. He had his work, she had hers. They supported each other. It felt calming. Once he'd visited Fortune in summer, seen how beautiful the area was, he'd probably also overcome his dislike of the country and find some positive things to say about that, too.

She and Val met for a long, giggly lunch at a new place near the Museum of Modern Art. Val took the afternoon off from the exhibitions department, because she wasn't busy. They drank a lot of wine. Val revealed that she'd joined a fitness club – not because she wanted to exercise, but because a friend at the Museum had told her the place was full of cute young guys – and now she was lusting after the instructor of the spin class.

"Wow, what thighs," she said, rolling her eyes. "Solid muscle. But he makes me keep pedalling and pedalling until I'm ready to cry. The guy's a fucking sadist."

"And you probably get off on that, you wicked lady," Adie said, chuckling, taking a big swig of her Merlot, remembering Val's fling with the pool bar guy in the Virgin Islands.

"Yeah, I fantasize about him tying me to one of those torture devices they have in the exercise room but," Val sighed, "he's young enough to be my grandson, and I think he's banging the chick at the reception desk. She looks all of eighteen. Cute as anything. All long, dark hair, pert little tits and big Bambi eyes. Tough competition, cherub."

Val shook her head and laughed. She picked up the empty bottle.

"Shall we order another?" she grinned.

"Yes, let's."

Mildly drunk and emboldened by the turn in the conversation, Adie said, looking down at her glass, "I had a little fling while I was up in Canada, Val."

"What, you? You're kidding me, cherub."

"No I'm not. He… um… he owns the property next door to mine. We met in the woods."

"Sounds very romantic. Tell me more. Did he fuck you up against an oak tree in the snow?" Val leaned forward eagerly. "I want all the grisly details, cherub."

"No, we lay down by his woodstove. On a polar bear rug."

"Well, cherub, you are a dark horse. Was he good?"

Adie blushed. "Yes, very good."

"You seeing him again when you go back?"

"No. I discovered that he's married but cheats on his wife with all kinds of women."

"Well, don't they all?" Val said. She threw her head back and barked with laughter. A young couple holding hands at the next table looked over in a disapproving way. Val poked out her tongue and took another swig of wine.

"Don't let his dearly beloved stand in your way, cherub," she added. "If you got off on him, go for it. Fuck 'em and leave 'em, that's what I say. After all, they do that to us, don't they?"

As she wobbled back to the apartment in the late afternoon, the boozy glow wearing off, Adie decided that Val was right. Yet could she treat men as nothing more than a quick, satisfying fuck? She concluded that she wasn't brave enough. Shep popped up again out of his deep, dark hole as she got off the subway and walked up 90th St. She ordered him to get back in. *Go, now. Get lost down there. At this very moment. And don't come out again, country boy. I'm not going to waste any more time daydreaming about you.*

The next morning, waking with a cracking headache, Adie checked her email. Her heart jumped. There was one from Shep. A brief neutral message about a polar bear he saw falling through the ice. The animal scrambled out safely. He sent a blurry picture of the huge, lumbering animal, taken with his cell phone. Three days later, he emailed again: a link to a YouTube video about a moose jumping over a fence by a highway and scaring some hikers.

Then a week after that, just eight words:

"I hope you are well. I miss you."

She trashed all three emails.

Thirty-one

One evening around the middle of April, Michael came home from Columbia drunk. An unusual occurrence. During the working day, he never imbibed. At home or on social occasions, he stuck to wine, but always in a restrained way. He hated to get hammered, he'd always told Adie, because he remembered what too much booze had done to his dad. In all their years together, she'd only seen Michael overdo alcohol two or three times, invariably after an argument with her.

Yet that afternoon, he smelled of scotch and had the vacant, silly grin of the inebriated on his face. He slumped on the sofa without bothering to take his shoes off. The raccoon specs clung crookedly on the end of his long, thin nose. His check shirt was unbuttoned. He was singing, his voice cracking.

"Ha ha de ha. Ha ha de ha. Tra la la. Am I happy, am I happy. I've been at a bar on Broadway with Dan Wagstaff all afternoon. We got into their single malts."

"What's going on, Michael?" she asked with a smile, amused by this out-of-character behaviour.

"I'm… er…" he hiccupped, "…celebrating."

He tried to get up off the sofa. Thought better of it. Sank backwards. Continued to grin stupidly at Adie.

"What about?"

"Well, get this," he hiccupped again. "I heard today that the Tate is planning a major travelling retrospective on the Pre-, Pre-Raffell …" he stumbled over the word and gave up. "This time, they're giving particular emphasis to the art movements that influenced them and they're devoting a major chunk of the exhibition to the Nazarenes. But you know what the best part is?" He beamed. "They've asked me to play a major role. I'll be putting together the *catalogue raisonnee* of the Nazarenes' works. Guess what that means?"

He tossed a sofa cushion into the air.

"I get to do some travelling on the gallery's dime, ha-ha. Go to Europe. Revisit Frankfurt, Vienna, Brussels, Berlin, maybe even get to see a glorious painting by Johann Friedrich Overbeck in the Porziuncola Chapel in Assisi. Because it'll be my job to find and catalogue everything the Nazarenes did. Then the Tate will pick the ones they want to include in the exhibition. Much of their work has never been catalogued properly before, you know. It's scattered in various museums and schools. Just think of it, Adie. *Europe.*"

Michael drew a deep breath and sighed. His eyes lost their boozy blur for a moment.

"I'm so happy. I can't tell you how much I'm looking forward to being back in London."

"That's wonderful, Michael. How exciting, I'm thrilled," Adie said.

"Yeah, me too. It's so fantastic. Catch." He tossed the cushion at her. She threw it back. He reached for it but missed, then shrugged as it hit the kitchen door frame. He collapsed back on the sofa, still grinning.

"God, I'm drunk," he said, pressing his fingers against his temples. "My head is going round and round. I'll have one helluva hangover tomorrow. But Adie, Adie," he looked up anxiously at her, "you'll come with me, wontcha? For part of the trip, I mean. We could meet up in London. Revisit all our old haunts."

"Yes, I'll bet we'll find them changed." There was the pub in South Kensington where she and Michael had hung out with his university buddies in the summertime. What was it called? The Gloucester Arms? He in bell bottoms and a tie-dyed shirt, she in a white mini and clunky sandals. What happy days those were.

"When exactly do you have to go?"

"Soon, two or three weeks, when I've finished the current semester."

Her face fell.

"But Michael, I can't come then. That's... um... when I was planning to go back up to Canada," she said.

The positive mood between them evaporated like mist pumped into a dry room.

"You don't want to – is that it?" Michael said, looking down, twisting a tassel on the cushion between his fingers. "You'd be bored spending time with me, huh?" He looked up at her. "I guess I am boring. You'd sooner hang around with your girlfriends. I'll bet if Val asked you to go with her to Europe, you would."

"No, no, it's not that," she said. "Of course I'd like to come. It's just that the guy who's renovating the house expects to have all the major work done by then – and I have to go see him."

And *pay* him, she thought. So far, she'd sent Knock an electronic funds transfer of only twenty per cent of the estimate. Yet he'd probably spent far more than that on the materials.

"And you know," she added gently, "I need to get started on my own project too. You remember, I hope," she looked at him quizzically, "that I'm illustrating this big book for Sumac on native plants?"

Adie felt a twinge of resentment. Why did men consistently think that their work was more important than anything women did? In the midst of his excitement about the commission to research the Nazarenes' *oeuvre*, Michael had obviously forgotten that she had important work to tackle herself.

He looked uncomprehending for a moment.

"Oh, yes, your… um… book," he said, playing absent-minded professor now, his usual cop-out when reminded of something he'd forgotten. "I didn't realize you had to start work on the book right away."

"But Michael, you saw the contract. I have thirty-five huge illustrations to…."

"I know, I know, but can't you play hooky for a couple of weeks? You could come over to London from Canada. There must be lots of flights from Toronto."

"Okay, I'll try. But it's a big project, Michael. And if I can't come," she decided to turn the tables, irritated by his self-absorption, "perhaps you can fly back to New York via Canada? I really want you to see the house – *our* house," she corrected herself. "Our summer house. It's going to be yours as well as mine, you know. And it will be beautiful, I think."

"Mmm, I guess so," he said, twisting the tassel again. "But I can't commit to anything."

Michael's head was bursting with Europe. The sophistication of its cities. The veneration of art. The way Europeans preserved historical buildings, instead of tearing them down. The wonderful variety of restaurants in London. He knew already that Adie's rural hideaway would be no match for the glories of his favourite part of the world. Humouring her was important, he was aware of that. Yet staring at her face, now scrunched up with irritation, he sensed a gulf deepening between them, as if they were going through the motions of marriage simply because they presumed they should, not because they really wanted to be together or had much to share anymore. He privately thought the project to renovate her uncle's house was foolish and doomed to disaster. He sensed it would end badly. He had no desire to get involved himself. The backwoods would only remind him of his childhood. His hated childhood. All those years stuck in the ass end of the Adirondacks, waiting, hoping, for the time he could escape to a big city. He wished he'd paid more attention when Adie inherited the house. Perhaps he could have talked her out of the idea.

"Let's discuss this another day, huh?" he said, heaving himself up from the sofa with a supreme effort. He felt like a sailor now, his ship going up and down in immense waves. He wanted to topple over the side of the deck and sink to the bottom, to end the sensation. He staggered off to the bedroom, tripping over the bedspread.

"Sorry," he called back at Adie, "but I gotta go lie down."

In early May, Michael left for Europe. Frankfurt first, he said. He looked so happy, Adie felt happy too. She kissed him goodbye at the apartment door. They hugged. She promised to meet up with him somewhere, knowing in her heart that she wouldn't go. And Michael headed to the elevator, mouthing "See you in Canada," as she stood waving in the doorway, yet thinking, too, that he was unlikely to go and see her.

Adie prepared to depart herself. She hauled her two precious amaryllis plants over to Val's for safekeeping. Emptied the fridge. Washed the sheets. Put new ones on the bed. Drew the drapes. Locked the apartment. Told the super they'd both be away, but she wasn't sure for how long.

She headed out to Newark on a grey day. Flying into Toronto, the sky looked even greyer and full of rain clouds, the city a boring monochrome of browns and more greys below. She picked up a cube van that she'd reserved on the Web and felt bold and adventurous, signing the forms, then driving the big, white vehicle away to the freeway. On her two previous visits, coping with the heavy traffic, she'd been frightened in the little red rental car. The van changed that. Then suddenly, there was a furious honking behind her. In the rear-view mirror, she saw a taxi driver in a turban, weaving his yellow vehicle from side to side, inches from the van. She honked back indignantly and gave him the finger as he slid out into the adjoining lane and tore by, pulling a face.

"Fuck you, Mr. Turban Man," she yelled, although she knew he couldn't hear. "What's your goddamn hurry? I'm already going way past the speed limit, aren't I?"

And then she laughed, because that was the problem with cities. All cities. Everyone was always rushing. So rude. So impatient. So intolerant of people who weren't sure where they were going. Michael loved cities. Yet she couldn't wait to escape them, to settle into her quiet house in the woods and start painting.

First, though, there were things to buy. She turned off the freeway into an ugly suburb somewhere west of the airport and found a room in an even uglier motel. Yet it was clean, convenient and cheap, and she'd be gone after a couple of nights. She had no interest in heading into Toronto's downtown. First on her list was a big box store selling art materials. She bought an expensive metal art table, two desk lamps, a stool with a back support, a credenza on wheels and enough watercolour supplies – two large, wooden art boards, paper, pencils, brushes, dozens of tubes of pigment – to last her three months. A cheery young sales clerk with a Mohawk haircut carried everything to the van for her, then refused a tip. What nice people Canadians are, she thought, even when they work for some corporate giant who doesn't give a shit about them. This wasn't like New York.

Next, she tracked down an IKEA outlet, a massive barn of a building painted blue and yellow, located beside a busy road, and bought a few basic items of furniture: a table and four chairs like the ones she and Michael had used for years; a futon and frame; sheets, towels, dishes. All strictly functional stuff. Knock would undoubtedly be appalled at her choices and the shoddy way the pressboard furniture was made, but they would do for now. Making the interior of her Victorian house look elegant, like something out of the home decorating magazines she saw in racks at supermarkets, could come later. If she found the time, that is. But she probably wouldn't – because what she wanted to do more than anything was paint.

It was a glorious morning, cool but sunny, as she drove out of the city. Getting onto the freeway again, flustered by speeding trucks, she turned on the radio and discovered the Metropolitan Opera broadcast was playing. The strains of Cavaradossi's heart-rending aria during the first act of *Tosca* filled the cab and the emotion in the music made her think of Shep. Was he back in Fortune now? She switched the radio off. Threading the van through dense traffic was difficult enough. She didn't need thoughts of the country boy buzzing around in her head as well. Opting for silence during the entire drive, she resolved that the first thing she would do, after meeting with Knock – and maybe making a quick mug of tea – was go exploring her woods with her sketchpad. The elusive trout lily that Maggie McCorkindale had told her about was her quarry.

Yet a surprise waited in Fortune. One that put a dent in her plans.

Thirty-two

Snow. A mini-blizzard enveloped the van as she turned off the freeway. Adie was shocked. Chilled, in spite of the van heater. She kicked herself for not wearing gloves. Wasn't it supposed to be spring? Buds on trees and fresh green stuff coming up in farmers' fields, that's what she'd expected to see – it was early May, after all – yet, fat wet snowflakes were splatting on to her windshield. She turned the wipers on full, cursing. There would be no trout lilies – or any other paintable plants, for that matter – sprouting in her woods yet. Presuming she could start work the moment she arrived was just a pipe dream.

She passed the spot where she'd gone into the ditch in February and shuddered, remembering. How embarrassing. How foolish. Nothing more than a fantasy now. She pushed the country boy firmly back into his deep, dark hole when he made an attempt to pop out, and she drove on into Fortune village. This time, she decided, she'd stop and get acquainted with the woman who ran the general store.

The store was empty. It always seemed to be. Yet the sad-faced woman she'd seen before still sat at the counter with her neatly-permed hair. She was watching TV again.

"So you're back and bringing things with you, I see," she said, taking note of the van, craning her neck in a nosy way towards the window. She pressed the Off button on the TV. "I guess that means you're staying now, eh? Well, I better introduce myself. I'm Gracie Piloski, but you can call me Gracie. I run this... um... hole. And I get to be Fortune's postmistress too. A heck of a lot of work, I'm telling you. But there it is."

She smiled and held out a hand with surprisingly elegant fingernails painted red. Adie shook it.

"Want a coffee? Mine's real good. Peanut butter cups? I seem to remember that you liked those," Gracie said.

"Sorry, but I don't eat candy anymore. I lost the taste for it. And I don't want coffee right now, thanks."

Feeling she should buy something, she added, "What do you have that I could cook for my supper?"

"Oh, lots of things, dear. Hot dogs, chicken pot pie, breaded chicken strips, beef patties, frozen french fries. The cod in batter is good." Gracie waved at a big old chest freezer in the corner. "Go look, eh? And you'll find mac and cheese over there."

She nodded at two shelves of packaged and canned foodstuffs.

Adie settled on a chicken pot pie that had freezer burn and an iced-up bag of frozen peas. She felt relieved that Michael wasn't standing at her side, gnashing his teeth about carbs. Both purchases, she noticed, were well past their sell-by date, but she'd arranged to spend her first night at Tish's, so she wouldn't have to eat them, anyway. She and Tish were on friendly terms once more, the tense evening over the steak and kidney pie forgotten. She was actually looking forward to seeing Tish. She knew so few people in the area yet.

Driving the van up Fortune Hill felt strange. Exhilarating, but strange. She opened the window. Inhaled sharply, hoping to smell her woods as she approached, but got slapped with a faceful of wet snow instead. She wiped her cheeks, laughing. So this was it, finally. She was arriving at her house. Her home. The place where she could do exactly as she pleased and be beholden to no one. It was a thrilling prospect, despite the weather. She couldn't wait to see what magic the Mennonite renovator had wrought inside.

Wires still dangled out of walls. The bathroom tiles weren't laid. Six tall, traditional kitchen cupboards hand-crafted from cherry wood by Mervyn Baumann stood on the floor of the living room, waiting to be hung on new drywall. There was a pile of construction debris in the front hall. Yet Adie realized, looking around her, that Knock had pulled off an amazing feat in a comparatively short time. It all looked so different from her first visit in the fall. And while the downstairs wasn't finished, her large spacious studio, with its windows facing east to pick up the morning sun, was ready for use.

"Thank you, thank you. I love it," she told Knock, wanting to hug him. Suspecting that he was too reserved to respond to such effusiveness, she offered her hand instead.

He took it, gave a little formal bow and said, "We've a ways to go yet, of course, but it's liveable now, Mrs. Adie. You can move in. And notice how warm it is inside the house?"

"Yes. Quite a relief, seeing as winter's still here." She glanced out of the window, dismayed by the still-falling snow.

"That is your new high-efficiency furnace at work," he said with pride. "I had it installed three months ago, so we could carry on here all winter. It runs on propane and will keep you quite comfortable. But if you do get the urge to go chopping firewood," he motioned to the woodstove with a wry smile, "I kept the old relic, just as you asked me to."

The big, black cast iron stove still stood on a metal platform in the living room, its top plate and curlicued legs flecked with rust. Unlike his cousin, Knock clearly wasn't a fan of old-style heating. She pictured Gully sitting in front of the stove. His last hours. Sipping the scotch. Taking the pills. She hoped that, wherever he was, he had finally found peace.

Flavian was at Tish's, to her surprise. He stood at the kitchen sink peeling potatoes and stayed for supper. The other guests were a middle-aged couple who had reserved at the bed and breakfast for a week. They were hunting for a hobby farm in the area and had grown tired of driving back and forth to Toronto every day. They had the pink back bedroom. Adie didn't care if the trucks kept her awake all night in the noisy blue one. Tomorrow she'd be spending the first night in her own house. She couldn't quite believe it was happening.

The evening was lively. The couple produced a bottle of wine – Tish didn't drink and kept no liquor in the house – and the man, a radio announcer with a red handlebar moustache and big, booming voice, told Adie not to get depressed about the new fall of snow.

"You wait. It'll be probably be gone tomorrow," he said pouring more wine. "Welcome to our crazy Canadian climate."

Overnight, the handlebar moustache man was proven right. The temperature shot up an amazing eighteen degrees. By mid-morning every smidgen of white had melted. It was as if the snow fairy had dropped by, waved a wand and said, "Enough. Away. Be gone till next year, my pretties." Adie headed back to her own house along the lake road, thrilled to see bare, brown earth and uncloaked trees as well as bright green grass on a couple of lawns.

Flavian came by shortly after noon. He'd volunteered to help her unload things from the van because his store was closed on Mondays. With the thermometer climbing, it didn't take long for them both to get sweaty, carrying the boxes into the house. So they took a rest on the front steps, shafts of sunlight coming through the dark spruce, hitting their faces and winter-white arms. The air smelled fresh. Adie looked around her and realized that spring was lurking in the wings, in spite of the surprise yesterday. The overgrown garden at the side of the house was piled high with dead brown stalks of weeds and flowers flattened by the snow, yet she spotted shoots already coming up. Some of them looked like the wild catnip she'd picked last October. She made mental plans to buy a wheelbarrow, clean up the mess, then try growing some vegetables and other herbs. Gully came to mind again. She wondered out loud if her uncle had liked having the garden and if he'd planted anything in it.

Flavian shook his head.

"Mom says he wasn't a happy man," he said. "He just went through the motions. He didn't seem to particularly like or do anything."

"But he was fond of your mom, I hear."

"Yes. Seems so."

"Do you think they were involved with one another? You know, lovers?"

Flavian looked hard at her.

"Who told you that?" he asked sharply.

"No one. I just wondered, that's all."

He got up off the steps immediately and glanced at his watch. Then headed indoors.

"C'mon. let's unpack your boxes," he called out to her. "I have to get back to the store soon and do some paperwork."

In the living room, surveying her mini-mountain of purchases, Flavian rubbed his forehead and sighed.

"Boy, I hope there's an Allen key in one of these," he said with a chuckle. "You know how it is with IKEA. They make you assemble everything yourself, and then you discover that you need an Allen key and you can't find one."

The elusive Allen key was located, taped to a piece of cardboard in the box containing the futon bed frame. They hauled the box upstairs to a back bedroom. Adie intended to sleep on the futon temporarily, until she found time to buy some proper bedroom furniture. To her relief, Flavian proved adept at putting her acquisitions together. He'd had plenty of experience – and frustrations – he told her, setting up shelving from IKEA in his bookstore and also at his former apartment in Toronto. She was content to watch, grateful to have a male helper, and resolved to drop in and buy more books soon as a thank-you. She tried out the futon. Lay down on it, feeling moderately satisfied with the feel of the polyester stuffing under her back. It would suffice for a while.

They found the old chest of drawers next. Knock had stored it in the adjoining bedroom. But the Victorian antique weighed a ton, so they decided to take all the drawers out before trying to move it. Adie yanked at the top one. It slid open easily, unlike the time she'd explored the house with Shep, when the place was damp and unheated. Now it was dry and warm. To her surprise, she found clothes stashed on a pile of shelf paper.

"Wow, these must have belonged to my uncle," she said, laughing, pulling out old, greyed underwear, mismatched navy blue and brown socks full of holes and a crumpled plaid shirt with frayed cuffs. "When the township cleaned the house out, they missed these, I guess."

She sniffed a sock. Pulled a face at Flavian.

"Smells like hamster cages. Mice have been living in this drawer, I think."

She put the clothes on top of the chest and peered in the drawer. As she suspected, there were a few black specks. But then she noticed something else, sticking out from underneath the liner paper at the bottom of the drawer. An envelope. A white one, square, the kind used for greeting cards. She pulled the envelope out. It was addressed by hand with a blue ballpoint pen, and she recognized the handwriting at once. Oh, no. The letter was from her mother.

She sank down on the futon with a shiver of dread. What was this? Inside the envelope were six sheets of thin, pale blue airmail notepaper, neatly folded into quarters. They were covered with the shaky, spidery scrawl of someone either very old or very ill.

"Dearest Gully: The black dogs are circling now. I can feel every bone in my body crumbling with this cancer. And half of me is ready to go, but the other half wants to stay, although I wonder why. My life has not been happy, when I look back on it.

But I mustn't be dramatic. You always told me I was too dramatic about everything. That I took things too seriously. But you did too, didn't you? And that was what got us into trouble. We were so young – at least I was – and I couldn't let you go. And now there's something I must tell you, a secret I've kept to myself all these years.

I believe Adie is not your child. I insisted to you that she was because I wanted to hang on to you. I couldn't bear to see you forget me. I never loved Derek, as you know. I was pressured into the marriage, because Dad noticed right after you came over to England that something was happening between us, and he wanted to put a stop to it. But we couldn't stop, could we? And then after Adie was born, I kept on insisting that she was yours, because I wanted to believe it myself. I loved you so much. And I did intend to run away and come to New York to live with you, but in the end I couldn't do it. I'd become a mother, my life had changed, Philip had come along and both kids needed me. I wanted to give them a normal life. I thought I'd made the right decision. but now I wonder, because not a day has gone by when I haven't thought of you. My life has been so lonely. So lacking in passion. And love.

But I feel terrible about misleading you and Adie. She and I have not been close since I told her about you. I advised her not to have children. Now I think she could have, even if you were her father, but fifty years ago, less was known about incest. People said that awful things could be passed on to both the children and the grandchildren. They might be born with a cleft palate or sickle *cell anemia or hemophilia or mental problems. And though she turned out to be normal, I couldn't bear the agony of worrying about such things appearing in her children. I've always been so muddled about everything. So confused about what I wanted out of life and I...."*

The letter went on for another two pages. It was dated November 16, 2008, two weeks before her mother died and about a month, Adie estimated, before Gully died, too. So he probably had killed himself, after getting this missive from her. She felt sick and decided to read the rest later. It was all too much to absorb at once. Oddly, she didn't want to cry. She felt quite calm now. Her mother's words were a punch in the gut, but also a reminder of how self-absorbed she'd always been. All her "I" this and "I" that. Her never-ending "I, I, I." Adie ached for her and also for Gully – it was painful to read about their unfulfilled lives – yet she also felt something approaching disgust. Because now she remembered how it was. Mummy first. Always first. Mummy, Mummy, Mummy. Her stomping off to cry about some hurt in her bedroom, so Adie and Philip had to tiptoe around the house. Her leaving them with babysitters to go off to London on the train, all dressed up in high heels and a silly hat with a veil. Her saying, "Bye darlings, so sorry to leave you. Be good," when she didn't mean a word of it. Her upset about this. Her upset about that. And Daddy retreating into his greenhouse to get rid of the whitefly and deadhead his begonias, because he wanted to get away from her black moods. Why could she never move on? For a few years Adie had hated her mother for saying she shouldn't have children. But then she'd put it all behind her. Filled her life with other things. And Michael had never been attracted to fatherhood anyway. So why couldn't Mummy move on, too? Why couldn't Gully? What had prevented them from finding some other happiness in their lives?

Flavian stood waiting politely beside her as she read the letter. She looked up at him with a wan smile and held the letter out.

"Here," she said. "You may as well read this too. It's not that private, I guess. Doesn't mean much now. And your mom might be interested. It explains why my uncle came to Canada. He was my mother's half-brother, you see, and they fell in love. She was only fourteen when they met. He was twenty. It went on for years. They were utterly obsessed with one another. Never able to let go, for their entire lives. All very sad."

She sighed and thought fondly of her gruff Scottish dad, who'd had red hair like her. She'd always regarded him as her father. Knowing now that he almost certainly was, she wished he were still around to hug.

"I'm going to find a garbage bag downstairs for Gully's old clothes," she said, eager for something to take her mind off what she'd discovered.

Flavian nodded and read the letter himself, standing by the window. When she came back into the room, he had a strange expression on his face.

"You know, this is weird," he said, "but I guess it's time to reveal my own little family secret, even though Mom made me swear never to tell anyone. She was worried about the gossip in a small town. But you'd better know, I think."

He swallowed hard. "Your uncle was my father."

Adie's response surprised him. She took the news calmly.

"I thought as much," she said smiling. "That's why I raised the subject when we were sitting on the steps. But did he know?"

"No. Mom says she never told him. What happened between them was very brief, I think. I get the impression that it might have been just one night," he grinned and raised his eyebrows, "because she'd gone over to see him, upset about being dumped by some guy. And she told me that she always knew that there was something haunting your uncle, probably a love affair gone wrong, so she didn't want to burden him with the news that she got pregnant."

"But perhaps he suspected. And that was why he left her money in his will."

"Yes, I've thought of that. But it may have just been because he liked her."

"Life can be so sad sometimes," Adie said with a deep sigh. "Perhaps if my uncle had known about you, it would have shaken him out of his depression and made him forget my mother. And your mom could have used his help financially. I don't know, Gully and Mummy…." She sighed again and shook her head. "What a sad business – and so stupid, when you think about it."

"Yes but that's love. I think that when we fall in love, it's out of our control," Flavian said, remembering Jean-Paul, how they shared nothing, but he'd adored him anyway. "Love just happens. And often it IS stupid. Totally stupid."

Adie thought of Shep, then. She'd behaved stupidly with him. Was that love? Maybe yes, maybe no. She couldn't help wishing sometimes that she could see him again.

Thirty-three

Yet the country boy wasn't around. The other Victorian house on Fortune Hill seemed uninhabited. In the next couple of weeks, as Adie settled in, she discerned no sign of life over there, a hundred yards or so from her own home, through the dark spruce. No green pickup truck went by at the end of her long driveway. She didn't hear the *vroom-vroom* of an ATV starting up outside his drive shed. Nor the sharp crack of firewood being split. Half of her wanted to run into him. The other half didn't, because it would probably happen unexpectedly and be awkward for them both. So she stayed away from the trail that led to his house from hers, sticking rigidly to her side of the stream. And when she went out on forays with her sketch pad, searching for the native plants on Blair Rountree's list, she took a detour to avoid going near the cabin.

The plants she sought were no-shows too. It was too early in the year. So she spent the time getting organized. She returned the van to a U-Move franchise in Marsh River, then walked one block over to a truck dealer's. The experience was fun. She felt like a farmer strolling around the lot, inspecting the latest models, wishing she had a green-and-yellow baseball cap with John Deere emblazoned on the front. Amid the big, black vehicles, shiny with chrome and silver stripes, she spotted a smaller blue second-hand pickup. It had minor rust under one door and a dent in the back fender, but looked in pretty good shape. Even better, it was equipped with four-wheel drive – a necessity in winter, the salesman told her, when she explained that she'd recently arrived to live on Fortune Hill. She paid cash and mentally thanked Gully for the sizeable bank account that she kept dipping into, chiding herself for thinking badly of him.

Driving the truck gave her a sense of power. She loved the sensation of being up high on the bench seat, lording it over all the compact cars on the road. She was turning into a country girl, for sure. Everyone, men and women, drove pickups here, and they all looked like they got a charge out of it. The thrill was almost sexual, she thought, wondering if she'd run into Shep, driving his own pickup. She fantasized about a random encounter on a dirt road somewhere and him pushing his hand into her pants again as he planted kisses all over her face and neck. Then she laughed out loud. *No, you idiot. Stop it. It's over.*

She made several trips in the truck to Marsh River to buy stuff for the house and, at an electronics store, signed up for Internet service. A young guy with long, skinny legs and bright red acne welts on his cheeks came out to Fortune Hill the next day, driving a white van with a ladder on top. He clambered like a spider up onto the roof and installed an antenna and dish, patiently explaining the ropes to her. She was surprised to discover that everything worked just fine. Yet, connected to the world again, via her laptop, she wished she didn't have to be. Life was simpler and calmer without the intrusion of the Internet.

Knock's crew came every day except Sunday to finish the interior of the house. She made them coffee and heard about their lives. They were a nice bunch of guys who all lived in the area. If she felt lonely after they left for the day, she visited Tish. She dropped by Boddington Books several times, too, to buy a book or simply chat with Flavian. The discovery that they were blood relatives had inspired a kinship between them. She also met Chrissie Tanner one afternoon on her way out of the bookstore, but didn't blush or feel embarrassed now.

They exchanged greetings, Chrissie giggled, and they went their separate ways.

She wondered how Michael was doing. Emailed him.

"I have surprising news," she wrote. "It was in a letter from my mother. Will tell all when we meet. When R U coming? A."

He didn't reply, but she did get an email from Maggie McCorkindale.

"The trout lilies are blooming in Vermont. Go see if you can find them on your land. They're probably coming up now. Here's the text I'm sending to Blair."

The Word file attached to her message contained four short, succinct paragraphs. Adie read them thinking, Yes, Maggie could indeed write, as Blair had said, and that this was going to be a fruitful collaboration. She was dying to get started on her contribution. Maggie added this footnote:

"See if you have *Hepatica Americana*, too. It's very small, often concealed under dried-up maple leaves. Has clusters of flowers. Usually white, but also lilac or bluish-pink. If you find some, I'll tell Blair we want to include it, because it's a pretty plant – and a North American native."

Two days after that, her heart jumped to the clear spring sky. She found both plants. A clump of trout lilies appeared magically overnight in the place where she'd thought they might grow, under a bare maple bordering Joe Perri's land. There were three solitary stalks, each with a yellow, nodding bud, emanating from matching pairs of greenish, pointed, mottled leaves. Their whole shape was so dainty and distinctive, backed up by the maple trunk, they already looked like a watercolour painting executed by George Ehret. She couldn't wait to put her own stamp on the flowers, to depict their bell-like beauty in her own, far bolder style.

Then, fifty yards away, near where her property line met the stream, she rummaged in the leaf litter under another maple.

And hallelujah, there was the Hepatica. This one had small, white flowers, with leaves that were liver-shaped.

Which to paint first? She opted for the Hepatica because the trout lilies weren't quite in bloom. Yet there was no time to lose. Both plants were classified as "spring ephemerals," meaning they wouldn't stick around for long. She raced back to the house for her painting gear. It was a fairly long jaunt through the woods, and she returned out of breath, carrying her portable paint box, brushes, a watercolour block and a folding stool that she'd brought from New York. Then she settled down to produce a series of brief watercolour sketches, glad of the stool, remembering the hassles with the broken lawn chair on her first visit. Some of these sketches would be close-ups of petals and stamens. With others, she'd show in detail the structure of the entire plant. These would be the basis for the large final portrait that she'd execute in her studio and give to Blair.

Her fingers shook with excitement as she picked up a pencil. Then she felt her body go trembly all over. Her heart started jumping up and down, as if on a trampoline. With excitement or fright, she wasn't sure. She glanced behind her nervously.

Because she heard the distant roar of an ATV coming towards her through the woods.

"So you're back," he said.

"Yes, I'm back. And so are you," she said, looking up but not smiling.

"I've been up north for weeks. Came down south yesterday. When did you arrive?"

"Um, a while ago." She looked down again at her sketch pad, willing him to go away.

He didn't. Wouldn't. He'd parked the ATV a few yards away. Now he stood looming over her as she squatted on the stool. His clean smell that she'd liked – of unscented soap and country air – hit her nostrils.

"I saw you rushing through the trees from your house just now. I have deer eyes," he said.

"Oh, and what are deer eyes?" she asked. But she wasn't really interested. It was just something to say. She tried hard to shut him out and concentrate on the Hepatica, keeping her own eyes glued to the sketch pad balanced in her lap.

She heard him chuckle.

"All hunters have deer eyes," he said. "We train them to see every movement in the woods. Although," he laughed louder, as if making a noise might encourage her to look up at him, "I confess that your red jacket was easier to spot than this one. Is it new?"

She didn't answer.

He placed his hand on her shoulder. It felt heavy. Then he tweaked the black polyester jacket that she'd bought at Modell's before leaving New York.

"Nice," he murmured.

She ignored him.

He jerked hard on her sleeve now, so that the pencil fell out of her hand.

"Stop that, Shep," she said. "Please go away."

"No. Just look at me, girl," he commanded. "Will you put that damn drawing down for a minute and look at me?"

She did. His face betrayed anger but also bewilderment, as she reluctantly unfolded herself from the stool and stood up, her face inches from his.

"Why didn't you reply to my emails?" he said, sounding as plaintive as a middle-aged man with a deep voice can. "I waited and waited to hear from you. I thought that we liked each other."

"Well, I do – I did like you, Shep," she said. "But you're a sneak. And you run around with a lot of women, I hear."

"Who told you that? I'll bet it was Tish."

"Maybe it was. But I also heard you talking on the phone to your wife the morning after I… I slept at your house. That was sneaky."

"It was? I asked Mary Ann if she wanted to come over and stay at the house while I was away, that's all. We have an… arrangement because we don't get along. I didn't say anything to you because I knew it would upset you. And you know," he paused, "if you suddenly got a call from Malcolm, or whatever his name is, I wouldn't throw a hissy fit. I'd be an adult about it. I'd realize that you had stuff to discuss."

"Oh, so I'm not an adult?"

"I didn't mean that."

"Well, I have nothing to discuss with you, and I have work to do. So go away, please."

"Come on, girl. I don't think you really want me to. Do you?"

He put both arms around her neck now and turned on the penetrating gaze that she both loved and hated. Her insides went all quivery. She felt her legs dissolving beneath her.

She allowed him to kiss her.

"Will you come to the cabin with me?" he said, opening his eyes after the kiss, boring them into hers. "The polar bear pelt is in there, you know. On the floor. Waiting for us. You won't hit your head on the bunk this time."

He chuckled when she blushed.

"Come on," he said.

She wriggled out of his grip and pushed him hard in the chest with both hands.

"No, no, no." she said, squinting up at the sky. It was clear and blue, the sun's rays penetrating through the maple branches and creating long, attractive shadows on the Hepatica flowers. "This light won't last long. Please, Shep. Go away. I have to get these sketches done. I have a very demanding assignment. I'm working on a book of illustrations."

"Well, all right, girl," he said. "I'll go."

He started to turn but stopped and grinned at her wickedly. And though she turned away, looking flustered, he sensed victory, because there was that familiar spark in her eyes.

"But I'll come over to your place tonight, shall I?" he asked.

He detected a glimmering of acquiescence and persisted.

"I'd love to see what you've done with the house," he said, as she still looked away. "I'll bet it looks fantastic."

She hated herself for being weak. She turned and said yes.

So Shep went to Adie's house after dark. He left the ATV at home and bounced along the trail through the woods, freshly showered and shaved. Clean underwear, socks and a new pink shirt as well. The works. He hummed to himself. Felt happier than he had in months. In his jacket pocket was a bottle of chilled Sauvignon Blanc, the wine women always liked. He kept one hand on the bottle, clasping and unclasping its neck to reassure himself. But then he wondered why he worried, because wine – and especially this wine – always worked.

And so it did. After they'd finished the bottle, they climbed the stairs to Adie's bedroom, unable to keep their hands off each other any longer. They made love awkwardly, clumsily, for a long time, on her IKEA futon.

Then, as they lay together afterwards on the too-narrow mattress, Shep realized he'd been right that night in the cabin, when he was terrified she was going to die. He needed this woman in his life. He loved her more than any other woman he'd ever known. He wondered what the heck he was going to do about it.

Drifting off to sleep, squeezed beside her, he also wondered if he'd ever get to have sex with her in a proper bed.

Thirty-four

And so it went. An idyll of sorts, with no questions asked, no weighty issues raised by either party. During the day, Adie worked like a madwoman on her watercolour plant portraits for Sumac. At night, she saw Shep, and they made love. Sometimes at her house, on the uncomfortable futon, which made his back ache. But at other times, when she didn't like the texture of the light or it had rained, making everything too wet for her to sit sketching out of doors, they rode out to Wolf's Glen on the ATV in the late afternoon and stayed there till long after dark.

With the sky the colour of smoke above the cabin roof, he lit the oil lamp and a fire in the woodstove, and they lay naked on the polar bear pelt, their bodies golden and soft-focused as a gelatin print in the flickering light. He inspected her methodically for mosquito bites, peering in her armpits and ears, pushing her thighs apart gently to check her tender parts, running his fingers up and down her toes, kissing every one of them as he went. And because it was spring, and she was unused to being in the woods, she had plenty of bites. He dabbed calamine lotion on the nastier welts from a bottle that he kept in the triangular cupboard and ordered her to stop scratching. And sometimes she obeyed, but other times the bites itched so badly, she couldn't help clawing at them with her clipped nails. That's when he scolded her and threatened to spank her and called her a silly city girl who had a lot to learn about living in the country. And a thrill went through her at his forcefulness and desire to fit her into his world, which was so different from anything she'd known before.

Occasionally, they took sweet snacks – rum, cans of Coke, his ever-present chocolate chip cookies – along to the cabin. Then they sipped and nibbled while listening to the Eroica, or the orchestral music from *Der Freischütz*, with the old phonograph cranked up high. Once they even tried timing their passion to the crescendo at the end of the Eroica's third movement, but it didn't work. The tempo was too fast. She collapsed on top of him, and they rolled over and over on the thick, creamy-white fur, laughing their heads off, getting gritty crumbs of cookie stuck to their backsides. She grew accustomed to his plump body, how he blended it so skilfully with hers, caressing, pushing in, lifting her to places she'd never dreamed she would go. She adored every inch of him. And he adored her, couldn't get enough of her, and continued to wonder what he was going to do about it.

It was a suspended kind of happiness, the best kind, without a future, without consequences. She no longer asked him about Mary Ann. He never mentioned Michael or suggested that she come over to his own house. They didn't discuss what Tish had said about him. Adie stopped going to visit the bed and breakfast in the evenings and felt guilty, but made excuses on the phone that she was working like crazy on her paintings – and though Tish probably thought that was another case of horse feathers, she didn't care. Shep didn't care, either, because there is no one as selfish as two people in love. Sometimes Shep's daughters and Tyson the Terrible – a nickname dreamed up by Shep – meandered into their conversations, but when it happened, they both sensed that their words might lead them somewhere they didn't want to go, so they stopped and changed the subject.

The only thing they allowed to come between them was Adie's painting. Being with Shep made her feel so young, so energized, so bursting with inspiration, she couldn't wait to pick up a brush every day. She banished him during the long hours spent in her studio or when she sat on the stool out of doors doing her preparatory watercolour sketches – and he went away without complaint, but most days crept back quietly at around one p.m. with something for her to eat. Then he would disappear again until the evening, leaving her to nibble absentmindedly from the plate of snacks, hardly paying attention to what she was putting in her mouth because the work absorbed her totally. She produced the portraits of the Hepatica and the trout lilies in record time. And they were spectacular. Even she liked them. Then she found wild North American ginger down near the stream and painted that, too. And when she emailed Blair and Maggie digital images of the three paintings, they were both over the moon.

"Absolutely wonderful," replied Blair. "Can't wait for more."

"Found any Jack-in-the-Pulpit yet? Dying to see what you do with that," wrote Maggie.

The next day, she did stumble across a jaunty Jack. Its brown-and-white striped hood reared up under a clump of tall pines deep in the woods. She rushed out with her sketchpad and stool, relieved not to have to go looking for the plant in Marlene Knockenhammer's garden, because heading there would have meant disrupting the magical space that she'd slipped into so seamlessly with Shep, and she dreaded doing that, because then this fevered burst of creativity might dry up and disappear. And he praised every sketch, every painting, every scribble, every single thing she produced with a pencil or a brush. If she'd scrawled a line on a blackboard with a piece of chalk, he'd have praised that, too. He called her the most amazing woman he'd ever met. He ached with love for her.

Then one morning a crack appeared in the fortress they'd erected around themselves.

An email from Michael.

"Dear Adio: How are you? I was at Tate Britain this morning. That's what they call it now. I sat on a bench looking at Millais's Ophelia for a long time, remembering how we met. How exactly like Lizzie Siddal you were. And then I went to the gallery cafe. It's all different now, of course – quite swanky and upscale, no Cornish pasties on the menu! I guess other people hated them, too. They had plenty of low-carb offerings, I'm glad to say. I had a good wild bass ceviche for lunch.

"But I missed you. I wished you were here with me. I've had a great time in Europe. Didn't get to Assisi, but I spent several days with Gerhard Krumholz, the Nazarenes specialist at the Staatliche Museum in Frankfurt, and it seems we can borrow several great pictures for the show at the Tate. There's one of a black-and-white cat that I know you'll love.

"How is your own painting going? And the house? It's been good to have some time apart, but now I'm looking forward to seeing you. So I've booked an Air Canada flight from London to Toronto for June 21. I presume you can come and pick me up at the airport. You have likely bought a car by now. Love, Michael."

June 21. *Three days from now. Yikes.* The pickup truck. That's what Adie thought of first. She couldn't picture her urban, country-hating husband folding his big, angular head and beanpole body into the cab alongside her. He'd surely recoil in horror the moment he spotted the navy blue four-by-four with the chrome fenders and big wheels in the parking garage at the airport. Then he'd shake his head. Say she was nuts. Ask her why she'd wasted her uncle's money on this gas-guzzling emblem of the rural culture that he so despised and lecture her that she should have bought a sensible little Toyota or Mazda that wouldn't cost much to run.

Panic set in then. About Michael. About Shep. About her work. The house. The truck. Everything. She wanted to scream with confusion and fright. How was she supposed to handle all this?

A bed. A proper bed. Queen-size with a firm mattress. That was the immediate answer to some of her problems, she decided. She was going to break permanently with Michael, she truly wanted to; she just couldn't face doing it yet. For one thing, she and Shep hadn't discussed the future, and for another, she was so focused on her painting. The spring ephemerals didn't last more than a couple of weeks. She wanted to capture as many of those as possible before they disappeared. So for now, she reasoned, she'd just put up with Michael's visit – he wouldn't want to stay long anyway, hating the country as he did – but before he got here, she needed to go out and buy a bed, simply because they'd always shared one. And he was such a creature of habit, her husband. He'd expect her to have a bed here. They wouldn't be doing anything other than sleeping in this bed, yet he'd fuss about having to squeeze beside her on the futon. It would make him complain. Endlessly. All night she would have to lie there and endure his grumbling that he couldn't turn over properly, that he was nearly falling off the edge of the mattress. And that he couldn't sleep a wink.

With regret, she stopped working on the portrait of the Jack-in-the-Pulpit and washed her brushes off. She lined them up to dry. When Shep came by the studio with a tuna fish sandwich for her lunch, she told him that she was going out to buy a bed that afternoon.

"You are? Great. About time," he said. "Shall I come and help choose it? That lumpy futon has been hell on my back. I can't wait to be in a proper bed with you."

He leered in a jokey way. As she bent over the credenza to put the lid on her watercolour box, he came up behind her and pinched one of her buttocks.

"I love your ass," he whispered, his lips brushing her ear. "When that bed gets here, I'm going to make you kneel down on the mattress, come up behind you and fuck you senseless."

Yikes. This declaration that once would have made her wobbly at the knees with desire filled Adie with fright now. She turned around to face him. Wasn't sure what to say. Dithered. Debated. Churned inside. Decided to just plunge in and be honest.

"Shep, I got an email from Michael this morning. He's coming here in a couple of days. I wish he weren't. But alas, he is and that's why," she paused, dreading his reaction, putting on what she hoped was her most appealing smile, "I have to go out and buy this bed."

Shep wasn't sure he'd heard right. He stared at her, uncomprehending.

"You're kidding me," he said. "What the fuck is this? You'll drop everything to go out to buy a bed to sleep on with your husband, but you're too busy painting every day to do that for me? I don't get it. I've had to make do with that fucking futon every night and I haven't complained. I don't get you, Adie. I really don't." He shook his head. "You're unbelievable. And may I ask," his eyes blazed with anger, "if you intend fucking Malcolm on this bed? I guess you do. That's why you're going out to buy it."

"It's not Malcolm, it's Michael," she said with a feeble grin.

"Malcolm. Michael. Think I care what his asshole name is? Fuck him. Fuck you. You're too much, Adie. I'm outta here."

Shep banged out of the studio, colliding with the credenza on the way. Brushes, tubes of paint and the tuna fish sandwich went flying all over the floor. Downstairs, she heard the front door slam. She wanted to run after him, to grovel, to say she was sorry, to ask him to forgive her, to whine that everything was such a mess, that she loved him madly but had no idea what to do.

She didn't, though. She took the coward's way out. She restored the brushes, jar and tubes to their rightful places. Tidied up the remains of the tuna fish sandwich and threw them in the garbage.

Then she drove out to a Sears store in Marsh River, took a deep breath and bought a bed.

Thirty-five

"You look different," Michael said, kissing Adie's cheek in the airport terminal, then pulling her close. "You have a glow about you."

"Do I?" she said, alarmed. Could he tell?

She extricated herself from his arms and avoided looking at him. She fiddled with the strap of her shoulder bag, pretending to be interested in two dark-skinned children, pretty as dolls, who had followed him out of the arrivals door. They were being mobbed by a clutch of sari-clad women, all chattering like a flock of starlings in Hindi.

"Look, Michael," she said to distract him from the topic of her. "Aren't they cute kids?"

"Yeah, I guess so." He turned around briefly to look. "They were on the plane."

Michael, never interested in children, wondered what had prompted Adie to make the remark. She didn't usually get gushy over kids. One of the women, rotund as a barrel, draped in a flowing, orange silk robe, scooped up the smaller child, a boy of about three and started kissing him all over in a frenzied way, making smacking sounds with her lips. The boy screamed and tried to push her away.

"Let's go," Michael said, wincing. A shrieking child always reminded him of a parrot in a pet shop. "I'm more interested in you. You've changed since I saw you last. You're full of smiles and… um… a certain *joie de vivre*."

His smile was almost a leer as he linked his arm in hers. "Must he, all that clean country air."

"Yes, could be. But my painting is also going well," she said, biting her bottom lip, hoping he wouldn't notice how on edge she was, not wanting to continue with this kind of conversation. "Did you have a good flight?"

"Oh, not bad. I forgot to order a special meal, and there was some awful breaded chicken thing, full of carbs, so I left most of it. The trip was okay, though. I persuaded the flight attendant to give me a pillow. Slept most of the way."

"Good. You look rested."

In truth, Adie thought Michael looked tired and pale, his cheeks sunk inwards, his Adam's apple bobbing up and down, like an enormous boil on his long neck. She'd become used to Shep's cuddly, plump body and round, unlined face, often pink from the sun. She wished Michael would stop his obsession with low-carb eating. He was too thin. She couldn't imagine curling up with him, spoon fashion, like she did with Shep. She crossed her fingers that he wouldn't get any ideas once they were lying together on the Queen Simmons High Loft Beautyrest, which two brawny men from Sears had hauled up the stairs only an hour before she left for the airport. A panicky thought came into her head. Had Shep left any half-eaten bags of chocolate chip cookies lying around in the bedroom? Or, even worse, his socks or underwear? He wasn't very tidy. And it had been such a mad rush, putting sheets on the new bed, shoving the heavy futon out of the way by herself, getting everything shipshape before departing.

The truck didn't bother Michael, to her surprise. He seemed more curious than anything.

"You know, I've never actually been inside one of these ridiculous monsters," he said, folding himself like a praying mantis into the cab. "My dad didn't like trucks. He always preferred his Chrysler sedans. You like it?"

"Yes, it's fun to drive."

He shrugged.

"It's your money."

He turned his attention to the view as they headed out of the city on the freeway. Toronto's suburbs looked exactly like Long Island's, he told her. Same subdivisions, same shopping malls, same billboards, same cars everywhere. He showed vague interest in an exit sign that read "Mississauga" and mumbled that it sounded Indian. Then he mumbled again that the country outside the city was flatter than the foothills of the Adirondacks. After that, Michael fell asleep, his large, pale head lolling against the side of the cab, the raccoon specs falling forward on his angular nose.

They reached Fortune Hill in mid-afternoon. He woke with a start and immediately admired all the spruce trees on either side of the road. They reminded him of the mountains, he told Adie. It was all trees, nothing but trees, in the Adirondacks. He'd studied the different kinds of trees at school.

"They are collectively known as conifers. I do remember that," he said with a chuckle. "But my favourite was the tamarack, which loses its needles in winter. It looks so beautiful in fall. A brilliant yellow."

Adie felt disturbed by this talk. Michael seemed to be warming to the place. She prayed that he wasn't going to stay long. Her nervousness increased when he expressed delight at the house.

"It's a wonderful example of Victorian architecture, Adie. You were smart to save it," he said, putting his arm through hers as they headed up to the front door, which Knock's men had painted forest green. "But is it warm inside, I wonder?"

Adie told him about the new propane furnace.

"Well, times have changed in the country I guess," he said, with a dry laugh. "My Dad had a three-storey clapboard house with a smelly oil furnace in the basement that never worked properly. We froze every winter."

They toured the interior. He made positive comments everywhere, to her consternation. She suggested something to eat when they were back in the kitchen, but he recoiled, griping once more about the breaded chicken, saying he couldn't stomach a thing. Adie was hungry, though. No, she decided, I'm *starving*. She thought of Shep constantly. Wished he were there, opening a bag of cookies or chips that they could both dip into. For the first time in months, she had the urge for a Reese's Peanut Butter Cup. She wondered, staring at Michael, what on earth she was going to do to entertain her husband for the rest of the day and evening.

They went upstairs to her studio. Michael bent his head to look at her completed plant portraits. The mole with the wiry hair under his left ear was getting bigger, Adie noticed. It stuck out now, oozing over his shirt collar, a squashy, pinkish-purple protuberance that looked repulsive. Then she felt guilty for thinking such a thing, because Michael turned around and said her paintings were fantastic.

"I especially like the Jack-in-the-Pulpit you're working on. Such an odd-looking plant," he said. "But it will sure make an arresting illustration. I predict that this will be the most popular one in the book." He paused and looked around the studio. "And working here obviously suits you, doesn't it? So if you want to get back to painting tomorrow, that's fine with me. Don't feel you have to play hostess and entertain me. I need to go through a ton of my material about the Nazarenes and email a few people back in Europe."

Well, good. Relief again. Life with Michael had always centred around work – his and hers. She didn't know what else to do with him anymore.

"What about a walk in the woods before dark?" she asked, because the light was waning outside the studio window. "There are trails everywhere on the property – and it's lovely down towards the stream."

"Sure," he said. "I need to stretch my legs after being cooped up in that plane. The seats seem to get smaller every time I fly. Or am I just getting old?"

He laughed. She did too.

Outside the back door, Michael's mood changed. He swatted away a mosquito. And another. He walked into a spider web. Cursed. Flapped his hands around his face, muttering that woods in the country were always full of bugs waiting to trap you. Then he stopped and listened, frowning at the sound of a machine starting up. *Vroom-vroom. Vroom-vroom.* The noise came from somewhere fairly close by. He stuffed his fingers theatrically in his ears and turned, grimacing, to Adie, who was walking right behind him. His expression – and the noise – made her heart sink. Oh, God. What awful timing. The ATV. Shep was obviously taking his boy toy out for a spin. She hadn't seen him since their blow-up, and half of her wanted to be honest about him to Michael. Should she tell him right then and there, standing in the woods, that their marriage was over, that she was in love with Shep, the guy who drove the ATV? No, she just couldn't face it. Not yet. Michael would be so shocked. He wouldn't believe her. He'd fly into a rage. She needed – as she always did – to pick the right moment and rehearse what she was going to say.

"Well, rural life sure hasn't changed that much," Michael said scornfully, taking the fingers out of his ears. "The heating's better, I'll grant you that, but there are still those awful yahoos racing around on those things."

He peered into the woods, in the direction of Shep's house.

"Who's making that racket now, I wonder?"

"Oh, it's just a neighbour," said Adie nervously. "And he is actually quite a nice guy."

"Is he?" Michael snorted. "Well, I don't want to run into him, thank you very much."

He retreated towards the back door,

Adie didn't want to run into Shep, either. Not right now. She prayed that he wouldn't materialize on his machine in front of them.

"Let's not go out for a walk," Michael said.

"Sure."

They sat again at the IKEA table, the whine of the ATV only faintly noticeable outside the kitchen window. She made tea, apologizing that it was just teabags, but she couldn't get loose tea in Marsh River. He shrugged and said not to worry, he knew this wasn't Manhattan. He told her about his research, how it had taken him to Frankfurt, Brussels, Berlin, Vienna and Rome – but that he'd ended up in London and still liked that city best. He showed her a photo he took with his cell phone outside Tate Britain, looking towards the Thames.

"I wished you were there to be in the picture," he said. "It still looks as beautiful as ever."

"Yes, it was too bad I couldn't make it."

"So, what's this interesting news you have to tell me," he asked, picking up his mug. "You mentioned it in your email, didn't you?"

"Oh yes, I forgot."

She went over to her new, tall, cherry wood kitchen cabinets, built by Mervyn Baumann. They were what she liked the most about the updated kitchen. Such smooth, beautiful wood with a lovely grain. She retrieved from a drawer the letter written by her mother.

Michael put his mug down. He read gravely, clutching his spectacles, dropping the pages one by one on to the table, as she watched in silence. Then he rubbed his eyes, looked up at her and reached out to clutch her hand.

"What a sad letter, Adie. I'm sorry you had to find it," he said gently. "Your mother was always such a neurotic. But getting seduced by her brother at fourteen must have screwed her up for life. So difficult for them both. And you. What a mess. Um," he regarded her in a speculative way, "did finding the letter upset you?"

"Yes, at first. But I'm over it now."

"Well, I'm glad, because I did wonder at the airport when you made the comment about those kids we saw...." he paused. "Adie, do you regret that we didn't have children?"

She thought, with an inward chuckle, if only you knew, Michael, why I distracted you with those kids.

"Occasionally I guess I do, but not often," she admitted. "And we all have regrets in our lives, don't we? But did you want kids?"

"No, never. Not after what my parents did to me." He shuddered. "I didn't want to ever make children feel guilty about who they were and what they wanted out of life. I see so many parents doing that. They have these expectations," he sighed, "and then they get disappointed when the kids want something different."

Michael squeezed her hand again.

"Rest assured, I have no regrets about kids."

They picked up their tea mugs again and smiled with genuine affection at one another.

This rare intimate exchange – one of the few such exchanges they'd had in years – made Adie briefly wonder why she'd plunged into the mad affair with Shep and whether things would have turned out differently if, in fact, she and Michael had become parents. She felt so detached from her husband now, as if she were marooned on one ice floe while he occupied another. And though they were drifting further and further apart, out into an open sea, pulling close together again was out of the question. Yet Michael was basically a nice guy, with whom she'd shared a lot. They'd been together a long time. Would kids have anchored them together into their old age? Was there still a chance that they could reach one another across the ice if they were both willing to try?

She thought so, holding his hand in hers. But then something happened to remind Adie why they'd drifted so far apart in the first place.

Thirty-six

At eight o'clock, Michael yawned. He wanted to go to bed, but was still strung out from the flight. He worried about jet lag.

"I always wake up in the middle of the night, after these transatlantic runs," he said. "And I don't want to disturb you."

"Well, have some catnip tea," Adie urged. "It's a mild tranquilizer and sedative, and I've discovered the stuff grows wild in the garden here. I often have a mug."

She didn't say what she'd also discovered. That most nights, catnip tea wasn't necessary. That the best sedative in the world was having hot sex with Shep. She always fell asleep immediately afterwards.

Michael pulled a face. He hated herbal teas. He only liked his tea black.

"Well, just try some, won't you? It's great with honey. And it will help, I'm sure."

Adie went out into the darkness around the house, searching for catnip. She cursed the lack of light. She hadn't yet got around to screwing a bulb into the light fixture Knock had installed outside the back door. The garden was still an overgrown mess. She scrabbled around and located a clump of catnip on the west side. She pulled off a handful of the pale green, furry leaves and, back indoors, tossed them in a jug, poured on boiling water and left the brew to sit for a few minutes. She gave Michael a mug of the green liquid to take upstairs, adding a spoonful of honey to cut the bitterness, but avoided telling him about the honey, because he'd fuss that it was full of carbs.

When she joined him two hours later, the mug was empty on the floor beside the bed. He was already asleep.

Well, good. It worked. The last thing she wanted was him snuggling up to her. She crawled under the covers quietly, careful not to waken him, relieved to hear his rhythmic breathing. She had an erotic dream about Shep, then woke up in the early hours, mumbling to herself and feeling hot all over.

The next morning, the sky was puffy and grey. It looked like rain. But Michael was in a good mood, singing the praises of catnip tea. He'd slept well. Over breakfast, Adie told him about Tish's brief tryst with Uncle Gully, then about Flavian and – big excitement – the realization that she and Flavian were cousins.

"We should go into Marsh River today, so you can meet him. He's a lovely guy, with a great bookshop," she said.

"Sure," Michael said. "What a surprise. You have a cousin here in Canada, of all places. And how brave of him, opening that shop. In my experience, people who live in small towns aren't big readers of books."

"Oh, you'd be surprised. He's doing pretty well. And after you meet him, we could go across the street to the Kaffee Klatch for lunch."

"The Kaffee Klatch?"

"Yes, I know it's a dumb name, but the food isn't bad. They make great sandwiches on homemade bread."

"Um, sure," Michael hesitated. "But I'd prefer a salad without any bread, if you don't mind."

Adie wanted to throttle him.

They both worked all morning – him at his laptop at the kitchen table, her in the studio upstairs – then headed in the truck to Marsh River. Turning onto the main street, she wished the downtown was putting on a brighter face for Michael's arrival. In the drizzle, the row of stone buildings looked decrepit and dark, almost like the façade of some old, grey Victorian prison. The indoor lights in the store windows were half-hidden by wet maple leaves hanging low. and only two – the Kaffee Klatch and Boddington Books – exuded a warm, welcoming air.

"Not a very good day for your introduction to the joys of small town life," Flavian said, shaking Michael's hand, looking out at the rain. "But good to meet you anyway. Can I offer you a coffee?"

"Thanks, but Adie tells me we're going to the Kaffee Klatch."

Michael cast a sceptical look in the direction of the café a few doors down. Its lights were blazing. He could see a row of people sitting on stools in the window.

"Oh, don't be put off by the name," Fabian laughed. "You won't just find a bunch of old ladies gossiping in there. I've discovered belatedly that their food is very good."

Michael meandered around the bookstore. Prodded by Adie, he bought a coffee table book on the art of the Renaissance. Then they crossed the street and went along to the café. They found two free stools in the window. To his relief, a grilled chicken, avocado and sundried tomato salad was on the menu. Even better, it cost half what he paid for a similar salad in Columbia's cafeteria. And to his further surprise, the waitress said, "No problem, sir," when he asked her for a side order of beet salad instead of a Kaiser roll.

The waitress was a voluptuous, middle-aged woman with fat, white arms, who wore a baby-pink smock. With a grin, Michael whispered to Adie that she made him think of Rembrandt, who'd always wanted a wife with that kind of physique. They both ordered tea. It came in a large pot, made with tea leaves, not bags, accompanied by their own small jug of milk.

"This is a nice place," he said, as Adie poured the tea. "I like it. Thank you for bringing me here."

"See. Told you, didn't I?" she teased, tapping his bony knee.

She bit into her chopped egg sandwich. "It's not all burgers and hot dogs in the country nowadays, you know. Things are more sophisticated than you think."

She rubbed the steamed-up windows so they could see out to watch the passing pedestrians. There weren't many, because of the rain. Everyone was bent over, carrying an umbrella. Adie slid off her stool to go the ladies' room down in the basement and left Michael looking out.

His attention was drawn to a girl without an umbrella. She appeared out of nowhere and darted across the street, over to the bookstore. His mouth fell open in surprise.

He asked the Rembrandt waitress if she knew who the girl was.

"Ah yes, that's Chrissie Tanner. She works in the hairdresser's a few doors up. She cuts my hair for me. Lovely girl, isn't she? She lives around the corner, I think, with her boyfriend."

Michael stared until the girl reached the bookstore door and retreated inside. He tried to watch her behind the plate glass window, but the drizzle made everything blurry. He turned back to his salad.

The next day, standing in the doorway of Adie's studio, Michael announced that he'd like to go to the Kaffee Klatch again for lunch. There was a broad grin on his face.

"Today? Now?" she said. "It was that good?"

"Yes, I enjoyed myself. Great food. Pleasant lady serving us. And my eyes are tired from working at the laptop. I need a break."

"Well, sure …" she hesitated, glancing up at the clock on the wall of the studio. It was barely noon. "But I won't join you, if you don't mind. I'm at a critical stage with this watercolour. You okay with taking the truck?"

"Sure," he laughed. "It will be a new mid-life adventure for me."

Adie listened to Michael starting the pickup. She pictured him in the driver's seat and chuckled, wondering if he'd find his way into Marsh River along the twisting lake road. But there was a map in the dash, she remembered. Thankful he'd gone, she continued to work on the painting stapled to her drawing board. She floated in a wash of diluted Hooker's Green over the three leaves of Jack-in-the-Pulpit, her heart in her mouth. The performance of this wash was critical. When it was starting to dry, she tipped the board sideways to encourage the pigment to flow and not puddle at the edge of the paper. If that happened, she might be stuck with the nightmare that all watercolour artists dreaded: the phenomenon called back run.

Yet there was no back run. The wash dried perfectly. No unsightly oozles and blossoms marred Jack's portrait. She layered in another wash, feeling hungry afterwards and longing for the routine she'd established with Shep. He always managed to bring her something to eat at exactly the right moment. And while he might have left some snacks in the fridge downstairs, she couldn't remember. But was Shep still mad at her? She hoped not. That he'd understand. She thought seriously of going off along the trail to check if he was around, because she was starting to feel desperate about not seeing him. If she had to eat humble pie, so be it. She'd done it often enough with Michael. Perhaps Shep would have something good for her to snack on over at his house.

But, no. Too risky. Michael might come back and wonder where she was. She went downstairs. The only thing edible in the fridge that didn't require cooking was a tub of unsweetened goat's milk yoghurt, which Michael had insisted on buying yesterday at a health food store in Marsh River Mall. She hesitated but spooned some down, standing at the sink, gagging at the strong flavour. She thought what a bore her husband was. Shep would have brought her yummy sweetened yoghurt, with bits of peach and strawberry at the bottom, accompanied by some kind of cookie.

After three mouthfuls, she couldn't stand the goat yoghurt any longer. She returned to the rigours of depicting Jack preaching in his little pulpit.

Michael settled into a window seat at the Kaffee Klatch. He ordered the same salad as yesterday and a pot of tea. The tea was a good excuse to stay as long as possible in the café. He intended to sip it very slowly. The waitress with the Rembrandt arms probably wouldn't mind how long he stayed, anyway. He placed the weighty Renaissance art tome on the counter in front of him and thumbed through some pages.

But he barely glanced at the book. He kept his eyes glued to the street outside the window. It seemed like ages that he was waiting there. Becoming impatient and anxious, he jiggled his long legs against the stool, wondering how many hours he could stay. As the café started gradually emptying after lunch, he worried that he'd have to depart, too. But then the place started to fill up again. New customers were coming in, ordering coffee and slices of a lurid red cherry pie displayed on the counter by the cash desk with a label that said, "Homemade today". He wondered if it would be necessary for him to order some of the loathsome, calorie-laden pie in order to keep his spot in the window. He asked for a fresh pot of tea instead. The Rembrandt waitress complied and said he was welcome to stay as long as he liked.

Then it happened. Her. The girl. The one he'd been waiting for. There she was, at precisely 4:04 p.m., walking along the pavement across the street, past the bookshop she went into yesterday. The girl named Chrissie. The one the Rembrandt waitress told him worked at the hairdresser's. This must be the time she finished work.

He leaned forward on the stool, his mouth open. Remarkable. He'd been surprised at the resemblance yesterday and seeing her again confirmed his initial assessment. Chrissie was exactly like the girl in New York. His Sid. His luscious Sid. He marvelled at the fact. There was the same glorious mop of carrot-red hair, and she moved in the same brisk way, exuding the same confident air. The hair, flowing around her head, looked like molten copper. Michael felt his heart leap, watching it. And she had a lovely face too, kind of like Lizzie Siddal's. What a bonus. Michael stared openly, savouring the fourteen seconds that she was in view across the street, just like he used to back home. He fixed an image of this new Sid in his mind, so he could daydream about her whenever he liked.

But he didn't want to daydream. He wanted to watch her in person. So he would come again tomorrow.

"I think I'll go to the Kaffee Klatch. Have a late lunch this time," Michael announced early the next afternoon.

"What again?" Adie said and laughed. "I think you've fallen in love, Michael. That woman with the Rembrandt arms has put you under a spell."

"Yes, maybe." He grinned. "You don't mind?"

"Not at all."

She carried on putting the finishing touches to Jack-in-the-Pulpit, wondering, after Michael left, if she should have joined him. Perhaps he was getting bored with being stuck out here in the country. But it was a relief to have him gone again, because now she would risk going to see Shep. The moment the truck disappeared at the end of the driveway, she pulled on her hiking boots and hurried through the woods to his house.

To her surprise, Shep was at home. He opened the mudroom door immediately. He still looked angry.

"Oh, it's you."

Yes, it's me. And I'm sorry, Shep. So sorry about um... him showing up like this. Can I come in?"

"I guess."

They stood awkwardly side by side in the kitchen. Shep didn't offer her anything to eat or make any move to touch her.

"Did he like the bed?" he demanded, looking hard at her. "Did he fuck you on it?"

"Oh, shut up, Shep."

"No. When's the guy going?"

"I don't know." She sighed. "I wish I did."

"Well, you better get rid of him, girl, or that's it. We're done."

Adie wanted to challenge Shep about Mary Ann's whereabouts. After all, she could be in his house, couldn't she? Wasn't he in the same predicament as her? Why was he being so nasty? Yet she shrank from the cold glare, the lips clamped together, willing her to leave. She slunk back along the trail, wondering if Michael was home already, waiting for her at the house, agitated by her disappearance.

But he wasn't there. He didn't show up till dusk.

Thirty-seven

Adie didn't question Michael about his absences. The truth was, she barely noticed. She was too busy. Producing the portrait of Jack so absorbed her, she felt glad to be alone. So Michael continued to patronize the Kaffee Klatch. He went the next day. And the next. And the one after that. He climbed into the truck and headed into Marsh River at about two p.m.

On the fourth day, she thought that he definitely must be bored. How else to explain her husband's sudden infatuation with a small town coffee shop? That was it. Boredom. He was a city boy and spending all day on Fortune Hill, in the silence of the woods, didn't enchant him the way it did her. Michael needed the bustle of people coming and going behind the steamed-up windows of the most popular gathering place in Marsh River. His attraction to the place was still mildly puzzling. If he felt that bored, why didn't he go home to New York? But she neglected to think further on it, because during his fourth prolonged absence in town, she made an amazing discovery while on a walk in the woods: a clump of wild lady slipper orchids. They were blooming among cedars that someone had cut down to stumps years before. Out on the eastern edge of her property. Adie knew from her botany books that the yellow-and-brown *Cypripedium calceolus* preferred to bloom on cleared land, but even so, it often didn't. It was a temperamental diva, at best. So her heart soared. This was her best wild find yet. The erotic-looking flower that the French once called *Sabot de Venus* was now extinct in Britain and becoming rare in North America. Yet here they were, flourishing on her land! How exciting, how utterly sublime.

She told Michael that evening. He complimented her on her sharp eyesight and encouraged her to head out there as often as she needed to, doing the preparatory sketches. He insisted that he didn't mind at all, because he could always go to the Kaffee Klatch.

So Adie hiked out to the wild orchids for five days in a row, producing sketch after sketch of their charms: the provocative yellow pouch called the labellum, the sexy slit at the centre, the bizarre twisted brown ribbons dangling down the sides of the flower. Then she came back to the studio to work on its final portrait. When she was out at the edge of her woods, Michael vanished from her mind. Even Shep did. All she cared about was capturing the essence of this exquisite little flower on paper.

Heather, the waitress with the Rembrandt arms, became accustomed to seeing Michael. He was one of her regulars now. A good one too. He always tipped well, better than Marsh River locals, who tended to be cheap.

"Welcome, sir," she said, early every afternoon, smiling as he pushed open the door of the cafe. "I've kept your stool by the window. Your usual?"

"Yes, please," Michael said. Then he sat. Waited. Watched.

For Chrissie.

Michael went for nine consecutive days to the Kaffee Klatch. On the seventh, he grew bolder. He decided to follow Chrissie and take a photograph with his cell phone. Forget the bustling, overcrowded Upper East Side. This small town where nobody walked anywhere was a far better place to snap that picture. Here, he'd finally get what he wanted. He wouldn't blow the whole thing by getting jostled by some jerk, then tripping like an idiot and breaking his ankle.

The next day was windy. Michael sat waiting on the stool in his usual spot. Chrissie blew into view across the street, his goddess-like Sid, red hair billowing out in clouds around her turquoise jacket. So heavenly, so ethereal she looked. Even better than his old Sid in New York. He couldn't wait to do it. He picked up his bill and tried to leave in a hurry, but there was a line-up at the cash desk and Sid was already down at the end of St. David's, disappearing around a corner, before he made it outside. He practically ran after her and spotted her red mane proceeding up a narrow, hilly street behind the stores on the other side of the street from the Kaffee Klatch. He followed. Her destination was a modest building at the top of the hill. It stood isolated, a square, red box of brick, with trees on either side. The building seemed to be divided into four units. He walked fast and found himself gasping, trying to keep up with her. As she pulled open the big plate glass front door of Hilltop Manor Apartments and disappeared inside, he held back and watched.

So this was where she lived. He hung around for a few minutes, half-hidden by the trunk of a wide old maple. He looked back, down towards St. David's for a doorway to hide in or some other secluded spot from which he could snap the photo tomorrow, but there wasn't anywhere suitable. This was frustrating. He felt a physical ache now. Must do it. Must get her great mop of red hair on to his laptop. He'd kept the desire in check for months, but now it was back, possessing him, haunting him. Then he relaxed. He came to the conclusion that, in reality, all he needed to do was leap up from his stool at the Kaffee Klatch the moment she appeared, follow her up this hilly street, hold up his cell and go *click*. Because the street was quiet. No one would see him. This wasn't New York. He didn't need to hide.

The next day, it rained heavily. She didn't show. He felt even more impatient. But the day after that, on a warm, dry afternoon, there she was at precisely 4:04 p.m. striding along the street past the Kaffee Klatch. He hurried out of the cafe, profusely apologizing for his hasty departure to the waitress with Rembrandt arms.

"No problem, sir," Heather said, thinking he was an odd fish, obviously new to town, coming in every day from Lord-knows-where, always ordering the same salad. Yet she pocketed his tip, hoping he'd be back tomorrow, and cleared his plate away, fingering with pleasure the American ten-dollar bill in her pink smock.

Michael pursued Sid up the hill, pulling his cell phone out of his pocket. He held it up high and snapped several pictures. He pressed the button to review them, examining them closely through the big raccoon specs. They seemed a bit blurry and indistinct. He cursed under his breath. Had he put the phone on the wrong setting? Well, not to worry. He'd try again tomorrow for better ones.

Yes, tomorrow. He turned and headed back down the hill.

Michael didn't realize that the girl had gone in through the glass door but then come out again.

And she was looking hard at him.

Chrissie Tanner went into the apartment that she shared with Tyson Sprauge. She told him what she'd seen.

"There's some weirdo out there," she said, going over to the window, pulling the drapes back, peering out. "And he's stalking me. A tall, old, skinny guy with big, black glasses. I think he's trying to take my picture. He sits in the window of the Kaffee Klatch every day, waiting for me to come by. Then he leaves and follows me up Hill Street."

"WHAT? You're kidding me," Tyson said. He leaped up from the sofa where he'd been playing a video game. He roared like a wounded lion and rushed to the window. "Where is he? How long has this been going on?"

"A week. Maybe longer. I just realized for sure what was happening the other day."

"The fucker. I'll fix him, babes. Don't worry. That son of a bitch won't know what hit him. Is he out there now?"

"I don't know."

Chrissie sank down onto the sofa. Tyson jammed on his hi-top sneakers, not bothering to do up the laces, and hurtled down the corridor stairs outside the apartment two steps at a time. He went around the block twice, then down to St. David's, past Boddington Books and the Kaffee Klatch, and up River Street the other side. He rushed through the circuit a second time. When he returned to the apartment, he was red-faced and panting.

"Couldn't find any trace of him," he said, gasping. "But I'll get him, babes. You said he comes every day?"

"Yes, seems to."

"Well then, I'll get the fucker tomorrow."

"Aw, Tyson, don't do anything rash," said Chrissie, picking up from the coffee table her Martha Stewart book about floral arrangements for weddings. "I'm all right now. Just get me a Coke, will you? He's probably harmless."

"That's for me to decide, babes," Tyson said, grabbing two Coke cans out of the fridge and glugging down one himself. "Just you leave this to me."

The next day, Michael went to the Kaffee Klatch as usual, feeling so glad he'd come to Fortune. With Adie busy painting all the time, he was free to watch Sid every day, sitting in this pleasant cafe, nibbling slowly on a salad he enjoyed, served by a friendly lady who didn't mind how long he stayed. It was so much better than hovering at the apartment window in New York, worrying all the time that Adie would notice his harmless little activity and get upset about it. He headed to his usual stool to wait, full of anticipation.

Tyson waited, too. Minutes before Michael disappeared inside the Kaffee Klatch, he'd concealed himself in an alley on the other side of the street. And once the door of the café shut, Chrissie's fiancé crossed over. Heather approached as he went in. She was holding out a menu, smiling, ready to show him to a table, thinking what a good-looking young man he was – and how great that the café was attracting some new customers who weren't all over fifty. But Tyson didn't smile back. He roughly pushed her aside, his arms flexed and ready to fight like a boxer's, his face contorted with rage. He went straight up to where Michael was standing, about to sit down on his customary stool.

Without saying a word, Tyson aimed a blow at Michael's back, right between the shoulder blades. Michael staggered. He thought for a second that a light fixture had worked itself loose from the café ceiling and fallen down on top of him. He turned around painfully, incredulity registering on his face. Who was this? This hick? This thug? This total stranger, whom he'd never seen before in his life. What the hell was going on? Had he been mistaken for someone else?

Michael tried to put his hands up to defend himself. He was about to say, "Wait a minute, buddy. You've got the wrong guy," but he didn't get the chance. Because Tyson hit him again, this time in the face. His fist smacked solidly against Michael's bony jaw.

Heather yelled, "What's going on? Hey, stop that!"

Tyson ignored her. He started pummelling now with both fists.

"You fucker," he shouted. "You perv. You son of a bitch. You stay away from her, do you hear?"

In a rage, he kept on hitting. Michael staggered backwards, blood pouring from his nose, down his shirt. The raccoon specs fell on to the floor. Tyson stamped on them with both feet.

More punching. More blood. Panic flooded through Michael,

and he raised his arms to his face, trying to protect himself from the maniac in front of him. He felt only searing pain as his thin body bent backwards, like a ballet dancer's, over the top of the counter. He flung out an arm to try to steady himself as he toppled, knocking over a mug. The mug sent a stream of pale brown coffee mixed with blood down his jacket sleeve, then smashed into pieces on the tiled floor.

A woman screamed, cherry pie falling out of her mouth. Several people leaped up from their tables and stood immobilized, uncertain if they should intervene.

Tyson kept shouting, "You perv, you perv," over and over again. Michael was drifting now, only dimly aware of a man's voice and a blurry figure with a face contorted in fury. And that fist. The relentless fist that kept coming at him. One of his eyelids split, and the blood trickled down into his eyes, blurring his vision. Then it travelled on down, over his cheek and into his mouth. Time shifted backwards. He saw Ponnetville. His dad drunk in an old, brown armchair. His mom wielding a hammer over the wiener schnitzel. A black Chrysler parked beside a dried-up lawn. A baseball game, with him gingerly picking up the bat, and his dad standing on the sidelines, looking grim. Then Adie's hair, thick and very red, billowing out in front of Nelson's Monument on the Thames. He wondered why Adie wasn't with him now. Where was she? It occurred to him then that he was probably going to die, and he wished he could see her before he went, but he didn't worry that he couldn't. Death was a surprise. It seemed quite welcoming, almost friendly. There was no reason to fear it. You just had to agree to go, and it carried you along. As Tyson's fist struck him again, Michael's head crashed against the plate glass window behind the counter with a loud crack, and he wondered if he had been shot. Yet he felt no pain. Nothing now. He was floating, somewhere up near the ceiling of the café. His eyes closed as the massive sheet of glass behind him split, top to bottom. A chunk fell out into the street, crashing on to the concrete sidewalk, narrowly missing a woman who was pushing a baby in a stroller past the café. Then his head and long, thin neck slumped into the gaping hole, settling on top of the jagged edge of the glass.

"Call an ambulance and the cops, for God's sake," a man shouted, staring at him transfixed, unable to move.

"Someone stop him! Stop that madman," the waitress, Heather, yelled, dialling 911, as Tyson raced out of the door. Two men pursued him, but no one could catch Tyson. He was young and fit, racing down St. David's with the agility of an athlete. Then up Hill Street. Back home. Back to his beloved Chrissie. She hadn't, at his insistence, gone to work that day.

Heather and a middle-aged man pulled Michael away from the hole in the window. She tried to cradle his head, not very successfully. It lolled sideways, as heavy in her hands as a bowling ball. Blood was spurting upwards from his neck like a fountain. It kept splashing on the white wall of the café and trickling down on to the floor.

Heather heard a rattling noise then, coming from the back of Michael's throat. It sounded loud in the silent café. A couple of other women started to cry, realizing what that sound meant.

They stared in horror, clutching each other. The jagged edge of the broken window had gone deep into Michael's neck.

Thirty-eight

It took only three minutes. When glass punctures an artery, it can be that quick. Two paramedics arrived, tearing along St. David's in a white-and-blue SUV. They rushed into the Kaffee Klatch, toting heavy bags of gear. Michael lay sprawled like a rag doll on the tiled floor, Heather holding his head in her lap. He was already dead.

One paramedic kneeled down and grabbed Michael's wrist.

"He's gone, isn't he?" the waitress said, tears falling down her cheeks, hoping the paramedic would say no, but knowing he wouldn't.

The two men didn't answer. "Let's just wait for the police, ma'am," one said.

Then the cops arrived, screeching up in a black-and-white cruiser.

"Who is this man? Anyone know?" the older cop, Dave Millgrove, demanded, peering at Michael lying on the floor. Dave had lived in Marsh River all his life. He knew just about everyone, but not this stranger. People shook their heads. A portly old man who visited the Kaffee Klatch every day for a slice of pie said the stranger had only started coming to the café about a week ago.

"Where did his assailant go?" Dave asked next.

"Up there," said one of the men who had rushed outside after Tyson. "He ran off up there. Hill Street I think."

"No one leave the restaurant yet, please," the younger cop, whose name was Matt, said, as the cops hurried to the door.

"Everyone stay right here. And can someone find the manager?"

Without waiting for a reply, Dave and his partner jumped into the cruiser and sped away, siren blaring.

Heather straightened up, sliding Michael's head gently off her lap, aided by another waitress in a pink smock. She steadied herself with her hands on a table top, barely able to stand – her knees kept buckling. Her front felt wet, and she looked down at her lap. The pink smock was soaked with blood. So were her fat, white arms. There seemed to be blood everywhere – on the table, mingling with the coffee on the floor, splatted on the walls, the table tops. A splotch, very red, slowly dribbled down the edge of the broken window. Everyone stood staring at the blood, numb, horrified. It had all happened so quickly.

The owner of the café, a middle-aged woman with brassy blonde hair and turquoise eyelids materialized then, her high heels clattering down the wooden stairs behind the cash desk. Told what had happened, she rushed up to the stunned Heather, her hands outstretched.

"My God, love, you'd better go to the hospital yourself," she said, putting her arm around her, oblivious to the blood. "C'mon, I'll take you. You look pretty shook up."

"Yes, but I'm not hurt," Heather said, rubbing her eyes, smearing more blood over her eyebrows and forehead. "Not like him. Poor guy. I don't know who he was, but he was real nice. And now he's gone."

Two more cops arrived. They began the tedious business of questioning witnesses and collecting evidence. Attracted by the commotion in the street, Flavian locked the bookstore front door and hurried over to the coffee shop. When he entered, he heard the people in the café talking in hushed tones to the cops about the "tall, skinny man who sounded American" and realized at once who it must be. He'd seen Adie's husband heading solo into the Kaffee Klatch several times. He identified Michael to the police. Half an hour later, Flavian was heading up Fortune Hill with them in their police cruiser, charged with helping them break the news to Adie.

But she wasn't there. The house was unlocked. Michael's closed laptop sat on the IKEA table beside a pile of his research papers. There were dishes in the kitchen sink. The trio looked around. Called her name out back. Ventured a few yards into the woods, still calling, "Adie! Adie! Mrs. Coulter! Mrs. Coulter!" No response. Her truck wasn't in the driveway, either. One cop said she must have gone out. Flavian disagreed. The truck was in Marsh River, he explained. Michael had driven it there. Adie had no other vehicle. The cops shook their heads. Said they couldn't wait any longer. They'd come back again later. She had obviously gone out with a friend.

They tried Shep's house next. but he was gone, too. Minutes before, he'd received a hysterical call from Chrissie, then driven down to the police station in Marsh River to be with her.

Tyson was already in a cell there. He was about to be charged with second degree murder.

Shep did everything he could for his daughter and her hot-headed fiancé. So did Mary Ann. She was already with Chrissie when he arrived at the station. She'd sped over in a taxi from the home decorating store.

The three of them sat together, presenting a united family front for once, while the cops explained the charge against Tyson. Shep called his lawyer. A bail hearing was set for a week hence. Until then, Tyson had to stay in jail. Chrissie, weeping, went to his cell, accompanied by Mary Ann. Shep held back, remembering what Charlie had said about Tyson. He didn't want to see the kid. Not yet. After they came back, Mary Ann said Chrissie was going with her to Hanni's house for the night.

So Shep went home. Alone. Back to Fortune. Proceeding at a crawl along the twisting lake road. Finally able to think about the impact of all this on the woman he loved. Did she know that Michael was dead? The cops had told him no, not yet. They'd gone up to her house right after it happened but hadn't found her. If he could help in any way, they'd appreciate it. A cruiser was scheduled to try again in a couple of hours. They thought she must be out somewhere.

But Shep knew Adie hadn't left the property. With his deer eyes, he'd watched her early that morning, through the spruce trees. She was heading out to paint the lady slipper orchids.

He found her down among the stumpy cedars, squatting on her stool, as the sunlight was starting to fade. He went there on the ATV. She was huffy with him at first, telling him to go away, until he insisted. "Please, you have to listen. I have some dreadful news." Then she just kept saying, "Oh God. Oh God," over and over again, after he told her. About Michael. About Tyson. He pulled her to his chest, and she wailed like a child.

Back at her house, she recovered sufficiently to call the police detachment in Marsh River. They told her she needed to go down to the morgue and identify Michael. Shep drove her there. She was dry-eyed now, but numb. They hardly spoke on the journey into town. Or when the ordeal was over.

He asked what she wanted to do. They were standing outside the hospital in the parking lot. The morgue was in the basement. The sun was going down.

"Go home, I guess," she said. "But come with me, will you? I don't want to be alone."

Nor did Shep. He held her hand and ached for her as they drove to her house. Then he searched her refrigerator for some wine and found an open bottle. Held it up with a questioning look. But she shook her head.

"No, no. No alcohol. It would make me throw up," she said.

She was wondering what to do with Michael's body.

"What I'd like is some catnip tea," she added. "Will you make it?"

"Catnip tea?" He almost laughed. She'd offered it to him a couple of times before. He hadn't taken her seriously.

"It makes a good tranquilizer, Shep. Truly. And a mild sedative. It's totally harmless. No side effects, like pills."

"I could use something like that myself right now," he murmured, realizing he felt like a wrung-out dish rag.

"Well, let's both have some," she said. 'It's out in the garden, around the side of the house. Look for stalks with small, furry green leaves. Go collect some, if you don't mind. There's lots out there. You just pour some boiling water on the leaves and let it steep for a few minutes. You can put them in that."

She motioned at a white jug standing upside down in the dish drainer.

"I'm going to have a shower. I think I stink of formaldehyde. It was so... so awful being in that morgue with him. Seeing his beat-up face. Poor, poor Michael," she said, starting to cry again.

Shep went outside. It was getting dark. He tried switching on the light outside the back door, but there was no bulb in the socket. He floundered around in the dusk and bent down, searching for Adie's catnip. There were so many green things growing there. He didn't have a clue what any of them were. But his big hands eventually settled on what he presumed she wanted.

He went back indoors and made the tea in the jug. It was waiting for her when she came out of the shower, refreshed, calm again. They sipped it sitting at the kitchen table even though he hated the taste. It was so bitter. He almost spat his out. But then, he'd never liked herbal teas. Adie smiled at him, shook her head and said, "Oh, Shep, you and your sweet tooth," when he wrinkled his nose. She motioned at a jar of honey, told him to add another spoonful, insisting that the infusion would be good for both of them. So he did what she wanted and emptied his mug,

She emptied hers, too. They sat in silence, him holding her hand, squeezing it now and then. She stared ahead, still looking as if her mind weren't really there. Then she turned to him with a sad smile and said, "Why don't we take a ride out to the cabin?"

He was taken aback.

"What, now?"

"Yes, now. I don't want to just sit here, being miserable. Let's go listen to some Beethoven. He always calms me."

Thirty-nine

Monkshood is a manifestation of Mother Nature's dark side. Devilish. Despicable. Deadly as a hunter's bullet. Every part of this beautiful plant is poisonous. Ingest it, and you are probably finished. Even handling the leaves is dicey and will cause a rash, some say, because the toxins can penetrate the skin. Monkshood slows the heart until it stops beating. People sometimes call it the devil's helmet, because of the way it looks. Yet in truth, the deep purple flowers, piled one on top of the other on long, graceful stalks, perfectly resemble the hoods of monks – and look as shadowy and mysterious. It has claimed victims since Roman times.

It claimed two more that night.

Adie had painted monkshood once for a gardening magazine. Loved the assignment, too, because its statuesque stems and flowers were so spectacular to depict in watercolour. She also knew how dangerous the plant could be because – although she was a city girl – she'd read up about monkshood in a botanical encyclopedia before starting to paint. At the time, she'd been shocked at its ability to kill so swiftly.

Yet the country boy had never read a botanical encyclopedia.

After a lifetime spent hunting in the woods, Shep knew deer and their habits like the back of his hand. He was aware that they came for the corn in Joe Perri's field. That they ripped the bark off trees when they were hungry in winter. That they liked the young shoots of sumac and apple trees in spring. He'd even scattered radish seeds in a back field once, because he read somewhere that they were drawn to the young, green leaves.

Shep missed one thing, however. Deer never touch monkshood. They're wise to its ways. They recognize it. They won't go near it.

And he was in a hurry that evening, so anxious to give comfort to Adie, so desperate to make her feel better. Out in the overgrown garden, as dusk fell, he found all kinds of leafy stalks, in various shapes and sizes. He couldn't make head nor tail of them. Some leaves were big and bright green, with sharp, toothy edges. Others were greyish and shaped like boats. Still others were soft and small and grew close to the ground in clumps next to the back door. Which ones were her damn catnip? He had no idea. He couldn't see properly, either, in the growing darkness, because she'd never gotten around to installing a light bulb in the socket outside the back door. He forgot what she had said – to look for the leaves that were small and furry. So he groped around and grabbed a bunch at random, hoping for the best. Then he went back indoors and followed her instructions.

Mixed in with the calming catnip were half a dozen bright green, serrated leaves of monkshood – plus one elongated leaf of wild foxglove, which can have deadly consequences, too.

Adie thought the tea didn't taste the way it normally did. Yet she didn't question Shep. She thanked him for making it. He couldn't find a tea strainer so they both swallowed leafy bits with the liquid. Then they went out on the ATV. She wrapped her arms around his waist and leaned her head against his back, so relieved to have him there. She was still dazed. She couldn't think about anything. Riding along on the ATV in the half-light, her cheek pressed into Shep's denim jacket, she felt only a sensation of floating, of being lifted above the world.

Charlie Cousins found them. Not until the following day, when the sun was high in the sky, blazing over the cabin. Chrissie called him just after ten because Shep hadn't shown up to meet Tyson and the lawyer at the police station. She asked if he would go by her dad's house and check, because she wondered if he might have been distraught, drunk a whole lot of rum, then overslept. He did that sometimes, when things worried him. She knew he wouldn't have abandoned her.

The house was empty, of course. But Shep's familiar dark green pickup stood in the driveway. And Charlie, skilled hunter that he was, alert to any change in his surroundings, noticed fresh ruts in one of the trails going out through the woods, behind the house. So he followed them. Walked all the way out to Wolf's Glen.

He came across Adie first. She was face up, naked, floating in the stream. A faded Ophelia, her long, pale hair splayed around her, hands poking stiffly above the surface of the water, as Lizzie Siddal's were, in Millais's painting. Her body, very white and ghostly under the shadowy spruce, had come to rest against a cedar trunk. Her eyes were open and glassy. One foot was tangled up in some weeds. Afterwards, people speculated as to why she'd wound up like that, in the stream with no clothes on. It seemed mighty peculiar to Gracie, who hinted that perhaps something had happened between her and Shep, and…. Yet there were no marks on her body, no evidence of any kind of fight. And the coroner wrote in his report, when toxicology tests had confirmed monkshood and/or foxglove poisoning, that ingesting monkshood can affect people in many ways. Sometimes it prompts profuse sweating. He reasoned that perhaps she got disoriented, that her body felt too hot. So she'd waded into the stream to cool herself down and died there.

Shep was slumped over the bench seat on the ATV, wearing only a shirt. The report said that he had vomited a couple of times – once on the path, then again over the handlebars of the machine. After that, he'd probably passed out and not regained consciousness. Perhaps, the coroner surmised, he was attempting to get on the machine and go for help. He seemed to have died after Adie.

The coroner estimated that they'd both lived from four to six hours after drinking the tea. Charlie found the LP of Eroica on the phonograph. The battery had gone dead, so the turntable wasn't spinning around anymore, but the needle still rested on the black vinyl disc. There were two small, empty glasses and a half-full bottle of rum on the floor of the cabin. Their clothing lay scattered about beside the polar bear pelt. When he bent down, Charlie also a detected a small, fresh stain on the pelt that the cops missed.

Charlie didn't tell anyone about the stain. He concluded that Shep and Adie had made love before they died.

He wiped away a tear and felt glad about that.

Epilogue

Her book came out a couple of weeks ago. Well, it's not really her book anymore. She did only five of the illustrations. The publisher had to scramble after what happened and find other artists to produce the rest of the paintings. But hers are the ones that stand out. It's all over the Web that they are the most extraordinary depictions of plants anyone has ever seen, particularly the Jack-in-the-Pulpit and the lady slipper orchid. The New York Times called her the best botanical artist the world has ever produced – better, even, than the famous ones who were around in the 18th century.

Chrissie emailed me, asking if I wanted a copy of the book. I said no. She says Flavian is getting a few for the store, although he doesn't expect to sell many. Most people in Fortune and Marsh River feel the same way I do. They'd rather forget that she ever came. And now that I'm back in Africa, on the new aid project in Senegal, I have other things to fill my thoughts. So many hungry children, so many people with sadder stories than ours. As I said, I don't think we ever really forget. There's no such thing as closure. But I have moved on.

Chrissie is amazing, though. Still there, in the middle of the memories, waiting for Tyson to be released. And so calm about it. The charge was reduced to manslaughter after the truth came out, and the judge took into account that he was young and a first-time offender. So he got three years. If he behaves himself in jail – which he seems to be doing – he'll be out in a few months.

Then they intend getting married and living on Fortune Hill. I couldn't stand it, but Chrissie is already fixing the house up. She loves the place. Always has. She's like Dad. She even intends keeping Wolf's

Glen. Says Tyson will love it for hunting with Charlie. But Mom is buying a new bungalow in Marsh River with the insurance money the air ambulance service paid out after Dad died. She never liked living in the woods anyway. And she can't be blamed for wanting to put the past behind her.

The old recluse's house next door is empty again. Someone from the township office came out and boarded it up. Just like before. She left no will. It seems that she does have a brother somewhere, but Bill Wickenheiser's office is still trying to track him down. Chrissie hopes they can't find him. Now that it's been revealed that Adie was Flavian's cousin, Chrissie wants Flavian to inherit the property, instead. She says he's been wonderfully supportive since Tyson went to jail and that he has a new man in his life. A cop called Matt, who likes hunting. She thinks they'd make wonderful neighbours.

Gracie gossiped for a while, of course, bragging that she'd been right all along about the mystery relative coming to Fortune. But then she surprised everyone and retired. She sold the store to a young couple from Bangladesh. They made all kinds of changes and are doing well with take-out food they cook themselves.

When I next go home, Chrissie wants to take me there. She says their samosas are awesome.

Author's Note

A first novel is a daunting task. Self-doubt dogs the writer every step of the way. It is so easy to throw up your hands and say, "Why am I doing this? It's utter rubbish. I quit."

Although I had seven non-fiction books under my belt, this fictional story – inspired by my fascination with the two different worlds of city and country people – proved a particular challenge. I am profoundly grateful to everyone who encouraged me to keep plodding on towards the finish line.

My thanks go to:

Carol Cowan, Carolyn Forde, Sara Katz, Anne Kotyk, Kathe Lieber, Liz Primeau, Aldona Satterthwaite and Sandra Shatilla, who all read the first draft and suggested ways to make the story better.

Mary-Fran McQuade, who came up with several wonderful improvements, and then took on the tiresome chore of editing those inconsistencies in language, spelling and punctuation that slip by any author; Chris McCorkindale and Sue Breen, who did the cover design and typesetting; Barrie Murdock, who helped with the production process; and Steven Biggs and Robert Rotenberg, who provided valuable advice.

For their support: Susan Day, Josephine Felton, Marjorie Harris, Julie and Bill Henderson, who invited me to stay at their apartment in Manhattan so I could make sure the New York locations were accurate, Ann Huber, Jessica Ing, Phyllis Rawnsley and Marlene Wynnyk.

For insights into hunting: Dave Baxter, Barrie Murdock, Tony Vanderheide, Dr. Bob Wright, as well as David Carpenter, author of *A Hunter's Confession*.

For information on plants and painters: *Botany for the Artist*, by Sarah Simblet; and *Botanica North America*, by Marjorie Harris.

For introducing me to Weber's opera, *Der Freischütz*, at a performance in Toronto: the innovative and entertaining Opera Atelier. (www.operaatelier.com)

For exhaustive background on the Pre-Raphaelite painters: several books, including *Lizzie Siddal*, by Lucinda Hawksley; the massive tome, *Victorian painting*, edited by Lionel Lambourne; and *Desperate Romantics*, by Franny Moyle, which was made into a BBC TV series of the same name.

To see Pre-Raphaelite art in North America – plus the red-haired ladies they loved – I recommend the Wilmington Art Museum, in Wilmington, Delaware (www.del.art.org). They have some great examples. In the U.K., the best collection of their paintings continues to be at Tate Britain (www.tate.org.uk). It includes three by the idolized Lizzie Siddal herself.

Please visit my website: www.soniaday.com
Facebook: https://www.facebook.com/soniadaywriter

Other Books By Sonia Day

*Tulips – Facts and Folklore about the
World's Most Planted Flower*

The Urban Gardener

The Urban Gardener Indoors

The Complete Urban Gardener

The Plant Doctor

*Incredible Edibles – 43 Fun Things
to Grow in the City*

*The Untamed Garden – A Revealing Look
at our Love Affair with Plants*

*Memoir
Middle-Aged Spread – Moving to the Country at 50*